THIRST

VAST COLLECTIVE BOOK IX

Nicole Hayes

Iona Print

Library of Congress Control Number: 2022909924

ISBN 978-1-7378379-5-4 (Hardcover Edition)
ISBN 979-8-9908310-2-5 (Softcover Edition)
ISBN 978-1-7378379-7-8 (Ebook Edition)

Printed in the USA

Iona Print
nicolehayesauthor@gmail.com
https://nicolehayeswriter.com/

THE VAST COLLECTIVE SERIES

Last of Daylight
By the Pale Moonlight
Asylum in Firelight
Nox's Verse
Glass Chains
Pyrite Prison
Restraining Silver
Korac's Verse
Thirst
Levee
Flood
Xelan's Verse
Cascading Light

Life rewards those of us who hold onto hope. Never let go.

TRIGGER WARNINGS

Please consider my entire series 'Rated R.' These books are meant for readers sixteen years and older. Read with the following triggers in mind:

- Graphic Violence
- Graphic Language
- Psychological Warfare
- Graphic Sex Scenes
- Allusion to Off-Page Sexual Assault
- Horror Pregnancy
- Stolen Agency
- Theft of a Cheesecake

CONTENTS

ACKNOWLEDGMENTS

Batman, I know nine books is a lot, and as I'm writing this you're beta-reading book twelve. Here I am trying to tell you how much it means to me, and I can't find the words. Each book hapens because you told me to sit down and start writing, and each book is finished because you give it your stamp of approval. Thank you for making them a reality.

Firefly, I know this was an odd one to get through, but we made it. Xelan and Korac are on page together because of you. Thanks for keeping the Silver General with us.

Rebeca, thanks once more for an amazing cover!

A PROLOGUE TO DRINK

{Pil}

"**I am Icarus, Aegis, Master, and Slave.** This is my closing and farewell for now."

The recording replayed its ending scene. Blared from every shop, food vendor, and vice den on the stroll down Pil's exceptional promenade. Enticing patrons to venture inside and listen. Like this restaurant with its fancy diorite bar and glass booths. All around the establishment, contraband entered the ears and minds of the impressionable public.

The irritated man gritted his teeth and asked for the check, careful to keep the hood of his carbon fiber coat closed. Couldn't let the locals see his face. After paying a ridiculous amount of credits for grilled mushrooms he didn't even touch, the man stepped away from the bar and headed for the door. Flexing, he felt tight in his own skin. This compression setting bunched his muscles to discomfort. He resented it. But how else would he hear the Verse illegally broadcasted across the Vast Collective for himself?

Take care not to lose sight of your own well-being. Because if the great King Rayne—Killer of Night—falters, how will the Shadow push on?

Be brave. Your army is coming to rescue you. Leave some for the rest of us.

That elegant cadence matched with that arrogant charisma—The Atheneum. Accomplice to his brother's demise, Korac, the former Icarean General, knew very little of shame. Much like these shop and restaurant keepers who fearlessly sold admission for listening parties. Hence the expensive vegetarian meal.

Profiting from infamy. How positively capitalist of them.

Korac and the Aegis slayer known as Sagan or Seamswalker mocked the very laws they offended with this Verse while recording it. Congratulated one another for their indiscretions and claimed the side of the righteous in their constant lovemaking.

Children.

The frustrated man flexed his fists again. As he passed the bar, people attending from all eleven planets muttered excitedly.

"I can't believe how little I understood of Cinder's suffering."

"His woman sounds hot. Maybe hotter than the Silver General, himself?"

"I wonder what the Tritan's want with the Aegis Dyson's Sphere?"

"Have you found a copy of Nox's Verse? I hear it implicates Primary Rem in more atrocities—"

And so the speculation went on.

This amount of provocation did not bode well for the irritated man's cause. Nor the others'. He left the venue to find more of the same on the street. The bustle of people hushedly discussing the significance of Korac's Verse.

Outside a botanical shop, a Caprent man and a Mon3 drone wondered aloud, "And the Progeny were charged as traitors without appearing before the Tribunal. Three out of the four Eminents agreed."

The drone frowned at this. "That was two months ago, right? After the disaster which closed all the conduits to Gait?"

Slyly, the Caprent looked around and lowered his voice. "My cousin was indentured to the Pain Curator. The Progeny freed him. Gait was no accident. That was the Seamswalker and her vengeance on ol' Razor."

Eyes wide, the drone swallowed hard before verifying, "Your cousin is safe, right?"

"Oh, yeah. Works in the Lamian porn industry now. But you know... he doesn't have any idea what happened to the Progeny after. Just the same rumors we all hear of their sabotaging slave industries Collective-wide."

Normally, the irritated man would interrogate the Caprent about his cousin. In fact, he planned to do exactly that.

Later.

Now was the time to breathe away from the others. As unhappy as they were. With him. With Gait's destruction. And with the Progeny. Never mind the loss of a genius they never fully appreciated—

"Looking for Razor?" A Pil Dwarf appeared from a black hole of a den. Dark and vacuous, it smelled of molded cheese.

When the question sunk in, the annoyed man tilted his head to the side. "What are you on about?"

Slinking big blue eyes left then right, the Dwarf encouraged the irritated man to lean closer so he could elaborate. "I worked on Gait when it went to pieces. I stole some of Razor's equipment, see? Set up my own Emporium of Exotic Experiences in here. You want it, I got it. Including Rayne's pain."

Fascinating. Knock-offs of the Pain Curator's once great empire. That brilliant young man contributed more to the Vast Collective than any single mind in existence. Nacres, memory exploration, access to all manner of vice—And this is what it amounted to.

"Get lost and take your counterfeit pain with you."

The Dwarf scoffed before offering, "May Elden forgive you, mister, for aggrieving a humble merchant with such venom."

Now the man was angry. No amount of breaths or heartbeats would span long enough to let him calm down. He stormed back to the Dwarf and snatched him before the short man could escape. In his face, the angry man spat, "Elden was a sociopathic opportunist with no regard for those in his life who loved him. He cared only for prolonging his people. Which sounds noble, until he disregarded his advisers, pushed his wife away, and abandoned his daughter. The only reason you even know the pagan's name is that he got very, very lucky once and the Vast Collective has paid gravely for it ever since—"

Tears spilled from the Dwarf's eyes, tripled in size. He was terrified, but not of the angry man's words.

Fuck.

The hood fell back and revealed the angry man's pale blue skin with deep blue striations. A clear film that passed for eyelids slid over his black voids with every blink. No lips, nose, or ears—No way to mistake him for anything but a Tritan.

A crowd gathered and gawked.

Wonderful. Just spectacular.

Tired, so very done, Remorse deactivated the compression field on his orb to zero percent. Within seconds, he stretched to his full height of sixty-five feet and substantial breadth.

Time to take out the trash.

After decimating the promenade, he'd convene with the others to resolve this situation caused by freeing the Verses into the Vast Collective. Civil unrest wasn't the right word for it. No. This shit stank of revolution. And with every attack on their supply lines, despite Imminent's discretion, the Progeny gained more ground in this war. The efforts of the clandestine organization couldn't afford this exposure. It hurt Enki's research of the Mother to revitalize the reproduction of the Tritan race. Only one young woman satisfied their requirements thus far, making her the most likely candidate in Enki's ambitions.

And then there was Silence. Her eyes kept careful watch on Remorse to repay the *kindness* he showed the powerful female when the Primary left her for millions of years in stasis. With that threat looming at all times, Remorse deserved a fucking break.

Yes.

Senseless, stress-relieving destruction now. Imminent anti-Progeny campaign later.

They would start with Tameka.

ONE

BLEED YOUR ENEMIES DRY

{LACCEIRUS-CAPRA}

GREEN BLOOD AND ORANGE MUD CLUNG TO TAMEKA AS SHE SURFACED FROM THE UNDERGROUND LAKE. The knife in her teeth was sharp and sliced through the throat of her nacre-less opponent. After narrowly dodging several of the Caprent's acid attacks on land, she tackled him into the unclean water. This eliminated his acid-spitting advantage as much as removing his nacre eliminated her ability to drain his life from it.

The Caprent lost.

Tameka swam for the lake's lofty banks, pulling roots from mud, trying to climb her way out. Entire trunks slipped easily from the slimy, stratified sludge.

Great.

Defeated her enemy, only to find herself trapped in this shit forever—

"I got you." A gray hand with slender fingers reached for her. The arm attached to it was bound in muscle, displayed by his trademark black tank.

When she gazed up, Tameka wasn't surprised to find his signature grin. Only this was the first time she saw it on a battlefield. "Thanks."

Xelan easily lifted her from the muck. "Nice move, by the way. We should fight the Caprent soldiers underwater more often."

"They're pawns. Not soldiers." Tameka's voice sounded harsh even to her, but she was disgusted with how Imminent discarded lives so casually. "Only cannon fodder for their masters, sent to distract us from our mission. And—" She glimpsed some slimy swamp plant entangled in her short red curls. "Oh… oh no. How is my hair?!"

For the first time in two months, Xelan laughed so hard he held his ribs.

Tameka wanted to glare, but the relief overrode her personal hygienic crisis.

"Your face is priceless. It's only Rentroot. Here." With those dark eyes sparkling, he stepped into her personal space and removed the offending flora. His warm fingers brushed her chilled and sensitive neck. She shivered, and his hand lingered on the skin left exposed by the plunging neckline of her combat suit.

Time slowed down. The swampy cavern of Lacceirus-Capra melted away. Her pulse skyrocketed, and her breath caught in her lungs. This close, she gazed at the midnight ring surrounding his black eyes. They stopped shining with humor and ignited with a familiar longing. One they both endured over the last two months.

Of course, for Tameka, almost three years passed since they last—

"Yo, you two okay in here—Oh. Sorry." Bones, well-meaning and a solid teammate, stomped all over the moment. Ruined it, in fact, marked by Xelan stepping away. The good-natured Icarus left as quickly as he entered, but the damage was already done.

Swallowing hard, the love of Tameka's life—her soul mate—turned his back on her before stating the obvious. "We'd better head back. The mission is nearly finished." Xelan disappeared into the next tunnel.

Tameka looked to the cavern ceiling. Pink minerals veined the pale blue, almost translucent rock. Moisture sweat from the swamp's humidity and left a sheen on every surface.

What was she hoping to find by looking at the rock? The key to good timing? A permanent solution for Imminent? A guilt-free babysitter who could liberate both parents for some X-rated exercise?

The thought of Pax, their sweet son, returned the smile to Tameka's lips. Safe back at the Villa, she hoped he gave Iuo, Lamassau, Twenty-One, and Andrew a run for their money. She offered a prayer to Elden that they'd tire each other out before the A-team returned.

Holding onto that positive thinking, Tameka left the cavern to join the others. The mouth of the connecting tunnel opened at the top of an impossible chamber. She detracted her wings while marveling at the subterranean city below. Dissolved by Caprent acid, the people basically barfed their city out of pale blue rock. A rainbow of minerals scattered along every surface in a beautiful display of determination.

"Thank Elden for Kombuchi," Tameka muttered to herself. A Caprent warrior and friend located this ancient hideaway for them. The Shadow would never find it without him. There he was, in the acropolis' center, with the spectacle of his joints bent backward as he waved for Xelan. On magnificent wings, her soul mate joined the Caprent for the last phase of their plan.

"Time to go."

With a deep breath, Tameka dove into the humid air. The mist collected in tendrils of her dirty hair as she plummeted near half a mile deeper into the planet. It smelled earthy and alive. A second from hitting the rock floor, she batted her wings and let them carry her to the acropolis where her people waited. The A-team was comprised of her, Xelan, Kombuchi, Bones, Lynn, and Devis. The remaining Shadow were scattered across the Vast Collective doing Elden's work. That is, uniting the heroes against the villains to protect the people caught in the middle.

Amen.

Massive pillars of the pale rock supported the miles of sediment above from collapsing on their skulls. Tameka alighted between two of them where Xelan, Kombuchi, and Lynn waited. Off to the side, Bones stood like a muscled wall over Devis and their target. A Mr. Bort Les.

Lynn waved as her deep brown eyes scanned their perimeter. Nothing would get by her, evidenced by the viridian blood coating her umber skin and combat suit.

Tameka returned the gesture before whispering, "Does he have the information we need?"

Kombuchi nodded at the dark—almost blue-complected—Progeny interrogating the dazed Caprent with glowing purple eyes. "Devis is still searching his memory. This ability, how many other Progeny possess it?"

Suppressing a flinch at his direct question proved more difficult than Tameka wanted to admit. They kept their secrets closer these days after learning no small percent of their initial Shadow were traitors all along. Technically, three Progeny—ancient and recent—shared the ability to access nacre memory banks. Sadly, Tameka wasn't about to volunteer that information. Kombuchi established his trustworthiness on the battlefield.

But so did R, Smith, and Lucas.

"A few." She eventually minced the words out before changing the subject. "Anything else of note in this impressive citadel?"

Stuffing a black loc behind her ear, Lynn earnestly looked to Xelan for permission to share. She smiled warmly at his encouraging wave. Must be good news.

"We found a geological site where slaves mined soil deposits for Imminent the old-fashioned way. The site is roughly two million years old."

Two million… Well, that would put it around the same time as—

Tameka's eyes flared. "Umbra's atmospheric disturbance?" The one the Tritans made him detonate during Korac and Nox's first mission forever ago. It ruined L. Capra's atmosphere. "It's still obtainable?"

Pride flickered in Xelan's eyes at her correct assumption. "That's right. Deep in the soil bed, and they supply it twice a Collective year to Imminent."

Holding out a small, sealed container, Lynn elaborated, "Because it doesn't take well to blasting, it's difficult to excavate."

Tameka peered through the glass with narrowed eyes until they met with glowing purple rock. "Is it radioactive?"

Xelan explained, "Highly toxic."

"That's why they only deliver it twice a year." Lynn preened a bit in her role as the current exposition expert.

Tameka smiled at her, but Kombuchi's frown gave her pause. "What is it?"

He pointed at the container with his elbow bent backward. "Every Caprent knows that stuff is highly volatile. If mined incorrectly, it reenters the atmosphere and risks a new disturbance. I'm ashamed of any member of my species willing to endanger us all for Imminent favors—"

"Those favors promised me a life beyond the existence of time and confined reality."

The three turned and faced the clustered group of men. Bort, the enemy, glared at them with seething eyes that matched the soil sample. Devis' true-green eyes flared as he stepped away and went to Lynn's side. He trusted her the most after they survived the attacks on Iona's Arsenal together. Dutifully, Bones stepped beside Xelan, his Prince and the Shadow's leader, for all intents and purposes.

Tameka wondered why the men left the villainous Caprent unattended until she noticed the hole in his gaping chest. Violet, luminescent blood poured from the throbbing wound.

It was done.

Bort coughed and gargled. Blood sprayed through his teeth as he grinned. "You think... you've gained anything?" More heaving breaths between coughs. "Imminent will never cease... you ensure only your end—"

Tameka's blade went through his skull, and she left it in his brain. Dead. When she turned and faced her friends again, she expected shock or disdain.

Instead, Xelan offered her his hand with a pained expression, saying, "That was the right thing." Understanding framed his features.

Learning from her unrelated sisters' experiences—Sagan's and Rayne's—Tameka refused to give their enemy time to spill their poison. No talking. Ever.

Shaking off the cold-blooded murder nerves, Tameka took Xelan's hand and peered between the faces of her Shadow.

Kombuchi pointed at the dead man's blood. "Mutated by the mineral deposits. Volatile stuff. Be careful with it, Xelan."

"I'm familiar with it, and thank you. I will." The Icarean genius held his hand out to Bones. "His nacre?"

After the exchange, Bones stood and walked over to Devis. "Are we ready to head home?"

Devis tied his long locs back with a frown. "Are we certain Imminent never planned for us to confiscate his nacre? His memories may be tampered with."

Xelan held the amber pearl in his index finger and thumb against the artificial lights. "I'm almost sure of it, but that's why we have Pablo and the Mrs. here." He winked at Lynn.

She beamed. "With your help, Devis, along with Ross and Kyle—We can do anything—"

Thunder echoed throughout the underground city.

They peered around and at each other before Lynn pointed and cried out, "A pillar! It's—"

It happened in an instant.

One second the pillar was solid and firm, ancient and reverent.

The next second, it slipped.

Maybe an inch or six, but it was enough.

"A dead man's switch." Xelan's voice was already triplicated in pitch, and his eyes solid midnight blue in Atramentous. "BANANA!"

A million years of dirt sighed and shifted, ready to collapse. On them.

Well, screw that. There was no way Tameka would let them die so soon after resurrecting Xelan.

{LACCEIRUS-CAPRA}

As a frightening groan resonated and trembled the subterranean acropolis, Xelan's instincts screamed for him to grab Tameka and escape on his wings. Every muscle in his body strained with the impulse.

But he was more than his instincts.

With a quick scan of their surroundings and a few deep breaths, he calculated their odds of survival. Seventy-two percent if they left now. This afforded them a ten-minute window of flight the way they entered.

Time to go.

Coordinated and trained, the Shadow assumed their escape formation. Wings out, Tameka held Lynn. Bones clutched Devis, who looked terribly dejected by it. Kombuchi reached out for Xelan, his flight partner.

The Traitor Prince of Cinder spared one precious second to catch Tameka's gaze. Eyes green and sharp as stained glass. Beautiful and fierce. Mud and viridian blood covered every inch of her. So very ready for the worst-case scenario because she lived it repeatedly.

Without him.

So young but so tired, he knew from Tameka's memories that her short life was far too eventful. And Xelan abandoned her to it. Their son to it—

Another groan broke his self-flagellation cycle, and with a sharp nod to his Shadow, Xelan gripped Kombuchi before embarking on the emergency flight. Speaking of eventful—

Lynn cried out as their flying pairs narrowly spiraled away from falling boulders and showers of dirt.

Bones growled when a slab sheared his legs through his armor. "Your highness, this shit went sideways!"

Yes. It did. But they expected this. Every Imminent supply chain met them with some element of danger. It's no surprise the most guarded so far in their hierarchy of malignancy would deliver the most devastating pitfall yet.

As the world above threatened to bury them in an extremely deep grave, Xelan prayed to Elden they'd see Pax again—

"We'll make it." Tameka's endless well of optimism surpassed even her capacity for nacre energy.

It made Xelan look back and grin at her.

She beamed at him before her eyes widened in terror.

"Look out!" Devis shouted and pointed ahead of them.

Kombuchi shuddered and convulsed before spitting a vat of acid onto a crashing boulder. It dissolved mere heartbeats before it could crush them in Xelan's distracted state. "This time, 'I got you.'" The Caprent chuckled at his use of a catch phrase the Prince unknowingly adopted.

"Thanks." For letting Xelan see his son again.

They rushed on in silence, aside from occasional grunts and cries. The rocks fell heavier and faster. The groans louder and sounded more frequently. Before they breached the tunnel, a deafening rasp burst from behind them. Each spared a glimpse and did a double-take.

Weakest in the center, the ceiling cracked wide enough to allow the looser silt to deposit in an impressive cyclone that meant to bury the city.

Xelan urged, "Faster."

The tunnel welcomed them with its own battery of debris. Rocks ricocheted in tumbles from the wall, targeting them. But between their aerial maneuvering practices and Kombuchi's deadshot acid aim, the Shadow found their way to the surface without another noteworthy occurrence.

Black rain fell from a brown sky filled with a toxic stench. Wind—howling and angry—long ago peeled away the vegetation from the barren rock. The planet's tears dissolved animal life on the surface back when Umbra decimated L. Capra's atmosphere.

Xelan only learned that from reading Nox's Verse. The Tritans ordered the atmospheric disturbance all for the mineral that eventually led to the Prince creating the Progeny—

"It's working!" Tameka cried excitedly.

The rain made to dissolve their flesh if not for the fortified nanite barrier Lynn developed over the last two months. She beamed at them from Tameka's arms. "It's converting it into H_2O." Lynn stuck out her tongue. "It even tastes good!"

Xelan smiled at her enthusiasm. All of them, brilliant. They grew so much over the last two years—

L. Capra let out a bellow of pain as it funneled beneath them. From the sky, they watched the planet bury one of its ancient treasures. A gorgeous city reduced to dust. Fortunately, it was in the opposite hemisphere from the rest of Caprent civilization.

Kombuchi straightened his toga where it bunched in Xelan's clasp. He huffed. "Our friends on Pil will help us recover it. Whenever this is finally over."

Xelan moved them vertically, standing in the air while he hitched the harness on Kombuchi's belt. Secured, he observed the ruin. "The crawlers and excavators recovered my stronghold on Earth. We can lend a hand." But in all honesty, he preferred the mine stayed buried. He was sure now of Imminent's intentions, and those designs endangered them all. "Once we end Imminent, we'll unearth the city." Not a moment before.

Adjusting Devis in his arms, Bones checked his watch. "We're early for the rendezvous. Do you think B-team made it?" All the while he spoke, he dodged the other man's billowing locs where the winds slapped them in his face.

"We are most doomed if not." Devis in Bones' grip kept his arms folded, looking uncomfortable with the harnessed arrangement.

Xelan opened his mouth to offer a non-committal assurance when Tameka answered with a firm, "Absolutely."

Her optimism was infectious.

Lynn hitched onto the other woman and smiled vibrantly in response. "No way Sagan would let us down."

It wasn't Sagan Xelan was worried about.

{REIPON}

"That's it. We're broadcasting."

Korac was relieved and exhilarated by Tumu's proclamation. The entire Vast Collective paid witness to the story of Korac's life for however long they circulated it. Every dirty secret. Well, aside from the ones Sagan wanted redacted. He smirked at her through the glass separating the studio from the Enki-tech sound booth.

Said gorgeous young blond badass raised the most adorable thumbs up with a goofy grin to match. Her eyes—the most perfect violet—sparkled, reflecting the diamonds that freckled her face and adorned her hair. The carbon stones armored the otherwise mesh slip of a mini dress. Not to mention the incredibly sexy, adamantine-studded collar that spelled an important word between them.

GENERAL.

As in, he, the former, and she, the current General of the Two Worlds' Armies.

Today they corrected a befouled memory for Sagan. The two of them danced all evening at some Prince's elegant birthday party. Stole the spotlight, really, but that might be their attire. Or maybe their description fit two of the most wanted fugitives in the Vast Collective. Minus the two signature axes, of course.

It was a crime to possess white hair, pale eyes, and more charisma than the entire planet famous for its monopoly on the porn industry.

Korac straightened his silver tuxedo jacket with diamond-crusted lapels before turning to back to the blue alien in the room. Tumu. The sound of Korac's voice played all around them. Only slightly unsettling. "How many are we expecting?"

The Gargantuan Tritan, once a Primary now a double-agent Officer, shrugged inelegantly. He blinked the clear film over his eyelids twice—A tell. Tumu was nervous. "Sixty at the festivities. Two hundred on the way. At least.

The Reipon Lamias take their role as the Vast Collective's official historians seriously. Frighteningly so. And you just upheaved public understanding of what that history is, and exposed it as propaganda.

"They will not be happy."

From her vantage point at the window, Ross cried into her earpiece, "They're coming." Her brown waves bounced wildly with excitement.

Through her mic, Korac heard Jack mutter to the young woman, "You can do this. We can both do this." He gazed at Ross for a longing second before she turned and sought Korac through the sound booth's glass divider. Ross dipped her hazel eyes as she recognized the now-familiar habit of seeking the Icarean General's approval.

Ouch.

Elden deliver Korac from unintended victims of his charisma—

"It's time." Tumu sounded a lot like Xelan with that cryptic dramatic shit. "Sagan, are you ready?" He meant was she ready for an emergency Seamswalk exit. Just in case.

Both men left the booth to join the rest in the adjoining studio with a view of Reipon's capital city. Sagan nodded firmly for both of them and the younger Progeny in the space. Her voice came across the airwaves in their back-and-forth reading of the Verses they wrote two months ago.

At the memory of the transcribing, and perhaps to deter Ross' crush, Korac cupped Sagan's chin and pecked her a kiss. A promise of what's to come.

Damn.

Sagan shone him a killer smile, and kept it, even when the doors blasted open. Smoke filled the air despite the entrance the intruders so rudely left open. Nice view of their transport. Fucking crawler knockoffs.

Korac kissed Sagan again. They were ready.

Ross touched both their shoulders and closed her eyes. The male and female Lamian soldiers that stormed the galaxy's largest transmitting station fell to their knees mid-step.

Gait. Child slave. Assaulted and abused. BDSM. Umbra. Icarean royal guard. Planet invasions. Lyriki betrayal. Planetary domination. Earth. The Vacating. Death matches. Second Earth invasion. Volcano Day. Prison. Razor. Sagan's torment. Gait's destruction.

Earth. Grade school. Middle school. High school. Training as a Progeny, inheritor of an ancestral burden. Abusive boyfriend. Emotionally irrational girlfriend. Invasion Day. Volcano Day. Exploring the Vast Collective. Razor. Razor. RAZOR. Gait's destruction.

All of it slammed into the nacre banks of the attacking forces. The Shadow watched on as the soldiers knelt or fell paralyzed when they absorbed Korac and Sagan's entire histories. That afforded the Shadow enough time for the last phase of their plan.

"Jack."

The young man—King Rayne's brother—glanced at Korac with hesitant hazel eyes before he raced up the stairs almost too fast to see. Each of them—Ross, Korac, Sagan, and Tumu—gazed at the ceiling where the base of the transmitter protruded from the glass at the very top of the open lobby. After a few strained heartbeats, a metallic screech and a glass-shattering groan shuddered the several-hundred story space-scraper. The base of the transmitter vanished from the roof. Through the hole, they watched Jack toss the entire antenna off the building.

After five minutes, the outlawed King Regent returned from his long sprint down the tower. A little breathless, he smiled at Ross. "Has it landed yet—"

"Yip!" Sagan startled when the antenna plunged onto the enemy's crawler.

Although the Reipon soldiers left the machine thirty meters away, the ground cracked and shifted until the fissures reached and rocked the building. All the glass blew out and showered them from above in tiny cubes. Korac pulled Sagan into his jacket and sheltered her. The debris tinkered off their backs and arms, which they preferred over stabbing shards. Especially for the unconscious Reipon guards just doing their jobs.

Once the impact settled, Ross crossed the room to the closest guard. She knelt beside them to check their pulse. "Will they be okay?"

Jack swept his impeding brunette fringe back and checked the unconscious guard nearest him. "I think so. You were amazing." He stopped glowing at Ross long enough to spread the gushing. "We all were. I wish we had to time celebrate this victory. I think we earned it."

"No time." Tumu was such a fucking buzz kill. "The Tritans, Lamias, and Imminent will retaliate, but feel free to ask Xelan at the rendezvous." Now he offered a smile Korac would call conspiratorial. "Lam and I would appreciate the off time."

Sagan snickered into her hand, saying, "Don't you mean '*on* time?'"

Ross blushed.

Korac tried to rid himself of his most recent unwanted mental image.

Jack beamed at the group. "We did it. They can't hijack our signal. Do you think the others are okay?" He peered at Sagan as the authority.

She graced him with a warm smile meant for a well-loved sibling. "We know Xelan and Tameka delivered. I can't wait to see what Imminent was doing on L. Capra. Pehton is a soldier to the core. No way is she failing. And Matt and Lucy... well..."

No one stopped that crazy couple of conscience-absent sociopaths.

{ENKI}

"Ginger. This is Morning Star. Have you cleared that sector? Over."

Matt's lips pulled automatically into a smile at the sound of Lucy's sweet voice. It evoked images of her dark blue eyes, silky blond hair, and soft pink lips. Memories washed over him of how deeply she often kissed him when they stood in fields of bodies and flames, soaked in the blood of their targets.

Their favorite kiss.

"Ahem."

Puk's voice was less welcome.

Humored nonetheless, Matt turned to his Monarch 3 partner, and both looked to the sky where Lucy waited beyond Razor's old Emporium of Exotic Experiences sign. She, along with a team of Pil engineers and former Gait employees, operated from a shrine stationed outside the unstable orbit of Gait's remains.

One half of the broken planet flung into the star at the heart of Enki. The other half hurled toward one of many oceans in the Dyson's Sphere, threatening imminent destruction.

That's where Matt and Puk spun, clinging to the bisected planet's rogue half. Dressed in suits designed to the keep their insides contained, the Tritans hired their team to salvage materials from key institutions such as the prison and the Emporium. That was one objective to their mission. For their second objective, they set charges to blow the planet into smaller, less apocalyptic chunks.

Matt was pretty sure Enki stole this idea from a movie. Unfortunately, his familiarity with films ran to the obscure. So he couldn't recall the name of it. Puk, who loved all things Earth pop culture, wouldn't tell him which one. Now they made a game of his guessing.

Lucy came over the line again after Matt's intentional delay. "Ginger. Come in. Over."

He took every opportunity to soak in her voice before her day-shift ended. "Morning Star. Ginger here. We filled three bins with Emporium material. We need two more. There's a lot of goods in here. Over."

Puk chuffed as he pulled an entire control panel from a Divine Booth. "You can fucking say that again."

If Matt knew he'd have to clean up after the Emporium's destruction, he might've reconsidered the decimation. Then again...

Light from the setting sun broke through shards of whiskey stained-glass windows and filtered the jagged horizon of collapsed space-scrapers and warehouses in a mind-bending serenity.

Matt understood the scenery was breathtaking. He could appreciate sights aesthetically. Smells aromatically. But he couldn't understand the emotion behind them. The only time he felt something—anything—was when he clutched someone's skull in his fists or when Lucy looked at him. Breathed near him. Cried out for him—

"Nice work, Ginger. We'll send another bin. Any requests on today's transport? Over."

Her.

Matt almost requested her.

"An ETA on our sanity? Is that something you can give us, Morning Star? This inertia is killing me." Puk smiled broadly through his needle nose, and the expression glittered in his multi-faceted eyes. "But I'll settle for some more anti-nausea meds. This planet spins too fast for my nacre to keep up with. Over."

The Mon3 drone needed an upgrade. Matt would mention that to the group if they ever rendezvoused again. The Shadow was up to some serious shit all over the Vast Collective. Until then, Matt pushed his auburn fringe from his face and grappled with another panel of Divine Booth technology. A white one. Inside, he found a drive.

Rayne's pain.

Razor charged billions of credits a night for the elite rich to experience their King's trauma. So much wealth stored in a tiny capsule that Matt easily fit into his suit pocket. The Shadow held stories. Personal and raw. This one deserved some privacy for a while—

"Ginger. Sorry for the delay, but a broadcast interrupted our channel. It's... I'll relay it." Lucy didn't finish with "over" because she held the mic to another speaker. The voice coming from that speaker turned Matt and Puk to one another.

They both grinned.

[SS]: Korac's chuckling and now full on laughing. I have to know why. "What is it, babe?"

I'm just ruminating that the way Nox reacted to Razor is very similar to how I imagine Rayne would. To treat the Pain Curator like a buzzing insect, too insignificant to pay more attention than it would take to swat him.

[SS]: I smile with him because I've thought the same thing about you, Rayne. And it is oddly similar.

They did it. They fucking did it.

Puk propelled across the space and landed a snappy high five with Matt. The Mon3 drone kept his reactions soundless. Enki surely monitored the comms, and it'd be a shame if the Tritans marked them now.

There was still so much work to do.

"Ginger. Your transport ETA is two hours. I drew the short straw for watch tonight, so I'll keep you through the dark. If you need me, call. Over and Out."

Matt always needed Lucy. She was his conscience, a guiding light of sorts, and he loved working with her.

Puk rolled his eyes with a groan. "You've got that look on your face again."

The ginger human went back to his salvage and muttered over his shoulder, "What look?"

"The 'I love Lucy' face." Puk lent some extra muscle to the task.

With a grin, Matt reminded his comrade, "Well, I *am* her husband." This was the first mission Matt and Lucy worked as a couple. No, they weren't married. Yet. But they sold their story as a married pair who worked for Razor. He did security, and she coordinated operations.

Easy.

Puk had worked with Matt as Emporium security, so not that much of a stretch.

Together they infiltrated the Tritan's emergency effort to save their collective asses. Pun intended. A hundred people scoured the planet for goods and set explosives over the last couple of months. But the deadline was closing.

Enki faced destruction in one week.

The twenty-one-year-old human considered their work. Solid. Xelan orchestrated this efficiently, and Matt hoped they delivered to Wingmaster's expectations. With Korac's Verse on the airwaves, it only meant the others were well on their way.

Matt prayed to whoever was listening that the distraction bought Pehton enough time.

"Yo! Was it 'Deep Impact?'"

"Not even close."

{LUKEMORE}

When the silo's remnants crumbled in an explosive cloud of shrapnel and dust, Pehton's heart stopped.

Oleen was still inside.

"What do you think you're doing, Pehton?!" Miy shouted over the roaring destruction.

To be honest, the orange-feathered Lyrik wasn't sure. Even as Pehton burst from the plateau and soared on orange gliders to the collapsing structure, her instincts screamed for her to retreat.

More of a frenemy and not at all self-sacrificing, Miy stayed behind, guarding Lukemore's entire slave force, freshly liberated from Imminent's design. Blow-back from an explosion swayed through Miy's orange and black feathers as she grimly declared, "There's no way she survived!"

"I have to try."

How very Shadow of Pehton. Guess she was fully integrated into the hive mind now, because all she thought about—all she wanted—was to find Oleen alive and safe.

Pehton's kerosene blood boiled with it until the surrounding air shimmered and rolled with a smoke of her own making. A ball of fire engulfed her. An integration of ignited nanites formed a forcefield around her that combusted incoming shrapnel.

The Siren's Gale.

Pehton was one of only two Lyriks in their history with this gift. And she mastered it. This was an entirely new and untested use of it. No time for weapons testing. The former Executive Warden of Gait barreled into the explosive cloud, determined to recover a teammate.

Flames and fractured silo billowed in a spiraling arc that hindered her descent. Hot. Sweat dripped from her pitch-black skin as this badass Lyrik fought fire with fire. It occurred to her—so very much to Pehton's own irritation—that her courage would impress a certain gorgeous white-haired half-Aegis, half-Icarus.

But that was the anxious desire to distract from her disastrous thoughts talking. Coping mechanisms were nifty because not for one second would she allow herself to believe Oleen was dead. That would mean giving up on her.

Teeth clenched, Pehton finally breached the lower levels of the silo, deep beneath Lukemore's surface. Imminent's trap buried any evidence of the bases below the slave apartments. They nearly buried the slaves with it.

Abresson's pre-recorded image had projected from the Tantamount with barely enough time to warn them the weapon was hidden below. Not that it was intentional. No. The indigo Tritan tuned in for a gloat session with only fifty seconds left on the countdown.

"Shadow, say farewell to your understanding of mercy. No haven will shelter you. No name will pass your lips that we won't hunt the owner and leave them for you to find. You will learn how much mercy we've granted you, for only in its absence will you see. Your lives are ours."

Thank Elden for dumb, smug Tritans. His lack of impulse control had saved their lives and the lives of the people Imminent enslaved. He bought them fifty seconds. Fifteen survivors of the great female race constructed by the Tritans led six million workers to freedom from the Wrong Side of Eternity. From exhaustion, from starvation, and from pollution, they escaped with or without wings thanks to Xelan.

The Traitor Prince of Cinder borrowed from Enki tech to create massive skids and programmed them to ferry across the silo fields where Sagan left conduits. Conduits that opened to all over the Vast Collective. Caedes guarded Kyle as he screened the workforce for memories implicating Imminent involvement. After which, the former slaves selected their destinies and received hundreds of thousands of credits each, courtesy of hacked Emporium accounts. Once again, a gift from Xelan, who established the accounts for Razor.

Freedom.

Or at least closer to it than these people ever knew. Some abducted, some sold by their families, but all of them endured more than enough suffering for three lifetimes.

So had Oleen.

The Lyriki existence wasn't all misery, but they never lived for themselves. First, they guarded the Tritans and answered their every whim. Eventually, they came to serve Gait as its wardens. Their numbers dwindled when their leader, Gale, set the Pantheon on fire during a spontaneous combustion episode. As punishment, the Primaries ordered decommission of all non-Warden Lyriks. Terrified, the female race sought strength in their newly designated leader and Executive Warden, Triss.

Fucking Triss.

Corrupted and selfish, the first Executive Warden infected the others with her malignancy like a vicious cancer. Before long, the fourteen Lyriks under her leadership committed terrible atrocities and forgot shame.

Pehton took it upon herself to reeducate them. She forfeit their volition to Razor and donned the mantle of Executive Warden, unaware it was another of Imminent's ploys. With their will under his command, the Pain Curator subjected the women to the same horrors they inflicted on the prison's slave labor force. Poetic justice? Absolutely. But Pehton still wrestled with the moral dilemma.

Oleen was special. She was warm and gentle. The Lyrik showed the most compassion when Pehton rescued them from Razor's control. Eventually, she brought the others around in time to help the Shadow with this grand stratagem. Even Miy, who stubbornly refused to admit her complicity in the torture of innocent children. But Oleen started to crack that thick skull.

Pehton wasn't ready to lose her voice of reason. Her second-in-command. Pehton believed Oleen when she claimed to know an alternative way out of the silo. The woman insisted on pressing the Tantamount's countdown to retrieve the damning evidence that linked Imminent to the catastrophe. Evidence Kyle discovered when he memory walked with the silo's chief operator. Pehton tried to assure Oleen that six million witnesses were enough. But off she went.

Pehton *must* find her.

Tectonic plates shifted beneath her and disrupted the charges set around the silos. Fire blazed around her, and only her nacre, converting the smoke into oxygen, kept Pehton breathing. Hopefully, it kept Oleen breathing, too.

"Oleen! Oleen, where are you?!"

In a ball of flames, Pehton spun into the bottom level of what remained of the silo and circled it. Hard to see with no light. Even her built-in night vision struggled in these depths with this much smoke. Desperation choked Pehton until her voice broke with it as she screamed, "Oleen! Please!"

Korac's Verse was playing on the airwaves by now. They had been listening to it before they discovered the Tantamount. He spoke of the lost Lyrik. Of how she tamed his temper and his need for control. At the time, it made Pehton chuckle to imagine that the most gentle Lyrik once educated the Icarean General in BDSM, but in some ways, the Vast Collective proved actually quite small—

The train of distracting thoughts ceased, crashed, and derailed.

There was no alternative way out, and Pehton supposed Oleen realized that. Or knew all along. She tucked herself into a flexible duct. It rode out the worst of the tectonic activity, but it did nothing to deter the flames.

Tears spilled down Pehton's cheeks. They evaporated with the heat before they could mingle with her sweat. Contained in her fire shield, she glided from the silo's center to the interior wall and crouched into the duct.

The smell...

Pehton would not gag, but she'd choke on the raw emotional lump in her throat. There wasn't enough of Oleen left to bring back and bury. Only her yellow eyes remained like stones amid the char. Hard as gems, Pehton collected them with hands that shook. Raw, she rasped, "I'm sorry, sister."

As she made to leave, the ash succumbed to Pehton's Gale and revealed something. It shined. Alloy? Glass?

Holy. Shit.

The amber hue of nacre glass nestled in the curve of Oleen's shriveled remains. The brave Lyrik found the evidence exactly as Kyle described. Oleen guarded it even in death.

Fresh tears fell, but the instability of the fault below grew more violent. There wasn't enough time to honor her with Eternity rites. Squeezing the eye-stones in her hands, Pehton said goodbye. "Thank you. We will never forget you."

The flight challenged her sanity, but she eventually broke free of the fallout. On the way to the others, she hoped the home team welcomed a funeral. Although by now, Andrew, Lamassau, and the others expected casualties from the battlefield. But it seemed no matter how many times they lost soldiers, they never expected to lose someone close to them.

Pehton and Caedes now had one more thing in common. They both lost a friend to that arrogant, bloated, scarred shit of a Tritan.

Abresson would pay.

TWO

DRAIN THE POISONED WELL

{REIPON}

ANDREW SNEEZED INTO A TISSUE.

"Uncle Andu! Someone t'inking 'bout you," Pax called from the tree growing in the center of the living room. Its multiple trunks of charcoal gray climbed high through several stories of the Shadow's Villa. The toddler employed this as a means to travel between floors.

Only three years old, but more closely matured to five, Tameka and Xelan's son combined adorable smallness with incalculable intellect.

"See!" Lamassau stomped in from the hallway. The only green Tritan pointed a long finger at the toddler. "This is what I'm talking about. How does he even know that idiom?" Since everyone started co-habituating together, the Chef suspected Pax of putting on an act. "He's diabolical, I tell you!"

Said sinister child hung himself upside down on a branch. Pax's red curls swung with him as he showed all of his tiny teeth. "Hee!" With a grin that would do his dad proud, the baby Progeny fired his little fingers like guns at Lam.

The Chef gasped, clutched his chest, and spun to the wooden floor to his dramatic end. "Brought down in my prime!" Tritans bared sharp quills for teeth when they smiled. Even the conspiratorial wink in Andrew's direction couldn't temper the ferocity of the sight.

Andrew tasted Lamassau's intentions. Sure, this was invasive. Downright rude. But after the hell Lucas subjected Andrew to, Conscience's conscience couldn't care less. His ex-lover left behind the shattered fragments of Andrew's heart and some trust issues.

I hope Tumu returns safely. I wonder if I can convince Andrew to make snacks. After this game, it's time to put Pax down for a nap…

Okay. Maybe Andrew's conscience cared a little. Lam's innocent intentions shamed him. Leaning across the diorite counter separating kitchen and living room, Andrew offered, "Who wants Pil shrimp wraps?"

Despite his convincing act as a corpse, the Chef perked at the mention of food. With a hand raised, he called, "Me! What about you, Pax?"

The toddler's face was purple from hanging upside down for so long. In a voice giddy from the blood rush, he requested, "Sweet tatos."

Andrew grinned at him while shaking his head at the incredulous cuteness. "Those are your mom's specialty, kiddo. We'll—"

"I can make some," Twenty-One volunteered from the stairs.

He dwarfed the Lamian Prince beside him in bipedal form, who offered, "I'll help. I'm starving."

Both men pounded down the extra wide staircase with heavy combat boots and five hundred pounds of muscle between them. Twenty-One blended in with the warrior caste of Icarean society, dark brown eyes and long black hair. Only his size, almost as formidable as Nox, set him apart. Iuo was a black and blue-eyed gentleman who moonlighted as the Vast Collective's very own Porn Baron.

Yes, that's an actual title.

So far, only Twenty-One and Puk starred in a film over the last two months. Miy volunteered, but the Shadow agreed it was best to keep the endangered species incognito until after they won the war. A rumor spread throughout the villa that Pablo and Lynn commissioned a private filming session for a professional home movie. Supposedly it involved a trapeze.

Desperate times called for desperate distractions.

Andrew invited both men into the spacious kitchen with him. The big guy fetched ingredients from the higher cabinets made from a matte black material. The snake prince grabbed some sweet potatoes to peel.

While cleaning the shrimp, Andrew laughed at Lamassau's attempt to retrieve Pax. "Come on, kid. You'll faint at this rate. I can't even see those freckles on your cheeks anymore from all the blood in your noggin."

Enjoying the casual family vibe, Andrew asked his two sous chefs, "How is everything upstairs?"

They glanced at each other before answering in a way that prompted Andrew to check their intentions after their answers. luo went first. "The residences are still free of Imminent carvings, spyware, and people. Aside from Bethany, who is still unresponsive."

"The recreational floors are clear as well. Except that *woman* keeps shouting at me to free her." Twenty-One's face scrunched in distaste as he set the potatoes on the flameless cooking surface. "Triss is truly tenacious."

With their answers ringing as truth, Andrew still scanned their intentions. The gnawing pricks of anxiety all over his skin itched at him until he gave into the impulse.

Pax likes extra sour cream in his potatoes. The calcium will strengthen his bones. I should start the bacon.

To say Twenty-One was a surface thinker insulted his military skill. The Icarus lived millions of years with a suppressed nacre in the warrior caste. He was still coming along, but his kind intentions, once more, left a twinge in Andrew's guilty heart.

But that didn't prevent him from testing luo.

My people will never forgive what I've done. Even so, I pray to Elden one day they see that the truth saved this

Vast and wonderful Collective. And may history prove more merciful in its account of my deeds.

Shit.

Was everyone here a fucking saint?

Well, of course they were. They were Shadow.

Irritated in his shame, Andrew went extra aggressive on mincing the shrimp into a paste.

Fuck Celindria.

Fuck Imminent.

And fuck Lucas!

How could that Icarus live with Andrew for two years and lie to him every day? The man even betrayed the Progeny's location on Cinder that fateful day when Nox killed Xelan. The day he brutalized Rayne.

And why—dear Elden—why did Andrew still want to hear from *him*? To listen to what the Icarus had to say?

"Keep your faith in me a little while longer."

Was Andrew a bad person because he wanted Lucas' last words to mean something?

John died because of this shit—

A warm tininess wrapped around Andrew's leg.

Pax squeezed his tawny freckled face against the adult's tactical pants. The child promised, "It'll be okay, Uncle Andu."

Only then did Andrew glance at the other faces in the room that he forgot even existed. For a minute there, it was only him, the knife, and his survivor's guilt. The other men unabashedly watched and withheld nothing from their concerned and understanding expressions. Iuo gripped Andrew's shoulder. Twenty-One patted the other bicep.

And then there was Lamassau.

The crazy Tritan abruptly hopped onto the counter and scrambled across it to kiss Andrew on the forehead. With a cheeky wink, he jumped back off. "Listen to the kid."

Andrew averted his eyes and looked down at the shrimpy pulp on the cutting board.

Time.

He needed time they never seemed to have enough of—

"Can you believe they only sent two hundred to stop us— Hey guys!" Sagan walked into the room looking amazing in that dress.

Tameka, who filed in behind her, answered, "Well, at least they didn't install any pitfalls on the likelihood of their deaths—Oh, come here, my handsome little man! Let me squeeze you for a bit!"

"Mommy! Daddy!" Pax released Andrew to run into his mother's waiting arms. "Sweet tatos."

Xelan ruffled his son's hair and kissed his crown, where Tameka held him in her arms.

Sagan focused on the eats spread across the counter. "That sounds wonderful. I'm starved."

"You're always hungry, amos." Korac fixed her with a melt-worthy smirk.

She poked his nose before kissing him and teased, "Aren't we lucky my appetite for you is truly bottomless—"

"Stop!" Xelan shuddered. "Please, we talked about not doing that around me."

Andrew hid a snicker.

Sagan pecked Korac another kiss. "Sorry, Wingmaster. I'm off to retrieve Pehton's team. I'll be back in time for food, so don't eat without me." The Seamswalker backed into a conduit with a finger pointed accusingly at the group. "Again."

Twenty-One bowed his head to Korac, who nodded at his soldier as he retreated up the stairs. The former Icarean General's intentions lay bare as if he couldn't contain his concerns.

Sagan looked so tired. The nightmares are getting worse. I'll draw her a bath after dinner…

Remorseful, Andrew closed Korac's intentions out. The couple deserved their privacy.

Still whipping the potatoes, Twenty-One asked, "Where're the rest of the teams?"

Tameka sat Pax down on the counter and tied his shoes while answering, "Sagan took them upstairs first. Everyone needs a shower." She glanced over at the nearly finished meal. "Thanks for cooking, guys."

Iuo drained the potatoes and muttered over the water pouring, "Always happy to play house-husband."

Xelan mused, "I'll get you an apron with 'Kiss the Chef' printed on it."

"Make that two," Lam ordered.

Everyone laughed.

Andrew snuck away from the conversation to hide under the open stairs. He tried to rely on this coping mechanism less lately, but every now and again, he tested it. The coin flipped in the air before landing on the floor.

Side.

Again.

Ever since Silence arrived at the pit in Cinder, even before she betrayed them and stole Rayne, the coin stood on its side. Time to find a new way to explore the Probability Matrix. Or this shit rendered Andrew useless. There was too much at stake. The Shadow and Rayne. Plus, whatever Para, Karter, and Chris endured under Celindria's command these last few months.

Until Andrew regained control, pain, violence, and death awaited each of them.

{Enki}

"Has anyone ever said you're about as funny as you are sane?"

It took everything in Chris' power to ground out that little quip. All up in his head, sweat dripped from his lip and doused his taupe skin across his naked body.

Celindria liked to keep him that way. *"I appreciate the aesthetic your fit physique brings to the chore of piloting your volition."* She had confessed on the third day of this nightmare.

Chris only hoped Remorse let the Valkyrie keep their clothes, but highly doubted it. Karter was gorgeous, tall, and built like a warrior with ample curves in all the right places. The woman rocked a rainbow mohawk. 'Nuff said. Para was tiny for a Valkyrie but tall for a human woman. Short blue hair and a cute penchant for cut-off shorts and leather harnesses. The pair of them spent the last several million years together and generously welcomed Chris into the relationship within the last three years.

There was no way in Hell Primary Rem wasn't using them to torment each other.

And god dammit, Chris couldn't do shit about it. So he needled his jailer to rail against his impotence.

"Remorse is a demanding lover. I think he often considered himself generous when his actions came across more as pitying his partners." Celindria turned away from the visual outside of Chris to glare at those bright blue eyes in his direction. "I'm sure the anatomical barb gave the old Tritan a complex. Us Vast Collective women weren't constructed to tolerate the painful extension.

"Demanding."

Venom. Poison. This bitch loved nothing and hated everything.

On all fours, Chris spat the sweat and Celindria's taste from his mouth. She forced his body to service her every three hours—although, he honestly lost track of how long he spent in this mental inferno.

Rape.

Chris recognized this as rape.

One refuge he found in this firestorm was that Silence kept Para and Karter too busy for Remorse or Abresson to make similar physical time with the Valkyrie. Knowing how the Shadow gossiped about Kyle's feelings for Silence, Chris prayed the young man saw some decency in Silence that granted charity onto the enslaved women.

One other consolation was that Chris never, *ever* doubted their people would rescue them. It was a matter of leverage and opportunity. In the meantime, he endured Celindria.

Chris peered through the screen of his eyes. T.A.O. returned them to the continent in Enki. Wearing yet another

Mad Max dominatrix ensemble, the small Seamswalker idled off to the side of Celindria's lab. With every surface covered in nacre glass, the sterile space held a floral fragrance carried in from the connecting tunnels. Purple-leaved, orange-blossomed flowers lined the black cave system that surrounded them.

They called the continent New Cinder.

The room boasted several slabs, cold storage, and some odd machinery Chris didn't recognize. A cage lined the south wall. Inside, Celindria imprisoned a young man with dark skin that matched hers. He kept his hair in short twists. But it was the prisoner's teal eyes that shocked Chris.

The man could only be Andrius, Andrew's ancestor, and Celindria's brother. She was so family-oriented.

When the ancient male Progeny first laid eyes on Chris, tears spilled from them. Choking from the emotion, Andrius said, *"In my deepest regrets, I beg forgiveness from a stranger for all you'll endure because I was weak. I am so sorry."*

The last two months tested that proclamation.

Unwillingly, Chris and the girls staged terrorist attacks and planted evidence implicating the Shadow across the Vast Collective. Remorse forced Karter in her role as Eminent to vote in favor of outlawing the Progeny, convicting them of charges without them coming before the Tribunal for trial.

Despicable.

The proceedings divided the people of the Twelve Worlds. For them, the Progeny extended Elden's legacy. They fought for good, and the Tribunal were infamous for their cruelty.

In that vein…

With everything in Chris, he lifted his head and gave Celindria the full force of his gaze. "You will never achieve your aims, woman. We will stop you. Give it up, and maybe we'll consider mercy for you."

Celindria returned her gaze to the view, disregarding him. Her actual body stood across the room at a lab table comprised of several Enki projection screens. Along that wall, the evil mastermind covered every square inch of glass with her notes and formulas.

Although it pained him to admit it, Celindria worked her psychotic ass off with a passion that only the truly crazed indulged. Unfortunately for their team, she excelled at it. Strategy, weapon and defense design, politics—she possessed an arsenal of damaging intellect. And every day she dedicated it to destroying Chris' adoptive family.

The woman in his head ceased abruptly, and her body across from him stood alert.

Primary Rem stormed into the glass cavern, looking awfully displeased. "The Shadow made their move, and I am sore to admit that I'm impressed with the extent."

Celindria stepped away from her obsessions noted in the clenching of her fists to cease the work. "Damage report."

"So far I only know of the diversion." Remorse slammed a drive on the tabletop. "Load it." He settled in on a stool, leaning an elbow on the table. His body language suggested it wasn't casual, so much as frustrated.

Korac's elegant tenor filled the lab with hope.

"I am not the monster you once thought me to be. But I'm not sure I qualify as a man. I have always been lesser, and my gravest fear is that the ones I love most will one day see me for what I am.

"A slave without a people. A slave without a home.

"Rayne, your majesty, whereever you are, if you can hear this—I hope you recognize the unmistakable charm and magnificence in my voice."

Chris would bet a million credits that when the psychotic bitch played the drive, she never suspected how much it would reaffirm Chris' faith in his people.

"A Verse?" Celindria hissed.

Remorse nodded, propped on his hand. His voice sounded tight as he elaborated, "That's right, and Nox has one they released into the public as well."

The woman's brows shot up before she squeezed them back into a frown, which did nothing to hinder her ethereal and deceptive beauty. After a few seconds of consideration, Celindria murmured, "Did you acquire that as well?"

The Primary stopped leaning into his hand and stood to pace the room. "No. I staged a Shadow attack on Pil's capital promenade." He wandered over to T.A.O.'s idle body and gave her an assessing once over. "Send the Seamswalker out for a copy of Nox's Verse. The public opinion claims it implicates me. I can only imagine what it says about you."

Celindria said nothing. Just stared at her work.

"There's a nasty revelation regarding Abresson in Korac's Verse." Remorse faced Celindria once more. "I haven't decided how to proceed with this information, but I'm certain you'll want him dead. Leave his punishment to me."

"I will exist eternal once this is over. Why should I care about one imperfection?" She turned and gave the Tritan a stare devoid of light or feeling.

Ignoring her, Primary Rem went to the nacre-deterring cell along the south wall. "Andrius. How are you faring?"

"As much as I'm certain it concerns you, my mental health suffers immensely watching my sister manipulate my gifts to torture these innocent people." The Progeny shimmered like Karter, implying he underwent Enki surgery at some point. They interwove nacre filament into her bones and skin after she nearly died in a cave-in. Andrius' filaments wove along the opposite grain, leading Chris to assume he was sliced and diced in the past.

Was there no one Celindria wouldn't torment?

"You're too astute," Celindria said.

Shit.

Inside Chris' mind, he squared off with the version of her stored within. Alert of him once more. She always dressed like an angel, a seraph of pain, in all white, breezy ensembles. Celindria approached him with a smile he could only describe as violent.

"Remorse will leave. Then we will continue your lessons."

Fucking. Awesome.

Celindria glanced back at Chris' external vision and addressed the Tritan as herself. "I'll listen to Korac's Verse once I read Nox's. It seems only right to experience them in order. Until you return with it, I wish to remain undisturbed in my work. I am close to a breakthrough with the Seamswalking capsule."

As Celindria went back to her devices, Primary Rem stepped up behind her and clasped the table on either side of her, his front to her back. He was careful not to press contact even as he muttered into her ear, "You wouldn't be dismissing me so you can play with your new favorite doll, would you?"

"What business is it of yours?"

Gross. Now the Tritan was purring. "You know how much I enjoy watching you work. Silence keeps the women too busy for me to find time with them. Indulge an old lover."

When the Celindria in his mind grinned at Chris, he knew this was heading nowhere good, but at least the girls were spared.

Thank Elden for Silence.

{ENKI}

Silence was home.

All around her, monoliths of white stone reached for the terraformed sky. The imposing casings housed tome after tome of Tritan and Aegis history. Floral thyme carpeted the ground in fragrant white drifts. Chrome waterfalls poured into reflecting pools throughout the stacks. Overseers whispered overhead, scanning for intruders in Pil alloy shells. Black clouds swirled against the saphiric, artificial atmosphere. A storm loomed over the continent containing the Pantheon.

Her father brought Silence here many times in her childhood. She never once recalled unsettled weather here. Father said it was to protect the volumes from rain. As the ancient Icarean female gazed at the storm, she almost heard his deep voice amid the white stone. It filled her with peace.

Almost.

An azure pulse rippled across Silence's dark gray skin.

Abresson, plain Tritan of average human height with indigo skin, flashed the white scars hidden beneath his robes when he gestured wildly at the sky. He reasserted, for the thirtieth time, "There is no way Rayne can affect the weather in Enki. It is monitored and controlled."

Smith "humphed" in response from his station by the Progeny King's side.

The young woman slept in a glass coffin filled with her own blood, aptly named the Martyr Complex. To prevent the detonation of her Weapon and to supply Celindria with samples, they connected plumbing to the exsanguination mechanism. Every hour on the hour, golden razors drilled into Rayne's back, pumped nutrients and sedatives into her while draining her of her blood.

Silence ordered Lucas and Smith to guard her. The Icarus hid more than he let on behind those molten gold eyes. After his arrival in Enki, he stopped with the impeccable dress and donned a suit so pitch black and perfectly crafted it looked seamless. An abyss melted over his attractive build. Shorter than Silence, Lucas still carried himself with confidence and purpose. Diplomatic and sincere, he easily infiltrated the Shadow. Perhaps more than he'd intended. Now a depth was cast in his gaze.

Lucas was lost.

Ever since the human defected, Smith sported a telling smile, but what that smile told, Silence had yet to discover. Medium build dressed in combat gear, medium brown hair in a stylish cut, and medium brown eyes lined in kohl. Smith was handsome but not gorgeous, so he blended well into a crowd. Soldier and spy, the perfect assassin, and an agent of Imminent.

Silence suspected Smith of placing his bet on the Shadow. Specifically on King Rayne.

"I warned you not to underestimate her, Abresson." Lucas liked to provoke the Tritan. By the way he leaned against a column that flanked the Martyr Complex, he appeared casual, but Silence noticed the tension in his muscles. Like a coil waiting to spring, Lucas wanted a fight.

Now this was because he either disliked the short Tritan which Silence commiserated, or because regret wormed its way inside and made a nest in the golden-eyed Icarus' heart.

Smith, still with that smile, looked between the Icarus and the Tritan before winking at Silence. Apparently, he noticed as well. He shifted at the ready, where he sat against another column opposite of Lucas.

Abresson showed tremendous restraint when he ignored the provocation and simply approached the Martyr Complex on its dais. He traced the gold filigree in a way neither Silence nor Lucas could. Icarean nacres reacted negatively to gold.

"Her beauty isn't written on her bone structure. Nor her muscles and curves." The Tritan also enjoyed toying with Lucas and Smith, two men who spent so much time as Rayne's guard. "The sleeping King's biorhythms sing in perfect harmony to the Probability Matrix. All Probabilities lead to her. In tears. Alone and afraid."

Smith watched him, but not like an Imminent soldier. No. The human's eyes sparked as he peered at Abresson like he wondered what the Tritan's skin tasted like.

This was entirely too much tension for a room filled with warriors supposedly fighting on the same side.

Not at all like the Shadow who treated each other and Silence like family.

Sat on a bone-white throne, Silence glimpsed her confident reflection in a nearby waterfall. Gray skin and mid-length black hair with a blue stripe that bisected her bangs. Full lips softened the severity of her high cheekbones. When she smiled, which wasn't much lately, all her white teeth showed. The absence of the expression drained the light from her gunmetal gray eyes. But that's not what caught her attention.

Finally.

Clothes that fit her. Her asymmetrical skirt clung to her hips, covering one leg and revealing the other. The top was a slash of material that covered diagonally across her breasts and one shoulder. Barefoot, of course. Icarean warpaint contoured every striation of her muscles and completed the ensemble.

Once upon a time, Elden insisted on painting her skin before battle. It was one of few ways he showed affection for his estranged bride—

"I come bearing news of the Shadow." Although the voice came from Karter's mouth as she approached, the words were from Remorse.

Para walked alongside her from the conduit, presenting something in her hand.

The men straightened and gave their attention to the Valkyrie. All except Abresson. He kept his gaze on Rayne's unconscious body. Silence's skin pinched when not even naked Icarean females could divert Abresson from his obsession with the young King.

At the first opportunity, Silence would kill him.

Remorse forced Para to kneel before the throne. How like a small-minded creature to assume displays of submission meant anything to Silence. "Stand."

Lucas took the device from Para's hand. After examining it, he proclaimed, "It's an audio recording. Would you like me to play it, Mother?"

"Please—"

"I wouldn't recommend that around Rayne." Karter sounded firm with Remorse's commanding tone. "It's a Verse. Korac's. He uploaded it to the entire Vast Collective, and they've distributed copies of Nox's Verse. Something we weren't aware existed."

Silence kept the knowledge from her gaze and noted that both Smith and Lucas also hid their awareness. All the Shadow knew of Nox's illegal Verse.

Rayne slayed Silence's grandson. Celindria said her descendant deceived him, manipulated his feelings for her, and usurped Cinder's mantle from him.

Over the last two months, Silence stared at the Martyr Complex and thought on the matter. One element made little sense. If this girl was capable of such vile deception, why would the Shadow follow her? Why would Kyle—

The knife in her heart twisted until Silence almost gasped.

Too much. She must avoid thinking of the two men who never left her thoughts. The two men she betrayed, for all intents and purposes, but one day, history would understand. "Locate and obtain a copy of Nox's Verse. I care little for Enki's reputation or your Tribunal, Remorse. I care only for shifting the paradigm. Has the release of this information impacted the Probability Matrix?"

Remorse shook Karter's head. "We still can't see events beyond Rayne's destruction."

"And the artifacts?"

"All stagnant. Not one indicator reacts to this Probability with any foreknowledge. We travel blindly." After answering, Para spared a glance over her shoulder at Rayne. "Uncertain for the first time."

Karter grinned.

Abresson copied the expression.

Smith's knowing smile broadened.

Only Lucas gazed down at the trapped King with caution in his eyes.

Silence thought more like him. This wasn't the chaos she sought. This was someone's calculated pandemonium, and only the Shadow could sort it out.

Kyle entered her thoughts once more, and Silence hoped he survived the Tantamount Abresson set earlier on Lukemore. With that in mind, she ordered, "Abresson, join the Valkyrie to retrieve Nox's Verse. And Remorse? Be sure to dress them so they blend into the crowd."

"Yes, Mother." The indigo Tritan pulled the naked bodies of both Icarean females against him with an arm around each as they exited to the conduit. "I promise to behave myself."

As they left, Lucas caught Silence's glance. They shared a brief transaction in perfect understanding.

"Ahem." Smith slipped the device containing Korac's Verse from Lucas' hand. "Mind if I...?"

All three of them looked at Rayne.

Silence took a moment to consider her options. Yes. This one caused the most trouble, and in choosing it, this strained trio stood little chance of surviving. What would the Shadow do?

"Play it."

"With pleasure."

{LUKEMORE}

Kyle was having a bad fucking day. The faintly green smoke from his joint drifted through the open conduits leading all over the Vast Collective. Thirteen Lyriks helped millions of people file through them. Millions of souls in his head. Childhoods, adolescences, first experiences, adulthoods—all of it in pain. Abducted and reduced to nothing but work, day in and day out.

Fuck Imminent.

Pot mellowed out the headaches, but it couldn't cleanse Kyle's brain of this outrageous fever. The throbbing in his temples almost buckled his knees. It only worsened when Pehton returned holding two citrine gems.

Another loss.

Kyle liked Oleen. She was nice to the Shadow and optimistic about their strategies. Another adopted stray.

Now Pehton carried herself in the same way as Caedes. Both heavy in the shoulders with their heads down, shuffling as if their feet weighed too much to lift them. The Icarus still proved formidable in a fight after losing his best friend. More so even. He was quicker to kill.

Pehton was older, though. She understood the futility of mourning casualties. "The good ones go first."

"You're wrong." The gravel in Caedes' voice rattled deeper than usual as he corrected her. "When all you have are good ones, the grief is the same. We've surrounded ourselves with mines of bereavement. Each one fallen is an explosion of sorrow that rattles our house of nacre glass."

Wow. Even through his screaming temples, that made sense to Kyle.

Miy stirred from where she watched beside him to glance over her shoulder at the pair of real upbeat types. Usually, she spoke in a sharp, harsh tone. Dissatisfied with everything. On this cliff overlooking freed slaves, Miy softly pressed, "Then what are we to do?"

Kyle turned then, feeling a little woozy from the pale yellow horizon twisting around. He wanted to hear how the Lyrik approaching Caedes answered. The Icarean warrior kept his back to her. Pink, yellow, and blue blood coated him from bald head to combat boot. Caedes always dressed like a serial killer, wearing a black turtle-neck sweater and cargo pants, but he added warpaint to the uniform after...

Well, Kyle couldn't think of a word that described this level of aggression.

Caedes would fuck anything up that got in his way to Abresson.

Except Pehton, apparently. The short Lyrik only came to his bicep and gently squeezed it. With perfect restraint on those killer instincts, the bald Icarus peered down at her.

To answer Miy's question, she said, "Destroying Imminent is worth every one of those sorrowful explosions. We know the fallen feel the same."

That's right. Everyone who died fought the good fight. But god damn, Kyle was tired of losing people. Not all of them to death, either.

Lucas, Smith, and...

A cruel smile crept onto Kyle's lips. He couldn't think her name without a burn in his chest that Kyle had become far too acquainted with over the last two months.

And then there was Rayne.

Kyle took a solid hit on the joint as his thoughts drifted to the sleeping King. She wanted this. Told them so.

"This is the only way inside. Trust me. Please."

Okay. But now what? How did they communicate with Rayne once she found herself inside? How did they rendezvous with her to synchronize missions? And dear Elden, someone please tell Kyle this wasn't some self-fulfilling prophecy bullshit. The thought of her dying alone and afraid after all of this—

"Story Taker!" Miy cried out as she rose to her feet to help him.

More footsteps rushed across the dirt toward him, but Kyle couldn't see. Fallen to his knees, he squeezed his eyes closed and held his head in his hands. "Too much... light."

Light? Yeah, right. Try guilt and anguish.

But they bought into his bullshit. "Keep your eyes closed. I'm sure the stench from the pollution and fire isn't helping."

Caedes growled when he spoke. Not out of anger, it was just his voice lately. "Sagan will arrive soon—"

"I'm here."

The Seamswalker appeared beside them and whistled at the conduit activity. "Your team finished early, and wow... what a sight."

The exodus migration trickled to a herd of two-by-two now. It still made for an impressive view.

"Almost finished," Pehton assured.

Miy huffed beside her. "Tell the Seamswalker about the price."

Not again. No more talk of death. It was too much.

Kyle's head pounded, pierced, and—

"Well, I'd say six million is his limit. I've seen him in action. He doesn't take breaks. Story Taker just pushes through the pain and smokes more to self-medicate. I—He's awake." Pablo's frustrated voice switched to professional concern. "Hey, can you open your eyes yet?"

The smell of cinnamon gum assaulted Kyle's senses and twisted his empty stomach. If not for his nacre, his upchuck reflex might've won all over the Doc. "Dude. Please." Kyle gagging in his face helped push Pablo away.

"Sorry. Sorry. Lynn likes it." He possessed the good grace to sound abashed. "Is that better?"

Someone giggled.

Kyle cautiously cracked a squinted eye. Black tile floor, white-plastered walls to hide the nacre glass frame, and fiber optic lights twinkled along the black ceiling like a starry night. Combine that with a fairly comfortable bed, and Kyle knew he was laid up in the infirmary.

Sagan and Tameka both smiled down at him. Alive and well.

The blond went first. "You passed out shortly after I arrived. Sprung a leak in your nose, too. How are you feeling?"

The redhead checked his forehead next. "We may have to bench you for a night. Doc Pablo was just giving his orders."

"Bed rest." Pablo gave a firm nod. "You outdid yourself today. Amazing work, and we're celebrating—"

"The other teams? Everyone's all right?" Kyle couldn't wait anymore to find out. "Nothing happened on L. Capra or Yu?"

Tameka's voice softened as she confirmed, "No other casualties."

With warmth in his brown eyes, Pablo elaborated, "R's eternity rites on Yu went quietly, as they should. X took R's kids to stay on Yu with Legir. They should be safe there."

Safe. *Safe.*

Sagan's violet eyes met Kyle's green ones and a sad exchange took place. Was anywhere truly safe anymore? He opened his mouth to say so when a familiar elegant voice sounded disembodied throughout the room.

One night I leaned in the drawing room's entryway while Nox and Xelan told their stories to the delight of our guests. Devis had left the room and when he returned, stood opposite of me in the arch.

Devis folded his dark arms, well-honed from working at his forge. Back then, his head was hairless and shiny. And he had trouble being still. Dusting off his clothes, pulling on his earlobe, rubbing his head—anything to fidget.

It grated on my nerves.

"Wow," Kyle croaked through his tight throat.

Pablo hopped up and offered, "I'll get you something to drink. Water or juice?"

"Juice."

Sagan sank onto the foot of the bed, and Tameka mirrored her. The Seamswalker beamed proudly. "We did it."

Tameka shared the same appreciative smile. "We made it."

Kyle let his head fall back on the pillow, exhausted. But yeah, the relief was catching. "Phase I complete." His brows pulled together in a frown. "Now what?"

"Rest."

The girls looked back at the door. Xelan stood in the frame, shrank it really, looking a little tired himself. Which helped Kyle's ego some. "Hey, Wingmaster."

The biggest pain in Kyle's ass drifted into the room with a tightness in his eyes. Xelan's voice was so sincere as he said, "I apologize. We underestimated the number of people kept as slaves beneath Lukemore's surface."

"No problem. They're free now." And only one person had to die for it. Kyle winced at his internal crassness. "I uh... can I get some rest?"

The girls hopped off the bed, and he felt the absence of their warmth instantly. Tameka came to his side, surprising Kyle. "What you did today was nothing short of amazing, and I don't give praise lightly."

For the first time in three years, Kyle felt a bridge between them. It made him smile for her.

Sagan called from the door. "Yeah. It'll be one of the first things I tell Rayne when we see her. Good night, everyone. I need a break, too."

At the door, Xelan squeezed her shoulder and assured, "You earned it."

They shared a warm smile before she disappeared. Tameka followed Xelan outside with a lingering wave.

Pablo returned with that drink, exercising some perfectly discrete timing.

"Thanks, Doc."

In a white lab coat that flattered his Nicaraguan complexion, Pablo held up a finger. "Because you overdid it and passed out, you're staying for a few hours."

That sounded reasonable to Kyle. "Sure. Standard operating procedures—"

"On Lynn's first night off in two months."

Oh. Fuck.

The wicked grin that crossed the doctor's noticeably full mouth unsettled Kyle even before Pablo announced his sinister plan. "So we're listening to Korac's Verse all quarter-night long."

Someone blow Kyle's brains out already.

Fuck.

{REIPON}

Pablo left Kyle to sleep to the dulcet sounds of Korac's voice.

Fat chance.

The former Icarean General's charismatic storytelling translated too well to audio. No one was sleeping in this house tonight, and not only because most of the residents were couples enjoying their first night off together in months. No. Everyone had homework to do.

With that in mind, Pablo went to check on his other patient. He opened a whisper of a crack to her room. Perspiration gleamed all over Triss' pitch-black skin, exposed from the tossed blanket. On. Off. She couldn't get comfortable, evident by her gritted teeth and occasional groans.

Triss knew Pablo was checking on her. He could tell by how she tried to control her irregular breathing and the flutter of her lashes as she squinted in agony.

The pregnancy wasn't going well.

Korac told the story of his life even in this room. Until Triss told Pablo to turn it off, he'd let her listen. She might learn something to assure her that the Generals adopting her unborn daughter were indeed decent options for parents.

One could only hope.

Securing the door, the doctor returned to the labwork he needed to run on both his patients. So much work to do. Pablo sighed and permitted himself a moment to hang his head. Once the stress settled in, he couldn't make it stop. He pulled on his neck with both hands and blew the hair from his cheeks.

What a fucking day.

And now he wouldn't get to spend the night with Lynn. He rubbed the tattoo of gold-laced circular text over his nacre.

Never endanger this. Never risk yourself without me. Never leave without coming back.

As far as Pablo was concerned, they were still making up for breaking their vows during the attacks on Iona Medical Ecology and Iona Arsenal two months ago. No making up tonight, though.

Then there was the strange interaction with X and Legir on Yu. Against the backdrop of the most beautiful planet Pablo ever saw, X whispered his vow to the Shadow, *"Tell Wingmaster, our Traitor Prince, when he finds the courage to hunt down his own creation, we will be at his side."*

It bothered Pablo ever since. Were they implying that Xelan hadn't killed Celindria, not because he couldn't, but because he chose not to? Or were they implying that *Imminent* was somehow Xelan's creation? They were so cryptic.

"I should ask him," Pablo proclaimed to no one, but it was a good idea. Ask tomorrow after Xelan and Tameka shared some family time together.

In the meantime, the doctor resigned himself to researching the rest of the night. He'd thought to check the blood they took from Rayne before Imminent snatched her. It was contaminated with the virus that was in Silence's blood. The virus Pablo created. That meant Rayne's nacre was possibly fortified against any attempts to deweaponize her.

When Pablo shared this discovery with Xelan, the Icarean Prince vowed, *"We'll figure it out."*

The young doctor cautioned against building up false hope. *"Wingmaster, I feel I need to stress how thorough this virus is—"*

"I'll find a way."

So would Pablo. He worked in tandem with Xelan to cure the virus and further simplify Rayne's nacre. The doctor was two hours deep into his research when Thubgy, resident Hellkitten and big purr motor machine, scratched at the door. Pablo cracked it. "Hey, fella. I know you usually sleep with Kyle, but not tonight. His room needs to remain sterile and you…" He inspected the six-limbed critter with a crocodile snout. Mud covered every red-scaled inch of him. "Are not that."

The kitten scurried away with a "huff" toward the veranda. Through the cracked door, Pablo looked up at the nacre glass pool above. Sounds traveled down the open staircase and through the infirmary wing. Uhm. Oh. Those kinds of sounds—

"Do you think Tumu and Lamassau know everyone can hear *and* see their naked asses?"

Caught spying, Pablo opened the door for Andrew. "I was just… I thought I heard—"

The Progeny chuckled. "You and the rest of the house can hear it. I hope Thubgy jumps in and ruins it for them." He tilted his head to the side. "You know what? I take that back. I'm just bitter and maybe a little jealous." Lucas' betrayal hit the entire Shadow hard, but it must be killing Andrew. "What about you? No 'Lynn time?'"

Why was the doctor trying to blush? He was a married man. Who made a professional sex tape. Besides, when Pablo told Lynn of his on-call duties, his wife was *most* generous with their good night parting. He pushed aside his bashful reflexes and grinned. "I promised to make it up to her later."

"Is it cool if I take advantage of your on-call time?"

Pablo straightened and let Andrew in. "Of course. How can I help you?"

The infirmary was comprised of four research stations, each with a pair of projection terminals borrowed from Enki tech. Instruments littered the black countertops. White perimeter lights kept it bright enough for work, but not so bright that Pablo suffered from fluorescent light syndrome. There was a built-in cot in the corner, which he often resorted to during their more dangerous operations.

Andrew leaned on a counter and folded his arms. He seemed uncertain about how to proceed.

The doctor sat on his rolling stool and waited patiently. No need to push here.

After a few heartbeats, the Progeny opened up. "I can't see the Probability Matrix with my coin anymore. It's stagnant and been that way for the last few months, but I think... I think I can trance my way into it."

Pablo's brows shot up as he considered how to approach this. "What do you need from me?"

"You won't like it." At the doctor's encouraging wave, Andrew finished, "I need you to kill me."

The Progeny was right.

Pablo didn't like it.

THREE

WASH AWAY YOUR SINS IN MY RIGHTEOUS BLOOD

{???}

THE TORRENT BATTERED THE BEACH'S WHITE SANDS IN A CEASELESS BARRAGE FOR OVER TWO MONTHS. Concession stands, beach loungers, and sandcastles all drowned in the deluge. Lightning struck violent waves, and thunder rumbled the heavy clouds. The scent of ozone and foam permeated the air. An island beyond the riptide erupted, and a small cone formed from the molten rock. The fiery liquid poured into the raging sea, inviting the lightning to taste the ash there.

Manifestations of her grief and rage, Rayne soaked the rain into her pale skin. Curled her toes in the wet sand. Let the water drip from her long black hair, fingertips, and clothes. Despite the long sleeves of her tunic and the full length of her tights, a chill settled in about an hour ago. Now Rayne was numb. Even hugging herself under the downpour offered little relief.

None of this was real.

Well, almost none of it.

"Rayne."

Nox was real. More real than the combat boot sinking into the sand behind her with his single tentative step toward her. He was the only thing real in her simulated conscience. "Come back inside. We must discuss the stratagem to greater effect."

Lightning struck when Rayne looked over her shoulder at him. It splintered in the reflection of his black eyes. The wind danced with his dark hair, dryer than her own. He lingered, dressed in black, between her constructs—the strategy simulator and the beach.

War and sanctuary.

Nox stood where Rayne's worlds collided, and he asked her to join him in war.

She straightened and closed her eyes with her face upturned to the troubled sky.

Deep breath.

Ever since Abresson killed John, their people betrayed them, and Imminent took her, Nox and Rayne discussed strategy for days on end. Occasionally, she educated him in construct manipulation. But every fourth day or thereabouts, she wandered outside of the dry simulator with its mauve projections of their fronts and into the storm that embraced her with clarity.

Rayne fought for the Shadow, for Earth, and for Cinder. To make Xelan proud and to create a safer galaxy for Tameka and Pax. She did not fight for hate or revenge, but lately she struggled with a gnawing need.

Violence.

She wanted to hurt those who hurt her family.

"Rayne."

The sleeping King opened her eyes. It was like Nox knew, and he found productive ways to distract her from it. Elden, her sanity owed him for it.

Rayne spun fast enough that her hair sluiced water in an impressive arc. Soaked, she glanced up—all the way up their eleven-inch height difference—to meet Nox's gaze. Slightly—so timid in their interactions with each other—he nodded to her with respect, plain for her to see.

"I'll regret it until I'm gone, until I'm dust, and long after."

Even with every awful sin Nox committed against her and Earth—when she looked in his eyes, Rayne believed he'd confessed his truth to her months ago. So they collaborated to work on that whole "safer galaxy" aspiration. And he didn't question her objectively odd behaviors. Elden knew the man had a few of his own.

"Let us begin with Silence." Nox followed her into the room, touched the projection, and brought Silence's outline to the forefront.

Rayne sighed as she recited perfectly from memory, "Surra. Your mother's mother. Wife of Elden. Originator of Imminent referred to as 'Mother of my People.'" She paused a moment as she reflected on the name "Silence."

Three days into their relocation to Enki, Nox and Rayne eavesdropped on a conversation between Smith and the Icarean female.

Smith sounded both curious and hesitant. "Forgive me for asking, but if Surra is your name, why do we call you Silence?"

"My father named me 'Surra.' My husband named me 'Silence.' And Imminent named me 'Mother.' Elden said that in council, I wielded silence as a weapon. And as his enforcer, he wielded me. I was his Silence."

At Nox's curious brow, Rayne continued her recitation. "Uncle Vinco's Verse described a deity or an apparition bearing Surra's description. She would appear at night to soldiers that would die the next day. 'Before your death, there was Silence.' Known for saying, 'On your death, a world ends with you. Know the stars will fall still and weep for you.' As a member of Imminent, she saw outcomes of battles through the Probability Matrix. We believe this was her attempt to absolve her conscience."

Rayne understood this. What she didn't understand was war in Elden's time at all. "I thought Elden's time was a golden era?"

"This predates my grasp of our history as well. Karter might know." He hid a wince at her name by thrusting his fingers into his hair as if frustrated.

Again. Rayne understood. They both listened as Abresson and Remorse complained without end about how the Valkyrie were always too busy to commit them into the breeding program. Silence assigned the female Icari on missions and frequently reminded the men that Karter and Para were infinitely more useful without their wombs occupied, hindering their agility, speed, and strength.

The constant insistence on their unavailability sparked something in Rayne. She felt so stupid when she realized it was optimism. As if Silence was more than an agent of Imminent? Upon this realization, she'd spent another week standing in the storm to wash away the shame of hope.

Nox shifted the image to Primary Rem. Rayne stared up at the three-dimensional projection and hated it. He tortured every King of Cinder into capitulation. Made monsters of them. Although, Umbra was still on trial as far as she was concerned. Rayne didn't know enough of his story. Glancing at Nox, she reminded herself it was easy to hate what one didn't know, but once someone's entire story unfolded, hate often slipped from her and into the ocean. Like the magma from that island, it cooled and eased.

Maybe the same was true for Remorse...

"Nox, when the Progeny first met Primary Rem, he told us a version of Cinder's history. He said the Tritans weaponized Li after they discovered Elden established an army set on scouring the galaxy for the source of his nacre. 'The foreigners.'"

As he listened to her story, Nox folded his arms over his chest with his eyes narrowed in concentration. When she finished, he gravely shook his head. "That contradicts everything I know of our people. My entire childhood, mother—Savis—told us that Umbra formed Cinder's first warriors, the Valkyrie, in my lifetime. Given your source, I struggle to credit this alternative history."

Rayne opened her mouth to question him when he held up a finger. She nodded for him to continue, and only then did he elaborate.

"But given this new information we have and your interpretation of the timeline of events, I am willing to reconsider it. I'll have to sort through Uncle Vinco's Verse. When he mentioned battles in his history, I always assumed he referred to some time after Li's expansion but before my earliest memories. Now, we must know what came before Elden's fall—"

I am not the monster you once thought me to be. But I'm not sure I qualify as a man. I have always been lesser, and my gravest fear is that the ones I love most will one day see me for what I am.

A slave without a people. A slave without a home.

Rayne, your majesty, wherever you are, if you can hear this—I hope you recognize the unmistakable charm and magnificence in my voice. This is my Verse.

Oh, there was no mistaking it. "Korac! Nox, can you believe—"

Nox stopped breathing. The former King of Cinder stared upward into the black emptiness, frozen. The intensity in his eyes only enhanced the ferocity that permeated every fiber of his being.

Korac's Verse, a recording of it broadcasted to the entire Vast Collective, continued, and Rayne changed the scenery. A couch, fireplace, and hexagonal walls lined with books. This transformation occurred around the massive Icarus without so much as a muscle twitch in acknowledgment. Now it was Rayne's turn.

"Nox."

He snapped to her without hesitation, and only then did he recognize the space. "Xelan's study in the stronghold?"

Rayne smiled sadly as she nestled into her plush corner of the leather sofa. Many nights she spent here reading her fallen mentor's diaries until passing out. In her scene, Nox constructed a matching armchair and sat across the coffee table from her. It was good practice to manipulate the space. They sat together in companionable silence, listening to Korac.

Well, until Rayne's tears. Korac's childhood and Sagan's reaction to it pummeled Rayne's heart. Prior to this moment, Nox gazed upward at the source of the broadcast, but after her first sniffle, he peered over at Rayne. To her surprise, Nox didn't hide his own distress at Korac's upbringing. There was a tightness to his eyes and a frown to his full mouth that implied regret.

"I suspected, but I never asked."

Rayne had to clear her throat before she could speak. "It sounds as though he appreciated the privacy. I think he viewed his time on Gait and his time on Cinder as two different lifetimes better kept separate."

Nox dipped his head to her logic and returned his gaze to beyond the ceiling. They listened in silence until the scene in which Korac introduced Pehton.

Do you remember Pehton, your majesty? As if you could forget. She and Tumu detained you for your Tribunal. That was one of your most impressive performances. I was proud to await trial beside you, sprite. I knew Xelan would be proud too, but I suppose you can tell him about it yourself when you two finally reunite.

[SS]: It's a day we're all looking forward to, Rayne. There's a pool going. Two thousand credits say Xelan will cry first. Of course, those are all Tameka's credits. I put five hundred in that both of you would cry at the same time. Don't let me down, babe.

Now it was Rayne's turn to freeze.

"Xel... Xelan..." Her words left on a breath, and her heart pounded in her chest. "Xelan's alive..." Every famous grin he ever flashed passed through her mind, including his very last—

The couch dipped beside her, but Rayne hardly noticed.

Every encouraging word during training. Every goofy name he'd always announced so proudly. All his hugs...

Every.

Last.

One.

"Tameka will lose the wager," Nox declared from beside Rayne.

Hollowed out to make room for this new revelation—a world with Xelan in it once more—Rayne looked up to meet Nox's eyes, blinking in shock.

The powerful figure on the couch with her reached over and caught a single tear as it fell from her cheek. He held it for her to see. "I'd take that wager. Sagan primed you to cry first. Tameka already lost. Do you want in?"

Nox's sudden good humor shocked the clarity into Rayne that she so desperately sought. After another heartbeat, she laughed. It was so absurd. "He's alive, Nox." She squeezed her eyes shut to allow the tears to flow freely. "Xelan..."

When his weight shifted on the couch, Rayne opened her eyes to find Nox leaning forward with his elbows rested on his knees. He worried his hands in a nervous gesture. Softly, he said, "We must include him in our calculations. He'll come for you. How does that factor into the stratagem?"

Rayne grinned, despite the tears on her face. "I can do this. We can reunite the Shadow, and I can still destroy the Tritans without destroying Enki or myself. I believe in us."

{???}

"I believe in us."

This sweet young woman. After everything the Tritans and Nox put Rayne through, she still harbored so much hope. It energized her. Weeping one minute and then the next—

Rayne hopped to her feet and stared down at him with her hands on her hips. A beautiful, encouraging grin amid those dry tears. Black hair still wet from the rain. Commanding his agreement with the enthusiasm of someone who survived one war, not several.

"I believe in us."

Nox believed in her.

And Xelan.

If anyone could infiltrate Enki and exploit its weaknesses to bring down the fall of an eon-long empire, it was Nox's little brother. Once Xelan learned of Nox's existence in Rayne's conscience, it would all end. And truly, Nox found justice in that.

So bring the battle and bring the strife. There was only one person in the entire galaxy who could thwart one-hundred percent Probability in the Matrix, and Rayne smiled with all the warmth of Li down on Nox at this very moment.

Rayne was capable of anything.

Meanwhile, the recording of Korac's voice continued the harrowing tale of his life. Nox's brother-in-arms and the only person he could call a friend. He'd suffered so much before Cinder.

Nox smiled for Rayne. Not a grin or a smirk. Something he hoped came across as reassuring, but frankly, those muscles were out of practice on his face. "As your majesty wishes, we will revisit the stratagem enlightened by this news. But as we work, I recommend we listen closely to what messages the former General of the Icarean armies encoded for you in this broadcast. A broadcast they risked life and limb to share with you."

Her smile crumpled into a thoughtful frown as she tilted her head, considering. "You're right. This was a dangerous ploy for them."

Nox nodded with solemn understanding. She sank back onto the couch beside him with the smile returned, unable to contain her excitement at Xelan's resurrection.

Again, Nox understood. Some part of him wanted to praise Elden and beg forgiveness from the brother he loved and perhaps misunderstood, but another part of him wanted to punch Xelan in the face for waiting so long after his death to revive as he obviously would. It was obvious to Nox, anyway.

Rayne reached over Nox to claim the pillow on the other side of him. He moved his hands away to let her by, and she smiled at him as she did it. Continued to smile as if nothing would ever take that expression from her again, even as Rayne curled onto the couch in the exact position Nox witnessed her curl into many times while reading Xelan's diaries.

The rites. The Weapon inside her—its fuse responded to pain dealt and pain received. Years ago, Rayne came here to hide that she'd inserted rites—Icarean torture devices—under her ribs. After tapping into Xelan's security feed at the stronghold, Nox watched her cut them out. And she knew.

"You have no right to be here. And if I find one thing out of place, I swear to Elden I'll cross the desert and cut your brain out."

Rayne also knew when Nox had spied her retaking Iona-29 in a bloodbath that Korac indicated Nox quite aptly enjoyed. He always appreciated her violence, but that wasn't the point. Rayne had smiled for the camera feed. With bodies littered around her, Rayne smiled for Nox.

"How did you know I was watching the feeds?"

The words rang in the silence and nearly wrenched that pretty smile from her face. Certainly not his intention, but his curiosity refused to relent.

Rayne remained curled against the armrest, but tensed. Her eyes flashed momentarily as Nox assumed she recalled the instances to which he referred. Eventually, she answered, "The Tritans programmed you as my target with a special tracking system—Your heart. I could hear it across the Vast Collective. Slow. Steady. I knew your whereabouts at all times, but I also knew when you were resting, exerting yourself, or afraid."

Nox frowned at her pause.

Rayne licked her lips and darted her gaze away as if concerned how to word the rest. Tucking a hair behind her ear in a nervous gesture, Rayne elaborated, "Your heart beats a certain way only for me."

Of course it did.

In an instant, Nox was on his feet, unsure as to why. His skin itched under this mental construct of a shirt. He needed to breathe—

A walk. A hunt sounded good. Not only because that was far too intimate a connection to process but also because it no longer mattered.

Dead. Heartless.

This was—

"Nox."

He hazarded a glance over his shoulder at Rayne still curled on the couch and comfortable in his presence despite their history of destroying each other.

"Listen. Korac is about to describe how he met you and Xelan."

That elegant cadence in his arrogant tenor resonated through the space louder and clearer than before. Nox looked at the black, empty void above and absorbed his best friend's words.

I caught the arrow before it pierced my throat.

I heard the youngest boy gasp, "Wow," from across the courtyard.

Yes. It was quite impressive.

[SS]: Korac smirks and winks at me. I'll let him be cheeky with no teasing from me. He's earned it. Although, if we don't take a break for food soon, he'll quickly find me in a less forgiving mood. Your girl gets hangry.

You know the rest of this story, sprite. Nox and Xelan took me to their royal chambers. I thought they were some upper echelon of the army, or looking for a slave. I stripped naked to let them inspect me, as this was always done.

How they reacted changed my life.

[SS]: He's no longer talking. It's been a minute at least. I'm letting him have a moment with his reflections. I initially assumed his childhood would be the hardest for him to share with me., but now I wonder if it's harder discussing what he lost on Cinder once he finally found it.

He's ready.

I wished for a people. For a home. To belong somewhere. Xelan, you self-righteous mad scientist, you gave me the robe off your back. Donated half your clothes to me. And your absolute lunatic head-case of a brother gave me status and purpose. Your mother procured my wardrobe, furnished my room, and educated me.

I'll never forget Nox's words. It was the first time in my life anyone spoke to me that way.

"No. None of that. No one touches you here. You fight. Kill them if you have to. I vow after you fell the first one, the others will not likely try again."

No one touches you here.

You've read in his Verse that Nox called Amolot into the room to supply my upgrade. He subdued her with one-hand—

How?! How else was I supposed to respond to these moments? Not only Nox's words, but his actions demonstrated integrity, nobility, and kindness. Foreign notions to me.

I responded in the only way I knew how.

When Xelan asked if I could take her blood, I looked to Nox for his approval before accepting it. As I would do countless times in the next million years.

Damn you, Nox, for recognizing the significance of that moment. For writing it in your Verse to Rayne. Sprite, you must understand. From the start of my life, I followed orders and did as I was told to keep myself alive. But on Cinder . . .

I found people worth fighting for. I would give up my life for Nox. For Xelan. And now for you.

Nox opened his eyes and grinned.

"I found a people worth fighting for, too." Rayne sounded so warm and sincere from her cozy perch. "He talks as if he thinks you can hear him."

Funny that Nox could. "Maybe Korac suspects." Now wouldn't that make things more interesting?

Rayne responded in silence, prompting Nox to turn and take in her shocked expression. Blinking, she gasped, "You don't think he knows? Do you? I mean... he's the only one who figured out I swallowed your nacre."

This was a dilemma. Nox knelt to ease her craning to maintain eye contact. "Rayne, if Xelan is alive, how will you explain this?" He gestured to encompass the room and himself with it. "To him and Sagan and Korac? Or won't you?"

Rayne held up her hands in surrender as she reasoned, "One thing at a time. I'll change the venue back to the strategy room. I don't think the study is working for you."

No. No, Nox needed to visualize. Within a beat of his absent heart, the room shifted form. Once more, he stood in the black room with lilac projections. Beyond it, Nox glimpsed a bolt of lightning striking the ever-present beach. Sand hardened to glass.

Rayne selected a projection of Xelan and stared at it, smiling softly. Hope brightened her already electric eyes, but the storm on the beach raged on.

"Why does it not abate?" Nox asked. In her elation, he expected the storm to fade.

As if chilled, Rayne hugged herself and turned her back on him to face the storm. Her words barely carried over the torrent. "I'm still grieving for John. But now there's more. My confusion and my doubt."

"Doubt?"

"What if this is a trap? A lie to lure me out of the box? Or let's say he *is* alive. Did I do the right thing sealing myself in the Martyr Complex? Hiding myself and you. Will I... Did I disappoint him—"

"Enough of that talk." Nox walked through the projection to stand beside her. They both gazed out at the storm. The island's eruption continued while Korac told a story Nox recalled with fondness.

Fluorescent lava drained through the freshly opened fault in an impossible vortex. The awesomeness of it glitched out my ability to comprehend it. This isn't what normal people stared at. And certainly not something they considered riding down.

I smirked.

My best friends laughed.

We were ready.

Nox took the lead, and I followed, with Xelan behind me. The current—there's no way to describe that fury. It took us through a vertical tunnel of spinning magma. The heat pressed and tested the limitations of our suits, but I had faith in them. The skids, however . . .

My feet felt loose.

I glanced at the other two to see if they were having the same problem. And when I realized they were fine, I knew I was in trouble.

Wasting no time on feeling ridiculous, I shouted, "Banana!" Such a stupid word.

Despite the literal clouds over their heads, Nox and Rayne peered at one another before bursting into laughter. She giggled sweetly, and he chuckled deep in his chest.

"It is such a stupid word, and I love Xelan for it." Rayne held her sides and looked back at Xelan's projection. "How can you keep that joke coming, and it never stops being funny?"

When Nox wrote his Verse, he focused on anything that might count as helpful to Rayne. Names, places, and events all bearing significance to the Tritan threat. But also because Nox often neglected any memory that offered normalcy. Promised hope. With every other terrible event in his life, how could he get lost in those fleeting moments—

Not fleeting to Korac.

His best friend clung to those memories and grasped the true promise in them. The hope for a home and a family.

Judging from the exchanges between Korac and Sagan, it sounded as if he finally found what he was looking for.

"They're happy together," Rayne offered as she listened on. "Hell, I'd say they're even cute together, but I hope he doesn't get too comfortable warming my side of her bed."

It was such a ridiculous and unexpected thing for her to say that Nox barked out a laugh so abrupt it dismissed his train of thought entirely.

Rayne grinned at him before inquiring, "So… you were fun once?"

The mischievous spark in Rayne's eyes told Nox they weren't getting any work done today, and he relinquished himself as her entertainment with an elated abandon denied to him for far too long.

"I believe in us."

With evidence of Korac's restored faith surrounding them, so did Nox.

FOUR

THESE SCARS BLEED TEARS

{REIPON}

SWEAT. Fatigue. The satisfying hush of spilling sand. And music. Anything other than Korac's Verse.

The tri-forked chain dart with its gold barbs struck its intended target and decimated the sandbag. With substantial muscle strained on her corded arms, Tameka tugged on the chain, returning it to her. It went under her lifted leg and, with a turn, spun behind her back. Cut to her chin, her red curls stayed out of her sight as she obliterated another target behind her.

Hours now she'd spent out here, and Tameka finally understood Rayne's obsession with running. If the Progeny, codenamed Fury, slowed down for even a single second, thoughts assailed her, skewing her perspective. They wanted to claim her optimism. Came here to assassinate her hope.

The constant exertion focused Tameka's concentration better than any meditation technique Xelan taught them—

Xelan.

The source of her concerns.

When they returned home from L. Capra, Xelan and Tameka had went through the motions of their post-mission ritual. Covered in mud, Tameka stripped inside the closet and went straight to the shower. Xelan gave her space until the water steamed enough to censor her. Through the obstructed glass, she watched him pull the pins from his hair. For missions, he twisted and braided it back so it looked cut short. She bit her lip as she considered which look she preferred for him. Pretty with it long. Handsome with it short.

The women around here were more jealous of the men than each other.

As if respecting her privacy, Xelan never once glanced at Tameka, even as she observed, "I couldn't drain their nacres because they didn't have any. Why was that?"

He set out the leave-in treatments she liked and the oils he preferred as he explained, "Imminent sealed the mines with nacre-deterring shields. That and they wouldn't waste a nacre on men and women sure to die while mining the volatile mineral." The considerate Icarus replaced her used towel with a fresh one and hung her favorite fuzzy robe within reach.

But what if Tameka wanted to walk around naked? To tempt him into a look, a glance—Something! Over the last three months since Xelan's return, they skirted around each other in this polite, comfortable but not cozy living arrangement. After depriving herself for two years while mourning him, Tameka was more than ready to revisit the ceiling with him.

Not that an opportunity ever presented itself.

The Shadow worked non-stop to sabotage and expose Imminent. With all their mixed talents and expertise, couples went weeks or even months split in rotations opposite each other. And while "we will always remain" was more definitive than ever, morale began to chafe from the separateness.

Together. They were all together.

Well, mostly.

God damn, Tameka never thought she'd feel sorry for Kyle. But here he was, working his ass off on the brink of hospitalization with no promise of a comforting hand to hold.

Fuck Silence.

Fuck Lucas.

And fuck Smith.

Tameka ripped the chain back, tearing through six bags on the return. Her teeth set in determination, and her muscles screamed in peak performance.

Was she the asshole now? Whining to herself that she wasn't getting any when she was fortunate to have her entire family under one roof again?

Five more bags.

By the time Tameka turned the shower off, Xelan had already left their suites for an errand not at all conveniently timed. Despite how much his swift exit deflated her, he took Pax with him for some father-son bonding and to afford her some time alone.

Pax. Her sweet son. He lit the house with his warm smile and clever adventures.

He's a quarter Tritan.

It showed. They weren't sure where to age him because his cognition sometimes presented more advanced than an adult, but it all manifested in childish humors. Like his understanding of Rayne's situation.

The lack of communication from her in their dreams weighed on Tameka.

Another three bags.

Losing Oleen.

The dart banked from a post and ricocheted through two more bags—

"Mommy kicking butt!"

Tameka loosened the tension in the chain and almost cried out from the agony in her arms at the sudden relief. It impacted all of her senses in a mini-blackout. Pax had already clung to her leg by the time it abated.

"I've seen no one so graceful with that weapon until now. Especially not with your force. Fury." From behind, Xelan breathed against her ear. He squeezed her sore shoulders in a gentle massage. "You'll need to soak this workout off."

Only if you join me.

As if! No one would babysit Pax on their first night off in months. Instead, Tameka stepped away from them both and sat in the training pit stands. "I'll take your advice after I watch you two for a while." Her smile was genuine.

Xelan returned in kind, and Pax beamed at them both. The Prince of Cinder squared off with his tawny copy. "Ready?"

Cheesy as always, the father dressed to match the son. Black sweats and white tanks. Black bands wrapped their knuckles and elbows. They were barefoot. Pax barely came to Xelan's waist, and the boy sported one thing his father didn't. A chain around his neck. He still possessed Rayne's emergency blood after everyone either spent theirs or had theirs spent for them during the betrayal.

Pax inhaled through his nose and lowered his hands. His feet were planted firm and square to the center of his balance. Those midnight eyes in that little face flashed with knowledge not yet afforded to him through experience. Red curls bounced when he gave a firm nod. "Ready, daddy."

Tameka's chest squeezed with the cuteness. Especially with the proud papa Icarus' chest puffing out.

This.

This was all Tameka needed.

{REIPON}

Xelan kicked first, slowed way down to give his son the opportunity to block—

Pax caught his father's foot and pushed Xelan back to stumbling while the little imp backflipped away. He stopped with his fists up, ready for more.

The Prince of Cinder smirked at his clever offspring. "Very good."

Tameka cheered, "Kick his butt, Pax."

That smirk broadened into a full grin, which Xelan let her see over his shoulder.

Her cheeks flushed under her gorgeous freckles from her workout. It made her eyes sparkle with humor until they shifted with mischief and a smirk for what sneaked up from behind—

Tiny arms and legs grappled Xelan's waist and shoulders. At his ear, Pax demanded in a rasp from the strain, "S'rrender, daddy." The boy clutched him in a tight headlock, and Xelan be damned if Pax wasn't applying the pressure correctly.

Spots dotted Xelan's vision, and when he went to one knee, Tameka stood with concern plain in her eyes.

"Pax?"

A three-year-old was putting down the Prince of Cinder in combat—

His weight disappeared with a swift suddenness that left Xelan coughing into his fist.

Tameka's warm hand brushed over the bared skin of his back that did more than soothe him. "Are you all right?"

"Hee, mommy. I beat daddy." Pax performed a little victory hop before appearing in his father's face. "I won, daddy."

Xelan coughed and rubbed his throat where the toddler's little fingers blocked his father's trachea in a demonstration of perfect technique. He reached out and ruffled the red mop on Pax's head while answering in a hoarse voice, "I'm fine, Tameka. Pax, where did you learn a choke hold?"

Pax shied and looked away.

Tameka and Xelan shared a look before he soothed, "You're not in trouble, son."

"No, baby. You did so good. We only want to know who taught you?" Tameka held her arms out to comfort the boy.

He rushed in and took advantage of his mother's tender kisses. "Auntie Kar and Uncle Chris."

Xelan relaxed. Of course, Karter and Para taught him some practical maneuvers. They started early with Cinder's royal sons, as well. Thanks to Karter, Xelan could break an Icarus' neck before he was five.

Tameka smiled brightly at the kiddo. "They did a great job, and you learned so well. You kicked your dad's butt. Look at him. He can barely sit straight." She winked.

Xelan resisted the urge to grin. Instead, he lowered his lids and coughed. "I still feel… a little… woozy…" Dropped flat on the ground, face first in the sandy remnants of Tameka's training session.

Eyes fake-closed, he waited while Pax gasped. "Mommy!" Little pats told Xelan the boy jumped up and down in excitement. "Daddy went to uncon'shush!"

Laughter belied Tameka's mock-surprised voice. "You'd better finish him then. Are you ready?"

"Ready."

Their shadows moved, and Xelan knew Tameka lifted their son for a final kick. Xelan waited until the last moment to burst from the ground and attack Pax in a tickle fit. She turned coat and joined the Prince in tormenting their squealing toddler.

"No fair!"

Xelan grinned and pulled back Pax's tank, proclaiming, "Yeah, well, neither is using secret moves on your dad." He took one big breath before blowing a massive zerbert on his son's stomach.

Tameka kept him from wriggling while giggling at his toddler cries. Xelan looked up to find them wearing matching smiles. Rare ones found only in genuine joy and bliss. These moments would grow less frequent over the coming weeks. So Xelan vowed to appreciate them while they lasted. "C'mon. Let's go back to the room and watch something."

Regal even when she winced, Tameka hid a frown as she reminded him, "Jack destroyed the transmitter. There's nothing to watch."

Right. To force everyone to listen to Korac's Verse, they ended all signals outside of their own untraceable source. And the only recorded videos in the house were Lamia porn.

"I'll read to you then." Xelan put off listening to the broadcast. He needed a break from world-shattering revelations. Nox's Verse reconstructed the framework of the Icarean Prince's entire life. And although his memory was nacre-perfect, it was easy to push aside any instances of Nox behaving as the exemplary big brother. Because, honestly, it hurt to remember a time in his life where Xelan didn't want his older sibling dead.

Korac's Verse would fare much worse.

After both freckled-faced redheads in his life agreed, the family wandered inside. The highest room with a three-hundred and sixty degree nacre glass ocean view, their suites comprised a sprawling bedroom and a cozy sitting room they converted into Pax's domain. A spacious bath accommodated their small family's needs.

"Pax, baby, pick out a book and get the fort ready. Mommy needs a shower after her workout." Tameka waited for his big nod and enthusiastic run into the next room before heading for the closet. "Xelan, why don't you tell me how the debriefing went?"

Before entering the bathroom, Xelan waited for the shower to run and the splash from behind the glass, indicating she'd started washing up. Even though he tried to restrain himself, he took in a glimpse of Tameka in the shower steam. She'd wrapped her fiery red hair in a white satin headband that matched the shower tiles. Her warm-complected curves blurred through the obstruction, enticing him. Despite the obscured details, he never failed to miss the tattoo on her hip. Gold-laced letters inked in a distinctive shape.

WINGMASTER.

Before their workout, it had taken every ounce of his self-control to stave his legs from crossing the dewy marble. All his discipline to hold his arms down from lifting her legs over his shoulders like the last time they were together. Remind her of how good they could be in the shower.

But earlier Tumu, Iuo, and Lamassau were waiting for a debriefing. Pablo, too. Everyone required Xelan's time, and the mission required his dedication. The two years gone did nothing to temper it. If anything, they needed his leadership now more than ever.

Not to mention, Tameka made a point of undressing in the closet. She might want privacy after killing so many Imminent soldiers earlier in the day.

Now Pax's cute humming prevented Xelan from joining her. Their son was in the next room, stripping their beds for sheets and pillows to build a fort fit to protect their reading experience. When was it appropriate for them to find time as a couple? Elden knew Umbra exposed his sons to entirely too much of his affairs in that way. Maybe it gave Xelan a complex—

"So how was the debriefing? Was Tumu intrigued by the mineral? How is Iuo handling the destruction of his people's precious propaganda machine?" Tameka asked reasonable questions.

Xelan gripped the edge of the counter and leaned toward the mirror.

Breathe in. Breathe out.

Too much.

And where the fuck was Rayne?!

Old habits crept in. The desire to retire to his basement labs and work until he thought of nothing else but how things worked and how to unmake them—

Tameka shut off the shower taps.

Moving combat fast, Xelan rushed across the bathroom and grabbed a fresh towel. He stretched it open at the shower's entry before she even knew he'd moved.

Tameka's bright green eyes blinked at him through the steam. She looked perplexed and a little sad.

Curse him for putting the sadness there. "Tameka, I know my timing is awful in confessing this. Our son is waiting for us. But when isn't someone waiting for one or both of us? Please know that I find you as breathtaking as our last time together. Which was—for me—only months ago. I know for you it's been much longer."

Tameka stared at him with her breath bated for him to finish, naked in that receding steam.

Xelan grinned at her. "Since then, I've seen the tattoo, and I can't wait to taste it despite the damage it'll cost me. I want you, Tameka. One day, we'll get the timing down right, and I promise, we'll bust that eighteen-hour record. Until then, I can't describe enough to you how badly I wish one of our people went into psychology as a therapist. Because I think we could all use it."

Tameka's eyes widened and sparkled throughout his impromptu speech, rendering him a nervous wreck. His speech certainly saw more eloquent days. And what if he'd confessed too much to her? Did he put any of it on her—

She stepped from the shower with every curve and muscle bared to Xelan. The air this far into the bathroom cooled her skin into goosebumps. Or maybe those were further indications of her thoughts, hidden behind heavy lids. Confident, Tameka swayed her hips with her steps and met his eyes when she stopped an inch from the outstretched towel.

Elden, she was perfect. Self-assured and adept in a way that was catching. Water traveled down her skin in rivulets that Xelan wanted to chase with his mouth. Especially when she pulled the towel from him and let it fall aside. Tameka reached for him, and he bent for her, an unsteady kiss, so when she pushed him against the counter, he fell back on it. Purring into their kiss, she climbed astride him and Xelan forgot his reservations.

This.

He was missing this.

Not exactly the sex, but more the warmth from Tameka's breasts and the solid weight of her hips gripped in his hands, avoiding the golden tattoo. Her soft moans. The grinding. Hell, the intimacy. This was all he wanted.

Her.

"Tameka."

"Yes, Xelan." She gazed down at him, breathless from their kissing. Her lips were fuller, and her cheeks rosier. Bright eyes left hungry for more.

"I—"

"Mommy! Daddy! The fort is done, and Thubgy got inside. We're waiting!"

They both groaned. But it was a happy sound, made obvious by the look they shared.

Love.

For them and for their son.

This was a step in the direction they needed, but the road might be longer than they thought.

Tameka hopped down and freed her hair. Fluffing her fingers through it, gloriously naked in the muggy bathroom, Xelan hoped it wouldn't be too long of a road. Unbidden, he recalled the sweat glistening on her strained muscles as she worked that chain dart with expert precision—

"I'll find a sitter for him." Xelan licked his lips as Tameka bounced into her jeans with only a black bra complimenting her breasts. "Tonight."

She beamed at him and climbed into one of Xelan's t-shirts, echoing an old tradition for them. Old for her. New for him. Relief transformed into guilt. "Am I a bad mother because I'm looking forward to it?"

Xelan took her hands in his and kissed her forehead. "Only if you think I'm a bad father for the same reason."

"Never."

"That's the right answer." He pulled her with him out of the closet and into the room, where Pax waited on top of his impressive fort. But the boy's eyes didn't move from the bedroom door—

A knock sounded.

"Prince Xelan, it's Iuo. I'm sorry, but I have unfortunate news that can't wait."

Xelan glanced at Tameka with a sad smile before dropping her hands and answering the door through the foyer. "What happened?"

The Lamian Prince averted his black and blue eyes and shuffled his bi-pedal formed feet before daring to answer, "A disaster struck the promenade in Pil's capital city. Leveled it, Wingmaster. Few survivors."

Millions. Millions frequented and worked in that district.

Dizzy. Sick.

Xelan was about to lean his head on the cool surface of the wall until he glimpsed the deeper frown on Iuo's face. Dreading the answer, he pressed, "What's the rest of the news?"

Iuo looked from Xelan to Tameka to Pax, who pretended not to listen under a sheet. With a conciliatory tilt of his head, Iuo finished, "The Tribunal is charging Rayne with its destruction. Xelan, they said she escaped her prison on Cinder with Tumu's help and attacked Pil as an act of terrorism against the Tribunal that punished her and ultimately against the Vast Collective."

Tameka took a step closer, her eyes wide and glittering with anger. He hated the waver of uncertainty in her voice. "Xelan, what does that mean?"

Clenching his fists to stop the tremors, Xelan shifted into Atramentous. Iuo took a step back while staring into his solid midnight eyes, but the Icarean Prince couldn't control himself.

Everything was wrong. Nothing was all right. And now Xelan must risk the last vestiges of his will or give in and lose to fate.

"Once the Tribunal convicts her, Imminent can eliminate her at will. They'll execute Rayne if we don't fall in line."

Laughter bubbled from Tameka. Iuo and Xelan shared a confused glance before she beamed at them with pure confidence and love.

"They'll try."

{Reipon}

Bones missed Colton's cheesecake.

The super badass Iona Lieutenant stayed behind on Earth with another badass Lieutenant, Cypher. Both were humans, but Bones didn't hold that against them. They worked with Tempest and Dolor to recover projects abandoned after Smith, Lucas, and Silence betrayed them. The traitors who took King Rayne.

Although Imminent declared the Progeny and their associates fugitives, Enki and the Tribunal still maintained a front of salvaging Earth and Cinder after the war. The Brethren were still "in charge" there. The Tritans stuck them with the wet work of distributing nacres to human kind.

Suspicious nacres.

Nacres that Bones suspected...

But of what?

Well, he didn't know. But the Shadow and The Brethren brainstormed a few terrifying possibilities. Volition control. Declined intelligence and increased aggression. Explosives—

Fucking everything. Anything.

It left Bones' feet itchy—

"You gonna call or glare those cards into a winning hand?"

Andrew chuckled at Kyle's snarky—and factually incorrect—intrusion of Bones' thoughts. He held *the* winning hand. And what a pool to win.

The last cheesecake. Kept frozen these last few months to celebrate a big win. A win with a high price—

Fuck.

Kyle was right.

"I raise you chocolate syrup and an exquisitely clean fork." Bones threw in his lot to the groans of defeat all around the rosewood lounge. Their censure nearly drowned out the dulcet sounds of Korac's Verse in the background.

Twenty-One threw his cards down, folding with a grievous shake of his head. His heft reduced the professional dealer's table to kiddie furniture.

Devis acted as referee. The First Wave Progeny took the job seriously with his powerful arms folded and eyes squinted at the players. He kept his mask up after Bones' raise, but excitement piqued in his glimmering eyes.

Jack and Ross spectated from the bar. They shared a grin derived only from youthful enthusiasm.

Bones gloated despite his inner monologue reminding him of Oleen's death. "That's right. I—"

A thud sounded from the ceiling. Another. The percussion sounds were arrhythmic and louder at times.

Andrew kept his eyes down with a knowing smirk. Kyle scowled at both the bet and the disruption. Twenty-One chuckled.

Ross murmured with her hazel eyes turned upward, "That's Caedes' room, right? Should we check on him?"

Bones, Andrew, and Devis all shared a look. Kyle blinked wide at his sister. A blush kissed Jack's cheeks as he explained, "Uhm… He's with Pehton."

Her eyes got huge, and that rosy flush reached her ears. "Oh."

Twenty-One cleared his throat into his fist. "I want to see this hand, Bonemaker."

Jack crossed the room and requested some music from the hospitality software. Obviously to help distract from the thumps above. Not that Bones minded. This was all the couples' first night off in months, and as far as he knew, every single one of them was working. Although Pehton and Caedes weren't officially a couple, they spent a lot of alone time together. That's their business, but he got it.

Bones missed Para, and it hurt to think about her at all. Elden only knew what Imminent subjected those beautiful Valkyrie women to. With the stakes raised, for the first time since Volcano Day, Bones worried they might not recover everyone.

Not only on time.

But not at all.

Hope cost a lot these days. Like an entire cheesecake.

Andrew tossed in some sundae sprinkles. "I'm all in."

Kyle looked upside his head. "Quit screwing around. We promised to split this cake—"

"Jack, how are the Iona recoveries?" Ross inquired low enough she didn't disrupt the bickering. "And the Verses?"

Half listening to Andrew and Kyle disrespecting the game, Bones focused on Jack's answer. Judging by their quick glances, Devis and Twenty-One listened along.

The fugitive King Regent of Earth had this smile—kind of a goofy, crooked smirk—that he only showed for Ross. The teenager was terrible at poker, too. "Six, Colton, and Cypher travel on Molly and Iron Hope, distributing the Verses with the nacres. They repaired the Iona Medical Ecology and Arsenal, which sit empty, waiting for us to return. The quantum communicator is running. Tempest oversees the establishment of global receivers. And I heard from Boklo two days ago—Andrew's agriculturist? The Vittle crops are thriving."

"What about Pisces?" Andrew kept his eyes low as he stared at the betting pool. Thubgy's mom, the Hellkite, brought much joy to the home Andrew made with Lucas in the Icarus' zeppelin. The Shadow couldn't bring her on the retreat because she impregnated herself again. Apparently, she schemed to populate Earth with Hellkittens.

Jack's smile warmed the room once he realized he'd captivated the entire audience. "Pisces is fine. I think Dolor is getting attached. There's one other thing." He met each of their gazes before elaborating, "Xelan's stronghold is fully restored." At their frowns, he nodded as they arrived at the same conclusion. "They're trying to draw us out."

Bones gnawed on this concern often. How do they ever return? Could they ever? What about the worlds they left behind—

Tameka swept through the door with a look of pure determination on her pretty face. It'd been two months since Bones saw her in anything other than a combat suit. The blue jeans and black t-shirt were almost startling, but casual suited her.

As if hearing his thoughts, Tameka beamed at him before announcing, "Fellas—and Ross—we need a morale booster. Andrew, do you still have the Iona-29 footage we kept for training?"

Andrew glanced around at all the eyes on him. "'Rayne's Reclamation?'"

Bones almost snorted when she recoiled gently as Tameka exclaimed, "You named it?"

"Not me, no."

Oh.

The way Andrew's face fell made Tameka step off. Softly, she stayed on topic. "I think we need to remind everyone exactly who's inside of Imminent right now." She turned and looked behind her where Xelan and Iuo wandered into the lounge. "And Xelan never got to see." Confident and proud, Tameka squared her shoulders and lifted her chin. "We won't lose. Rayne won't let us."

Jack smiled even brighter.

Ross leaned in and whispered, "I need to check on my sister."

He met her eyes. "Isn't she in her session with Korac?"

"Yes, but—"

Another thud sounded.

Tameka and Xelan looked up. Not Iuo. The Porn Baron made a show of looking at his notes. He'd recognized the sounds for sure.

The only redhead in the room asked, "So... what's going on in Caedes' room?"

Xelan read the room. He laid a gentle hand on Tameka's shoulder and raised a brow. "Pehton..."

A light bulb practically bloomed behind her eyes. "Oh."

Now. Bones minded his own business, but he often let his mind wonder as to Tameka's relationship with the bald Icarean warrior who stood by her side after Xelan's demise. Although Pax referred to the stand-in as "Uncle Caeda," one might say he acted as a father and raised Pax as his own. So what other roles did Caedes assume in the Prince's absence.

But that was none of Bones' business. He only observed a slight... tone... in Tameka's utterance.

"Anybody up for some carnage?" Andrew interrupted the tension. He loaded the capsule into the hospitality device and a screen projected a compilation of feeds from Iona-29. The edits cut together all the angles that captured Rayne in her retaking of the lost facility.

Keeping his eye on the cards and the cheesecake, Kyle rocked his chair back and put his feet on the table with his hands behind his head. The relaxed composure was a front that Bones saw through.

Only six people had ever witnessed this footage. Korac and Nox, at the time it was recorded, they tapped into the feed and watched a show intended to intimidate them. Matt, Puk, and Sagan said Razor played the feed to advertise Rayne's experience at one of his venues. And Lucas, who reserved the footage for "training purposes." Or whatever.

They lowered the volume on Korac's Verse and let Rayne's footage play to the music. Xelan stood closest to the projection and looked up as if seeing Rayne in person. This tugged on Bones' heart. He understood those two shared a connection special to guardians and their wards. In fact, as the display went on, Bones wondered if Xelan might not appreciate the level of violence Rayne demonstrated.

To the beat, Rayne smashed one human guard's head through a cinderblock wall, disarmed a combat knife from an Icarus, and rendered him unconscious with a mid-flip kick to his temple. Still singing, she slashed a human behind the knees and shoved the knife through the underside of the other Icarus' chin. Blue blood showered her face. She tilted her head to the side as if listening or reading something not heard or seen by the camera.

Xelan frowned and stepped closer with his eyes narrowed. "The fuse. She's calculating the damage."

Tameka stood back, emotions conflicted on her face. She looked as though she wanted to reach out to him, but thought better of it. In Ross' absence, Jack sat alone at the bar. He looked equally dismayed. Iuo recorded his observations. Only Devis and Twenty-One looked unbothered. Both men nodded along with each move, as if approving of her choices.

Bones was more in this camp.

Well, until...

Rayne gave a particular smirk to the camera as a guard pressed himself firmly against her. She ripped into the guy's ribs and opened them like butterflied chicken. He screamed as she tore one rib completely out and stabbed him in the eye several times with it to the beat of the song. After his screams died, she threw the bone shank across the room into another taker. It went through his skull.

Everyone in the room shrank back. Winces echoed throughout the lounge. Plenty of "ooo" sounds through tightly squeezed faces.

Xelan looked away and went still. Now Tameka reached for him. He let her smooth a comforting hand over his shoulder blade. Under her breath, she assured him, "Rayne is so strong and capable of anything."

"I never wished any of you capable of this." Xelan kissed Tameka's forehead. "But I understand now why you wanted me to see it." He returned his gaze to the projected images and noted his observations to Tameka in hushed tones.

Meanwhile, the rest shuffled back to the card table, granting the obviously strained couple some space. The men gathered around the cheesecake, and they smiled easier and relaxed in their seats.

Fury was right.

It was a morale booster. Rayne could kill anything, and no one could touch her. With Tameka and Xelan leading the Shadow, anything was possible. They would rescue Chris, Karter, and Para. After kicking Imminent's ass, they would return to Earth and integrate the Icari into human society.

They would win.

In the meantime, Korac's Verse provided Bones with some interesting insights. Like why Rayne smirked at the camera that way. Or why Caedes had such a stick up his ass pre-Tameka days. Thank Elden the Icarus was getting laid as of late.

They could all use the comfort right now.

{REIPON}

Pehton slammed into the floor. The breath left her this time, replaced with little black spots in her vision. Caedes took both her wrists in one hand and pinned her roughly to the hardwood. Sweat dripped from his bare shoulders when he lay down the length of her. She gasped at the intrusion.

A knife in her side.

Before he drew blood yet again, the kerosene of her boiled blood filled the air with smoke and fumes.

"I will not relent to your Siren's Gale." The gravel in his voice gave weight to the undiluted death in his dark green eyes. His opened wings cast them in shadow against the roaring firelight. "Are you prepared to kill me, Pehton?"

Pehton spared a glance at their silhouettes on the wall. They looked engaged in far more pleasant activities. This was life or death. A better warrior than she, his eyes never left hers through the roiling haze of her ability. His hands held her wrists steady despite the sear of his flesh. All the way to his bones.

The flames erupted with a scream from Pehton. A scream of frustration as she shoved her foot into his middle and flipped him over her head. Caedes took her with him, and Pehton landed on top.

Not all was well.

They both locked their eyes on the knife in her ribs, and she gasped for air around it. Such specific pain. Like a bruise that throbbed in her lungs—

"Ah!" Pehton shrieked when Caedes withdrew the blade from her and pushed her off of him.

She lay on her back, staring at the ceiling while he poured them both a drink. Unable to move until her soft tissue repair system kicked in, Pehton listened to his words. "You're quicker. Stronger. Have you noticed a difference?"

Yes. The pain hurt more.

Pehton's electric blue armor, grown from herself, covered her skin in a mesh weave. With expert precision, Caedes managed to insert the blade between the organic material, soaked now in her orange blood.

At least he wasn't without injury.

Only one of his hands committed their post-workout drink ritual. The other rested at his side, blackened to the exposed bones. Oleen's charred remains flashed in Pehton's vision until it blurred.

"Caedes."

He didn't bother turning around. "It'll heal. How is your wound?"

Pehton drew breath for the first time in five minutes without an agonizing suction. "Better." She could almost get up—

After our "success" at L. Capra, the Lyriks arrived. Back then, there were thousands of them across the Vast Collective.

But only one mattered.

Sorry, Pehton. I hope this story doesn't break your heart too much.

Me at seventeen, Nox at eighteen, and Xelan at thirteen. We attended the banquet to celebrate our new guests. One struck a curiosity in me. Black eyes. Orange feathers. She was their leader.

Gale.

Caedes finally turned and met Pehton's gaze with a quizzically raised brow.

"Yes. I like him. Okay?! Not only is he frightfully pretty to look at, but he also makes for a decent friend." Pehton hazarded to sit up and accepted Caedes' hand when he offered it. That well-honed arm lifted her with ease. She only moaned once from the recovering wound. It no longer sucked her breath away, and the pain dulled to a sharp ache. "Drink me."

Although Caedes acquiesced by handing her the glass, he hid a cheeky smirk at her poor choice of words. Some men were only charming when they were shirtless and bearing gorgeous wings.

Pehton made an exaggerated show of rolling her eyes as she snarked into her sip, "Icari. Elden, help me."

"You know your cheeks glow orange when you blush."

She choked on her orange juice. Oh, but the men in this house—her face was on fire.

Caedes chuckled into his milk. It was a warm sound filled with gravelly mirth. This was the first time she'd heard his laughter since Abresson murdered John—Caedes' best friend and brother-in-arms.

Ignoring Caedes, Pehton wandered onto the veranda in time for one of Reipon's suns to set. The other would take another four hours in this seventy-two hour day cycle. But already the third moon ascended, reflected in the calm waters of a forgotten sea where Xelan made their home.

Caedes followed her with his stoic presence.

What was with Pehton and taciturn men? She *did* like him. He was intelligent, respectful, and quite the physical specimen. These sessions were the closest thing to intimacy for her in millions of years. Not since Remorse fed her the dram and rendered her unconscious for his idea of breeding.

So many regrets, but never her children. Twins, a boy and a girl. Despite her perfect nacre memory, she couldn't recall their faces or the warmth from their hands. Razor took that away from her. Took them both away from her.

Pehton's heart ached enough to make her gasp, and a tear fell before she could compose herself.

Caedes lingered unaware behind her, taking in the scene. The sky above was a star-studded green to match his eyes. It faded to chartreuse until it blended with an orange-red on the sun's setting horizon.

Eventually, he broke the silence. "You're improving exponentially."

"Will we move to the training ground soon?" Pehton kept the disappointment out of her voice. She liked the privacy afforded them here.

He leaned on the banister beside her and answered in his way, "No."

Yes. That one word answered everything just fine.

A knock sounded, and he turned for the door, offering, "Miy's here."

"Miy?" Did Pehton sound as startled as she felt? When he paused with a frown, she assumed so. "Sorry. I didn't realize you were training with her as well."

Caedes' feathers rustled as his pinions closed. "I'm not. She asked to eat dinner with me tonight. Is that a problem?"

What was in his voice? Other than gravel. Something else knocked around in there. Sadness maybe?

Pehton ruminated longer than necessary, at a loss for words. "I... uh..."

Everything about him softened. Oh. Did Caedes figure it out? He rubbed the back of his neck in an awkward gesture that made Pehton cringe at her own vulnerability. "I thought... When we moved here, you grew distant. And with Oleen..."

Pehton squeezed her eyes shut and looked away.

His voice continued reasoning in that soft bass. A good bedroom voice. "I respect that you're not ready for... dinner with me."

That didn't mean others weren't in line and damn it, Caedes deserved someone after carrying a torch for Tameka for several years. Elden knew Pehton wished she was the one, but...

So long.

It had been so long for her, and now she felt exposed. Raw. She was afraid—

"I can ask her to leave, Pehton."

How pathetic she must come across to Caedes. With her voice thick from a bad fucking day, Pehton assured him, "You are absolutely right." When she took his hand to squeeze it, she ignored the strength in it. "Miy makes for truly stimulating company, and I'm sure she could use someone right now. She knew Oleen longer than I. Be a gentleman and walk me out?"

Pehton bolstered her facade with a smile to hide the wincing. Even with Caedes' unconvinced glances, she held her head high. Even through the blatant concern in Miy's voice—of all people. They got not one tear shed or word from a broken voice.

Not until the door closed on Pehton.

Miy and Caedes' voices mingled together in muffled conversation. The flirtatious Lyrik laughed, and he joined the chorus from his rumbling chest.

With one desperate glance ceiling-ward for strength, Pehton rushed down the hall to her room. She wasn't crying because she felt more than warm camaraderie for Caedes. That was enough for them to share a few amazing days in bed together—Weeks, even. The Icarus had stamina.

No.

Pehton was crying because Remorse and Razor damaged her in every irrevocable measure. They took from her. Children, friendship, hope, and understanding—two million years of her life. Only now did she realize how little she had left to offer another.

Maybe that's why her crush on Korac felt so safe. He was perfectly in love with someone else, and therefore unattainable.

If that wasn't worth shedding tears for, Pehton didn't know what was.

FIVE

SPACE TO HEAL

{REIPON}

"**DO YOU MISS THE PAIN?** Or the adrenaline from the abuse?"

Bethany blinked at Korac's back. He was the nice Icarus who took her for walks and let her follow in silence, aside from the occasional prying question. But he never looked her in the eye for longer than a few seconds. He mostly kept to himself.

Korac added without a glance over his shoulder, "It's all right if you do. I miss the thrill of killing a foe four times my size with a million or more years on me. Snuffing that wasted life out of existence." His signature smirk entered his voice. "I suppose that's why I don't mind working for the Shadow so much. Plenty of that to go around."

Walking along the tiered gardens, Bethany trailed her fingers across an ivy-covered balustrade. All the while admitting to herself that she missed everything and nothing about her time in Razor's Emporium of Exotic Experiences. Her mind wanted peace, but her nerve endings wanted fire. Boiled sugar. Her skin split under the strike of a whip— Each morning, she expected it from the moment her eyes opened, and feared each night when nothing came. That her purpose wasn't fulfilled—

"You stopped injuring yourself," Korac observed from her arms, neck, and shoulders bared by the crop top.

Or did Bethany commit to better hiding places? After all, this ankle-length skirt hid a lot of prime real estate, and her nacre healed near anything—

"I don't smell any blood on you, Bethany."

Oh.

Right.

He… made her want to put the effort in. Where Kyle and Ross lingered like a constant reminder of a time long lost, Korac shone like a beacon of a time she might yet find.

Hope.

Bethany stopped and stared at the setting sun. Its twin star loomed above, waiting for its turn. She could see two moons from here, some great distance apart. The other pair of lunar crescents graced Reipon's southern hemisphere at this hour. Four siblings separated by a vast sky so perfect a green it reminded her of Earth's grass.

Everything here smelled alive of exotic flowers and sea foam. Xelan selected a beautiful location for his villa. Although how he ever knew he'd need this sprawling vista was beyond Bethany. Sometimes she went a week without seeing the same person twice. She relished the privacy.

Korac leaned his elbows on the banister several steps away. Always several steps away. She never knew if it was because he wanted the space or thought she did. Either way, his calm presence was more than welcome.

Ross vibrated with expectancy, and Kyle pulsed with disappointment. Bethany broke both their hearts.

Zero.

That's how many words she'd spoken in the last four or five years. She was 324. She was the Numbered. Razor hollowed her out and replaced her with a pain-crazed fiend. Now a story played all around Bethany of how the Pain Curator did the same to his baby brother. The man next to her.

Confident. Refined. Deadly.

Bethany wanted to be just like Korac when she finally grew up—

"Hi! Sagan said you were out here. The other girls are waiting for us." Ross followed the concrete steps down the tiered vegetation, looking carefree in her cut-off shorts and burgundy top that enhanced her hazel eyes. "How is the session going—"

Korac met her at the landing and muttered so low Bethany failed to hear him. All she heard was Ross' forlorn, "Oh," when he'd finished. To Bethany, Ross promised, "I'll find you before bedtime, okay?"

Bethany nodded. That was the extent of her ability to communicate, and even that took months to cultivate. She watched as Ross left, and Korac picked his way through the flower beds to the point they shared on the overlook.

"Ross worries. She doesn't understand," he offered this in a gentle tenor. "I know you don't hold it against her, but I think Kyle does. There's a tension there that you feel when you're around them."

Korac talked pretty, and Bethany liked to let him. She listened and appreciated that he knew without her telling. His smiles soothed her. Not because he was handsome, but because he could make them at all, given the memories she'd witnessed from him by accident. One day, Bethany could smile again too.

"Is it all right if I confess something to you that I've told no one?"

Bethany felt her eyes go wide as she peered at him. A secret from Korac. What could it be?

The Icarus changed out of the tux he wore earlier and into a white and black flannel shirt over a black tee and matching jeans. When he leaned further on the banister, the flannel fell a certain way, like he was sheltering himself. His voice was heavy with unease. "I'd rather not have the entire Vast Collective know my every weakness, my every trauma. But—and don't tell anyone this. Swear it." That pale gray stare turned sharply on her.

What else could she do? Bethany nodded.

He returned the gesture before finishing, "I hope it reaches more people like you. People that Razor hurt—that anyone hurt. I hope you take something from it, Bethany. Because you're no longer '324' anymore than I am '*contaminant*.' Do you understand me?"

Korac's words were sincere, but it was his eyes that moved her. Hard frost drifted in them, lost in the fierce determination set in his clenched jaw. A broken thing no longer. But it took him millions of years to find this, and an entire planet of people willing to respect him. Love him—

That's the point he was making, wasn't it? Even if it took a million years, Bethany already had the love of the people willing to find her.

No longer 324.

For Korac's understanding and grace, Bethany gave her best nod.

{REIPON}

"Pablo!" Lynn screamed through her husband's hand over her mouth.

He held her leg high by the bend of her knee with her back pressed firmly against a supply shelf. She stood on the tips of her toes to support what he took from her. What she gave. Hell, what she demanded.

And Pablo never said no.

Her husband let her down with a satisfied groan. "I love when you scream for me." He pressed those full lips Lynn incessantly desired against her throat. Both of them glistened across their brown skin that glowed from their lovemaking.

Lynn kissed the palm of his hand as he removed it, feeling especially thrilled from their hidden engagement. "Mmm… I'd hate to disrupt your patients."

"No, you don't." The smile Pablo gave her reminded Lynn of their earliest encounters. Sneaking around during the apocalypse to find one another alone in the convenient sense. Bashful, but determined.

Their lives were too full and not enough of it with their marriage.

Pablo cupped her chin and brought her gaze back to his. "Where'd you go? I lost you, and that's not allowed."

Although she tried, Lynn knew the smile she gave him was too soft and almost sad. "I missed you last quarter-night is all."

"And all the other nights?" When she nodded, Pablo kissed her before sharing, "Me, too. I discharged Kyle earlier. We have tonight. Assuming I can convince Andrew to wait another full day."

Lynn busied herself with reseating her shorts and throwing her t-shirt over her bra. "What about Triss?"

Pablo sighed and followed her example. She hid a smile as he got back into his scrubs. Even knowing he tired of them, she enjoyed how they enhanced certain assets of his. Something on a shelf caught his attention, and he reached for a gauze pack. "Triss has a special line to reach me. She's... she's not doing so good. If she calls, I'll come right away."

Raising a brow, Lynn amused, "Let's hope she doesn't abuse this power—"

His face.

Not since Invasion Day had Lynn seen every line of his face drawn so tight. He was distraught. "Pablo, I..."

He shook it off and cleared his throat. "It's uncomfortable treating a patient you know you'll lose, even with the amazing technology of nacres. I haven't really shared that with anyone."

Lynn cupped his face and brushed his cheek with her thumb when he leaned into it. "I'm here. You can talk to me."

Pablo patted her hand and shored up a reassuring smile. "Tonight. Right now, I've been away from my patients for an hour, and you're missing girl time."

"Do you think they heard us?" Warmth blossomed on Lynn's cheeks. Not that she was embarrassed. Pablo was her husband, dammit. But maybe she could learn to control her volume for the dying woman in the next room.

Shrugging into his labcoat, Pablo barked out a laugh. "Hah! I plan to get an earful from both patients as soon as I return to my rounds." He kissed Lynn's forehead. "I love you, my sexy screamer. Have fun." His fingers grazed the tattoo of their vows on Lynn's chest.

She shivered and laughed. "That's not getting rid of me, but I'll go. Tonight, we'll talk." Blowing him a kiss, she backed out of the infirmary—

And into the sound of two Tritans still going at it in the pool above. It took every ounce of Lynn's hypocritical energy to restrain herself from shouting at them to get a room. Instead, she mounted the stairs two at a time to the room with the most spacious en suite.

After two knocks, Tameka answered the door with dual dutch braids half-finished. "We're just getting started. Pick a station."

Lynn took in Sagan and Korac's ocean view corner suite. Their kind host and hostess left the windows open, so the wind breezed through their white curtains. Very beachy. It smelled fresh and serene, if a little salty. Korac's Verse played all around them.

Sagan braided Tameka's hair, surrounded by an assortment of tools. Ross set up a mani/pedi station. There was a spot for facials and another for makeup, both championed by two Lyriks. The other avian women ran hot water in the tub for feet soaking. Two other Lyriks Lynn passed in the hall went to retrieve snacks from the boys downstairs.

This grooming ritual was a tradition of the three female Progeny soldiers—Tameka, Sagan, and Rayne. They'd dedicated at least one night a week to primping and relaxing back when the war afforded them that kind of free time. Now Rayne was trapped in a box probably on Enki, and the other two girls were lucky to do this every three months. They were also kind enough to invite the other girls around the house, but some were missing.

"Where's Bethany, Pehton, and Miy?" Picking her way across the product and tool-littered floor, Lynn opted for the facial station. "I figured Miy would be down for this."

Sagan smiled and answered through the pins in her teeth. "Bethany is with Korac." Oh, right. The sessions. "And Pehton said she might come down in a bit. She was... uhm... recovering."

Tameka glanced up at her, and they shared a knowing look.

The yellow-feathered Lyrik steaming Lynn's pores explained, "Miy mourns. We all do. But hers is a private grief."

"Oh, I'm sorry." Of course. Lynn felt like asshole—

"While your apology is appreciated, it is unnecessary. There is much in this house tonight. It is easy to set things aside. Which is why we're here." She gestured to encompass the other Lyriks. "A welcome distraction."

A silence fell on the room. It was comfortable and focused on their shared experiences in grief and battle. This event was necessary. Even with Korac's recount of his truly dismal life playing all around them. Because he was proof-positive that this wasn't the end—

"Has anyone else heard Lam and Tumu getting it on non-stop since we got back?"

"Unfortunately, I saw it with my own eyes."

"Is anyone gonna limit couple time in the pool, or will they keep doing this until we start Phase II?"

"I heard Tritans could go even longer than Icari..."

Yes.

Necessary.

{REIPON}

Sagan loved having the girls in her room. She loved Korac for giving them the space to do this. It was his idea. She loved him even more because he spent his time away from the room helping Bethany heal.

Korac was so getting some tonight.

But Sagan also knew he did it to avoid people in the house. He avoided their conclusive stares now that they all knew so much of his truth. Korac was a big Icarus—very big—he could handle the exposure. It would eventually calm down.

Her lover was not the only person avoiding the story in the house. Even though it played in the room, Tameka distracted from it with discussion or activity. Xelan also seemed otherwise engaged. Sagan counted them as two out of three living persons she wanted most to hear it. Rayne was the third.

"Do you think Rayne's heard the Verse by now?" Sagan asked as she looped another one of Tameka's braids.

The redhead squirmed a little. "I hope so."

Sagan pressed, "What about Xelan?"

"Ah… he's been a little busy. I think he's waiting to catch it on the next run through."

Sagan's non-related sister tensed, anticipating the next question, but the Seamswalker didn't ask if Fury had listened to it. Sagan suspected it might prove difficult to listen to someone that Tameka detested discuss the father of her child in such an intimate fashion. Sagan only hoped she'd eventually grow out of it.

Xelan, on the other hand…

"I'm all done," Sagan said. "And I'll be right back. I have a quick errand to run for the boys."

Not a lie.

Tameka all but sighed with relief as Sagan hopped up and popped over to her desk. The item she wanted lay on top, packaged, and ready to go. She hustled out of the room with its soothing murmur of conversation. This was not something to put off.

Down the stairs and into the basement, Pax's voice heralded her arrival as he squealed and hid beyond a lab table. His freckled cheeks flamed with his toddler crush on Sagan. Living in the house with him was meant to squash it, but instead she occasionally wandered into a room to the sound of his "yips" and scurrying for cover.

It always made Sagan smile.

"Hey, Planet Breaker." It was Xelan's cheesy nickname for her ever since she broke Gait in half.

This also made Sagan smile. "Hey, Wingmaster. I hope you don't mind the intrusion."

They both gazed around the lab with its stations separated by glass walls: medical, tactical, and one specifically for Rayne's malady. Xelan had scribbled formulas and assumptions on every surface lit only by perimeter lighting that glowed along the gray ceiling and black floor. The white walls displayed some notes, but mostly they were covered in Pax art. Paintings, clay statuary, and models—all of which the father and son had created together.

Proud Papa Icarus.

Xelan stopped working on the next discovery that would surely save the Shadow's collective asses. "How can I help you? And what have you got there?" He raised an inquisitive brow.

Sagan gripped the packaged manuscript behind her back. The kraft paper wrapping crinkled under her nervous fidgeting. "Well, I... I couldn't help but notice you're not listening to Korac's Verse."

Xelan's face never looked angry or disappointed. Instead, he looked more understanding and open to listen.

Elden, she'd missed him.

"I brought you this." Sagan held out the only unredacted copy of the Verse. "I figured you might need persuading, so I kept this especially for you. You see, in the broadcast, I redacted most of the detail regarding you. And quite a lot of sex talk between me and Korac—"

Both of his brows shot up this time.

"—But that's neither here nor there. I feel uncomfortable knowing so much about you that you didn't volunteer, but I think some of it is worth mentioning to Tameka." Sagan quickly added, "I won't—Of course. But I... Well, I hope you understand the predicament I'm in. and I hope it helps you appreciate how much you're loved."

Xelan tilted his head to the side in that avian way that Icari sometimes did. As if he listened to some other force—Elden, maybe—on how to proceed. Then he held out his hands for her to pass him the tome.

Which Sagan did, excitedly. "You won't regret it."

"I'm most certain I will, but not for the reasons you assume."

Wow.

Xelan didn't frown as he said it, but something shifted in him. His eyes glittered with it.

"Xelan, what do these Verses mean to you, if you don't mind my asking?" Sagan hopped her butt onto a counter because she wasn't going anywhere.

"Hah!" With that sarcastic laugh, Xelan found a home for the Verse on a lab table beside her and leaned a hip against it. Meanwhile, Pax finished a chalk mural on the black slate tiles, humming a sweet tune only children know. "If I don't mind your invasion of my privacy? Yes. You're the only person I'll allow to ask me these questions because I promised you a talk months—years ago, I guess. But you know everything now, don't you?"

Sagan shook her head and tried to keep the respect in her eyes. "No. Learning from Nox and learning from Korac aren't the same as learning from you. If I'm pushing, please say so—owed talk or not. I don't want to make you uncomfortable—"

"All of this..." Xelan waved at the tome. "Makes me uncomfortable, but not because it's my life being exposed to the entire Vast Collective. That's... Honestly, that's 'whatever' at this stage of things. No.

"These Verses steal away what sense I've ever made of my life."

Oh.

The dawning of it all must have shown on Sagan's face because Xelan nodded with the recognition of it. "When I died, all I wanted was for Nox to die, too. For everything he did in my life and for everything I knew he could do." His voice took on a bitter tone. "I knew *nothing*. His Verse... it keeps me up at night. It keeps me busy down here. I..."

Sagan shifted a little uncomfortably on the counter. She knew there was more that kept him so feverish at work.

And since they all benefited from his fervor, she wouldn't dare criticize him for it. Except... "What about Pax and Tameka?"

For the first time since she lied about Justin abusing her, Xelan glanced at her with suspicion narrowing his gaze. It softened immediately, as did his voice. "I love them with everything in me—"

"Hee! I love you, too, daddy."

Xelan closed his eyes and soaked in his son's innocent eavesdropping. He sighed heavier than Sagan expected before continuing, "There's a 'getting to know one another' phase that never really took place. Tameka and I are working on it though."

Offering him a sweetened smile, Sagan assured, "I know you'll get through it." She glanced at the Verse. "And I think this will help. I want to hear your thoughts, and maybe it'd be good for you to talk to me about it."

Xelan's warm smile broadened to his trademark grin. "You're so tenacious, Planet Breaker. All right. Fine. I'll read it tonight."

"Good. Then you'll catch up with the rest of the Vast Collective." Sagan tilted her head as she considered asking him about their own research project. After Razor confessed that an "Icarus got the better of him" and that led to the creation of Seamswalkers, Sagan went on an endless pursuit to find the Icarus responsible. Xelan offered to help, but she'd taxed him enough for now. Instead, she asked a question that drove her crazy to think about. "Do you think Rayne's heard it?"

Xelan crossed the room to help Pax with his mural. He responded over his shoulder, "Do you want the logical answer or what my instincts are telling me?"

Sagan shrugged. "Both."

On his hands and knees, shading a lovely flower while his son chalked the moon, Xelan explained, "Logically, it would be unwise for Imminent to let her listen to it. And ultimately it's a 'let' situation."

Trying not to pout, Sagan asked, "And your instincts?"

"Rayne is capable of anything. If she could track Nox's pulse across the Vast Collective, she could hear Korac's Verse. And that's what my gut tells me to go with."

In Xelan's heart, he wanted Rayne to know he was alive.

Sagan beamed.

They'd be a family again soon.

{ENKI}

Lucy gazed out at the view from the shrine. A Dyson's Sphere with a tiny planet inside it, and the two halves of that tiny planet promised beautiful destruction. The star at the heart of Enki shone brightly beyond the shields in its orbit that provided some semblance of day and night.

It was night.

Lucy sat at a control panel of projected Tritan-tech to monitor the situation unfolding below, a ringside seat to Enki's obliteration. She let the others, a Collective-wide team dedicated to preventing the disaster, go to bed and leave them alone.

Them.

Lucy and a teammate, a Tritan guard named Yito. One such supervisor stayed with each shift. He constantly responded to a computer implanted in his palm, ever-vigilant of her and Matt's communications. At one point, Yito felt the need to say, "Damn, that human's a lucky man married to you and all. How did you two meet?"

Lucy, who had her back to him, plastered on a sweet smile and relaxed her otherwise straightened shoulders before turning around with the full force of her dark blue eyes and bright white teeth through lips plumped from her biting. "He knows he's a lucky man, too, Yito. We met at school during a big event and really hit it off."

Yito took in Lucy with an assessing stare. Her jumpsuit clung to her form. Not all men liked this. Too sexually aggressive of an ensemble could heighten their animosity, but these suits were standard issue. She did her best with the rest. No obvious makeup, only some mascara. Her blond hair stayed down and softened her youthful face. Her hair was long enough now that it hid any cleavage, only offering tantalizing glimpses. Men liked this.

Men like Justice Lee and Razor.

Lucy diverted the subject to Yito. Always good to talk about them. "Do you have someone special waiting for you at the end of this project?" She sat down across from the blue alien with an almost feature-less face to place them on a level playing field, but he didn't even know he was playing a game.

Her game.

"Nah." Yito dismissed her question with a wave of his gloved hand. "We're not permitted. Keeps us available for our work."

Brightening her smile, Lucy leaned forward, gaping her top and sweeping her hair away. "What kind of work do you do aside from stopping rogue planets? I'm so fascinated with Enki."

Yito chuckled with the unassuming nature of a well-distracted man. "It would dazzle you humans. It's a fascinating structure, no?"

Not that it was theirs. "It really is."

Something pulsed in his palm, and he shrank back into his reserves to answer it. "Excuse me."

From the Verses and the Progeny girls' accounts, Lucy imagined a lot of Tritans could play her game. But maybe not this one. He only seemed to possess the usual curiosity straight men had for women, and he was polite, which she didn't expect from his kind. Maybe he was a better candidate for—

"Morning Star. This is Ginger. We received the bins. Over."

Matt.

Elden, Lucy loved the sound of his voice. The confidence and the easy-going tone of it, but most importantly, the undercurrent of unrestrained danger. A predator lurked here. She almost left him on the hook long enough for him to speak again, but she was monitored and needed to play it safe.

"Ginger. Good job. Are the heavies on the way? Over." The full bins returned to the shrine for inspection before some Tritan fetched them for the trove hidden deeper in the Dyson's Sphere's maze.

"Affirmative, Morning Star. ETA forty-eighty hours. And—what, what do you want me to say? Oh—Puk says thanks for the inertia kits. Over and Out."

That Monarch 3 drone deserved a hug for putting up with all this nausea—

"You three make a decent team."

Decent was not a word Lucy would use to describe them. She faced Yito with a pretty smile. "Yeah. I guess we do."

He returned her smile in the way that showed all those Tritan teeth, sharp rows of them. "I'll request to set you for a permanent detail. No sense in keeping strong players apart."

"Thanks." Yes. Yito would make a fine addition to Lucy's mission. Tilting her head so her hair fell softly from one shoulder, she inquired innocently, "Any news I should worry about?"

The Tritan sighed. "The Progeny King and our rogue Officer, Tumu, destroyed the promenade on Pil, and other Shadow agents apparently killed a bunch of slaves on Lukemore in a tectonic attack. I swear. We were all routing for the Progeny, but this kind of guerrilla activity hurts everyone against Imminent. Do you know what I mean?"

Lucy nodded solemnly. "I do. Working for the vice industry taught me all about how terrorism works against the common good."

Yito gestured at her excitedly before diatribing, "Exactly! You get it! It's so polarizing these days. Team Shadow. Team Imminent. But what about Team Vast Collective? What about our rights? What a mess… It'll just end with Enki putting down all the fun. That's what they did in Elden's day."

Barely concealing her double-take, Lucy controlled the surprise in her voice when she asked, "What do you mean? I'm kinda young."

A black flush graced Yito's cheeks as he abashed and explained, "Oh, right. Humans are so recent. Back during Elden's glorious revolt, when imminent silence threatened our stars, the Primaries did their worst to stop him, and sucked the fun right out of the Vast Collective. None of the old Tritans have relaxed since. Now we all pay for it, and us younger ones are frozen and trapped here in Enki—Oh, sorry." Yito looked around as if remembering where he was and who he was talking to. "You're a good listener, and it's been a while since I talked to anyone about this. Thanks."

Lucy beamed at him. "No. Thank you."

A fine addition, indeed.

SIX

CALM AS WATER; STILL AS SHADOW

{REIPON}

XELAN CLIMBED THE STAIRS OUT OF THE BASEMENT WITH PAX CRADLED IN HIS ARMS. The unconscious boy was draped in the abandon only the young managed, and his father was almost overwhelmed with emotion from the journey to now.

How long before Xelan's son became a soldier and fought in the same war Xelan fended off his entire life? Before he ripped people apart and smiled in a crazed frenzy for the love of violence—

Xelan was unhappy about the Iona-29 footage.

Rayne was a brilliant sapphire in the terrible beauty of combat, but it showed in the tarnish of her soul. She slept in a box of her own blood, refused touch, and reveled in death.

What happened to his little girl—

Pax stirred and curled onto his side in Xelan's arms. They weren't far from their suites now. He took them the long way to avoid Tumu and Lamassau's extreme public display of blind abandon.

Honestly, Xelan was jealous of it. The memory of soft purrs and rushed breaths during his and Tameka's near miss earlier distracted him from work. She looked so relaxed today for the first time in a while, thriving among their people. Her pep rally fostered this casual atmosphere they'd enjoyed since. Tensions melted, relationships regrouped, and some people poked around in other people's affairs.

Pax held Korac's Verse in his hands for his dad, hugged it tight as if protecting it. Xelan wasn't upset with Sagan. He cherished the trust they had, which made her comfortable enough to come to him like that. He only found it hard to face her with what she might know about him. They did ask for his consent before broadcasting it. At least, there was that.

"Okay, Pax." Xelan laid his son out in his tiny bed next to their room. "Good night, son. Mommy will kiss you soon." He kissed the boy's red curls and mused to himself how grateful he was that Pax inherited Tameka's hair.

The child tiredly blinked eyes that matched his father's as he reached for a strand of Xelan's unbound hair and let it slide through his fingers. "I like your hair, too. G'night, daddy."

Xelan frowned as Pax rolled away onto his side. It reminded Xelan that there was so much the parents didn't understand about their child, but now wasn't the time for this derailment of his train of thought.

The Prince of Cinder took his former General's writing to the veranda and found a seat under the second setting sun. More stars twinkled in the green velvet sky as he slipped off the twine and unwrapped the kraft paper.

Off the top of his head, Xelan could list at least ten thousand things he'd rather do with his free evening—

Sincere violet eyes and a soft smile filled with kindness flashed through his conscience.

Of course, he would read it.

Xelan was finishing up chapter one when a beautiful sight stepped onto the veranda. Tameka tamed her wild red coils into two braids that emphasized the delicate arch of her brows, the gentle curve of her jaw, and the soft plush of her freckled cheeks. She'd changed into a white Lukemore silk robe that left her long legs exposed. Out of the Progeny, Tameka kicked the hardest in training, and it showed in the muscle tone of her naked thighs—

"My eyes are up here."

"I don't want those wrapped around me, Tameka." After considering what he actually said, Xelan erupted into a fit of laughter.

Her soft giggles joined him in a happy chorus.

This was comfortable.

He pat the big outdoor sofa beside him and flashed her the bound manuscript. "Sagan's assigning me homework now."

Tameka ignored the cushion and stepped between his knees to perch herself on one of his thighs. Her warmth bled into him, and she smelled like bergamot and expensive moisturizer. She peered at the book. "Can you study with a partner?"

Welcoming her almost shy smile, Xelan kissed her braids. "We could do other things..."

Playfully, Tameka nudged him, but it actually forced a huff from him. She half-laughed as she chastised him. "Sorry, but I won't let you use me to avoid this any longer." Contrary to her words, she kissed him, soft and sweet, before snuggling into him. "We can do this together and talk it through. I want to know you, Traitor Prince of Cinder. No more hiding. Deal?"

"Deal." Xelan adjusted Tameka in his lap and encouraged her to take one half of the book. "This will be the chapter when Korac came to Cinder. When he met Nox and I."

"What did you learn from the first chapter?"

"That I'll have to save my reactions for my Verse."

They read for a long time in silence. Well, not complete silence. Pax's soft snoring drifted through the window occasionally, lighting their eyes with precious delight. They made that little bundle of congested nasal passages. His nacre would correct it in a moment.

After finishing the scene where Nox slayed Gale in what Xelan once considered cold blood, Tameka stirred in his arms. They eventually shifted to lay out the length of the cushions with her snuggled against his side. She looked up at him. Those bright green eyes sparkled with curiosity.

"Get it out of your system."

"Well, I'd hate to know any spoilers before you write your own Verse, but your speed threw me off in Nox's Verse as well. Xelan, you held out on us during our training. Muchly." Tameka poked his nose to keep her observations casual, but her voice held something deeper.

Xelan nodded and set the book aside to trail his fingers along her arm. His gray complexion contrasted against her tawny brown skin. "I was still earning your trust, and I worried about intimidating you without nacres. But that's not what bothers you. Go on, Tameka. You can tell me."

She looked away and spoke against his chest. "You moved so fast, then. How did Nox and Korac ever best you? Why did you resort to the self-destruct code in your nacre?"

Ah. Well. Something akin to shame tightened his throat, and Xelan had to clear it to explain, "If you remember, there was a garrison on the stairs behind Korac and Nox. All I could think was how to stop them from pursuing you and Rayne. I could fend off my broth—Nox—and I'm not sure Korac's heart was ever in the fight. After reading these, I'm more convinced it wasn't. Not really. But I'd never defeat them all. Nox was always stronger than me. I knew this even before I read how much he withheld from us. I thought it was an appropriate time to test an experiment I wanted to install in our Shadow."

"The self-destruct sequence?"

Xelan squeezed her bicep. "Right." It became tougher to talk. "But... I miscalculated. I overestimated the blast radius and the rate of my repair systems. Not only did the explosion miss Nox, but I didn't heal fast enough to recover and escape as I'd intended."

Tameka remained silent. Her fingers walked over the exposed skin of his stomach.

Her contemplation concerned Xelan, so he tried another approach. "It was a risk. If we'd known about Pax, I swear I wouldn't dare. I don't know what I'd do differently, but I know I'd come out alive for you. All of you." His voice softened to almost a whisper. "I blame myself for so much of what happened—"

Tameka's finger planted firmly on his mouth. "No." She straightened to stare down into his eyes, so he'd see how serious she was. "No talk like that. I swear to Elden, Rayne is your daughter in all but direct lineage. She never confessed it to me, but I know she blamed herself for what happened to you. We are not blaming anyone but Imminent. I'm not even sure I blame Nox anymore."

If Xelan winced, it's not because he disagreed with her. It's because hearing that truth aloud, his own truth, further fragmented his delicate understanding of reality.

Tameka continued to echo his thoughts. "Remorse abused and used every King of Cinder, turned them into hateful weapons. I mean, you trained Rayne like a weapon to kill Nox, but I know it's not the same."

Ah. Full wince. Xelan took her hand in his and gave it a gentle shake. "No. What I did was out of hope. I wanted the world behind Rayne so that once she defeated Nox, it would break the Probability Matrix and free her from dying alone and afraid."

"Did it work?"

Xelan sighed, heavy with the uncertainty. "We'll know in time."

Tameka reached over him to retrieve Korac's Verse. "Until then, will you read to me?" She settled back against him, not at all aware that her robe shifted higher to reveal more of her thighs. Almost to her—

"Read, Icarus." Xelan met her sparkling eyes and her brilliant smile. "I'll give you a present afterward."

"Yes, ma'am." He opened the book to the three Icarean teens racing across the Ignis Desert, and an old wound opened into a past life. "This will get rough."

Tameka's smaller hand slipped into his and warmed Xelan at her touch. "We'll get through it together."

Together sounded good.

{REIPON}

Ross closed Bethany's door after finding the girl already curled in bed. No need to wake her. She was often tired after her walks with Korac. Although Ross understood they weren't intensive in terms of conversation or baring one's soul, even wandering in silence next to such a force of personality with so much experience would exhaust someone raised on Earth as a human. Especially a human with a recent history of torture and abuse.

Maybe one day Bethany could write a Verse and share it with her family.

In the meantime, Ross traveled from room to room, pervaded by the sound of Korac's voice with the occasional remark from Sagan. What a horrible childhood, mixed adolescence, and questionable adulthood.

It sent Ross retreating to the lounge with her brother and the boys. Sure, they listened to the Verse here, too, but they also moved on from games to critiquing action movies. Anything to distract from the lonesome quiet of the night hours around the big place.

Andrew asked the room, "Martial arts or gun movies?"

"I'm a fan of sword fights myself," Jack confessed, with an approving nod from Kyle.

Twenty-One snorted, "Guns are inelegant and ineffective in combat."

Bones stood and hushed the room to say, "And no race appreciates how much deadlier their women are than the males like the Icari."

The remaining two—Iuo and Devis—shouted, "Cheers to that!" "Here, here!"

They all toasted their drinks.

Ross grinned at them as she shook her head incredulously. Now that they finally agreed on a Mon3 film, she grabbed a sweater that hung past her shorts and slipped onto the balcony with the door left open. The comforting din of their banter and raucous laughter filled her with warmth and love.

This was family.

With Ross' heart wide open to the feeling, Oleen and John strayed into her thoughts. Pehton looked scooped out when she presented Oleen's citrine eyes at the debriefing. Xelan promised to pay Eternity Rites tomorrow. It wasn't long since the ceremony they held for John. They eventually carved him out of the ice, but, like Oleen, his nacre was too damaged to recover. Neither possessed a back up like Xelan.

Between Nox's Verse and Xelan's understanding of events, the Shadow guessed the Tritans somehow claimed his birth nacre that Nox had held onto for eight thousand years. There was still a question of how his hidden nacre maintained updates of the present, but that was one mystery that awaited them in Enki.

It was just another objective in their main quest to take down Imminent.

In the meantime, Ross downloaded memories from hundreds of people all at once, forcing them into unconsciousness. It was a useful ability, and one which Xelan encouraged her to exercise regularly. As much as she appreciated his guidance, he'd never understand what he asked of her.

"All those people with all their lives in my mind," she muttered to the green velvet night and its diamond littered sky.

A step sounded behind her. "What was that, Ross?"

Over her shoulder, Ross recognized Jack's tall shadow in the doorway. He held a snack tray in his hands and shrugged with it before confessing, "I know there's been little time to eat. I thought you might be hungry."

Jack was so considerate, and the longer Ross stared at him, the more she made out his handsome features.

Brown hair cut short but still soft, hazel eyes more brown than her own, and a pale complexion free of freckles or imperfections. He'd turned eighteen since they moved into the house, and every day his eyes looked older. Every day with Rayne's uncertain fate looming over him like a dark cloud.

Ross smiled easily for the man who worked so hard to find her sister while ruling as King Regent of a planet. "Thanks. I could eat. Will you load me up—"

"A celery stick with nut butter?" Jack gave her a shy smile. "I noticed you like these so much I wanted to try them."

Ross sat down on some patio furniture and took the snack from him. Simple and delicious. "Did you like it?"

"Not at all."

A snort clogged some celery in her throat.

Jack reached to pat her back and stopped himself. Awkwardly, he wrung his heads. "Sorry. I need more training before I trust myself not to knock your eyes out."

Right.

They both needed to work on their abilities. Softly, Ross asked, "What's it like for you? The strength and speed."

Jack's breath left him on a shiver. She wasn't sure if he was cold or unnerved. After a few heartbeats, he shared, "Sagan told me once what it was like for Rayne the first time. She was saving John's life, but she was also scared and self-conscious about it. Now I know it feels like that every time. You feel like a freak, but at least you're a useful one. You?"

Now it was Ross' turn to let out a shaky breath. "Exactly the same. A scared, self-conscious freak with a sprinkling of too many lives in my head."

"You wanna talk about 'em?"

Ross finished a celery stick and peered out over the sea, letting it sort the lives of those Lukemore refugees for her. "They were all very similar. Slaves raised by slaves or Gait Prisonborne or just unfortunates throughout the Vast Collective. Hard lives filled with strife and pain, abuse. And then nothing."

Jack sat down beside her with a confused frown. "Nothing?"

Ross nodded slowly as the gentle waves carried her attention toward the shore. "Xelan said the emptiness is when Imminent recruited them and coded all knowledge of their existence in the memory bank. If we had more time, we could collect their nacres and decode them, but Xelan was sure we'd find them all the same. Imminent hires only desperate and downtrodden people and provides them with cryptic briefings on their objectives. They leave no trace of incriminating evidence behind."

Jack caught on quick. "And like the guy we caught once in the Ecology, the nacre might hide a trap or trigger of some kind and endanger us. I didn't realize the Reipon soldiers were Imminent."

Chafing her arms, Ross corrected him. "A few were. Sleepers, I think. But the rest were all Lamias bred for their station. Good soldiers doing what they thought was honest work. No holes in their memories or any real indecency. Just the wrong place at the wrong time."

"Like so many others in the Vast Collective. Born to terrible circumstance. I want to help." Jack's sincerity never ceased to impress Ross. She opened her mouth to say so when he suddenly looked away from the night sky and faced her with an earnest purpose in his eyes. "I have an idea, and I want to run it by you before I bring it to the Phase II meeting with Xelan and Tumu."

Infected by his excitement, Ross grinned. "What is it?"

"I think we should confiscate Enki and redistribute it for the good of the Vast Collective."

Oh. Well, there's an idea.

{Reipon}

"That's right, Jack. Keep your distance—"

"Kyle, what're you on about?"

Andrew's nosy intrusion startled Kyle from his perch at the bar where he watched Rayne's little brother lure Kyle's little sister in with the trademark Callahan charm. Grumbling, he dismissed the other Progeny. "I'm looking out for Ross."

The other man humphed. "Well, I'm sure she appreciates you invading her agency and privacy."

Disgusted, Kyle turned all the way around to give Andrew the full force of his irritation. "It's not like that, man. I don't want her to think that because we're in the predicament we're in that she has to settle—"

"For the only hot teenage boy who happens to be the strongest person in the house and shares Rayne's more endearing qualities? Oh, my, do save her from disaster." Andrew slapped the back of his hand to his hairline and feigned a faint. "Whatever will she do?"

"Fuck. Off. Holt. Nobody asked you."

Andrew pointed out the door like a chump. "And she didn't ask you."

Rolling his eyes, Kyle turned back to his drink. "It's implied with the job description. This is how big brothers act." That should've been enough to put Andrew in his place, but apparently—

"I think your other sister needs your attention more than the grown woman outside enjoying a grown man's company."

Oh. That was so not the place to go. "You've never come closer to me wrecking your entire understanding of the here and now, dude."

Andrew's teal eyes flashed at the threat. "Bring it, Roberts. I'll have you bent over kissing your own ass—"

"Lady and Gentlemen! We invite you to the newest update on the Vast Collective's Most Wanted!"

Thank Elden for Bones' good timing and the perfect diffusion of his terribly amused voice.

Korac walked by the door of the lounge in time to catch the announcement, with Sagan at his side. Excitedly, she bounced. "Oh, goodie! I wonder what they raised us to this time?" The blond Progeny jumped over the back of a sofa and laid out on the cushions. Korac leaned on the couch with an endearing expression for his girl. It was a display of affection that Kyle had grown accustomed to after moving into the house. The couple were sickeningly sweet to one another all over the place.

And Elden, could Kyle be more of a jealous sourpuss?

He turned back to Andrew and, despite every combative fiber of his being, muttered, "Sorry, man. I wouldn't really rearrange your memories."

Andrew squeezed his shoulder. "Good. I really didn't wanna see you kiss your own ass."

Ross strolled in with the perfectly upstanding and fine young man that Jack Callahan grew into over the last three years. But that didn't mean Kyle had to like the notion of those two together. Maybe this was therapy-worthy.

Devis and Twenty-One watched from their armchairs with drinks ready to cheer. Iuo and Bones took to the center of the room. The three-dimensional projection illuminated from the Lamian Prince's palm.

First up, Andrew.

Bones read the bounty aloud. "A whopping ten million credits for 'Conscience, the Will Twister.'"

Andrew grimaced. "'Will Twister?' Sounds like a male stripper's name."

Kyle burst into laughter.

Iuo shouted, "Not so fast, 'Story Taker, Memory Raper.'"

Andrew snickered as Kyle frowned and searched the laughing faces in the room. Grumpy, he quipped, "Who came up with these names? Xelan?"

"The Tritan in him demands ridiculous monikers," Devis explained while ribbing Twenty-One, who frowned.

"I like those names."

Kyle dismissed the hefty Icarean soldier with a wave and waited for his bounty.

Bones proceeded once they hushed, "Kyle, you're worth another ten million credits. Not bad. Not bad."

Iuo blinked his black and blue eyes. "This has become such a strange custom. Next is..."

Tameka appeared in the three-dimensional projection.

"Fifty million credits!" Bones whistled while the others cheered. He promised, "Fury a.k.a. 'Powerhouse!' If it gets much higher, I'm turning you in myself!"

Korac huffed. "Good luck."

Sagan beamed at him for bragging about her sister.

"Oh, Pehton. Timely of you to show because I believe you're next." Bones waved for the orange-feathered Lyrik to wander further into the room.

Korac offered to get Sagan and her a drink. "Please!"

"Orange juice for me."

The former Executive Warden appeared in Iuo's palm as predicted. "Twenty-five million credits. Very impressive, 'Rogue Warden.'" Bones hammed this up entirely too much, but it dragged a smile out of Pehton, who Kyle knew needed it after losing a soldier today.

In fact, that's what all of this was about: trying to find some levity in this shit. Kyle understood and indulged in the good humor.

"Seamswalker, you're next." Bones grinned at the blond peaking over his shoulder.

"C'mon. What am I worth?"

Pulling her against his side, Korac assured, "More than they could ever offer."

Sagan kissed him. So much kissing. It was gross. Pehton's orange juice sloshed as she took a step back from it—

Iuo gasped, and Bones gaped before announcing, "A whopping seventy-five million credits for the destruction of Gait."

Ross clapped, and Jack whooped.

Sagan high-fived Twenty-One and Devis. "That's right! I'm the best—"

"Not even close..."

The hushed tone turned them all to Bones. He wasn't smiling anymore and the blue blood drained from his complexion. Iuo swallowed and took the spotlight from the spooked Icarus. "The Tribunal is offering six hundred million credits for Korac, 'Silver General of the Icarean Armies.'"

Quiet.

Only their breathing filled the room.

People were desperate in the Vast Collective, many of them born to slavery in all but name. Six hundred million credits could buy a moon on Yu. Or a palatial villa on Reipon, much like this one.

Tumu's image projected next followed by Rayne's. Everyone stared at the new bounties with lost, wide eyes and shaking hands.

Kyle wet his lips before breaking the quiet. "Bones, what are they offering for them?"

He shook his head, too stunned to answer.

Iuo replied, "Tumu, Escaped Officer, and Rayne, War King—"

Xelan's image appeared at the last.

"—Traitor Prince of Cinder. No credit amount given. Instead, it says, 'Hazard risk level black. If provided any news as to their location, compensation will exceed the responsible party's family line three-fold. Approach with caution. If apprehended and returned to Enki alive, compensation will exceed the responsible party's family line five-fold. Do so at your own risk.'"

Enki offered freedom from generational poverty for a woman trapped inside their Dyson's Sphere by Celindria, Remorse, and Silence—

Don't think about her.

—Rayne didn't even destroy the promenade on Pil.

"This is fucked," Kyle offered to no one asking for it.

Iuo's next words left a chill in the room. "Our goal was to unite the Vast Collective against Imminent, but now Imminent has united the Vast Collective against us."

{Reipon}

"No. That's not the case at all."

Stiffly, the room focused on Andrew, who continued, "This isn't a popularity contest. This is a revolution. Our sources tell us the people know better than to believe these stories—That Rayne's a King of War and that Kyle rapes people's minds. It's all bullshit. What the people know is that Enki is reacting rather desperately to Korac's Verse. Now I say this grants the broadcast even more merit. Their response made it more of a threat by admitting the story of one man's life endangers the hegemony of an empire."

Andrew read that word in a book once. It seemed enough to impress their people. Korac squeezed Sagan's shoulder, and she reached for his hand affectionately. Her face was open with pride and warmth. Korac's eyes smoldered with intensity in a way that Andrew didn't want to appreciate so much.

Her intentions.

I know we can find a way through this.

His intentions.

Under fire. Fugitives. It doesn't matter. Once we complete Phase II, I'm asking Sagan.

Pehton looked less convinced, lost, and a little hopeless, but Lyriki intentions proved impervious to his scans.

Twenty-One stood and pounded a fist to his chest.

Conscience is right. This is the best course for the Shadow.

The depth in Bones' complexion returned as he mimicked the gesture.

If one of the Progeny with a bounty on their heads can muster up this much resolve, then Elden, dammit, so can I.

Ross and Jack beamed at each other. Their heads filled with thoughts of Enki, of all places, and made the least sense of anyone in the room.

Jack's right! Enki is the key.

All we need is to take the Dyson's Sphere. I can't wait to tell Xelan. Ross looks cute in those shorts.

Moving on.

Kyle put the joint he was leaving the room to smoke back behind his ear and leaned into the frame, nodding to the vibe.

This is exactly what they needed to hear, but how can we manage this? And if Jack looks in Ross' direction one more time…

Devis shrugged, folded his arms, and muttered, "The Shadow are all crazy. Surrounded by omens and alerts, and you give brave speeches. Brave and annoyingly infectious speeches. I am in." Did the First Wave Progeny always speak what was on his mind?

Iuo blinked his black and blue eyes, widened with an epiphany. "Not crazy." He went to work on the implant in his palm.

Sagan frowned at his frenzy. "What're you doing?"

"I'm sending an official response from my rank and station that each of you is on a separate planet. Sightings of you all around the Vast Collective—"

Andrew liked this idea. "Send them running in circles!"

Korac countered, "More than that. The official channel will spark contradicting sighting reports to compete with Iuo's missive."

Jack's mouth fell open. "All two hundred-plus princeps will receive notice. Collective-wide notice."

"They'll never find us." Pehton's grin returned.

Andrew had retreated from their smiling faces and celebration an hour ago. He was happy he restored the jovial atmosphere, but it took too much out of him to watch them function like normal people while he barely held together which life he led. Even with the wealth of optimism and mutual respect in their intentions, how could he trust anyone without knowing which Probability the Progeny faced.

Up in his bedroom, Andrew stared out over the gardens in a house that didn't exist. There was no road to here. No utility. Everything was self-contained. All things served a purpose. Those flowers were medicinal specimens Xelan collected all across the galaxy. The statuary harnessed wind energy. Organic materials from the ocean provided matter for the replicator to convert into food ingredients. And the nacre glass walls and roof gathered solar energy from the dual sun system.

But Andrew needed to see ahead of everything to feel secure. All this techno-luxury wasn't enough. Pablo agreed to help with the Probability dive, but only if Xelan agreed to monitor it.

Okay. Fair.

The next time Xelan emerged from his suites, Andrew was all about asking. But if Xelan said 'no,' Andrew would try without Pablo's help, and pray that he revived himself somehow.

He *needed* to see.

One way or the other, after the Phase II meeting, Andrew would die to see tomorrow.

{Reipon}

A knock at the infirmary door made Pablo stop rubbing his eyes and answer. Xelan stood on the other side with a warm, if slightly sheepish, smile.

"How is she, Doc?"

Pablo stepped back to let the Icarus in as he explained, "She's pretending to sleep when I can tell she's listening to Korac's Verse. I thought you'd be doing the same by now."

The tall alien shook his head. "Reading it, courtesy of Sagan, but I got to the invasion of Earth and needed a break. Tameka fell asleep, so I thought I'd check on our resident patient."

Knowing his face fell at the mention of Triss, Pablo tried to hide it by busying himself with his research on Rayne's fuse. "Feel free to check on her. I worry she doesn't sleep much. Her blood work is abnormal for a Lyrik. Too thick."

Xelan's warm hand fell on Pablo's shoulder and nearly brought tears to his eyes. Softly, the Icarus assured, "You're giving her excellent care, Pablo. She couldn't have a better doctor. I'll go in and see her now if you don't mind?"

Pablo could only nod. He resisted the urge to eavesdrop. Xelan occasionally visited Triss. It posed some unnerving implications, but Tameka never doubted his motivations, so why should Pablo?

Instead, he returned to the work he and Xelan constantly kept at. Reversing nacre programming to remove the Weapon in Rayne.

A few minutes later, Xelan reemerged with a sad smile. "You're right. She's definitely listening. I think she might even be comprehending it. Increase her sedatives another twenty CCs. How is the research?"

"I'll need to check with nacres that Legir kept over the years from previous Enki experiments. Like the men Bin helped before Nox came along in his Verse. I think the determining factor is there." A thought occurred to Pablo. "Xelan, when I was at R's Eternity Rites, Legir and X said something unusual. About you."

Xelan leaned against the counter casually, as if this wasn't cause for concern. "What'd they say?"

Pablo wet his lips before saying, "They'll come to help you when you're ready to hunt down your creation."

The smile faded from Xelan's face, and Pablo winced at the change. Xelan said, "No, it's fine, Pablo. Soon, I'll explain what they meant. I'd rather tell everyone at once. Is that fair?"

"Absolutely." Xelan made to leave until Pablo touched his arm. "And about Rayne? I know the Iona-29 footage is scary and that it was intentional, but Lynn and I cleaned up the aftermath. We found two men in the basement, killed precise and neat with restraint and discipline like you taught her. The rest was only her showing off for Nox's benefit."

"That's what concerns me."

SEVEN

VINDICATED IN BLUE EYES

{???}

RAYNE WAS CRYING AGAIN.

Nox smelled the salt of her tears, more diluted than the salt of the sea. She stared out at her beach from the strategy room with her back to him, her hair draped over one shoulder. He wondered if she cried outside this mindscape. Did her eyes weep within the Martyr Complex? Did the storms rage on in Enki, or were they reduced to a downpour?

Korac finished describing the end of his relationship with the Prince of Cinder, and Sagan responded in kind.

Oh, amos.

[SS]: I might be crying for him.

He's pulling me in for a squeeze and brushing the tears. Comforting me for commiserating with his younger self.

I wanna know if you cried, Rayne. If it reached you, too?

So much compassion in that big heart of yours. Don't worry, Sagan. The young man in that story is doing just fine.

Yet in that moment, I was lost. My King and my once-lover at odds and mostly as the result of an evil genius' machinations.

Although for Nox the relationship between his brother and his best friend ended eight thousand years ago, the lost promise of Korac's words today drew from his heart. Even knowing the General found happiness with Sagan in the end, the regret twisted a knot in Nox at how badly Celindria manipulated them all. But Rayne needn't pay for this.

He lowered a projection of Enki and called to her softly so as not to startle her, "You weep for Korac and Xelan."

"And you."

Rayne startled Nox instead. Her words left on a hushed breath, shaking with her emotions. Left exposed from her backless tunic, the tattoo of Elden's Verse trembled with her quiet tears. It was enough to break his heart.

"Rayne, no better ending awaited our story." He took a step through the projections toward her. "My brothers are alive and happy, working together to save the Vast Collective from Tritan tyranny. And I'm in a better place than I belong—non-corporeal existence notwithstanding." By the time he finished speaking, he stood beside her, feeling like a giant. "So why would you cry for me?"

Looking down at her profile, a small smile spread across Rayne's lips as she said, "When I said, 'and you,' I meant you also cry for Korac and Xelan." Faster than the lightning strike, Rayne reached out and caught a tear falling from Nox's face. "You appreciated seeing them happy together, and I'm glad that you see them happy now. But it seems, even knowing the present, Korac's Verse is still worth a tear or two. Even from the most feared Icarus in the galaxy."

For the first time since his death, Nox found an occasion to smirk, seeing that Rayne caught him in a tangle. She preened proudly beside him as she continued to cry. An idea struck him. "I tire of seeing you in tears, your majesty. Let's listen to Korac's Verse while we partake in some mental exercise. Shall we?" He indicated at their right where nothing but emptiness sprawled to the figmented horizon.

Rayne quirked a brow at him, twisting her smile with playful suspicion. She faced the abyss and took a step back. "Be my guest."

Visualize, build on the foundation of conscience and reason, and the construct will form. Abandon self-conscious notions of doubt; this prevents the formation.

Swells of igneous rock manifested on the edge of Rayne's ocean. The erupting volcano there found the course and streamed into basins, filling with liquid rock. Some cooled into obstacles for the river, but it flowed downstream where a cliff spilled lava into the ocean further away. The lightning from her construct graced his creation with a formidable greeting.

Facing him with a broad grin, Rayne vibrated with excitement rather than sadness and grief. "Really?!"

At their feet, two skids formed, one for each.

"Yes. Really." Nox opened his wings and stepped onto the skid. "Are you up to the challenge, your highness?"

Gossamer wings spread from her back, twinkling with chips of gold forming a circuit board. Rayne tossed him a hair tie with one in her teeth as she scooped up the black weight of her hair into a quick braid.

When her clothes shifted, Nox looked away to tie his hair back. His shirt confined him, but he wore it for her comfort. The jeans would suit the occasion just fine. He turned back to find Rayne waiting for him with a mischievous smile, wearing the same armor from their battle years ago. Kindly without the gold elements. While he examined her, she climbed onto the skid and strapped her boots in.

"Even though this isn't real, I'm still nervous."

"No need. I have a feeling you'll take to this naturally. Quite in fact. Drop and let the skid skate over the lava without friction." Nox knelt and checked her straps that didn't truly exist, while Rayne peered with curiosity at his actions. Her eyes shone brightly from down here, prompting him to stand and return to his skid. "Consider this practice for the real thing." He strapped himself in before gesturing at the precipice. "I'll go first to show you how it's done."

She stared at the lava without blinking.

"Rayne."

Snapping to him, she swallowed hard before managing, "Hmm?"

"I have faith in you."

Nox dropped without waiting to see how she responded. He trusted her to follow. The inertia from the drop dragged him down, so he formed a chute with his wings to buffer him, slowing the descent. He gave a triumphant "woot" when the skid met the magma river's surface and repelled the friction, as was its way. Every time.

Xelan invented one hell of a sport.

A similar cry sounded behind him, and Nox turned to find Rayne's skid alighting the lava. Her skin glowed pink in the firelight, and her eyes sparkled with it. Or was that—

Joy.

Rayne looked free, alive, and ready. He could tell by how fast she—

"Getting slow in your old age, Nox." She stuck her tongue out as she passed him in a crouch on her board.

He chuffed. "Amateur." Although she managed to find her balance, she swished through the magma rather than glided. "Sloppy!"

Unprecedented, Rayne spun the skid to face Nox as she continued backward down the river. Arms crossed and hip out with all the attitude of an undisciplined god with a martyr complex. "Then show me how it's done."

Youth.

Unable to contain the chuckle, Nox crouched and surged inches from her board. "Watch and learn, novice." With grace—a crucial element in the process—he glided around her without a drop of misplaced lava, opened his wings back until they narrowed into a more aerodynamic approach, and knelt until his hands almost grazed the river of fire.

All the while, Rayne watched and gave him an impressed nod. "Not bad. But I took dance lessons with Tameka. So watch me inject so much needed style into this secret sport of yours." She swept beside him, much better in form already than before, and smiled before twirling in a pirouette. Impressive, yes, but—

"Rayne!" Nox clutched her shoulders and spun her around his skid to the opposite side in time to miss a protruding boulder in her wake. Searching her wide eyes, he checked, "Are you with me?"

"I'm here. I... thank you. It's not real, but I don't have control over your construct. I tried to disappear it, but..."

"You're quite an impressive sprite, as Korac always says, but let's both give more attention to the course. It will worsen from here." Even as Nox said it, their skids gained speed, nearing the cliff. At Rayne's nod, he realized his hands were still gripping her shoulders and dropped them like they burned.

Because they didn't. Her shoulders were soft, and they were hers. But she wasn't his, and Nox didn't deserve this much of her.

Meanwhile, Korac continued to narrate his life to them.

It stung that we existed as brothers, but both felt disinclined to confide our lives in this way. Xelan a secret. Celindria a secret. Maybe things would be different if we'd been more frank with each other.

But he was my King, and I was his General. And this is how it was done.

"Too true," Nox muttered, while gliding between the rapids.

Rayne overheard him as she concentrated on the oncoming obstacles. "I like that you don't focus on what could have been. You accept your choices and those consequences, even with your regrets. I admire that about you."

Unworthy of her admiration, Nox elaborated, "I would change them if given the chance."

The river flowed faster, and the rocks clustered closer together.

Still, Rayne offered, "As I said, 'regrets,' but you focus on how to better the here and now rather than dwell on what wasn't meant to be."

Nodding along, Nox understood her now. "One can get lost that way. Try to better the situation you've made as you can with what you have at your disposal. I still wish I'd told Korac more. To hear how he responds to it..." Gritting his teeth, Nox ignored the emotion building in his throat and dodged a stalagmite.

"Korac loves you. You were the super cool big brother with all the strength and speed he aspired to have. If he could grow up strong like you, he could fight all his demons, no problem." Rayne's insights possessed the ability to choke Nox with his feelings.

Sorrow. Love. Home.

All of it squandered.

Fortunately, the world's edge fell away closer now. "We approach the lavafall, Rayne. I've lingered inside your mind long enough to know that you'll refuse to quit now, but prepare yourself. This will test you."

The electric blue of Rayne's eyes glowed with determination. "I'm ready."

Nox chuckled. What else could he do? She was so headstrong. "Trust the friction repulsion to take you down the drop. Hold your breath over the edge."

"I got this."

When Xelan's determination came out in her, Nox was inclined to believe her.

Side-by-side, they glided to the lavafall's edge. Below, the molten rock thundered loud enough to deter them. He constructed it to smell of proper ash and brimstone, and it was most potent where the magma met the ocean. Rayne looked fierce as she hyper-focused on the edge. Five seconds away.

Four.

Three.

Two.

{???}

Rayne reached out and gripped Nox's hand as they went over the edge together, both of them screaming. With delight. With the thrill. Abandoning their cares if only for a few quick seconds. And she squeezed almost hard enough to hurt herself.

Realizing Rayne must be hurting Nox, she let go as they surfed down the lavafall at a ninety-degree angle to the vertical drop. Standing upright while falling straight down was a sensation she'd never get used to if the broad grin on Nox's face was any indication.

Rayne was fine with that.

While the fall took less than the time to prepare for it, she swore it went on forever. It was possible Nox prolonged it for their entertainment, a welcome distraction from their cyclical thoughts and unexpectedly comforting interactions. He advanced easily through her construct lessons, taking both less and more time than she did with Elden.

Of course, it was Rayne's hope that in the land of nanites and nacres, somehow they could both manipulate the Dyson's Sphere external to their strangely cozy mindscape.

Scenic, too. While they rode the lavafall down, lightning struck an impressive wave only a few hundred feet away. Salt and ash mingled as the storm claimed both constructs' skies in clouds the color of Nox's skin. The heart of it as black as his eyes. Same as the igneous rock all around them.

Funny how that manifested in their internal processes.

Was the water the same color as her eyes? The sands the same pale shade as her complexion?

And all these components coalesced into...

Into what?

"Prepare yourself. Realigning to the surface will—"

The sudden and stark righting of the skid rattled Rayne's bones and chomped her teeth. The lava hissed and glooped where it plummeted here into the tide.

"—Suck."

Rayne laughed, unable to stop herself. It was so unexpected for Nox to use that word. "I didn't think that was in your vocabulary, former King of Cinder. How familiar are you with Earth slang?"

"Familiar enough." Nox beat his wings to slow his glide, and Rayne copied him. They both glowed from the adrenaline, far removed from her earlier tears—

We went to work for thousands of years. I created the exsanguination mechanism. And I'm not sorry. Celindria deserved to suffer. I hate that Rayne ever knew of its existence. I think I first regretted her fate when she came to the fortress for negotiations with Nox. So spirited and brave. Smart. An intergalactic leader in her youth, and I knew what we'd condemned her to.

For that, I am ashamed.

"I knew you tried to cover for him."

Nox looked away, seeming to concentrate on steering with his wings toward the riptide, where it swelled under the storm into an intimidating crest. He gave a satisfied nod. "This will do." He turned back to her and challenged, "Are you prepared for part two?"

Rayne flexed her wings, getting a sense of the steering, all the while feeling a grin spread across her lips. Even amid her enemies and crushed under the weight of her worries and grief, he found a way to make her smile. "I think I'm more than up for this. Thank you, Nox."

His anticipatory expression slipped into the faintest of frowns. At Rayne's smile, he shook it off and left it unacknowledged to buffer his wings into a sail. "Can you feel it?"

She copied Nox's actions, and the gusts glided beneath her wings. "I can."

"Now!"

They both surfed on their skids across the fledgling tide, catching it before it rose. And rose. And swelled.

Icy rain. Lightning strikes. Ocean spray.

Tactile sensations that felt good on Rayne's unreal skin. Beside her, Nox flattened his wings perpendicular to his crouching stance. At his nod, she mimicked him, determined not to need his help this time. All the while they rode the wave, Korac's Verse continued.

Back on subject. Nox took Celindria's death like a train wreck. His fixation on her transferred to any news I gathered of her descendants. And I encouraged the distraction to maintain the perilous grip on his mind. These are my sins. My wrongs. But I was caretaking madness, and I don't entertain excuses or placations.

I was less than a man, but not exactly a monster.

Nox kept his stare on the beach as they rolled toward it, so very high off the roiling sea. Rayne provided him with the arena for his betterment, and she refused to wring his emotions out of his careful reconstruction. But damned if she wasn't curious about what exactly took place in that mind of his—

"Caretaking madness…"

When he spoke, Rayne drew closer to let him know he had her attention. Meanwhile, Nox stared at the shore without blinking, despite the rain pelting his thick lashes.

That deep baritone of his softened as he ruminated unto himself, "Korac has a way with words, doesn't he? Eloquent and regal—Almost a talent for this. Already it's much better than mine." The smile Nox gave the storm was bitter from the feelings it restrained.

Rayne maintained her balance while staring at him. Once a few heartbeats passed, she smirked. "I don't think anyone expected this from either of you, and I can't wait for the Vast Collective to circulate your words, Nox. They were brave and unyielding. You opened that door for Korac." She let out a bright laugh, startling him. "Sorry. Can you imagine if Xelan writes one?"

Nox's raised a brow at the notion. "The galaxy would tremble." He nodded back at the surf. "We disembark here."

Right. They were totally in the middle of something.

Facing the shore, Rayne mimicked his stances to ensure a smooth landing. This was her construct. She couldn't manipulate Nox's build, but she trusted him with that much control over her conscience—whether or not he knew it. Regardless, she wanted to ride this out with respect to the wave. No cheating.

The crest lowered them toward sea level. Rayne balanced the skid until at the last minute she spun and rode the wave in reverse. "Woo! I did it!"

"Rayne!"

The ride got real bumpy—

"Oh, shit!"

As the wave washed away and joined the foam over the shore, the skid lost its indifference to friction and decided to once again give a fuck. Rayne's ass hit the sand and slid into the beach, her hands gripping the sediment to slow her roll. Literally. She landed with the skid over her head, laughing herself red in the face.

What in the name of yoga poses—

"I vow I've never met a woman more headstrong than you. You could control the entire landing, you realize that, don't you?" Nox's face appeared between Rayne and the sky. He looked the most handsome when in a tizzy.

Rayne filed that away for later. Right now, she needed to un-pretzel herself. "Ugh. I'll take my lumps and unwind this myself. You. Try to be less with the 'I told you so's.'"

Nox stared down at her with a brow raised in bewilderment. "You're absolutely right. You're not the most headstrong woman I know. Rayne Callahan, you're the most self-punishing, adamant force in the entire universe." He bent and offered his hand. "And I fell to you. So perhaps there's something to your method of banging your head against a brick wall until you break through." Shaking his head incredulously as she clasped his wrist, he pulled her easily upright on the skid. "Like water through a canyon, your majesty. Only much less patient."

Rayne dropped his hand and glared at him through narrowed eyes. "I take every one of those words as a compliment, soldier."

"As ever, your loyal servant." Nox dropped to kneel at her skid and unfix the straps confining her combat boots before unfastening his own.

Rayne watched him, fascinated by his unassuming nature around her and mesmerized by his careful measures to assure her comfort in his presence. She wanted Nox to know that she saw it. Saw him. But he only shirked any sign of gratitude she paid him, implying that she made him uncomfortable in doing so.

A soft impasse. A gentle obstacle.

One day, Rayne hoped they overcame it together. Until then…

The strips of battle gear covering Rayne receded and refashioned the constructed material into a long-sleeved backless top held together with strings. Wine colored. The matching wide-leg bottoms caught the sea breeze in a playful sway. Her hair, once freed, joined in the game, soaked and curlier than before.

Nox kept his eyes averted when she changed, as always. When he faced her again, he stared. He didn't mean to. Rayne knew because he looked away as soon as he realized.

The tension between them grew more comfortable with each passing day, and Rayne found herself easier in Nox's presence at the same rate. One day she could even see them happy here as friends.

Happiness.

Such a foreign concept to her outside of Sagan's arms or Xelan's warmth.

Especially considering the next segment of the broadcast.

[SS]: I have to clear my throat to speak. "Sorry. I… Razor was so twisted." It took Matt, Lucy, Puk, Pehton, Korac, and I sitting around like a support group discussing our encounters with him before I puzzled together exactly how badly he manipulated me. Never mind the actual support group the Lyriks established to cope with their very serious trauma.

Rayne, I'm sorry I wasn't more like you. I should have killed him the first time he smiled at me.

No. We are not doing this. Break time.

White magnesium heat flared through Rayne. The storm inside and out howled, reverberated in the chambers of her heart. She trembled with it.

How could her friends think less of themselves for being good people? For trusting? It's not their fault that assholes took advantage of their kindness. Continually! Sagan. Poor sweet Sagan—

"Is it time, King Rayne?"

Nox was why. His story. The hidden potential beneath the monster that generational abuse tried to make of a good Icarus. A story like his waited behind all their foes. But not everyone was worth saving.

Rayne gave Nox the full force of Li in her eyes, looked into his metaphorical heart, and begged herself to forgive the hope inside her. Inside Sagan. All their people.

Powering down took the breath from her. "No. Not yet."

Nox manifested a reinforced canopy and stood under it with an invitation in his eyes. "Come in from the rain," they said. He knew the solace she found here, but it isolated her even from someone inside her conscience. Xelan wouldn't like Rayne withdrawing like this.

Upon entering the canopy, Rayne enjoyed the sound of the rain on the roof enough to let herself dry for a while. Swallowing, she managed to say, "I hated the shame in her voice."

"You've heard it in your own," Nox stated, not questioned.

Rayne gripped her hair and shook her head, frustrated. "Sagan thought she found an ally. She shouldn't blame herself."

Nox looked out toward the tide with his eyes narrowed, but Rayne knew he was carefully wording what he wanted to say next. "There is a certain education in trust. Her regret is valid. Yours is valid. The shame is part of the experience. Let yourselves feel it, take the lesson, and move onto the next."

After that, they sat in the sand, fell quiet, and listened more to Korac's Verse.

The death matches.

Ementa's demise.

Abresson and T.A.O.

Nox and Rayne ended their silence simultaneously, "I want to break that Tritan." "No way he lives." They both glanced at each other, a pact between them. Abresson was priority one.

The only external indication of the story's emotional impact on Nox was the thickening of his voice as he confessed, "Korac never told me how he earned his credits, and I... despise that he ever encountered that Aegis beast on my behest."

"I don't think he does," Rayne offered, hugging her knees to her chest and staring at the sand. "I think you were the best thing to happen to him. Until Sagan, of course."

Quiet descended once more. The story carried into Korac acquiring Cascading Light for Nox.

To an Icarus, under the weight of Li's deadly promise—Rayne—you, in that image, represented our true salvation. I believe that's why so many Icari easily accepted your leadership after the war. It was the natural order of things.

Nox nodded his agreement. "True." He returned to their comfortable rapport as Korac continued narrating the event.

Our King wasn't obsessed with the image of our salvation.

Nox was obsessed with the young warrior inside that fire.

That posed a complication I never predicted.

Months ago, Rayne would've tensed at Korac's words in Nox's presence. As it was, her Icarean companion stared intently at the horizon. But she saw.

He clenched the fist opposite from her until his knuckles went white and cerulean blood dripped from his nails.

"I'll regret it until I'm gone, until I'm dust, and long after."

"Nox."

Frozen, he hesitated before turning to her. "King Rayne?"

"Let it go. I did." She meant it. Not that she forgave him, because she couldn't. But she believed him to be a good man, confined by a lifetime of poor decisions—his and those who made him. The Icarus next to her deserved another chance to try, and so far, she was glad he took it. Better off, even.

Nox let his gaze slip back to the storm, and Rayne followed.

"In due time."

EIGHT

BOUND BY UNBREAKABLE GLASS

{REIPON | SECOND QUARTER NIGHT}

"PRINCE IUO SUBMITTED THE FIRST SIGHTINGS REPORT ON THE PROGENY, BUT HE LIED."

Remorse enjoyed Para's body as a vessel. Such a short, yet graceful form. Non-threatening despite the wealth of sculpted muscle. He envisioned her as a passionate and imaginative lover. Unfortunate that they should possess her body for three months now without discovering if he'd assumed correctly.

"Permit me to investigate him while you see to the Mother's request."

Abresson, uninitiated and presuming, sat across the table of shaved obsidian. Shining onyx encased the cafe at the heart of the Obsidian Palace, reflecting their discussion as a romantic encounter. With Korac's Verse blasting from every corner, Para's body provided a clever disguise for the ousted Primary. Much to his growing irritation. He'd even dressed her as Silence demanded. A simple carbon fiber jumpsuit.

Remorse laced her fingers and spread her arms flat along the table, appreciating her gray hands. Dispassionately from her sweet voice, he said, "No. I want to see the recognition on his face when he sees this Valkyrie." If the Primary could stomach it, he planned to drape the girl all over Abresson—

The other Tritan shone a poisonous grin with his noseless, lidless, lipless, browless face.

—Or not. Besides, Remorse was far too incensed with the troll to entertain his presence for long. Soon, Remorse would decide exactly how to punish his undisciplined acolyte.

As if conjured to further his ire, Celindria as T.A.O. wandered into the bar wearing immodest buckles and straps peppered with golden spikes and blades. A truly monstrous disgrace to the young woman she inhabited. As Abresson glimpsed her and all but salivated, Remorse's opinion of the ensemble soured further.

All the same, Celindria approached them and folded T.A.O.'s dainty arms. "Have you acquired your objective, yet?" At the unintelligent shake of Abresson's head, she continued, "Mother asks after it. She seems quite determined to read it. I want to help."

No.

This was a deception hiding some grander scheme. Remorse kept Para's face neutral. "No need to trouble the scientist from her important works. We will manage to find a copy while we ferret out treachery. Two birds, one very dense book."

Unsatisfied with the suggestion, Celindria shook T.A.O.'s head. "You're resting Karter at the lab. I can Seamswalk her and you to another location."

Ahh. So that was it. Celindria wanted the lab absent of Remorse's presence to exercise with her male human specimen alone despite their earlier games. "So be it."

Abresson stopped gazing at T.A.O. with ownership plain on his face and called, "Iuo comes."

Celindria Seamswalked back to the lab. As the Primary multi-tasked by preparing Karter for an outing, Iuo approached. And yes. His eyes widened at the sight of Para, sitting cozy with Abresson.

Treacherous snake.

Despite his station, the Porn Baron always dressed like a fighter or a manual laborer. Remorse respected that about him. Offering a courteous nod to both men at the table, Iuo took a seat across from Remorse. His black and blue eyes blinked sideways, hiding a world of answers Remorse wanted. How to remain civil? After all, Iuo kept them in soldiers, votes, and credits. Not to mention the porn industry doubled as a front for trafficking. Not that this upstanding citizen across from them even knew.

"Primary Rem, is that you?"

Abresson dismissed the question and demanded, "What proof have you that the Progeny dispersed themselves throughout the galaxy?"

Remorse rolled Para's eyes at Abresson's lack of tact.

Iuo answered anyway, "Security footage."

"Easily manufactured. Especially by someone in your industry." Abresson waved in the Lamia's face.

Like a true professional, the Reipon Prince didn't react. He opened his palm and activated the images. They displayed various members of the Shadow, slumming around some of the more industrial worlds. One was Lukemore, which Remorse confirmed the Shadow had attacked an Imminent base of operations there.

The Primary tired of this deception, but Iuo proved himself repeatedly as an ally too valuable to dispose. Hiding his disdain behind Para's sweet voice, Remorse ordered, "Transfer it to Abresson for analysis. I expect an updated report from you by next quarter night. Not here. We'll meet at the Queen's Fare. We're tripling security on Monarch 3."

The Lamian Prince did as he was told and dismissed himself as was proper.

Abresson watched him go, as he idly scratched a cluster of scars on his wrist. "I dislike him."

"You like no one."

The dark blue Tritan turned and faced Remorse. "I like one or two individuals."

"Courtesy of Korac's Verse, I know which *individual* gave you those scars." The Primary gripped the back of Abresson's head and slammed it on the rock table. Twice. On the last, he smooshed that dark blue face, blackened with Tritan blood, onto the surface and leveled Para's eyes to his bleeding black voids. "As a man with an ambiguous code, the Exalted's son protected you all these millennia from my wrath. Although I had my suspicions, I knew for certain when you looked at T.A.O. just now. She was under an ally's protection." Remorse punched Abresson with Para's strong and tiny fist. "Never." Another punch. "Disgrace me." Another. "Again."

Black blood soaked Para's gray fist with two sharp teeth lodged in her knuckles. The one or two other occupied tables emptied with discretion. This was a location of business, and, therefore, no one else's business but the two at this table. Abresson spit out another tooth in a wash of ink before whispering three words repeatedly. Remorse needn't lean in to hear. It could only be the single appropriate response.

"Forgive me, Primary."

Eternity deliver Remorse from incompetent minions.

"Incompetent followers learn from incompetent leaders."

At the helm of Para's control, behind her eyes, Remorse spared the owner of the object he inhabited a glance. In a voice devoid of pity or understanding, he threatened out of hand, "One more remark like that from you, and I'll see to it this body consoles that beaten Tritan. Several degrading and sickening scenarios come to mind that don't endanger Silence's orders to keep your womb empty."

The woman braced on all fours in her mindscape, unable to hold her head off the ground from the constant mental exertion to regain her will. Still, the Primary sensed her next counterargument. He wagged a finger at her and tsked. "Before you comment on my distaste for Abresson, remember that my censure knows no bounds. Even my disgust. Have you forgotten what happened the last time you tried to agitate me?"

Para, naked and exhausted, was shriveled in her pit of existential sweat. The poor thing shrank away like a frightened animal.

"If you wish Chris and Karter to remain further unmolested by your own hand, then keep your head down and your remarks regarding my leadership to yourself. And your thoughts at a minimum. It's enough overhead to glimpse your sorrow and guilt—All this useless angst you lower creatures carry around like a leaded weight. Ahh. There."

Remorse clasped his hands behind his back and sniffed a familiar and hot aroma. "I enjoy the taste of your murderous desire. That, I can appreciate. Loathe me, Para. It matters not. You and Karter are mine."

{MONARCH 3 | MORNING}

Hundreds of sacs pulsed, dripping viscous fluid to the vats below. Like bellows, with each pulse gas escaped, siphoned into the plant for processing. The operation encased the delicate ecosystem of Mon3 drones and their queens in nacre glass to prevent exposure and to keep the products pure. Of the sixty thousand Mons contained within, none of them knew a world outside this plant existed. They were all born here and could never leave or risk cross-contamination.

Remorse, wearing Karter, viewed through the glass with T.A.O. by his side, as some head security officer—a Mon3 drone—detailed each measure in place to protect their investment. Imminent employed millions of agents, but only a few hundred earned rights to initiate, and out of those, maybe one survived their usefulness long enough to touch Cascading Light and join the ranks of Imminence.

This security officer was working hard for it. "...And genetically locked, nacre-deterring shields at every entrance. There is no way an agent of Shadow could step foot inside this base."

Celindria made T.A.O. slink over to the security officer and draped herself on his side. He salivated at the tiny woman, unaware of the parasite inside. While Remorse was far from kind, he truly pitied what T.A.O. endured at Celindria's hands. Merited further by the look on the drone's face after she finished whispering in his ear.

Tears fell from his eyes they went so wide with terror. He stammered, but couldn't form words. "I-I-pl-pl—"

The First Progeny exaggerated the sway to her sister's hips as she walked back over, assuring, "They will reinforce their efforts for fear of failure."

Within the mindscape of volition, Remorse glanced away from the view to Karter. In all the times the Primary occupied one of these lesser beings, they remained sprawled on the floor in tears and sweat.

Karter stood proudly with her back ramrod straight, and her chin set high. A silent, toned statue. With her mohawk, she stood taller than Remorse's Earth height of seven feet. Her exotic eyes—one vertical half black and the other half green—sparked with knowledge. Reconnaissance—perfectly aware of their surroundings and conversations. She was a dangerous one to ever release.

Celindria suggested, "Should we stop by the Queen's Fare? See if they have a copy of Nox's Verse?"

A drink sounded good.

T.A.O. reached out a hand, and Remorse stared at it, considering it. Hesitated. Where Abresson was incompetent and a minion, Celindria was formidable and an opponent. Remorse refused to trust her, even for Seamswalking. She could easily abandon him on some rock. While he could open a conduit to travel for himself, that required time and Aegis blood. Two commodities Enki lost to Sagan's destruction of Gait. The vulnerability to rely on Celindria as T.A.O. unnerved him. Once more, he cursed Razor's failure to capture Sagan's volition. Not that he blamed the Aegis. In all Probability's before this one existed, Sagan fell to them. Now they all soared blindly with only one certainty.

Rayne still dies in the destruction of Enki alone and afraid.

With that comforting notion in mind, Remorse took Celindria's hand and let her walk him into the trunk of one of Monarch 3's continent-wide trees. Originally intended to house individual hives, this one died long ago courtesy of a certain Icarean King. At the heart of it, where once the sac throbbed, stood the Queen's Fare—Imminent's base on Monarch 3.

True, the upstairs served the public as a front. Beneath was a din of vice and hedonism catered by the Pain Curator long before his demise. In usual fashion with Razor's projects, the casino and restaurants boasted elegance, if a little more rustic than the typical pain establishment. Carved entirely of wood, the place was varnished and polished to a pristine shine from the bars, eatery, gaming tables, balconies, stairs, and the pin swing—A swing suspended five stories over a million, ten-meter-long metal pins. Spectators gambled on a prisoner escaping their bonds before the swing released and the captive plummeted to their death.

T.A.O. and Karter walked through the front door, garnering some attention. Icari were rare on this planet. Progeny even less common. Ignoring them, Celindria and Remorse walked through the crowded lobby and into the bar.

Korac's Verse replayed from the beginning. The crowd's reactions mostly pleased Remorse.

"Six hundred million credits—I don't give a shit that he's some kind of hero. I'd kill babies for that money."

"Hero? Hah! All the Icari are blood-thirsty monsters. We can set out on the hunt today and split the money."

"You're wrong. Think about the truth here. The all-mighty Tritans are frightened of a band of renegades. What have they to fear of them? The truth, that's what. Look deeper."

Most seemed eager to claim the reward and turn the Progeny in, but, for every two greedy bastards, one noble crusader gave a speech on how much the bounties merited the Verses' validity. This unexpected integrity bothered Remorse more than the predictable greed reassured him.

Karter needn't make a sound to voice her elation. Remorse felt her thoughts.

Not much longer.

No sense wasting time arguing with a brick wall. As long as she behaved, he refused to waste energy engaging her.

The bartender, another drone, came around for their drinks. Remorse drew the man closer to whisper in his ear. "We search for a book. You know the one."

He flashed them two fingers.

Celindria shook T.A.O.'s head, held up three fingers, and added, "Along with a bottle of Yu nectar."

The drone blinked big lids over multi-faceted eyes for a few seconds. He eventually nodded and disappeared behind the shelves of fermented delights.

Remorse raised Karter's brow at Celindria. "Three?"

She rolled T.A.O.'s eyes and downed a shot before answering, "Silence, me, and you." Before he argued, she shook T.A.O.'s head to stop him. "You are more responsible than I for creating that monster. You will read to understand what he thought of you because it interests me to know. Besides, you should prepare yourself for what Mother will learn about your liberties with her family while she slept."

That cut too deep. Remorse winced with Karter's face. An evil, purring giggle erupted from T.A.O. before she drank her second shot. The drone returned, sparing them from more unwarranted conversation. He produced three capsules and held up one finger.

Remorse loaded one hundred thousand credits to the bartender, who barked out a crass laugh.

"One *million*, darling. Each."

T.A.O. seemed unphased before rolling her eyes and transferring the funds. After the bartender left, Celindria frowned into her shot glass. "One disadvantage to these disguises is we aren't afforded the same courtesy as our natural forms. Even Eminent Karter is less recognizable than the rest of us."

Astute observation, but Remorse barely paid it any notice because an explosion happened inside Karter's mind.

"Call him Korac."

I understand Three Two Four manipulated Karter's recollection of our time together and of the delivery she survived. And I mourn for her. I am grateful for this opportunity to reach her with the truth.

"You… separated me from my son and kept his identity from me. You keep us separated even now. Primary Rem, I will see your ruin." Karter's words simplified her emotions with far too much elegance compared to the savagery of her rage. Every fantasy she entertained of killing him, Remorse witnessed.

It really was quite distracting.

{ENKI}

Primary Rem stood in his sanctum of falling Cascading Light and stared through the open space of Enki to the cracked prison hurdling in two directions across their well-won and rightful home. Hands clasped behind his back, he focused on the tasks within his mind. But in his meditation, the growing urgency of that pending apocalypse tested his restraint.

It was enough to lose Enki to All That Which Was Imminent. Remorse refused to lose it to a child's game.

All around him, the columns of his sanctuary trembled at his might—the force of his grip on this construct greater than the understanding of his kind—let alone that of lesser beings. Turning on his heel, he knelt and emptied a vial of Aegis blood into a line on the floor. Kinetic energy crackled along his skin, thickened the air, and begged for the end.

A bolt of lightning split the way into the shrine overlooking ground zero. The Primary stepped through and startled the young Tritan guard to stand at attention. Young, being relative to about fifty million years or so. A pup, really. The truly young human woman on shift took Remorse by surprise. She turned from her task at the terminal to blink big, dark blue eyes at him. Her blond hair fell softly around a sweet face. Otherwise, she seemed harmless at work on the demolition project—

The human girl smiled prettily.

The scales raised on Remorse's skin, and a chill went down his spine. He found it difficult to take his eyes off her even as the guard saluted.

"Primary Rem, sir."

As if breaking a spell, she glanced away, and every feature of her face softened into its least threatening position. This was far more alarming than the smile. Something dangerous lurked behind her eyes.

"What's your name?"

Feigning nerves, the human girl licked her lips and glanced shyly away. "Lucy, sir."

Remorse frowned as he pondered if that sounded familiar. Meanwhile, the guard hid his own anxious glances between the two of them. Returning to the situation at hand, Remorse made a note to run an investigation into Lucy later. To the guard, the Primary ordered, "Yito, report."

"All teams collect artifacts from the designated zones while affixing charges for demolition. We are two days ahead of schedule thanks to Morning Star here." When the guard nodded at the girl, Remorse glimpsed the respect and appreciation in Yito's gaze.

They'd bonded.

The Primary almost let his eyes narrow. How interesting. Lucy gave Yito an encouraging smile that further cemented Remorse's suspicions. Whoever this girl was, she moved fast. He offered a half smile in her direction. "The Tritan race commends you. Soon, I hope to offer you an appropriate accolade, along with everyone else involved in the venture."

Once more, this Lucy averted her gaze in deference to his station when she gave a little bow of her head. "Thank you, sir. I only want to serve."

Another chill.

Remorse was prey that Lucy chewed and tasted to see if he was the flavor she wanted, and when he refused the bait, she tried again from another angle. Who was this bizarre creature? And should they consider her for the breeding program? Lucy could serve that way.

"We shall see. Yito?"

The Tritan guard stood even straighter, if possible. "Yes, Primary?"

Hands clasped behind his back, Primary Rem stared down where the last Aegis held his grand finale. All that brilliance and potential drained into a half-bred beast, Korac. With Abresson, the only soldier left on Remorse's side against Celindria and Silence, the Primary was very unhappy. Fortunately, neither woman possessed enough majesty to set aside their separate personal goals to combine forces against him. That was an alliance the universe couldn't afford, never mind the galaxy.

"Sir?"

Of course. The soldier awaited his orders. Remorse kept him waiting no longer. "If we lose even half a day of this advance, notify Eminent Lance and Eminent Abresson. Mention to Abresson the names of anyone exemplary involved." He spared Lucy an acknowledging glance before continuing, "That we might offer them some hospitality."

"Yes, sir." Yito all but vibrated with excitement. The silly, trained child. "Several on the ground come to mind. I'll pass their names along as well."

"See that you do." Remorse nodded to Lucy before exiting the way he came.

She shone him a brilliant smile that dazzled with gratitude and the pleasure of pleasing others.

What kind of predator was she?

Back in his sanctum, Remorse disabled the path, resenting the waste of Aegis blood. Where would they farm a source of it now? And ore? After revisiting the hive facility on Monarch 3, the nacre glass-encased project reminded Remorse painfully of their reliance on Razor. Without him, they could resort to mining Thailea, but how would they even enter the planet?

That dilemma should fall to Celindria. She was the one who rendered travel there impossible—

What about Silence? What will she do to him if she learns about Savis? Nox? If the remaining Tritans learned Remorse sent to sleep their most viable option for breeding their race back into existence, they'd skin him decompressed. Not even Tameka offered the potential that was Project Surra. What race existed that wasn't born on that woman's back? She knew it, and soon she'd know everything.

Death waited here.

Remorse could leave. Escape and never return to this life of weighing odds and careful choices. There was no deliverance from deliberation, and tomorrow only promised one thing.

His home.

In pieces—

Remorse snarled into the sanctum loud enough that it echoed between the columns. So very empty. So very alone.

Into the quiet, into the loss, into that cursed fire that took his life, he confessed, "Vi, you were right."

But he'd never get the chance to tell her the last truth between them.

Remorse, Primary Rem, the highest being in the Vast Collective, lowered his head.

{Enki}

Celindria kept her bedroom off her lab. It was a room with a bed. A bed she currently took advantage of Chris on. By now, he was accustomed to it, and wasn't that a sad commentary? But it was SOP. She typically got herself off three or four times and then left him to recover while she resumed lab work.

The first few times, Celindria stayed inside his head for it, but then after an incident, she left him on autonomic response while she removed herself from his conscience. Chris preferred this time where she couldn't see his reactions, his aversion to her touch. That wasn't her kink.

Strangely, he suspected that what sent her away was the only time he'd watched her. As much as Chris hated her—deep, seething, writhing, loathing hatred—Celindria looked beautiful, impossibly so, in everything she did. Concentrating on her work, enjoying herself with him, hiding her displeasure with her comrades—all of it. Out of curiosity, he'd watched her. Afterward, she'd retreated.

Now, Chris used the time to think of Karter and Para, bragging about him while he cooked dinner for their throuple. How they walked around the house in adorable cut-off shorts which left a little curve of cheek exposed. The way they all covered each other like a people blanket on the couch—

T.A.O. appeared, and Celindria finished with a quick dismount. She received the capsule from T.A.O.'s hand, looking more pleased than a moment before.

Inside Chris' head, Celindria returned to pilot him out of the bedroom. Aloud, she confessed, "I want to read this with my own eyes. Good night, toy."

"Looking to see what your ex-boyfriend had to say about you in bed?"

Celindria laughed haughtily before purring, "My toy, why you may be sore about your lack of say, you would be lying if you denied enjoying it. And never speak so lowly of the Eternal Bind."

Too tired to argue with her about how half the enjoyment should be distilled from earning consent, Chris instead focused on the one iota of information she offered so far. "The... what?"

Celindria said, "A bedtime story before I put you to rest, then. In the theory of Probabilities, there exist two beings inexplicably attracted to one another. While all lives and events may vary within the Matrix, these two coalesce despite the dynamics surrounding them. If we can locate these two forces, we could, in theory, collapse all the Probabilities to one."

That could only mean...

No more conflicting realities with figures that travel between them. The end to Imminent, as they would never feed on the chaos of the Probability Matrix again. Her earlier words finally came together. "You... you believe you and Nox are the Eternal Bind? Why?! And how does the collapsing happen?"

"Toy, despite this handsome and incredibly well-equipped form of yours, you are still young and, therefore, uneducated. That is not to mock your intelligence. I am quite sure with time and the proper schooling, you would make for a lovely initiate. Until then, play nice and stop trying to coax intelligence from me. What you have, I freely gave. Do you understand?"

"That you are bat shit insane? Yes. I understand."

A bitter smile spread across Celindria's lips. "I am Imminent. Good night."

Against his will, Chris laid out on the warm floor and curled into his naked self. His eyes closed, unable to open them. Celindria disappeared from inside his head.

Outside himself, she read the book aloud and only then did Chris recognize it.

Did all the Shadow know Jack was reading from Nox's Verse that entire time to Earth? Because it seemed unlikely the King Regent would volunteer to read it if he knew who was behind it. Elden, Chris hoped Jack knew Chris wasn't behind the wheel when Celindria pulled the trigger on that nacre disabling rifle when she shot Jack in the face.

Damn, what a miserable life Nox had led. Even Celindria's voice went from smug and pleased to quiet and absorbed. Until a call came in on her wrist device, but Chris wasn't able to hear the other side.

"No. Don't worry. I'll see that everything turns out fine. I miss you, too. Continue to focus on Tameka. You're doing an excellent job. I'm so proud of you. Good night."

Who the fuck was that—

"Sleep. I'll work you harder tomorrow to erase the misery of this Verse from my mind."

Chris stayed awake the entire long night out of spite.

{CINDER | SIX MILLION YEARS AGO}

"Silence, I will not permit this."

Words that rang against the walls, floor, and ceiling, all honed of crimson rock.

Permit this? *Permit this*?! "You arrogant, mortal being! How dare you speak to me in such a way when I created you? Elden, I am your maker."

"Then stay." No gratitude. No platitudes. Only a demand.

Why? Tears streamed down Silence's face. *Why can't you say it? Just say it!* Fractured, she muttered, "You cannot cease what already comes."

Elden, in his black shroud that hid even his eyes from her, took no step forward. Lifted no hand to stave her leave. "I want no war with them. Do not unmake this paradise."

I beg of you hung in the air between them, but was never said.

On a shaking breath, Silence tried once more to make him understand. "Elden, your paradise is my prison. I must complete the mission."

"Then proceed knowing you risk your creation for chaos. The iron of your will could silence the stars. See the threat for what it is. Silence..."

She fell to her knees and opened her wings. Unbidden, she stretched her arms above her head and lowered her face to the red stone, subjugating herself. *Please say it. Give me a reason to stay—*

A baby's cry echoed from down the hall.

Savis.

"Is she not enough, Silence?"

She. Not we. Not I.

{ENKI | NOW}

The heart that broke that day never mended.

When the Martyr Complex glowed magnesium light, Silence understood hers wasn't the only heart that remained wounded. Lucas stared at the box, calm but at the ready. Smith grinned at it with an emotion akin to pride.

Rayne stirred, and all of Enki knew.

Storms erupted across every continent and blanketed every ocean. The girl was a prodigy. Silence would still bury her if she risked the mission any further.

Smith whistled at how much this impressed him. "The War King is unhappy."

"Three Two Four's mistreatment of Sagan upsets us all," Lucas declared. He stood there as if ready to greet her.

Silence agreed. The Seamswalker deserved better. All the women fallen prey to this nightmare deserved better. Still, Silence stood from her throne and walked toward the glass coffin on its raised dais meant for this moment. The woman who slayed night blinded them with her fury until the light receded back inside her young form.

This sucked.

Silence missed Kyle and Andrew. Chief Lynn and Dr. Suarez. And Twenty-One, of course.

Why?!

Why did she go and build a family while afflicted with amnesia? Why was she *drawn* to the Shadow? Every fiber of her being ached to gain access to their operations.

Now that Imminent had Rayne, of course, it made sense. But...

Why...

Rayne smiled. It was warm and not at all a response to Korac's Verse.

"She does that sometimes. We assume she's dreaming," Smith answered the unasked question.

Silence looked up to find Lucas' gaze intent on her, measuring. They all understood. The mission shifted, not changed.

Unleash Rayne on Enki.

Monitor the Atheneum.

Wait for the Shadow to locate Ishkur.

A simple itinerary. In the meantime, keep the others occupied with busy work. The Shadow needed time to understand what Silence was before they came after her. Legir and X should know the stories, but they didn't recognize her, affording her some anonymity. At the time, it was welcome as Silence still needed to capture Rayne. But now...

"How much longer, do you suppose?"

Lucas and Smith exchanged a look before the former cleared his throat to offer, "While the Shadow excel at their righteous endeavors, they take a gloriously endearing amount of time to puzzle things together."

Smith chuckled.

Silence gave in and sulked. "I grow tired of this waiting—"

"Mother, we return with Nox's Verse, as you requested."

Abresson delivered the capsule, flanked by fully dressed Para and Karter. There was something wrong with his face, but Silence didn't care enough to inspect it further. She wanted to flay him where he stood for violating T.A.O., but all in due time.

Lucas paused the playback of Korac's Verse, undetected.

Capsule in hand, Silence spared no time uploading it into her nacre memory bank. While she experienced her grandson's life, Lucas looked at Smith and Smith looked at Lucas. Both with similar expressions—*She's not going to like this.*

Elden dying.

Umbra rising.

Savis... oh, Savis.

And Nox...

Xelan...

Rayne.

All their pain and all their suffering at Primary Rem's hands. With Korac's Verse continuing its first run, more misery came to light with each passing minute.

Karter's delivery.

Korac's childhood.

Pehton... poor Pehton.

The children of Gait.

Countless, nameless slaves.

Sagan.

This was not the chaos Silence had intended when she first touched Cascading Light. Thus far, those she wanted to suffer most instead siphoned power off the lives of the people she slept to save.

"Remorse."

Even with her back to the two Valkyrie Remorse inhabited, Silence sensed the tensing and flinching of Karter and Para's bodies. Clever, so very clever, to use the Icarean females as shields. Deliverers of bad tidings. But the Primary underestimated Silence.

The Mother glanced at Lucas. He nodded to the Martyr Complex.

Surra glanced at Smith. He also nodded to Rayne Callahan, but with a wide grin and a sparkle in his brown eyes.

As the Silence in our Stars stared at the War King with renewed clarity and a deeper appreciation, she moved a piece on the board forward.

"Report on your progress with Tameka."

NINE

CAREFUL—TOMORROW WAITS IN FLAMES

{REIPON}

WAVES ROLLED, AND FOAM SPRAYED. Tameka's skin glowed with warmth from the sun—

Sun?

She awoke with a start, with one arm stretched across the patio chaise. Still dressed in only a short robe and matching panties, she smiled at the blanket thrown over her. But where was Xelan?

Almost frantic, Tameka sat up and glanced around the balcony, but there was no need. He was across from her with Korac's Verse in hand. Closed. Finished.

With his head hanging low, Xelan looked wrung out and left to dry on a bed of emotional glass. More firmly than she expected, he said, "I didn't want to wake you."

Tameka readjusted her robe and tied it on her way over to Xelan. "Always wake me." After she noted the crease lines in her arms and the state of her braids, she smiled. "I think I needed the rest, but so did you."

"I'll rest. I promise." Xelan looked up to find Tameka standing over him. "It's a new day, and it was quite a sunrise."

She sat on the ottoman beside him and assured, "I'll catch the next one." After a moment in silence, Tameka asked, "Xelan, how was his Verse for you?"

Xelan's back and chest expanded before he let out a heavy sigh. "Life changing, but I expected as much. Did you know Rayne used to sneak out at night to sing in dive bars?"

Tameka let her brows go up. "No way?!"

He opened to the scene and pointed at the page. "Way. But don't tell anyone. I think they redacted this part from the public copy."

"Oh, why?"

Xelan answered with a frown, "Because Korac implies Rayne was in love with Nox at the time and invited him to hunt her—"

"Please. No more." Tameka put a hand against Xelan's chest to stop him from speaking. "I'm so sick of that narrative. Did you know that three months ago, Andrew tried to convince me Rayne let Nox into her conscience? And that's why he kept making cameos in our dreams with her after she'd killed him?"

Xelan froze. Stiff and by inches, he turned to ask, "What?"

Tameka explained Nox's appearances in their dreams with Rayne, and how in Andrew's dream, Rayne said Nox was allowed in her conscience and was no longer a danger to her.

"I… No." Xelan stood and set Korac's Verse on the table firmly. "No. I refuse to give that thought anymore of my time. It's a new day, and we have a briefing to start."

Right. Phase II.

Tameka stood with him and held out her hand. "Ready for this?"

Taking what she offered, they walked inside their suites to prepare. "I am. We are. This will be the last phase before we storm Enki." With a grin and a crook of his brow, he asked, "Are *you* ready, Ms. Phillips?"

"Yip!" Tameka blurted as Xelan dragged her into the walk-in closet by her robe.

Catching her under the chin, he brought her eyes to meet his. "These last few months, I've put thoughts of you out of my mind to stay on mission, to bond with Pax, but right now all I can think about is the secret you've kept from me."

Did he know? Did Xelan see it somehow? A little breathless, Tameka whispered, "What secret is that?"

Xelan pulled the sash open on her robe and went to his knees, eliciting a gasp from her. With warm hands she'd missed so much, he glided up Tameka's ankles, calves, knees, and thighs before stopping at her hips. Specifically, where her gold-laced tattoo stood out in contrast to her naked brown skin.

WINGMASTER.

Tameka blushed.

Xelan beamed. "You honor me." Kissing above the tattoo. Below it. One side. Then the other.

All the while, she closed her eyes, inhaled his scent of honey and leather, and let out a shaky breath. The sight of Xelan was too intense to stare at. Like the sun. But Tameka wanted him to know she understood. "I know you're in the leadership role again, and you're so wonderful with Pax—Don't worry about me. Give to me what you want."

"At the moment…" Xelan kissed the inside of her thigh. "I'll take from you what we both need."

Tameka opened her eyes to snicker at the sexy grin on his face, but stopped as reality kicked her in the teeth. "What about Pax?"

"For now, we'll have to be quiet. Later, you can ask Sagan for a gag—"

"Boy, stop." Tameka swatted Xelan playfully and grinned at him as he settled on his knees. Her grin faded into an anticipatory gasp when his eyes changed.

"Quiet." He held a slender finger against his lips and shushed at the same time his free hand brushed against her panties, nearly buckling her knees.

Three years. Three years without sex or proper feeding, and there Xelan was shushing Tameka with that extremely self-satisfied grin on his face.

When he teased her with his tongue and raised a challenging brow, she said through gritted teeth, "Wait until it's your turn—"

"Mommy? Daddy? Where are you?"

Xelan barked out a warm laugh. "We'll need locks, I think."

Tears almost fell from Tameka's eyes. Frustrated tears. Happy tears. Loved tears.

This was a beautiful family. Now, if only she and Xelan could manage some mommy and daddy alone time. For love and for sex, tonight, Tameka would do the unthinkable. She would ask Korac and Sagan to watch Pax.

In the meantime, she spared Xelan a damned frustrated smile. "You run interference with the kiddo, while I get dressed."

"I got this."

She smiled with her back to him at the use of his catch phrase.

Before exiting the closet, Xelan called, "Tameka?"

"Yes?"

"Don't forget to change your panties."

The son of a bitch slipped out of the closet before Tameka could swat him another good one.

Sexy jerk.

{Reipon}

Pehton dragged herself out of bed. If it weren't for the big meeting today, she'd prefer to stay in and hide. She looked so miserable out among the others that Korac had pulled her in for a hug at the end of the night. Held her for a few seconds, and when they pulled away, a single yellow tear fell from his lashes and hardened on his face.

The badass Icarean General cried nacre glass. And smelled so good—For two seconds, all that peppermint and frost almost made her forget about losing Oleen.

There was something wrong with Pehton.

The mirror agreed. Dull eyes. Lifeless feathers. Armor covering every centimeter of her skin, leaving only her face exposed. She needed some life injected into her. A change.

Damn.

She'd missed makeover night.

Pehton bent at the waist and fluffed her orange feathers, grateful that she'd showered twice since facing the decimation on Lukemore. Now the light tresses bounced easily, as if revived. Next, she receded her armor to only a skimpy halter top and a miniskirt with some knee-high boots. Sassy. That's what she wanted. After applying some red lipstick and matching eyeliner, Pehton was prepared to face the group.

Including Caedes and Miy.

Out of the room, down the hall open to below, Pehton was delighted to find Pax playing in the gigantic tree.

The little monkey hung upside-down from a branch and waved happily at her. "Hi, Peh Peh!"

Pehton hid her wince. The boy always referred to her by the same name Razor used. Pax was the only one allowed to call her that. Hands on hips, she bragged, "Hey, there little daredevil. I heard you took your daddy down last night."

"Hee!"

"Tameka, did you tell *everyone* our toddler defeated me?" Xelan groaned from the corner as he turned. He spared Pehton a wink.

She smiled at the impossibly wholesome Icarus.

Tameka beamed at Xelan. "Setting the record straight is all."

Pehton reached her fist out to the upside-down mini Progeny. He bumped it with a giggle as the red of his face darkened. "Nice work, Pax. I can teach you some moves to take down bigger opponents." She was five feet tall and offered self-defense to all her height-challenged brethren.

"Yes, please, Peh Peh."

"We'll be in a meeting, kiddo. Barge in if you need anything." Tameka blew him a kiss before they all headed into the dining room.

For some reason, Xelan furnished it with the galaxy's longest table. Lacquered black, of course. Everyone sat at it, facing the front of the room.

Tumu and Lamassau were seated on Pehton's right, dressed in pale Tritan robes matching their partner's skin, followed by Ross and Jack. The teenagers dressed in casual shorts and tees. Devis took a meditation pose in the room's corner. Kyle sat beside Ross with Andrew on his right. Both looked plagued by the same stress-induced insomnia that kept Pehton up all night. Pablo and Lynn shared a chair, her snuggled in his lap. Korac and Sagan took up the opposite end of the table. The Seamswalker wore one of the war criminal's button-downs. He kept it casual with—shocker—leather pants and a silk t-shirt. Yes, that was casual to him.

Working her way back up the table on the left side, Pehton smiled at Bones and Iuo, always rocking the tactical gear. Iuo already set up his stenography equipment for meeting minutes. They waved to her and pointed at a free chair between them and Korac. Pehton quickly shrank away from the attention at the front of the room to sit beside them. As her butt hit the seat, Caedes and Miy walked into the dining room together and took two seats on Pehton's side of the table with Bones and Twenty-One between them.

Something—What was that? A niggling, irritating sensation on the back of her head—

Pehton turned to find Korac staring intently at her and then glancing at Caedes with something close to murder in his eyes. It was so absurd that she almost laughed. Pitifully, of course. Instead, she waved him off and shook her head. That's not how she wanted it, but it was disgustingly endearing that Korac should care.

"Morning, everybody."

Pehton stopped smiling at Korac and looked to the Traitor Prince of Cinder. He and Tameka stood at the front of the room, operating a device that projected an image of L. Capra in three dimensions.

Tameka opened, while Xelan sat his ass on the table to listen. "Here's what we gathered from Phase I intelligence."

They explained the Imminent sleepers in the Reipon guard. Discussed the evidence Pehton's team gathered to prove Imminent's involvement in perpetuating slave labor throughout the Vast Collective. After which, Tameka pointed to the L. Capra image.

"Here they mined this mineral..." Tameka explained while Xelan handed out the contained sample. "...In excess despite its difficulty to excavate."

Xelan picked up from there by switching places with Tameka, and Pehton had to admire the easy partnership between them. "This ore brings us to Phase II and confirms a fear I can't keep to myself any longer." He pressed a button and Monarch 3 illuminated in three dimensions. "Our next major target lies here."

Tumu nodded as if he'd already guessed. Pehton glanced beside her at Korac because he leaned forward with his elbows on the table, eyes narrowed. She and Sagan exchanged a glance, and both shrugged. But Pehton swore she glimpsed—apprehension? Surely not fear?

Xelan said, "Iuo, please let them know the latest from your Imminent contacts."

It was odd to have a verified Imminent agent in the room. Especially given how badly Lucas and Smith hurt them. Pehton hoped the leaders here checked and double checked Iuo's allegiances on the regular.

The Lamian Prince bowed his head before setting aside his equipment to address the room. "I met with Primary Rem and Abresson." Anger emphasized the 'S' in his lisp. He peered at Xelan before nervously wetting his lips. "Remorse was piloting Para."

The room went still and trained their eyes on him with bated breath.

"She's in good physical condition. Not pregnant—"

The air whooshed out of them in relief.

"—But I don't know how much longer that will be the case. He accepted my doctored footage of your sightings throughout the Vast Collective and ordered me to report to him in the next quarter night. We'll meet at the Queen's Fare on Monarch 3. He specifically mentioned they'd increased security there, three-fold."

Korac startled the room when he cursed. "They wouldn't."

Pehton shot a questioning glance at Sagan, but she was all eyes for Korac.

"They would. Have. Are." Xelan sounded the most grave Pehton had ever heard him.

Jack raised his hand and sheepishly asked, "What's happening?"

Tameka took the floor. "We've all read the Verses by now. Sagan, what's the significance of the mineral found on L. Capra? What was important about Monarch 3?"

Sagan frowned but recited, "The soil from L. Capra and... Oh, Elden. The gas from Mon3 hives—"

"And the ore from Thailea created the Progeny," Tameka finished with a quick glance at Xelan.

Gasps around the room. Some gaped or blinked wide eyes.

Tumu cut through the din. "But if Imminent is operating in Enki, where are they hiding this army—"

"Army?!" Jack's eyes doubled in size.

"—Lamassau and I haven't noticed this activity."

Xelan hushed the crowd with a push of his hands. "I know it's a terrifying hypothesis, but that's been my concern for some time. Ever since Enki first assigned the Icari to those planets. Tumu. Lam. While you haven't noticed it, we can all agree Enki is enormous. It's easy to hide an evil organization where there's only thirty of you in a sphere the size of several million suns."

Pehton felt small in a room full of giants. She'd lived a while, but her experience amounted to very little compared to even the young Progeny in this room. The history between them spanned millions—hundreds of millions—of years. The Tritans made her people and forced them to serve in Enki. When they gave them missions outside the Dyson's Sphere, it was all Enki-oriented—

"Pehton?" Tameka called her name as if she'd said it more than once.

"Yes?"

The fierce Progeny woman shifted the three-dimensional image to Enki. "In your time here, did you ever engage or interact with a project of this nature?"

Pehton shook her head, half-disassociated from the overwhelming significance of this conversation. "No. But I wasn't popular with the Imminent-aligned Tritans. I worked more for Tumu, Wiw, and Lance." A thought occurred to her. "Has anyone tried contacting Lance? He must be one of the only decent Tritans left—No offense, Tumu—"

"Hey!" Lam took offense.

"—Someone should make an ally of that man while he's still alive and not exiled."

Tumu glanced away from Pehton to meet Xelan's waiting gaze. They both shared a curt nod before the Prince of Cinder confirmed, "Excellent suggestion. Sagan, can you and Tameka work on that? It's more Phase III related, but best to get a move on."

"Absolutely, Wingmaster."

Korac picked Sagan's hand up from the table, kissed her knuckles, and threaded his fingers through hers.

Elden. Pehton walked a fine line between disgusted with them, jealous, and just happy to share in the aura of their cuteness. When she returned her gaze to the front of the room, she glimpsed Caedes staring at her. Taciturn as hell, she wasn't surprised he contributed little to the conversation, but Pehton half-expected some cutesie stuff from the new couple. Yet they both managed professionally, far better than even the couple giving the lecture. Miy hardly looked away from the front.

After a few heartbeats, Caedes gave Xelan his attention once more, and Pehton could finally take a breath.

"So our focus for Phase II is Monarch 3." Tameka beamed with an enthusiasm that lit up her eyes. "If we can find whatever facility collects the gas, we can hit them three for three. No mine on L. Capra. No plant on Mon3. No more Aegis blood and ore from Gait or Thailea."

Xelan grinned down at her in another disgusting and perfectly heart-warming display of affection.

The Shadow was so... One could both aspire and throw up all at once.

Bones punched his hand and declared, "Let's find that damn plant!"

Pehton loved this idea.

{REIPON}

Korac looked around the room as people hooted and hollered their enthusiastic agreement. Hell, he agreed. He usually did with Xelan's strategies on a macro-level. As in millennia before, the Prince still trusted the General with the micro details—arranging squads, distributing weapons, organizing rendezvous, and so forth. It was so bizarre to be existing in this dynamic once more, but perhaps more unusual than that was how naturally it all fell into place.

Twenty-One cut through the good cheer to sober everyone. "Why can't they mine the Aegis ore from their tombs on Thailea?"

This should prove interesting.

Korac tried to stop it, but a smirk crept on his face as he leaned his chair back and propped his boots on the table. That's right. On the nice shiny table. The big vein in Xelan's head pulsed.

Lamassau stood to take the metaphorical mic. "About eight thousand years ago, a cataclysm befell Thailea. A blizzardous hurricane plagues the surface, planet-wide. It only thaws in the eye of the storm for a day, maybe two at the most. It's almost impossible to mine it."

Ross asked, "Befell?"

Kyle shook his head. "Don't ask." He and Andrew both kept their eyes away from Xelan at the front.

Devis chuffed and grumbled something.

This was enough. "Why don't you tell them?" Korac shot Xelan a challenging look across the table, big enough to compensate for issues Korac knew the decorator didn't have. Plenty of the people in this room deserved to know of the Prince's involvement in Thailea's devastation.

Xelan met the stare full-on and let an entire one or two minutes pass that way. Eventually, he said, "I will. One day. It's not relevant to this discussion."

Well, that was intriguing. Sagan whispered in a hush to Pehton, "A Verse?"

The entire room full of people with fairly decent hearing looked expectantly at Xelan.

Tameka cleared her throat and waved. "Let's get back to Phase II." She shot Korac a glare that made him want to cause even more trouble, but out of respect to her relationship with Sagan, he'd chill.

Sagan patted his thigh as if she knew.

Pehton giggled under her breath in a sound that truly relieved Korac. He was almost ready to rearrange Caedes' face when the bald Icarus walked in with Miy. Not that it was any of Korac's business.

Pablo raised his hand in a weird trait of American students before asking, "Will you need me this time?"

Xelan nodded as he switched the image back to Mon3. "I think there are people trapped here for the gas, and you could be useful if they require medical attention."

Lynn frowned, unhappy with the answer.

"Don't worry, Lynn. We'll keep him safe," Xelan assured something he couldn't and never should promise. "Here's what I'm thinking." He changed the image to Earth. "We need you, Lynn, Lamassau, and Andrew to meet with Legir, Cypher, and Colton on Earth. Lynn, can you see about transporting whatever you can from the arsenal to here? We're also worried about the nacre situation that's unfolding there. Grab some samples and bring them back for testing. I know we dropped that ball while running for our lives out of Earth and Cinder."

Lynn nodded. Lamassau tipped an invisible hat brim like a cowboy. Andrew asked, "Why do you need me there?"

Tameka took this one. "I think you can *suggest* people into forgetting you were there, if necessary."

Kyle laughed. "I didn't know you were a Jedi, Conscience."

Andrew nudged him.

Xelan possessed the good grace to look sheepish. "Well, yes."

Lynn grumbled something about dealing with the two of them for Phase II.

Sagan snickered against Korac, and he loved every second of the sound. Elden, she was steadily returning to herself. He kissed the top of her head to let her know how much it meant to him.

Xelan ran a hand through his hair as he went to the next planet, Pil. He looked less worked up and more distraught—

Korac almost straightened in his chair at the realization. Xelan had read Korac's Verse, and this was him compartmentalizing at his best. As the Traitor Prince went on explaining to Ross, Jack, Miy, Devis, and Twenty-One about their job to restore Pil with X, Korac wondered what exactly from his Verse put Xelan through the wringer.

Most likely the material that they'd redacted for the public broadcast. Korac owed Sagan a special favor for giving Xelan the only unredacted copy. All on her own initiative. He loved that honesty in her, and moreover—Elden, he couldn't believe he was about to admit this even to himself—he loved her for bringing him to a house full of people so like her.

"...And that's all. Recon about exactly what happened and establish a network to rebuild there. We can't let those people continue to go without homes and jobs with no effort from us to correct it." Xelan shot Jack a reassuring smile. "I know you can handle it. Miy and Twenty-One will be there to back you up."

Miy nodded to the big Icarus on her left. He returned the gesture. So many laconic people in one outfit.

"Next." Tameka changed the image to Reipon. "Home team. Bones, Pehton, and Caedes—Do you three mind staying here with Pax, Bethany, and Triss?"

Pablo spoke up. "I'll need to give you an overview of Triss' care."

While they talked, Sagan reached over and squeezed Korac's hand. He wished he could convince her there was no way Triss would die without having Razor's baby.

"Now time for Mon3 team. Sagan, if you don't mind sticking with us for travel?"

Xelan glanced at their hands clasped on the table for only a moment, but it was enough to make Korac smirk. "Where do you want me?" Because the two always worked together, and the phrasing was provocative enough to make people glance away. Too easy.

Tameka stepped up. "You two will take the plant. Pablo will be under your care. Kyle, this is your time to show Ross up. Her current record is two hundred and twenty. Tumu, you'll be keeping the children from misbehaving."

Korac glanced over in time to share a nod of respect with Kyle. They were absolutely misbehaving.

Gesturing at Iuo, Xelan said, "Tameka and I will scout informants to find the plant."

The room hushed once more.

"It's time to get the Valkyrie back."

After that declaration, everyone deliberated a while longer before breaking for lunch. During which, Korac lost track of Sagan, but he knew where to find her.

The nursery was off their suites with its crib, changing station, and dresser full of baby clothes. Stuffed animals lined the crib and matched the mobile hovering above. Everything was decorated sweetly in the colors of Korac and Sagan's eyes, silver and lilac. Soft.

Sagan sat in the middle of the floor, unpacking another haul of bibs and folded them neatly for storage, all while smiling and humming a tune in her work. Korac wanted to ask her now, but it wasn't the right time. Although this space represented a tremendous leap of faith for their relationship, it was also confined by the anxiety of Triss' impending labor. By her death.

Bittersweet.

The world deserved better than Gait's first Executive Warden. She was a monster, but raising her child—her and Razor's child—after she left this life was both poetic and criminal simultaneously. Perfect for Korac. Strained for Sagan. After all, there was a chance the little girl might grow to resent the people raising her who also killed her birth parents.

"Where'd you get those this time?" Korac sat on the floor beside Sagan, one knee up and one leg stretched out. Reaching over, he grabbed a few bibs to help fold.

She stopped humming. "Thank you. These are from Legir. They're made of fruit fibers in case little Echo decides to suck on them."

Echo.

The beautiful name tinged Sagan's smile with sadness every time she said it. It hurt Korac's heart, but he understood why she named the baby after Rayne.

Sagan changed the subject. "Can you believe Jack not only suggested that we take Enki for the Vast Collective, but that Xelan perpetuated the idea? Surely it's impossible to operate that thing."

Ahh… something Korac could help her with. "I suppose you think it's too late for me to ask my father for driving lessons?"

Eyes wide, Sagan stopped her work and turned to him, asking, "You would do that?"

Korac shrugged and took the stacks of bibs to the changing table while saying, "It's a secure facility, and with the Progeny, anything is possible."

"Wow… Imagine it. All of us under one enormous roof." Sagan ticked them off on her fingers as she listed them. "Earth, Cinder, Reipon, Pil, Mon3, L. Capra, Lukemore, Yu, the people evicted from Gait, whoever stays on Enki, and—Hey, is there anyone on Thailea?"

Korac shook his head solemnly and walked back to help Sagan stand on the floor.

She kissed his cheek, "Thanks. Wait a minute." Staring

at her fingers, she frowned prettily. "Are there only eleven planets in the Vast Collective? I've never noticed before, but I don't think I've heard of the twelfth world."

So she found the age-old mystery. Korac smiled ruefully. "We've reached the crux of the matter. No one has."

Those eyes stretched wide, and Sagan's pretty lashes fluttered with big blinks. "Seriously?"

"No one knows what the twelfth planet is or why the Vast Collective is always referred to as the Twelve Worlds."

Tameka walked by and stopped when she saw them through the doorway. "Hey, I was just looking for you."

"Tameka, did you know there isn't a twelfth world?" Sagan's incredulous disbelief made Korac smirk comically.

The other Progeny woman frowned. "Really? Girl, I'm not able to process any more revelations today. Not after what I learned about Rayne."

Korac placed his hand on the belt at the small of Sagan's back. He loved when she wore his clothes. He also loved the slight throb of the vein in Tameka's neck as she watched. She and Xelan shared similar triggers. Korac cleared his throat to ask, "Did you need us?"

"Oh, right." Tameka stopped staring and poked around the room as she danced around her purpose. "Do you think..." She sighed. "Could you watch Pax for us after the mission? We uh... need some alone time."

Sly. The smirk on Korac's face twisted and skewed to the sly. He glanced down at Sagan. She smiled up at him before answering for them both. "We'd be happy to. It'll be fun practice. Do you think he can handle being around me, though?"

Tameka kept her back to them as she assured, "Oh, yeah. In fact, I think this will diminish his crush once he's spent some normal time with you around the Villa. He's into piggyback rides and forts right now." She stopped fidgeting and straightened her spine, saying, "Thank you." When she faced them again, her eyes were full of something Korac couldn't quite place. "Both of you."

"Oh. No. Thank *you*." At Tameka's raised brow, Korac elaborated, "I can't wait to teach your youngling all manner of swear words and how to dress properly."

Sagan snickered into her hands. "Babe, I think you might give her a stroke."

"Mommy! There you are." Pax took a step in until Tameka held up a finger. "Oh. I forgot. Uncle Kor and Auntie Sagan, can I come in?"

Korac's heart expanded at Sagan, kneeling and holding out her arms. "Only if you give me a hug?"

Pax blushed to his red hair but waddled over like a bashful penguin. After jumping in her arms, Sagan made a sound which warmed Korac through when she squeezed and picked Pax up. When the time came, Sagan would make an excellent mother. Pax reached an arm out to Korac, who, despite his own doubts about fatherhood, immediately joined the hug.

"Uncle Nock misses you."

Stunned, Korac opened his eyes to meet mirrors of himself in Pax's midnight blue rings. Older. His eyes looked older than his body and mind.

"What was that, Pax?" Tameka asked, as Korac and Sagan handed him over to her.

The youngling glanced between the three adults, concerned by the shock on their faces. As if he did something wrong, Pax clammed up.

Tameka gave an apologetic glance to Sagan and Korac. "I don't know where that came from."

"The Verse, mommy," Pax said into her shoulder. "They miss each other."

Korac worked to keep the confusion and any potential suspicion from his face. Sagan held his hand, and he felt the tension in her small bones.

"Pax, are you spooking your mom with your dreams?" Xelan stood in the doorway. "Sorry for not telling you, Tameka. Last night, Pax woke up with dreams inspired by your Verse, Korac."

The toddler wiggled and reached for his father, who took him from Tameka and set him on the floor to jump on his daddy's back.

Tameka's frown melted into a softer expression. "I see." To Sagan and Korac, she offered, "We'll talk to him before you watch him tonight."

Korac kept his eyes on Pax. The boy communed with Rayne in his dreams, and rumors circulated over the last day that Nox often appeared when Rayne spoke to the Progeny in their dreams. What if…

"It's fine, really, Tameka." Sagan took her sister's hand and squeezed it. "Is everyone ready for Andrew's Lazarus experiment?"

"This should prove interesting." Xelan glanced between the girls before locking that ancient stare on Korac. "Do you girls mind going ahead without me?"

Korac narrowed his eyes at the Traitor Prince. Sagan glanced at him, and he assured, "Go. I'll check on Triss while you help with Andrew."

The women left with little waves and curious stares. Pax remained attached to Xelan like a ginger turtle shell. Quiet stretched between them.

Unable to take it any longer, Korac chuffed and found a wall to lean against. "What is it?" He folded his arms and crossed his legs at the ankles, settled for this battle.

Pax braided strands of Xelan's hair together as their leader confessed, "I finished your Verse."

"Did you want an autograph?"

Xelan made a disgusted sound and stared at the ceiling as if begging it for strength. Eventually, he asked on a groan, "You can't make this easy, can you?"

Korac's eyes narrowed further as he shrugged. "You read my life. Do you think anything in it was easy?"

"No. Elden, no. I wish…" Xelan placed his hands on his hips and stared at his tapping foot as he collected his thoughts into words. After a few minutes, he sighed. "I wish we'd communicated more. That I understood your background more. Hell, I wish for many things, Korac, but right now I wish we could get along."

Bitterness boiled inside Korac's heart. It stung. But near it—heart adjacent—came an unexpected spark. "You believed it?"

Xelan met his eyes then. "Every word. You weren't one for lies. I don't believe you'd lie to Rayne or to Sagan."

"Auntie Rayne and Auntie Sagan, hee!" Pax beamed at both men, and Korac be damned if that didn't melt his cool exterior. Some.

Korac held out his hand. "Maybe we start with trust."

Xelan clasped his wrist. As they shook, a smile spread across the Prince's face. "You're still planning to give me a hard time, aren't you?"

"Every fucking day, your highness."

{Reipon}

Andrew walked down the scape of his memory alongside Kyle, who highlighted the most recent accurate memories. Outside, they sat across from one another in the infirmary under Pablo and Xelan's careful watch. Tameka and Sagan hovered nearby for moral support.

"But why do you have to die?" Kyle held a joint even on this metaphorical plane and used it to gesture his point. "This seems unnecessarily risky."

Elden, he loved his family for worrying, but Andrew wanted them off his back now. "When I die, more Probabilities will form. I told you that this one went stagnant, completely unpredictable. This is a way to defibrillate it, so to speak."

Kyle hit his joint and let the smoke gather, shrouding his face as he considered. "So... will I die with you?"

Good question. "I doubt it. I'm sure it's fine. Are you ready? We have sixty more seconds."

His unrelated brother shrugged. "Nah. I'm not worried. Pablo and Xelan won't let us stay dead because

Tameka and Sagan will kill them for letting us die on their watch."

That's right. Andrew's pillars. No matter the Probability, Tameka and Sagan were always on the side of good. Rayne, too. They focused him.

He and Kyle bumped fists. Andrew said with a smile, "True that. Thank Elden for our sisters."

"Can you imagine Xelan explaining to Rayne—"

The scape glitched, and Andrew's heart jumped into his throat. Kyle was right there checking on him. "Hey… I'm here, man. Just… shit. Breathe or don't or—"

All around, the space inside of his mind blurred and multiplied, like being K.O.ed with a decent concussion. The walls split, the ceiling opened, and the hall of his memories exponentially aggregated and folded until a million formed and waited for him.

Kyle—a million Kyle's—rushed to his side—

No. Not all. Some stood and watched dispassionately as he died.

"I'm right here," several hundred thousand of them said at once in a choir of concern.

Andrew hitched and drew on air, but it was like his lungs didn't want it. Simply rejected it, and a horse kicked him in the chest, punching his heart. Finally, his breath stopped, and Andrew fell on his face.

Fuck.

God damn, dying hurt.

{ENKI}

"Was it *The Core*?" Matt asked as he set another charge.

Puk chuckled into the earpiece. It was much harder to walk on a rock while it spun at a dangerous velocity through space inside a Dyson's Sphere. "Naw, my man. But I bet Lucy would've guessed right by now."

"Fuck." Matt said it more for his friend's amusement than his own. Puk was all right. He seemed to get Matt and Lucy, or at the very least, stayed out of their way. It was unusual for Matt to work with someone other than her, so this was an interesting exercise in his ability to act like a person. "How many more ya got?"

The Mon3 drone made rustling noises as he searched his bin. "Uh... looks like fifty. You?"

"About twenty." Matt hovered his bin over to a cemetery in the prison's backyard. Puk was further down Mercy's Row, communicating over the earpiece. Into which, Matt asked, "Hey, will this even work? Are these explosives big enough? I thought there's supposed to be a drill involved." He tried his best to unlock his jaw and pop it. Handling explosives resurfaced his bad habit of teeth grinding under stress. That or worrying about Lucy's radio silence up there alone in a shrine with a Tritan.

Over the earpiece, Puk reassured, "Relax, Ginger. There's some big gun we aren't privy to because we're 'need to know.' Feel me?"

Yeah. Yeah. He got it.

A few minutes later, the drone returned to the comms. "You hungry?"

Not after his last sandwich only an hour ago, but Puk ate four times as often as a human. "I can take a break, if you want?"

"Yeah. This working around the clock business has my stomach growling—"

"Ginger. This is Morning Star. It'll be another beautiful day, boys. Over."

Matt instantly wanted Lucy.

Puk huffed over the comms. "Easy for you to say. You're not hurdling to your doom on a broken rock at fifty-six thousand klicks per hour, Morning Star. Over."

Lucy giggled—a sound Matt reveled in—before responding, "I'll send some more anti-nausea packs before I'm relieved for sleep shift. Yito, do you mind? No? That's wonderful. Thanks! Hey, Puk, I'm sending down a hundred cases of the stuff and some more charges. Over."

"Hell. Yes. Thank you, Yito."

Matt listened with a smirk on his face. Lucy was doing it. Building that support for her coup. Elden, he loved her. Boldly, he asked, "Can I get a kiss before you go to bed? Over."

Puk exaggerated gagging sounds through the mic.

Again, Lucy laughed sweetly, as much for him as for their audience, who never heard her giggle over bodies ripped apart by her bare hands. "No, but I will pass on Primary Rem's commendations. Over and Out."

That was it.

That was the Phase II signal.

Should their little cadre meet with any high-ranking member of Enki or Imminent, they shifted to the next stage in the design. Of course, they expected someone more like Eminent Abresson. A visit from *the* Primary Rem was a rare treat Matt hoped Lucy savored.

"Did you hear that, Matt?" Puk asked vaguely over the comms.

"Oh, I heard. Kudos to us."

"Cheers."

Matt placed another charge even further south before thinking to ask, "Hey, does the movie at least have a decent soundtrack?"

Puk chuckled. "One of the best."

TEN

POWER AND RESTRAINT

{REIPON}

PUSH. Push. Push.

Fingers laced, Xelan stood over Andrew and compressed into his chest while Pablo checked his pulse. He hated seeing the fear on Tameka's face in his periphery. The concern in Sagan's eyes. Lynn joined with an IV catheter ready to insert on their say—

"Now, Lynn. Get that adrenaline in him." Xelan knew his voice sounded harsh, but this was life or death, and there wasn't time to school his tone. He didn't dare stop the compressions, either.

Pablo pumped a milligram of adrenaline while staring at the heart monitor.

"What… what about Kyle?" Sagan asked, strained with her concern.

The doctor checked Kyle's vitals quickly. "He's fine. Still catatonic, though."

What if they gave him too much of the nacre disabler? "Scalpel. Quick."

Lynn handed Xelan the instrument he then used to slice open his wrist and shoved it at Andrew's mouth. "Take over compressions, Pablo."

"Got it."

Kyle startled beside them and jumped back as if electrocuted. "Oh! Oh, shit! Whoa..."

Sagan and Tameka pulled him back with them. "Are you okay?" "What happened?"

Blue Icarean blood, royal and spiked with a little Gargantuan Tritan, flowed into Andrew's mouth while their girls calmed Kyle down and Pablo pump-started Andrew's heart.

Kyle said, "He's right. A million Probabilities just opened up on us, like we were in an epicenter. And then... and then they collapsed. Because—"

Andrew gasped for the biggest breath. His spine bowed off the bed like the air punched into him. He gripped the sheets, grabbing purchase on this life.

"—He's alive," Kyle finished.

Xelan let Pablo help Andrew relax while he checked the girls. Their eyes glistened, and they were so relieved, they pulled Kyle into a hug.

Lynn put her face over Andrew's, still giving him space. "Welcome back. We worried we lost you for a second."

Andrew gripped his fists at his sides. "I was right! I died, and it opened more Probabilities. They closed when I came back. I saw... I saw so many things. But... Oh, Elden..."

"Take a breath," Xelan calmed him. "Give yourself a few seconds."

Abruptly, Andrew sat up and grabbed both Xelan and Pablo by their shirts, one in each hand. "No. I have... I have to tell you..." He swallowed as tears brimmed. "Every Probability presents various futures, but they all end the same. I can't see anything, not one thing, beyond Rayne's death in the Probability Matrix. Everything ends with her."

Xelan took another sip of his orange juice alone at the bar in the lounge. The juice sloshed in the glass until he stopped his hands from shaking. The girls opted to stay with Andrew and Kyle. Pablo and Lynn returned to prepping for Phase II. Xelan needed a minute alone, and the vitamin C should help with the shock.

"It starts with him *and ends with* her.*"*

"Mother, did you mean me and Celindria? Or did you mean Nox and Rayne?"

No answer.

And there never would be because their mother killed herself in a selfish, spiteful act that continues to haunt Xelan to this day–

A knock sounded on the door.

When Xelan turned to find Jack Callahan standing there, he realized it was a welcome distraction. This bright, promising star was one excellent reminder of why they fought. Already, he was a better leader than his sister, but that's because Rayne wasn't trained for leadership. She was always a weapon. One Xelan had a hand in creating–

"Come in, Jack. Have a seat. Can I get you some O.J.?"

"Sure. No ice."

Xelan grimaced and chuckled at the reflex. "Ew. Who puts ice in their orange juice?"

Jack took his glass and sat on the stool beside him. "Flight attendants."

Bewildered, Xelan laughed into his drink while taking another sip.

The young man stretched his glass away from him and played with it across the bar top. "Andrew's moving around already."

Of course. "I knew he wouldn't stay in bed like I asked."

With a solemn nod, Jack confirmed, "They grew up while you were gone."

Xelan hated they referred to his death as "gone." He lost a battle and paid the ultimate price. "I was dead." At the teenager's wince, he softened. "But do you want to know a secret?"

"What?"

"I'm glad they didn't grow up so much that they don't still need me." The Prince of Cinder tipped his glass at the King Regent. "Take you, for instance. You've come a long way from stealing money out of your sister's backpack for cigarettes. You know, she left that money in there for you on purpose?"

The teenager's hazel eyes nearly doubled in size. "Really?"

Xelan nodded along, imparting this one kernel of Rayne's love for her brother. "She said you needed it to look tough. To survive the people you were hanging around. You don't need it anymore, do you?"

"We're learning a lot about each other lately." Jack frowned and stared hard at his half-empty glass while saying, "Not all of it's good."

"Talk to me."

Sighing, the young man opened up. "Rayne gave me Nox's Verse to dispense in Story Circle. She lied to me and said it was anonymous. Everyone helped her lie. But you know? I can let that go."

Xelan placed a hand on Jack's shoulder and squeezed. "Good. She meant to spare you. Even I'm begrudging to admit there were some effective lessons in his Verse." He dropped his hand to help steady his glass.

"And that's fine." Jack sighed heavier, as if preparing for something momentous. "But what I can't stop thinking about is why did Nox kiss Rayne on the Volcano Day battlefield. Why do the less redacted copies of Nox's Verse read like a love letter to my sister and what exactly did she redact?"

Xelan wondered the same thing, and at the same time he knew the answer without asking. "It's complicated, Jack. Messy, even. More importantly, that part of the Verse is Rayne's business. That's why she redacted it."

"Was she in love with him? The man that destroyed civilization as we knew it?" Jack turned concerned eyes to Xelan, too vulnerable to dismiss.

"I don't think it's my place to say, but I hate the thought of you working yourself up with worse assumptions. Rayne confided in me that she cared for a version of Nox which he showed only to her. Now, whether that version actually existed or was part of his machinations, we'll never know. But you should ask yourself, does it matter? It's her business, and I think she handled it beautifully. I can't wait to tell her myself how proud I am of her. Like how proud I am of you, Jack."

The young man's eyes stayed heavy with this additional burden, but he smiled brightly with appreciation. "Thanks for talking with me. It's been on my mind for a while now."

"I'm here if you need me."

"In a house full of people who need you, don't you get exhausted?"

Both Jack and Xelan spun to see Tumu standing in the doorway with a bottle of single malt scotch. He tipped it at the bar. "Thought I'd return it now that Lamassau and I are finished with it."

Xelan grinned. "The entire house can once more swim in the pool after it's cycled through the filter."

"Jealous?" Tumu accused, as he replaced the drink. He smiled at Jack's snicker before reassuring, "Don't be, Wingmaster. You and I are the Eternal Bind. We can never part for long."

Jack's mouth gaped.

Xelan rolled his eyes and snorted into the last of his orange juice. "You wish."

"Does he, now?"

Ahh. Drama.

Lamassau leaned in the doorway with his arms folded, glaring daggers at his lover.

Tumu possessed the grace to look embarrassed as he spread his arms wide in surrender. "Lamassau. You know I don't—"

"Remember this moment the next time I'm playing strip poker with Bones and Twenty-One." The Chef turned on his heel and quit the room.

Tumu sighed. A good heavy sigh—

"You *do* love him!" Xelan couldn't keep the shock out of his voice.

Bewildered, the Tritan looked Xelan over but kept his mouth shut.

Jack broke the tension with a subject change. "How do you impress a girl when you think she's into someone else?"

Both men stopped staring at each other and looked at the teenager. This was about Ross, but her circumstances with Bethany strained things. With a non-brow raised, Tumu asked, "Well, who is she finding more diverting than our handsome King Regent?"

Fair question.

"Korac."

The Tritan's face puckered into a feature-less wince.

Xelan put his hand back on Jack's shoulder, more consolingly than before. Grimly, he let the boy down easy. "There is no competing with that."

Tumu solemnly concurred. "Buy a plot, rent a hearse, and bury that dream in the ground, kid, cause you are never getting her back from that."

"Damn."

{REIPON}

Lynn sat back and watched the unsupervised Progeny go at it.

"I'm fine, Tameka," Andrew argued for the thirtieth time.

Tameka responded logically, "You just died ten minutes ago. Sit. Back. Down."

Kyle passed his joint to Andrew, who accepted it eagerly as Kyle said, "He died. What good will sitting do?"

Sagan caught Lynn enjoying the show and winked at her, which made her snicker.

It was all light and harmless fun to burn off the nerves of impending Phase II shit. Pablo briefed Bones, Pehton, and Caedes on Triss' care in the next room while Lynn prepped the nacre disablers with lethal and stun charges. Things really were getting serious.

Despite all their research and discoveries, Imminent somehow learned of the Shadow's tactics. The last few runs they went on met with nacre-less enemies. That hurt their weapons, but also their defense. Tameka couldn't drain them dry, and the memory siblings couldn't overwhelm them. So, at Lynn's insistence, they started packing heat. Simple 9mm handguns. Tumu had sworn no space tech included projectile weapons because of their futility against nacre-imbued enemies.

Lynn doubted that was entirely true.

In the meantime, she looked forward to the trip back to Earth to stock up on better guns and ammunition. More so than their personal protection, she worried about the colossal Tantamount buried in Iona's Arsenal facility under the hundred-foot waves off of the Cape of Good Hope. Surely no one could access that vault without her DNA to open the hatch. Hence why Lynn killed all her copies so thoroughly dead during Abresson's invasion—

"You okay?" Sagan interrupted Lynn's thoughts.

She smiled at her friend while assembling another weapon. "I'm in prep mode. What about you? How are you doing with this Rayne business?"

The Seamswalker grabbed a gun and loaded it. Softly, she confessed, "I don't put much faith in the Probability Matrix, but I believe Rayne's strong enough to 'end everything.' Whatever that means. The only other person I think of as powerful enough to do that is standing in this room."

They both looked over at Tameka, who pushed Andrew back into the bed. Kyle tried to take his brother's side, but that so wasn't working. Powerhouse. Fury. Tameka could leave them both unconscious or mewing for their lives without touching them, but she hesitated to use it without more practice. Something about the suns imploding.

It was hard keeping up with the super powered types around here.

So Lynn and Pablo made themselves useful with weapons and medical care. Everyone contributed. Everything was fair.

Sagan asked, "Are you?"

Lynn blinked up at Sagan and asked, "Am I . . . ?"

The Seamswalker loaded another gun and laid it with the rest. "Are you worried about Rayne?"

Blowing the air from her cheeks, Lynn gave it some deep thought. Eventually, she said, "I worry about all of us, but I think—especially after watching that Iona-29 footage—I think Rayne is the safest out of all of us. There must be some other reason nothing exists after her 'death.'"

Sagan winced at the word, and Lynn reached out to squeeze her hand. "She'll be fine. You know if she were here, she'd tell you to 'Worry about yourself, keep your head in the game, and don't get dead.'"

"No truer words have ever been spoken." Pablo returned with a smile for the room and said, "Everyone, I must ask that you leave my patient now because my head can't take anymore of it."

On their way out, Tameka stopped to ask, "Hey Doc, do you mind joining us for a training session? I'm worried—"

He made a soothing gesture and nodded along. "Of course. Of course. I'll be there. Lynn, you wanna come with?" The little wretch licked his full lips, standing in the doorway looking delicious in those oxblood scrubs he knew she liked.

Lynn waved him off. "Let me get stations ready for testing those Enki nacres from Earth. You can tell me all about it when you get back."

Pablo blew her a kiss, and Lynn almost dragged him back for a session of their own. Instead, she continued working while musing about her husband and how lucky they were. Twelve guns prepped. One nacre station ready to hold about five test samples. They needed to access all the banks and functions. They might need Kyle for the memory—

"Dr. Suarez?" Triss called from the next room.

Lynn tried to reinforce her stomach to poke her head in. "Yes?"

Despite the pain tightening her striking face, Triss slipped into her cool and proud facade she wore like an armor. "Is the doctor in?" One fist gripped the sheets where she lay helpless in the queen-sized bed.

With a heavy sigh, Lynn stepped into the room, explaining, "He stepped out. What do you need?"

"Nothing from you." Triss faced forward, averting her eyes.

Unfortunately, Lynn saw the wince she hid. The woman was in pain and very pregnant. For a baby conceived only a few months ago, she looked full term. Pitiful and exhausted from the agony that kept her awake.

Hands on her hips, Lynn said, "Okay. You can be rude, but I'm about to pump you full of Yu juice to knock your ass out unless you tell me what you want. I won't have my husband upset with me for not seeing to you while he's out."

Staring forward with a stubborn set to her jaw, Triss rolled her eyes before asking with a sigh, "May I please have some water?"

That probably hurt. Such a powerful warrior reduced to hospice-level care.

"Sure. No problem. Cold or room temperature?"

Something must have spasmed because Triss' faced contorted in pain, and she breathed sharply through gritted teeth. Lynn poured a half liter of both temperatures and brought them to Triss, eager to leave the woman's side. Guilt and hatred tasted bitter, and she found it unpalatable for this long.

Lynn was almost through the door when Triss hissed through the pain, "Thank you."

A coward, Lynn closed it to avoid witnessing that woman writhe any further. Forehead to the door, she fended off conflicting emotions when a substantial weight settled on her foot. She looked down to find Thubgy, looking up with his tongue lolled out.

A welcome distraction from the worsening situation behind her.

"Hey, fella." Lynn bent to pet the Hellkitten, who no doubt came looking for food. "You know what, little man? Me, too."

Horrified by herself and the situation, Lynn left the infirmary, closing the door on the pregnant woman's screams.

{REIPON}

Tameka stood in the center of their training ground, an outdoor tiled space furnished by obstacles and decorated with cool weapons. Off in the tiered stands, Pax played with his toy train, Iron Hope. Andrew "rested" beside him. Pablo set down his emergency supplies and helped the toddler build a track.

Sagan stood at Tameka's side, grinning at Korac, who fought for the opposition alongside Bones, Twenty-One, Xelan, and Caedes. All of them smirking at their Progeny opponents.

Oh, yeah. Kyle was on Tameka's team.

"Are you ready to have your asses handed to you?" Tameka resented the enemy didn't shit talk in real life because she enjoyed the banter in training.

Xelan ducked his eyes for a second before returning with that fantastic grin. "Go easy on us, eh, Fury?"

Bones and Twenty-One opened their wings and flanked him. Caedes took the high ground to start. He looked ready to fight and not at all entertained by Xelan and Tameka's flirting. Was he still into her? She thought he was moving on with Miy or Pehton—

Not important.

Kyle and Sagan pressed their backs to hers.

Korac blew Sagan a kiss, and the girl practically melted.

"Ahem." Tameka jabbed her.

The Seamswalker promised, with an abuse of the catch phrase, "I got this."

Xelan barked out a laugh.

Tameka felt Kyle's eyes roll before griping, "Can we get to this?"

"Kick butt, mommy!" Pax shouted from the stands.

Okay, now everyone melted.

Voices muttered near the entrance before Tumu, Lamassau, Jack, Ross, and Iuo emerged. The Lamian Prince mused, "Good. We haven't missed a thing."

Lamassau bitched, "How dare you have a sparring session without inviting us?!"

Jack and Ross led the group to the stands, shaking their heads. The King Regent called, "Sorry. Sorry. I'll get them seated and shut up."

Ross vibrated with excitement. Once they sat down, she reached for Jack's hand and bounced with it. Tumu gave the moment a look and glanced over at Xelan, who nodded. Tameka assumed it had to do with the teenage boy's obvious crush on the teenage girl, but none of that mattered. All that mattered was—

"Fight!"

Thanks, Andrew.

Sagan opened a conduit. Tameka and Kyle fell back into it. They descended from the ceiling behind enemy lines. Meanwhile, Sagan squared off with Bones in hand-to-hand combat. At a shared nod, Kyle went right, and Tameka went left.

Twenty-One turned around right as Tameka emerged from the obstacle between them. He let out a war cry and brought both fists down to crush her skull.

She punched his side, her small fist fitting under his ribs.

He gasped for air, and she used the advantage to roll his hefty ass over her back. Once she laid him out, Tameka opened the well in her and took a sip.

Control.

Practice and control.

She only wanted to take enough to leave him unconscious—

Another heavy body tackled her and pinned her to the ground. Blows threw at Tameka so fast, she almost couldn't block them.

Who the fuck was fighting her so ferociously—

"I expected more of a fight from you, Sovereign Ambassador."

Korac's elegant cadence was enough to test Tameka's self-control, but the fucker swarmed her with his fists so she couldn't concentrate on her ability, leaving her with only one option.

Tameka took a blow to the face. Light exploded behind her eyes, and she bit the inside of her cheek. But this small sacrifice granted her a window to catch his next swing. She offered not one second of hesitation. Tameka took the light from Korac's impressed eyes until he lay out beside her. She fed his nacre energy to the audience, who gasped and sighed from the refresher.

Next up—

Kyle shouted and jumped from an obstacle to land on Caedes' back in the air and ride him down. Still no wings on Story Taker, but the boy managed without them—

Kyle barreled over Tameka's head, yelling the whole while.

Maybe "managed" was too generous.

He crumpled against the far wall and performed a stellar imitation of a puddle. Andrew and Pablo already made their way over to him while Tameka turned to face Caedes.

He was a fearsome sight in battle that made a black turtleneck and tactical pants intimidating without the distraction of hair in his eyes like the other Icari. This was their first fight, although Tameka often wondered about his style as an opponent—

Caedes twirled with spinning wings and opened with a roundhouse kick.

When Tameka narrowly avoided it, she took a spinning kick to the head. She rolled away in time to evade Caedes stomping the floor beside her head hard enough to crack the tile.

"Shit!" Tameka let out an unattractive grunt to roll onto her feet and catch another downward kick to her skull. This allowed her the leverage to push Caedes up and off balance.

Well, in theory.

With a flourish, Caedes let his wings steady him and went into another stance that left him loose and ready.

Leg work. The man was all long legs and powerful landings. In hand-to-hand, he was superior to her. Tameka missed her chain dart.

She took a deep breath and reached inside for that space in her nacre. Caedes noticed and ran to her with a spinning aerial kick. But she couldn't afford the distraction.

Open. Consume. Decide.

When she took from his nacre, her ability gave her a choice. Burn or dispense. Tameka knew if she let it, it would burn the brightest, hottest flash. This frightened her and made her hesitate to access it. Instead, she took a drink from Caedes and shared it with those in the stands until they filled.

Caedes fell to the ground, centimeters from kicking her cranium.

Only Bones and Xelan remained of the opposition. Tameka searched the training grounds for Team Progeny.

Sagan… where was she—Oh.

That was new.

{REIPON}

Ceiling.

Grounds.

Floor.

Ceiling.

Grounds.

Floor.

Bones grew tired of shouting some thirty loops ago. How the Seamswalker had ever managed to create a perpetual conduit—one end opened two feet below the top end—was beyond Bones.

All he knew was he was about… ten more falling loops from vomiting. Or passing out.

"I." One loop.

"Give." Another loop.

"Up." Last loop before the bottom conduit disappeared, and Bones mercifully sprawled onto the floor, a teetering mess.

He was so grateful for the solid, steady ground he kissed the white tile and let himself collapse to hug it. Nice and cool. Rest. Perfect spot, too. With his head turned this way, Bones got to watch the action closer than ringside.

And what action.

Sagan and Tameka faced off against Xelan, the last standing member of team Icari. Talk about saving the best for last.

Xelan opened his wings and let his eyes shift to Atramentous. He perched—dramatically, in Bones' opinion—on an obstacle like an enormous bird of prey.

A chorus of noise erupted from the stand. Boots stomped in a steady rhythm. The crowd wanted action, and they were about to get it.

The Prince of Cinder straight up disappeared. Bones never saw him move. He simply reemerged behind Tameka and Sagan and somehow sent them flying in opposite directions. The Seamswalker spilled into the stands in a clumsy attempt to catch herself.

Andrew, Kyle, and Tumu "Ooo"ed with a wince because landing in the audience was an automatic out. No hurting the bystanders.

"Fuck." Sagan stamped her foot with a cute pout.

Meanwhile, Tameka picked herself up, standing on the obstacle she'd landed on and opened her wings. She stared up at Xelan, who flew outside of reach in the room's center.

"Daddy so high!" Pax shouted.

The crowd cooed. What else could they do but fall at that toddler's adorably small feet?

Despite his son's distracting cuteness, Xelan kept his eyes on Tameka, affording her the respect of a worthy opponent. His voice projected with authority in three pitches. "You won't render me unconscious so easily. It's time to practice your ability while fighting. Are you ready?"

Tameka looked ready all right, but not to fight—once more, in Bone's humble opinion. Her chest heaved with excitement, not exertion. Her eyes shifted into Atramentous jewels. The woman looked ready to rip Xelan's clothes off and go to town—

Again, the Prince of Cinder seemed to disappear and reconstitute from the ether behind Tameka. It was that super fast speed of his which allowed him to move so fast the nacre nanite fields considered him a projectile. Wingmaster slowed down to deliver blows to avoid its rejection. He snaked his arms around her in a hold meant to knock her out.

But the redhead wasn't having it.

Tameka threw them both backwards against the obstacle's high wall, crushing their wings around them. In her efforts, she frowned with concentration—obviously working her mojo.

Which Bones was grateful he didn't endure this round. Although, he couldn't decide which was worse. The infinite falling loop or recovering from a drained nacre—

A cry brought Bones' attention back to the action. They grappled on the obstacle with Xelan on top, locking long legs and arms around Tameka to render her powerless.

Fury didn't like that.

She rolled them off the thirty-foot obstacle, leaving Xelan no choice but to release her in order to catch himself in a flurry of black feathers.

Tameka barely buffeted her wings before hitting the ground. She glared up at Xelan, seething now in a less-sexually charged manner.

Damn, Bones wished he had some popcorn. Or the will to get up off the floor.

Especially as Xelan's nose dripped a trickle of blue blood. The crowd gave a unified grunt, as was required with first blood. As more blood rushed from him, the peeps in the stand hushed with anticipation.

Tameka gripped her fists in concentration. Xelan let her take from him. Now this seemed less of a fight and more of a test of their limitations.

The surrounding air warmed and thickened. Hair stood up on Bones' scalp—for which he was glad something on him could stand at all. Sizzling energy nipped at his goosebumps.

What was this? It felt new. Although oddly reminiscent of that time, Rayne and Nox went blow for blow on Volcano Day—

Holy Thunderdome.

Lightning zapped the grounds only a few feet from Bones. Someone lunged and snatched him from the embers that sparked. Everyone ran to the exit, carrying the unconscious to safety.

Everyone except Tameka and Xelan.

They both fell to their knees across from the other in the ring. Xelan refused to give in, and Tameka siphoned from everything she could.

Suddenly, Bones surged with energy. Enough to stand and help with the others—

No. They all woke up now and huddled in the entryway with the rest. Those with Icarean and Progeny blooded shifted their eyes to Atramentous thanks to the influx of power. The rest zinged with it. So alive with it, as if the sun kept them awake—

Tameka cried out, and Xelan shouted, "I relent!"

They both collapsed.

{REIPON}

Kyle kept it to himself, but he thought it was so stupid to risk everyone in a training session before commencing Phase II. Now here they were in the infirmary with the couple responsible unconscious. At least Tameka was generous enough to disperse that nacre energy to help everyone else recover before imploding with her—boyfriend? Baby daddy? Lover? What exactly were she and Xelan these days, anyway—

"You fought so well. I learned a lot I hope to use from watching you." Ross' enthusiasm was both genuine and appreciated. Big brothers liked being looked up to by their little sisters.

Kyle never really grew out of that. "Thanks, but since you're on a simple rebound mission, I hope you won't need any of it." He'd talked to Xelan and Korac about keeping his sister assigned to less dangerous objectives.

"Everyone, please." Pablo held out both hands to stave the waiting fighters and spectators off and away from the infirmary door. Here, in this hallway, they could see through the glass pool and all the surrounding glass tiles of the main veranda. Light from both Reipon's suns shone through without all the toxic rays of Earth's sun that combusted the Icari. The light warmed the sincerity in the doctor's brown eyes. With his best reassuring voice, Pablo said, "I know you're concerned about our leaders, but they're in good hands. Please give the infirmary some space. I'll let you know as soon as they regain consciousness."

Kyle's concern bordered on mild. Nothing in this universe could put those two down for long. He was happy to leave to find some other form of recreation until he overheard Korac demand, "I expect to be the first person you inform. With Xelan unconscious, I'm next in command..."

The conversation isn't what stopped Kyle from leaving. It was the look on his sister's face as she pretended not to observe the interaction. Not to observe Korac, to be specific. Ross' eyes went all doe-y, and her cheeks glowed extra pink.

Aw. Hell. Naw.

"Ross, I want to talk—"

"C'mon, Roberts. Let's go eat." Andrew grabbed Kyle by the arm and dragged him from the scene.

The last sight he glimpsed before they rounded the corner was a hopeless look in Ross' eyes. Groaning, he said, "Fuck. I'd prefer Jack any day."

Andrew handed him a lit joint and said, "We wondered how long it would take you to notice. I lost a thousand credits because it lasted over a month."

Kyle took a hit and apologized on the exhale. "Sorry, man. Who's winning?"

"Iuo. He bet three months and swore that working in porn gave him an advantage to reading people—"

Kyle stopped dead in his tracks and met Andrew's eyes with all the seriousness that he could muster. "Porn had better not be involved with my little sister's crush on that Icarus."

Andrew laughed and shook his head. "There are worse first crushes. She'll grow out of it. Besides, I think Korac knows, and believe it or not, I think he's actively discouraging it."

"Good. Now where is this food you mentioned?"

One thing Kyle actually liked about Xelan was his unexpected abundance of chill. Take, for instance, this puffy white couch he and Andrew ate on. Messy shit like BBQ bore, but that Icarus would simply walk in, give them a wave, and leave. No big deal. It made the house more comfy.

Bones, Twenty-One, and Iuo joined them for lunch in the lounge. Lynn left the ingredients out for them in the kitchen before heading down to help Pablo. Everyone chatted about the training. Strategy, areas for improvement, the super impressive ending that almost killed them all.

Kyle was licking his fingers when Twenty-One remarked, "I want to train with the Valkyrie. They glide and dance with such grace."

Bones grunted his agreement.

Iuo kicked back in his armchair, saying, "They're legendary fighters. Everyone in the Vast Collective knows of their prowess."

"Do you think they're okay?" Andrew invited reality into the room. "I mean... they're tough, right?"

The softness of his voice made Kyle swallow his own concerns.

Silence...

Bones assured, "There are none stronger than the Valkyrie. They will soldier through this, and we are closer to saving them with every mission."

"Here, here." Twenty-One toasted with his plate. "Karter is a magnificent leader, and Para is capable of more than we could ever know—"

"What about..." The words left Kyle's lips before he could stop them and died because he couldn't bear to finish.

The room went quiet, and his friends mostly kept their eyes down.

Except Twenty-One. The hefty Icarus peered at Kyle with that avian head tilt. After a few heartbeats, he said, "We were soldiers our entire lives. Warriors. We fought for Elden before Umbra. Nox's Verse is contaminated with Tritan fictions."

"No offense, Iuo." Bones patted him hard on the back.

The Lamia nodded courteously. "None taken. But please, continue."

Twenty-One set his plate down and sat forward, staring at Kyle. "There was a legend, a haunting of sorts of a spirit that visited us in our dreams before a battle. This spirit was a beautiful Icarean female, often described as a Valkyrie with black hair and one blue stripe. Black wings with blue tips. The bluest Atramentous."

Andrew leaned forward, intrigued. "You knew?"

"I wasn't certain. You see, I'd never met her before that day at the Ecology." He shot Kyle an apologetic smile for mentioning the day he slept with the woman Kyle loved. "She only visited soldiers who died the next day in battle. It was unsubstantiated rumors and not far-spread. We aren't a terribly superstitious race, but... her features. They were so distinctive. Right down to the withering sadness inside."

Kyle swallowed again. Tried to say something. Choked. Looked away in shame and pain. He took a long hit on his joint.

"I don't believe she's evil."

Everyone in the room looked up at Andrew, who continued, "I read her intentions while you were under Celindria's control. She's scared of herself more than anything. I think Silence is some awesome power in this universe we've yet to completely meet, and with all that power, I think she fears her own capability."

Bones glanced at Kyle and wet his lips before asking, "So you think we can salvage her?"

Iuo and Twenty-One both perked at this.

When Andrew looked at Kyle, there was so much confidence and warmth that it burned him. "I know it."

Sagan entered the room, saving Kyle from the tears overwhelming him. "Hey everyone, Tameka and Xelan are awake and moving around!"

Hope lived in this house as long as they believed in each other.

Kyle could keep his faith in Silence a little while longer.

ELEVEN

HARBORED IN HATE—
THESE COMPANIONS OF MINE

{ENKI}

REMORSE STEPPED PARA'S GRACEFUL AND DEADLY BODY INTO A BLACK TACTICAL SUIT. In the mirror, her black eyes stared back with her thin fingers smearing black paint all over her gray skin. Careful with slipping on the fingerless gloves with gold set in the knuckles. More on the elbow and knee pads. They capped the boots with the metal, making it hazardous to tie them lest Remorse risk zapping Para and rendering her nacre useless.

"It may shock her nacre enough to wake her," Celindria had warned an hour prior.

It prompted a hopeful gasp from the distraught Valkyrie inside Remorse's mind.

He shook a finger at her. "Ah ah. Too much excitement over that, and I'll introduce you to the shield." The virus Dr. Pablo Suarez created to lock nacres against tampering. Ever. It was permanent, with no way to reverse it. At least not the last time Remorse heard news of it.

Para knew what he meant and deflated by lowering her head back to the floor.

"That's right, child."

Since then, he'd prepared her and Karter in separate spaces. They never let them near each other for long. Sadistic and cruel, but it served a practical purpose. Para gained a wealth of confidence in Karter's presence, and that was simply not allowed.

Meanwhile, Remorse tried his best to concentrate on anything other than Silence. Curse that Icarus for aptly naming her so. How often had Elden felt the ice of her quiet deliberation? That woman analyzed in a tundra—a vacuum.

Silence—Surra—read the entirety of Remorse's worst deeds against her family and...

Set it aside.

Compartmentalized it and saved it for later. Dangerous apathy, that.

The anxiety left him focused on these menial tasks and performing as many at once to produce a halfway decent distraction.

It wasn't enough.

Maybe he could entertain himself by beating Abresson senseless at Karter's hands. That should amuse for a time—

Why?!

Why didn't Remorse kill Silence the moment he first laid eyes on her?!

{Enki | 150,000,000 Years Ago}

"I call her Surra. Is she not the most beautiful creature to ever exist?"

Quet made for quite the impressive figure at fifteen feet, maximum decompression. He was the largest of the Gargantuan Tritan. Not only of the remaining, but of all that ever existed. To match his impressive size, a glow beamed from him. The pride of fatherhood.

Remorse, at thirteen feet, gaped at the swaddled bundle in his comrade's bed, overlooking the lake of Cascading Light supplied by a geyser of the black flame. The baby was a tiny thing with soft black fuzz from her gray-skinned head and peered at them with gray eyes that pierced with intellect contained within a reduced form.

Surra.

She kicked hard enough from her blanketed confines to loose a tiny foot with five toes. Something the toe-less Tritans knew nothing about.

"This . . . " Remorse struggled to meet Quet's beaming voids without exposing the incredulity in his own eyes. "This is the Project you've discussed with us the last two million years?" All their work to unseat the Aegis—weapons, strategies, traps, and learning to run the Dyson's Sphere—and this is what his brother wasted his time on?! Replacing the female population?!

"Fyyeeeooo," Surra managed as if answering Remorse's inner monologue.

He should kill her now—

A pulse surged under her skin, and her eyes changed to a blue that matched the singular patch of fuzz on her head. An intriguing change to her physiology.

"How many base pairs are in her DNA?"

Quet chuckled, and the deep sound thundered in his chest. "I knew you would come around. She has three trillion."

That was it. That was more than enough to seed the planets protected by the Aegis. Two already within their possession. Remorse smiled down at Project Surra and asked, "Is she programmed to consent?"

"There is no need. She was born for this."

{ENKI | NOW}

Indeed, Surra was, and she fulfilled her purpose. The body Remorse inhabited was proof of that. Everything about the Project ran smoothly until she escaped—

"What atrocity will you have me commit this time?" Para asked on a whisper.

Why were these women so fucking insufferable?! "Keep your mouth shut, Para. Or I'll force you to watch Karter perform on Abresson again. Will that render your obedience?"

Para seethed, but looked away, defeated. She was nothing like his Vi. Karter lacked in this as well.

No. Not since Savis had Remorse met a woman with the regal carriage of a true predator. Lethal only when intended, only after careful cunning, and only on her terms. Savis was an exceptional beauty with all the clever malice of a Tritan female.

Perfection.

At a high cost.

How terribly would Silence kill him for taking her daughter against her will at such a tender age? Tormented her grandson with malignant machinations? Ruined the fate of the Icari and veered them off their evolutionary path?

To that, Vi would say to Remorse, "You brought this on yourself. Now dig the hole deep enough to bury you both."

Yes, that was the way.

{ENKI | NOW}

Replenished with resolve, Remorse walked his body into Celindria's lab. He found the ethereal beauty with an intelligent mind gone rabid with power, admiring Karter's upgrades.

"So fascinating how the nacre glass and Pil platinum fibers blend with your skin. Aegis technology, you see? It's perfect," she said into Karter's face with Remorse looking back while Chris watched on.

This was quite a dizzying circus.

"Is the last one prepared, Celindria?" Remorse would never push her. She reacted negatively to pressure and often shut him out. As she was the only one left with enough ability to stand against Silence, he needed to repair the remnants of their relationship. "I sent Abresson ahead to the Queen's Fare to keep him occupied."

Celindria held out Chris' arms so she could slip a dinner jacket around him. The young human male cleaned up nicely. "Yes. Prepared. T.A.O. is also rested and dressed for the occasion. The Shadow anticipate retaliation."

Remorse inspected their soldiers with a glance in Celindria's direction. "Won't they be surprised when they receive something else entirely." He walked Para into the lab and lined her up with the rest.

Celindria loaded them up with rifles and capsules. "For all the Shadow knick away at our stone, they've yet to see the art within."

Her choice of words struck Remorse. Yes. The Vast Collective was his art. The Shadow thought they stood in the way without realizing their blood formed the palette from which he painted. "They will see it on the verge, at the brink, when nothing else can be done. They will see, they will understand, and they will cease."

"Remember what's mine."

How could Remorse ever forget? A soul wasn't something easily misplaced from his mind.

{ENKI}

Chris watched through his eyes as Celindria dressed him in a "coffee with cream" colored three-piece that complimented his skin. She trimmed up his fade, which he begrudgingly admitted had bothered him over the last few months. And lastly applied kohl to line his eyes.

The angelic wench even stood him before a mirror to admire her handy work.

"You are my favorite toy," Celindria whispered in his ear.

It sickened him.

She shook her head at Chris in the reflection. "Now, now. Hate me all you like, but even you must admit you clean up nicely at my hand."

The Valkyrie bothered him more. They were in tactical gear and war paint. Not to mention armed to their very sharp teeth. What was Imminent up to? And how horrifically would the Shadow suffer for it?

Draped over his shoulder, Celindria brushed her knuckles against Chris' face, down his neck, chest, and groped him.

With a serpent's hiss, she assured, "We don't want them to suffer. We want them to see as we do. Until then, they leave us no choice..."

But to what end?!

Celindria released him and walked T.A.O. to his side in the most clothes Chris saw her in since he'd got here. An elegant cocktail dress, displaying next to no cleavage. No ass exposed, either. Must be a strict dress code or Celindria wouldn't dream of covering this much of her sister. She stood them side-by-side like two dolls about to leave for a date.

"Oh, is that what you desire?" Celindria asked from T.A.O.'s mouth. "My sister interests you more than I?" She traced one of the woman's small fingers across his lips until he tasted T.A.O.'s skin.

Inside his head, Chris lifted his eyes to meet the controller. "No."

T.A.O. sank to her knees before him, and Celindria carried on from her mouth. "This is a curiosity I'd yet to sate."

Chris' skin shrank away from the small woman unzipping his pants. Elden, he didn't want this! How many levels of rape was Celindria willing to commit?

Still, she mused, "Perhaps gratification from both lovers would finally be enough?"

"Enough for what?!" Chris cried, strained from every fiber of his not wanting to do this. "What do you want, Celindria?!"

She stopped.

Not just the undressing him with her sister's hands. Everything shut down. Dark and cold.

For the first time in three months, Chris sensed the absence of Celindria's infernal majestic presence. Even T.A.O.'s mauve eyes went empty, unoccupied.

A sound broke through the confusing mess. Korac's voice recited the opening of his Verse. While Chris hoped it was less abysmal than Nox's life, Celindria's sudden disappearance unnerved him to the point of raising goosebumps on his skin. In the mirror, he followed a bead of sweat trailing down his face. He still couldn't move—

Holy. Shit.

In his reflection, Chris watched Celindria as herself appear behind him in a billowing of shadowy smoke. All flowy white clothes that flattered her significant curves. Black hair in braids and locs that flowed on a breeze of their own. Bright blue eyes that startled against her deep violet skin. On her tiptoes, she rose to whisper in his ear. Two words, but their meaning was lost on Chris.

"To. Feel."

Feel what?!

Chris went to shout as much when Remorse marched Para and Karter out of the lab. No. No! Where was he sending them? The Shadow!

No one heard Chris' cries or answered his questions. Instead, T.A.O. fixed his fly and stood. Celindria looked at him through T.A.O.'S innocent face, and Chris' heart wanted to break. He hated servicing Celindria, but Eternity help him—He couldn't live with himself if he'd violated that girl. Never mind Celindria controlled them both—Just, no.

"Some other time," Celindria promised from a mouth that wasn't hers, jeopardizing the very person who spoke the words. Threatened Chris with a sanity she knew walked a fine line.

"Hard to muster any sympathy for you when I know whatever you tell me is your scheme. Go to Hell, Celindria. The Wrong Side of Eternity."

From deeper in the lab, her real mouth said, "I was born there."

T.A.O. followed the other women out, presumably to cause some trouble, and Chris let his head lower to the ground inside his mind once more. Over and over, he repeated, "You don't know what you're in for." For hours, it seemed.

Until T.A.O. returned without the other women. Was that a good or a bad thing?

Celindria's authentic self also returned at the halfway point of Korac's Verse. It was as abysmal, if not worse, than Nox's life so far. She straightened Chris' jacket and checked his posture. "Enjoy your date with my sister. Since you seem so fond of her, I'll ensure a goodnight kiss at the end."

Chris almost vomited with his stomach roiling.

T.A.O. held out her hand to Chris. Despite a fresh aversion to touching her, he took it. Through the Seam, they stepped into a swanky place carved in polished wood. Abresson waited at the bar in his fanciest Tritan robes.

Outside was better. Chris could breathe here. Especially in public, where molestation was less likely to occur. The small woman next to him made it on the list of people he'd die to protect, but he wasn't exactly full of choices here.

Celindria manifested inside his mindscape once more, but with her back to him. A keenness shone in her bright eyes. This was professional work. Not something she mixed with pleasure.

"Eminent Abresson." The words came out of Chris' mouth.

The indigo Tritan with white scars looked anywhere but at T.A.O., which was fine with Chris. He nodded at the well-dressed human as they approached his booth. Discretely, he asked, "Are the others deployed?"

T.A.O.'s mouth answered, "They are. Retrieval is Imminent."

Celindria's puns killed Chris. Mostly because they were totally unironic. They sat, ordered food, and blended in with the crowd. Waited in their stakeout. Inside his head, Celindria kept sharp and watched the crowd, and paid no mind to the man enslaved to her unimaginative whims.

"I am inclined to introduce you to my imagination when we return to the lab."

Fuck.

The batshit insane woman intercepted his thoughts.

Why did Chris have to open his big fucking mind?

{ENKI | 150,000,000 YEARS AGO}

"Surra! Surra!"

Nothing would stop her. Nothing would cage her anymore. She would find her way from here.

These were comforting thoughts as she swam through the cosmic cloud of black flames.

"Never touch it," they said.

"It is forbidden," they said.

Well, they also told her happiness came from sacrifice, and after two million years, Project Surra refused to believe those fairytales any longer. Her life was misery and loss.

Not once.

Not once did they let her hold—

They simply took.

Enough of that.

Surra escaped via the lake of Cascading Light. Already they searched for her. Where could she go? Where would this lead her—

But Surra knew. Didn't she? The black fire told her. It whispered everything to her at once in all the instances in which it existed. Finite, but not permanently so.

Her escape alone shattered ten hundred thousand new instances. Ones where Surra was caught. Ones where she escaped. Neither interested her.

Only one instance promised Surra anything close to happiness, and she followed the light there.

The lake ended in a shrine to Quet's warded planet. A breathtaking sight of lush cranberry-colored trees, pools of ruby water swirling around mountains of black rock covered in blazing orange grass, soft and lush. Surra laid out on it after picking berries and languished.

Safe.

Finally.

Or so Surra thought.

The ground vibrated beneath. Not from tectonic shifts. Surra would see that in the Matrix. No. It was a stampede. As if manifested from her thoughts, a swarm crested over the farthest hill. Millions of them. All of them hungry.

They broke her heart.

Unafraid, Surra crossed the plain toward the front line, fell to her knees, and, with her hands raised overhead, bowed to the orange grass. Deep inhale. Easy exhale. Deep inhale—

The stars pulsed with Surra's being as her wings opened and the herd ceased. Stopped. Stared.

Surra straightened on her knees and assessed the people her father and the other Primaries committed to a life like hers. Misery and loss. New Probabilities formed in a star-burst reaction to Surra's decision. Yet, still, only one promised her happiness, and she pursued it.

Centuries Surra spent on the planet learning about her new people. After she'd introduced herself to this almost unintelligible army. Smart wasn't necessary for what Surra needed. The Icari were substantial, and that's all it took.

Well, it was, and it wasn't.

Centuries were a long time alone without communication. Surra trained them with gestures, but they seemed stubborn to evolve beyond that. She spent every night alone on the throne she carved to suit her solitude. Not hopeless, but not happy.

Until one morning, Surra awoke to a blossom as orange as the grass on the throne beside her. She smiled for the first time since leaving Enki. When she awoke the next morning, a pile of them awaited her. Their potent scent and the smell of sleigh fruit lingered. This went on for several nights until she resolved to catch the culprit.

The next night, a man, the tallest she'd seen of the Icari, carried armfuls of the flowers. He dropped them once he realized her eyes were open, yet he remained under her scrutiny.

"Greetings."

He went to his knees and placated himself as Surra did some time ago. Wordless, but somehow more intelligent than the rest.

A pet sounded nice. "You are mine now."

He never left her side and displayed more intellect than the rest. Surra talked to him often, and his comprehension of her words grew with each subsequent day. This new companion even helped her communicate with the language-less swarm of Icari who, until that point, signaled with their pheromones. This new alliance improved their odds against the Tritans exponentially.

Let them come.

{ENKI | NOW}

A knot of apprehension twisted in Silence's stomach as she pondered the reason for these surfacing memories. She sat with her legs folded at the base of the Martyr Complex and watched the girl inside listen to Korac's Verse.

Misery and loss.

What mother wanted that for her children?

"Not long, Silence," Lucas said from where he and Smith flanked the glass coffin.

The latter man smiled throughout the entire telling of the Icarean General's life. Each one varied. Sad smiles. Happy smiles. Even angry ones. Smith kept careful watch on everyone in the room, deciding for certain what he wanted.

Silence recognized that deliberation from her own reflection in the silver waterfalls. Follow the undetermined and unpredictable path? Or follow Imminent's new design? The Probability of her happiness long since ceased to exist. There was nowhere for her now, but there was somewhere for her children.

"It starts with him *and ends with* her."

Did Savis see it, too?

"Mother, we are nearing the end."

Silence raised a brow at Smith's choice of words, and his smile shifted to a sly smirk with a cavalier shrug. "I'm a sucker for drama," he offered as an unapologetic excuse.

Lucas tsked at his comrade. Both men waited for her to answer their unspoken question.

Silence stood and faced the Martyr Complex with her shoulders back and her chin held high. "Can I trust her?"

They glanced at each other before nodding in unison. "Yes." "Absolutely."

Placing her hands on the glass, avoiding the gold, Silence peered at the girl's smiling face. So much power in such a young thing. That same truth was said about Silence once. All Probabilities ended in Rayne's tears, her light. That the worlds should end in one girl's solitude wasn't an irony lost on Silence who bore this Vast Collective alone in the beginning. All her creations were poised on the brink.

"King Rayne Echo Callahan, do not disappoint me."

TWELVE

RIGHT OR WRONG—

THIS IS THE ONLY WAY FORWARD

{???}

"**SILENCE.**"

Rayne laid on her side in the sand, stared at the rain pelting the beach, and wished she knew what the woman wanted from her—What anyone in Imminent wanted from her. Why the leaders of the Vast Collective seemed hellbent to watch her die in this place.

"I'll disappoint all of you." That was a fucking promise.

Nox stirred for the first time in a few hours. He sat the entire time with one leg stretched out and the other bent, a wrist resting on it. His dark eyes stared out at the storm as they both fell into Korac's story. When the behemoth warrior stirred, it was to look down at Rayne with a nod that reflected his regard for her.

They would not die here.

"I want to meet my nephew," Nox confessed.

Rayne smiled up at him. "I'll bet Pax is just the sweetest mini-me of his mom and dad. I can't wait to teach him how to punch properly."

Nox chuckled and threw a seashell into the surf. "No doubt my brother refrains from using his full strength. You'll grant Pax the proper respect of a soldier."

"Damn straight." Rayne punched her fist. "Oh, and can't forget tickle fits. I know he's a squealer."

They fell quiet again. Comfortable and full of smiles. Well, she was smiling anyway. He still stared severely out at the storm. Softly, she muttered the thought on her mind, "You'd make a wonderful uncle."

A tinge of a bitter smile pulled at his lips before he said, "I know you'll make a fantastic aunt, your majesty."

Korac's Verse continued to provide awkward tension to their otherwise pleasant camaraderie.

It starts with him and ends with her.

That's what Savis told Nox she saw in Cascading Light on Thailea millions of years past. She meant Xelan, and Nox eventually took it to also mean Celindria.

But now I'm not so convinced.

[SS]: "You think it might mean Xelan and Rayne?"

Possibly. Or even Nox and Rayne. The end began with Nox's hatred for Enki that Rayne may one day finish.

The King of Earth and Cinder rolled on her back and folded her arms in a huff. "Is that all anyone can think about? Me dying?"

Nox finally switched legs and said, "Sagan seems to share your disdain for it."

Rayne's posture softened from bratty crossed arms to hugging herself around the ribs. "But not you, according to the rest of this scene."

They both listened.

And this way, I got to torment Colita incessantly.

"Oh, you mean you can't pull his attention away from a non-corporeal fire? Have you tried using your mouth?" I meant kissing, but judging by how fast her cheeks flushed cobalt, she thought of another activity.

"I'll have you know, General, that I've tried everything. The only solution is for you to remove the pyre at once."

I barked out a humorless laugh. "No fucking way. Staring into that image gives our King far more joy than these last two million years of your attentions..."

The muscle in Nox's jaw went to work before he spoke. "You've read my Verse, and you've experienced my life with me. You understand why. What your death represented. My freedom. The liberation of my people. But..."

"Yes, Nox?" Rayne graced him with the full weight of her gaze.

His baritone softened the cold in his eyes as he drifted into his memories. "During our first fight, I knew you'd let no one push you into dying here. At every opportunity you clawed from your very environment, means after means to overcome me. Flaming cinderblocks, beams, insulation—You burned me out, determined to win. Rayne, I can't know you and believe you'll die that way without a battle."

A word lingered between them.

Unless.

Rayne wasn't secure enough in herself to ask him for the rest of his thoughts, but she could always rely on Nox's juggernaut trait of forthright communication and his distaste for pulling punches. "Unless you put yourself to it."

Rayne rolled away, giving him her back. With her knees pulled to her chest, she almost hugged them. Curled in a ball, she laughed and it was bitter. "Some King I am."

From behind, Nox declared to her surprise, "*King* Rayne, you've already surpassed all of Cinder's rulers since Elden, and we were all known for a bout of petulance here and there—"

"Petulance?" Rayne sat up and glared at him. "Petulance?!"

He gave one solemn nod. "Yes. Your decorum is quite childish, but I'll accept it this once, given the state of things."

Was... was Nox picking on Rayne? Was that a tiny smirk on his irritatingly attractive mouth? And was it actually *helping* her???

It got her out of the fetal position, didn't it?

Unsure what to say, they sat in their quiet affinity.

Korac's Verse played a scene that explained why Sagan ever dated Justin.

So I was more stunned than surprised by how his blackmail unfolded. Sneering, Justin stepped closer so that he loomed over you. He put his face in yours and jeered, "Sure, you can say that about your own parents. But are you willing to put Rayne through that with hers? Can you guarantee they'll be as accepting? After all, maybe they saw themselves with a dozen grandchildren in their future. And you'll be robbing them of that."

So that's why. After all this time, Sagan was protecting Rayne, who never spoke to her parents about her relationship with Sagan. It seemed innate to keep it from them, along with all the other major changes in her life. Secrets that affected the world. Secrets worth protecting.

Shaking her head, Rayne clicked her tongue. "Have I ever mentioned how happy I was that Korac cut off Justin's head and gave it to Sagan?"

"A worthy endeavor," Nox said as he took to writing Icarean letters in the sand. After a pause, he confessed, "I was there the night you broke his leg."

Rayne's mouth almost fell open. "Really?"

Nox stopped writing to give her the full weight of his gaze. "It was after a sports event. He found you and Sagan together under the bleachers and threatened her. Fast—so fast for a human without a nacre—you sent him to the ground and stomped on his femur. A loud break that I enjoyed thoroughly even without all of this context."

Emotions stirred in Rayne. Some conflicted. Some mixed with shame. How should she take his compliments to her violence? Especially for that time in her life? In his? She concentrated on how it made her feel now, with this Nox and this Rayne.

Warm. Respected.

"I'd do it again."

Nox bowed his head to Rayne.

That's when things got awkward in Korac's Verse.

[SS]: You little vixen! I swear the next time I see you, I promise I'll chew you out. You said you only wore that for me! But I'm not admitting that fact to everyone, so... "She wore it when we went to concerts."

Well, it had the intended effect. Nox stopped glancing around at other people. Stopped frowning. Stopped breathing.

Especially once you started singing. And very well, if I may say so, your majesty. But you know exactly what you wanted with those lyrics and that breathy voice.

Nox took what I was sure was an involuntary step forward when you admitted you wanted to touch him. Sang you wanted to fuck him. Call me a liar, if you wish, when you see me next. But... He was there, King Rayne. He heard it all. He saw you.

With black lipstick, you kissed a lily and threw it into the crowd. Who do you think caught it? And how many people do you think he was willing to rip apart to win it? I was almost forced to intervene and hold him back.

That's when I realized that Nox's focus shifted from saving Cinder to being with you.

Nox cleared his throat into his fist and turned to look at the far horizon.

Rayne braided her hair to concentrate on anything other than the strained silence that stretched between them.

You left the backstage area of the dive bar and headed out.

Unarmed.

I knew what you wanted. I'd watched you after all. You wanted Nox to take the bait. To blow his cover and take you sooner than planned. Maybe you thought we could avoid the Invasion that way. Prevent the suffering. Or maybe you tired of the anticipation.

Either way, you put me in the terrible position of choosing for Nox, for Cinder, and for all of Icarean kind.

I lament this decision. Especially seeing that before Volcano Day, I begged Nox to reconsider and join your fight against the Tritans. Maybe if I didn't instigate the malice borne in him through Celindria's spite, things would be different.

Unable to contain it, Rayne let out a significant sigh that held the worst of the last three years. Simply breathed it out because nothing could change what had happened, and she was determined to only give her energy to the now. To what she could change right now.

"Nox?"

He faced her with a tightness around his eyes that touched her. Did he suffer the same as she?

They could change it. Together. "Remember what I said? Let it go. Things are not different, but I think they are getting better. We have to let go of all that lost potential and look forward."

As Rayne spoke, that tightness in Nox's expression loosened and allowed his black eyes to shine with clarity. "I couldn't agree more, your majesty."

Korac's Verse went deeper.

Tell me, Sagan, have you forgiven Nox for what he did to you during the Volcano Day battle?

[SS]: Korac asking me this question is the most thought I'd given it since the day it happened. The way Nox almost killed me… "I mean, it was painful. It hurt like hell, but the entire time he reassured me that everything would be all right. That he regretted the pain, but it was temporary and I would live. He knew. And now I've experienced him through the Verses, and…"

I drift off a bit. Thinking about the man that was Nox. How Korac remembers him. Even some of your stories, Rayne. It's all so tragic.

"Yes, I've forgiven him. I think I did when I woke up to you holding my hand on Cinder."

Korac sighs in relief.

I laugh nervously before asking, "Why? What's on your mind?"

I'm less of a wretch, then. I took the gesture of Nox placing your nacre into your hand as a show of forgiveness. Nox's way of giving us his blessing. And I found it distasteful to think that if you harbored any aversion to it—Understandable aversion.

[SS]: "Oh, trust me. You all need therapy. If Nox were alive, I'd suggest group sessions. But hell, who in this house doesn't need therapy right now?"

Rayne's brows shot up in surprise, and she nearly laughed when she saw an identical expression on Nox's face. "She forgave you."

"She truly is a benevolent creature." His brows dropped into a frown. "I have a sudden desire to crack Razor into pieces." *For hurting her* hung in the air.

This was a Nox worth knowing.

"His Verse is closing." Nox cocked his head, actively listening.

Even Rayne sat forward, eager to hear Korac's finale.

Rayne, you and I have our differences. For instance, I don't share an overwhelming desire to repeatedly sacrifice myself for those I love. Or endanger myself to their benefit.

But we are the same in that we will fight to see them happy. To avenge the ones we lost. And to right all the injustice in our power to do so.

Don't forget yourself, impressive sprite.

Take care not to lose sight of your own well-being. Because if the great King Rayne—Killer of Night—falters, how will the Shadow push on?

Be brave. Your army is coming to rescue you. Leave some for the rest of us.

The plan.

It was time.

Nox turned to Rayne, and she to him. They stood together and opened their wings. His black eyes shifted to mirrors and in them she saw Li—Cinder's very sun—burning in hers. Goosebumps prickled her skin, and a pressure built in her ears. Tight. So tense until lightning struck their canopy and burned it to ash, soaked it in the rain. All the while, the two stared at one another.

When Nox enveloped them with his wings, Rayne opened her eyes.

{ENKI}

Bright white light blinded Nox. In it, he felt Rayne's determination and hope, so pure it nearly sent him to his knees. Instead, it enveloped him in warmth and wrung from Nox his fealty and strength.

Rayne could take it all. Deserved it all. Earned every drop.

When the light receded, Nox stared out the window of Rayne's eyes with her beside him inside her mind. White stone floors and walls—no ceiling. The stacks of white tomes climbed into the silver sky above. Mercury waterfalls fell from their towering heights all around the Martyr Complex. The abomination lay on a dais, fit perfectly to its dimensions in the presence of a white stone throne.

Empty.

Old. Everything smelled ancient. Smelled? "I can smell."

Rayne giggled beside him before warmly explaining, "I shared my senses with you. You'll be open to most of what I experience. Not my thoughts or emotions, but everything else."

A better Eternity than he deserved, Nox nodded his thanks to Rayne.

"Is this the Pantheon?" She took a step away from the Martyr Complex. "Where is everyone?"

Calibrated.

Optimized.

Stabilizing . . .

Unable to stabilize.

Warning: Seventy-one hours and fifty-nine minutes until maximum destabilization.

The infernal fuse. Curse the Tritans for installing these Weapons. Rayne lost some color beside him, and it was enough to make Nox vow to ram his fist through Remorse's heart.

Softly, she said inside her head, "We have three days to complete our mission and put an end to this."

Nox took her cue for active pragmatism. "Begin with the knowledge and tools in your possession."

"Right." Rayne enthusiastically clapped her hands together in the mindscape. "We're in the Pantheon, deep in Enki. We're surrounded by books. Let's get to reading—Hey, there's something on the throne."

Although Rayne was the most powerful being in the galaxy, Nox still warned, "Approach with caution, your majesty."

Rayne rolled her eyes. "Yes, dad."

Taken aback, Nox crooked a brow at her, bewildered.

"I'll remember that one." With a sly grin, Rayne returned to her external sight. She said, "Hey, it's a gun. A rifle. Is this..." Checking the ammunition, she confirmed electrical stun charges. "This is like the weapons Lynn and Pablo made. They disable nacres."

Why would someone leave this? Was it for Rayne? Was she right to hope Silence, Smith, and Lucas were still aligned with the Shadow?

Shouldering the strap, she murmured, "Taking this can't hurt. Wait..." A piece of paper lay beneath it on the throne with a message written in gold ink.

KEEP YOUR FAITH IN ME A LITTLE WHILE LONGER.

Beneath that, lines formed a map. "These are conduits," Rayne said softly, with a sadness in her voice. "And these spaces are Primary Sanctums. See the Cascading Light?"

"Perhaps it's an ally, but it may also lead you astray. Tread cautiously." She opened her mouth and Nox cut her off, "And do *not* call me 'dad' again."

Her snickering charmed him, despite his stern facade. In the face of which, she confessed, "Okay. I won't, but tormenting you gives me a decent amount of satisfaction. Now let's hit these books."

"Careful for—"

Something metal clunked about fifty meters south. Rayne heard it and tunneled into a stack, hiding amid the gigantic volumes. A metal cube traveled overhead a few minutes later, scanning the area before continuing on its route. Inside her head, she said, "Security of some kind. I'll read a few before we follow the map. There must be a reason these books are throne-adjacent."

Nox approved Rayne's logic but disliked the mysterious disappearance of her jailers. The note and the rifle. Convenience irked him, and no one should be trusted here with her poised on the location of her predicted demise. This gnawed at him—

Rayne folded her long legs to her chest, bare from the same black beach top she wore into her isolated sleep. Since awakening from the blood-filled Martyr Complex, her nacre's nanites reclaimed the precious fluid. For a mighty warrior, she looked vulnerable, curled like that in a hiding place with a book larger than her body.

Truth be told, Rayne *was* more vulnerable now than trapped in that box, and Nox was in no position to support her on the outside. It vexed him—

"Okay. A Tritan named Quet wrote this. Do we know him?"

Nox read over the passage with her. "Do you remember the story of Elden's making?"

Nodding her recollection, Rayne stared at him with her undivided attention.

"The Primary that the Icari overwhelmed, whose nacre Elden consumed—That was Quet. The eldest, I believe."

They both turned back to the passages. Rayne pointed. "Here, he's referring to his attempts to replenish the female population. After calamity—hold on." She spun and grabbed an earlier entry. "Let's see if we can find... Hmm. What are these numbers, Nox? 1.5022.1325 | H?"

"Those are galactic years and dates. One hundred million Earth years will pass when Enki completes a single revolution around the center of the galaxy. Given what Korac described in his Verse, this entry occurred in the years prior to Tritan occupation of the Dyson's Sphere. It stands to reason they established this throne room with that dais more than a galactic year ago."

Rayne swallowed hard, and Nox understood. How could they know of the Martyr Complex so long ago? In a contemplative voice, she said, "Let's keep reading. We might find a weakness here."

{1.5172.1325 | H}

Primary Rem confessed to me that he and Vi are trying to conceive a daughter. Again. Primary Tumu and I cautioned against it since the last two hundred attempts left his spouse so gravely injured, but they are determined. Meanwhile, no other coupling conceived a female in the last one hundred thousand years. The people grow suspicious, and I cannot blame them.

{1.5173.6984 | H}

Vi returned to my hospital, dying. The labor nearly killed her, and the baby was not only born male, but he died shortly after meeting this world. Primary Rem is inconsolable. He seethes with impotence outside my lab even now. I hesitate to inform him or Primary Tumu of my recent findings, yet I despise bearing this burden alone. The burden of knowing we will never come back from this. The Tritan race faces extinction.

{1.5173.8722 | H}

Vi overheard my discussion with Primary Rem. She disappeared from her bed, and several other female leaders went missing, as Primary Tumu predicted. They can never know the truth. Not before we enact the program to correct our mistakes. Their compliance is required—necessary for the reconstitution of our people. If they resist, we will force the females. In the meantime, Primary Rem works for weeks at a time on the new engines. He fears the worst. I cannot say I blame him.

Primary Tumu says that we are wrong. For everything.

{1.5609.9158 | H}

Calamity drives us. The female population knows. They All Know. They are furious with us and demanded negotiations. We offered a window to encourage them to see reason. They countered with their own program to recover. The reverse of our suggestion.

It was Vi who said, quite regally, "Seeing as the men are responsible for breeding and manipulating our genes until no females are born, the women bio-engineers should hereby gain full access to your exclusive labs and reduce the male involvement to nothing more than bulls."

While Primary Tumu accepted her terms, for the first time, Primary Rem publicly disagreed with his spouse and recommended their compliance to maintain civility between the sexes. The women returned to their secret location within the station.

Our next priority is to locate it and rein them in. I will save our race.

"They lost their ability to make daughters." Rayne digested the concept aloud. "Their women sound quite fierce. I think I like Vi."

At first, it amazed Nox how she processed the entries and interpreted the people involved, but after a moment of looking at that smile on her face, he could only appreciate her manner—

"Oh, hey. There's a huge jump in the entries."

{1.6013.6899 | I}

We owe our very existence to the Aegis, but we cannot dally with our work. I strive even now in this luxurious facility they offered me to restore our race. Primary Rem and Primary Tumu argue at every turn. Primary Bol is preoccupied with Enki. Primary Lon and Xhi... well, it was for the best.

I am close. So very close to solving our dilemma. I only pray that Project Surra is successful.

That was it. That was the connection.

Rayne blinked at the entry and quickly flipped to the next page. There was nothing but torn pages in the spine. Someone removed them. "No!" she cried. "No, we were so close. Damn it." She threw it down and winced at the echo of its loud thud. "Shit."

It was Nox's turn to digest the concept aloud. "Quet is responsible for my grandmother, and she was his key to saving the Tritans. Surra—Silence—is older than Elden."

"She wanted us to find this. I'm certain of it, but what do I do with this information? I can barely process it." Rayne's frown crinkled her nose, and Nox looked away to regroup with a clearer mind.

What can this mean for the Icarean Prerogative Nox was recited his entire life by his mother? How much did she know? How did the Tritans come to find Enki and the Aegis? And where are the females?

Too many questions.

After a few heartbeats of Rayne's pacing, Nox stepped in her way. She looked all the way up at him and blinked with big blue eyes. Into that openness, he said, "Focus on the mission. This is solid intelligence to file away for later. In this moment, it serves as a distraction. Now tell me the mission, your majesty."

She ticked the itinerary off on her fingers. "Kill Abresson, Remorse, and Celindria after I force them to cure me of this Weapon.

"Locate Enki's control center—its bridge.

"Destroy the Dyson's Sphere.

"Go home and figure out how I can explain your existence in my head to the people I love.

"Hug Pax.

"Eat all the ice cream."

Rayne beamed at Nox, still only a step away. Warmth glittered in her eyes. It occurred to him she grew increasingly more comfortable around him in the recent months, and he relaxed around her in a way not afforded to him in his entire life. He felt free to laugh at her jokes, reward her kindness with smiles, and—

That was it.

Nox felt free.

Rayne asked nothing of him and accepted what he offered with praise and consideration as opposed to belittling or condescension—

He regarded her for so long that her grin eased into a gentle smile.

Inside her mindscape, Rayne stepped away from him and looked outside herself. Across the way, a mercury waterfall reflected her rather exposed appearance. Warmly, she mused, "What was I thinking, dressing this way? I didn't even paint my toenails. What do you think, Nox? Warrior-casual? Or comfy gear for all the traveling?"

Released from her spell, Nox spared Rayne an incredulous tilt of his head. "You're asking my opinion on your dress?"

More of that bubbling laughter he found astonishing that she could afford, given their situation. "I suppose you'd say I should fight this battle in something functional and ladened with weapons?"

"No."

Nox's terse response surprised Rayne. He enjoyed the slight widening of her eyes and the question behind them, the parting of her lips to ask it. Perhaps tormenting *her* gave *him* a decent amount of satisfaction. To draw it out, he said quite confidently, "As someone who fought you in every style of clothing imaginable, I can easily guarantee that you are capable of equal devastation no matter how you dress."

Nox meant every word. Rayne did her worst to him while wearing small dresses and heels with most of her skin exposed. She could kill in anything. It was a quality he found most attractive in her. He smirked, remembering Sagan's comment about them all needing therapy. There was something to that.

Rayne searched his eyes, perhaps following the same trail of thought, until she returned her attention to the mirror. She didn't need to ask. Nox looked away as his

King formed new clothes from a combination of Lyriki armor and Elden constructs, converting matter within her nanite field.

After a time, Rayne gave Nox permission to look. "There. Easy to get around in and definitely combat-friendly."

Dangerous.

That was the only way to describe how Rayne looked in the form-fitting, one-piece fight suit. Cobalt, the color of Icarean blood and Tritan skin. A thick matte black chain was belted at her waist. Smaller chains connected the outer seams, gaping open and exposing her pale skin along her arms, waist, hips, and down her legs where the seams ended in matte black combat boots. High-heeled, her favorite, Nox realized. She gathered all her long black hair into close-scalp braids and twists that loosed into a full ponytail.

Rayne turned to the left and then to right, checking herself in the mirror and played with her hair. Nox tried to not to react to experiencing the sensation of it in her hands as if they were his own. Instead, he said with sincerity, "You've outdone yourself."

"Thanks." Rayne let out a sigh and slapped her sides. "Welp. I waited around here all I can. They aren't returning for me to kill them."

Nox worked to keep the smirk off his face, but heard it in his voice. "Then you must seek them out."

Once more, Rayne shouldered the rifle, glanced at the map, and faced west. "Eighty klicks that way. Nox?" She faced him inside her mind.

He peered down at her and responded in the only appropriate manner, "Yes, your majesty?"

"What's your favorite flavor of ice cream?"

The question disarmed Nox and forced a smile onto his lips. Of all the things for Rayne to ask. Still, he indulged her, "I tried little of the stuff and only at Korac's insistence, but if I must name a favorite... Strawberry."

"Mine, too." Rayne smiled and prepped for a run. "Let's get to it. For Pax and strawberry ice cream."

Quite.

THIRTEEN

LIFE DOESN'T WAIT FOR WAR TO END

{REIPON}

SAGAN STEPPED OUT OF THE LUXURIOUS BATH AND RUBBED EXOTIC OILS FROM ACROSS THE VAST COLLECTIVE ALL OVER HER NAKED SKIN. Left her favorite silk bathrobe open as she swept into the bedroom. Korac was naked, waiting on the edge of their bed. She kissed him deeply, seeking the peppermint on his tongue. His frosty scent blended with her sweet watermelon, and he purred deep in his chest against her. Her fingers tangled in his hair, and she secretly reveled in the growing length. He cupped her ass with both hands, beckoning her to complete them.

Pulled to Korac, Sagan straddled his lap and stared into the dark gray flecks in his eyes. He coaxed her. She took from him what she needed. They gasped at their mutual satisfaction. Moved together until they found an intoxicating rhythm.

Breath catching, Sagan closed her eyes. So very close. He twisted his hips for her, and she lost herself. "Korac!"

He anchored her as she rode out the storm. Floating back down, she—

"Pain Kitten."

The purring voice was her lover's. The nickname was not.

Filled with dread, Sagan opened her eyes to find two sets of twin crescent pupils smirking back at her.

"Razor!"

Sagan startled awake from her nap, frantically beating the sheets to crawl away from—

No one. She was alone.

"Korac?"

After each of her nightmares, he'd soothe Sagan. Let her have some air before pulling her close and kissing her hair. So sweet and patient with her trauma.

Korac's absence troubled her, and she glanced at their axes hanging on the wall for strength. Sagan climbed out of bed from her Half Day nap and threw on a robe. Belting it this time, she went in search of—

Screams carried down the hall. They came from the infirmary. Rushing, Sagan found the Doc preparing a needle.

"Pablo, is it Triss? Is she—"

Another cry of agony followed by Korac shouting, "Now would be good, Doctor."

She walked with Pablo into the bedroom where her lover held down the mother of their future adopted baby. Triss' spine bowed and twisted. Her face was contorted in torment. Bone protruded from her elbows and knees where they bent backwards and punctured the joints.

The bone… It was amber colored glass.

Sagan cupped a hand to her mouth while Pablo tried to inject Triss with more sedative. "This is a last resort. It would put down a Hellkite, but it—"

The needle broke on her hardened skin.

"—Might require another delivery system."

Triss howled. Her belly looked less round and more square. Hard angles and straight lines. Like the baby was a gift, and she was the wrapping.

Momentarily coherent, Triss spared the breath to curse Korac. "You don't deserve this baby. None of you deserve her! AHH!"

Pablo hurried around Korac where he pinned her arms, waist, and legs. The doctor went to Triss' side. "I want to help with the pain. Please, drink this."

He poured the contents of the syringe into a cup, and she drank of it greedily. Her face softened in his presence. "Please. Please, Dr. Suarez. Make sure this baby survives. Please."

Pablo eyed the square in her stomach and the broken bones before returning his gaze to her. He said, "Triss, with your permission, I'd like to put you in a coma. One I can't promise you'll ever wake from. We can't leave you in this state, and these fits risk the baby."

Triss swallowed and shifted her gaze to the ceiling, as if considering her options. Another spasm hit, and she screamed.

Korac pinned her, but also stared at Sagan across the room. His eyes held a question. One she expected a week ago. One she wasn't sure how to answer.

It seemed like the right thing to do. But why? None of the people involved deserved their kindness, but dammit, they would do it anyway. It was only right.

Sagan nodded.

Korac met Triss' pained gaze. "Former Executive Warden, I'll upcycle Razor for one visit if you agree to the sedation."

Triss didn't hesitate. "Agreed."

Within the hour, because they really had little time, Sagan wrangled Xelan into chaperoning like when they wrote Razor's cameo in Korac's Verse. Tameka insisted on joining, and her support of Sagan warmed her heart.

"I owe you a debt," Korac said to Xelan outside of Triss' room. "She… Well, I know you're fond of her, so I wanted to prepare you for her condition—"

"She's dying." Pablo's voice and eyes were so hollowed out. "Every blood vessel is dissecting, and her bones are changing into glass. I'm beginning to think the Aegis young is a parasite that erupts from its host rather than births from it. There isn't time for conversation beforehand." He opened the door, walked inside, and arranged a chair at Triss' side. "I'm ready to administer it."

Sagan stared at the woman writhing in the bed with a visible cube warring in her womb and tried to muster some pity. But then she thought of how that same woman wanted to force Sagan into this very position against her consent to please the man she loved and...

Tameka's hand laced into hers and squeezed.

Xelan rushed across the room and soothed the dangerous predator in that bed. "Triss, I'm here." He touched her hand, and she grimaced a smile at him as he promised, "I'll oversee the visit."

While Triss responded with barely audible gasps, Korac sat in the chair with his hands on his knees and closed his eyes.

"I'm here," Tameka muttered to Sagan, who squeezed her hand back. "I hate to admit this, but that man adores you. He won't let anything happen to you and neither will Xelan."

Sagan wasn't sure anyone understood her trauma with Razor. It wasn't a physical threat he posed. Especially not after she cut him in half. The trauma came from every fiber of her being that wanted to convert him to their side, and when he betrayed that, her shame translated it into a failure on her part. A failure to protect herself, to see the monster for what he was. This was all Sagan's fault.

Korac opened Razor's eyes with their twin crescent pupils. Did he look at the mother of his child in pain? No. Did he assess Cinder's Traitor Prince to test his chances of escaping with Korac's body? No.

Razor stared at Sagan as if he *knew* her worst nightmares were about him. And he liked it.

"Sagan. Your eyes..." Tameka whispered.

Xelan held up a reassuring hand. "We're here, Sagan. You're safe."

While they checked on her, Razor finally acknowledged Triss and her state. She gasped and weakly reached out a hand he took with a gentle but earnest grip. He kissed the knuckles, and Sagan wondered what that was like for Korac.

Razor asked Xelan, "Who sees to her?"

Pablo held up a hand from across the bed. "I'm Dr. Suarez."

Xelan vouched for him, "He was one of my students."

Brushing Triss' hair back from her face, Razor acknowledged, "You're providing excellent care, but now she needs infusions of Aegis blood to help the conversion."

"I want to render her chemically comatose."

Razor recoiled in Korac's body as if slapped. "She'll never wake." Those eyes darted around in a panic, and Korac's face fell, crushed by the weight of reality.

"Hurts…" Triss gasped, and her spine bowed again. As the spasm released her, she breathed, "I… love you…"

Razor bowed Korac's head and whispered in such a way that Sagan realized he wished they were alone for this, "My siren, we are the Eternal Bind. I'll find you again."

Tameka and Sagan looked at one another after they glimpsed the hot tears rolling down Korac's cheeks.

Xelan clasped the man's shoulder in consolation. "We *will* look after her."

After another row where her muscles contracted almost off the bone, Razor nodded Korac's head and Pablo immediately set to pouring medicine into her mouth. "I'm sorry for the taste."

Triss didn't seem to notice much of anything. If this was Aegis labor, Sagan was grateful nacres allowed her the choice and saddened all the same she and Korac would never conceive together.

"She'll be as beautiful as her mother, Triss." To Sagan's astonishment, Razor stood and covered her mouth with Korac's. Tears and all.

Tameka whispered, "What do you think is going on in his head?"

Sagan wondered about that herself.

{Reipon}

Triss' eyes remained shut, never to open again, when Razor straightened Korac's body from their kiss. He gingerly touched her arms where her elbows bent backward. The orange blood from the punctured bone stained the bed and filled the air with kerosene. The source of her fire.

One Korac didn't mind seeing extinguished. When the thought entered their shared conscience, Razor glared across the black space between them. To which Korac offered a shrug. There was no love lost between him and Triss. Only tragedy remained.

"Show some respect to the woman who raised you, *baby brother*."

Korac circled the shackled man and reminded him, "You're no brother of mine, and if you hadn't abducted me from my actual mother's arms, I would never have suffered so much of Triss' 'tender care.'"

Razor ignored Korac and stared from his body down at her. "So beautiful even in her sleep."

"You loved her? Truly?" Korac didn't really care, but Echo may one day value that knowledge. He and Sagan both intended to keep their promise and tell their adopted daughter of her parents. This obsessive relationship they carried on for millions of years might provide the only positive anecdote about her parents to share with her.

In a voice deeper than a Gargantuan Tritan, Razor vowed inside this space, "I will find her in Eternity." He stepped Korac back to let the doctor set her bones. Softer, in his usual voice, Razor demanded, "She agreed, and now she's gone. Cycle me."

"Not yet."

Razor whirled on Korac, fuming in his narrowed eyes and clenched fists. It looked completely futile and unintimidating with him shackled in Korac's conscience.

Xelan brought him back to the scene. "Razor, we want to ask you some questions. Would you like to talk in another room?"

Fuck, the Prince of Cinder was generous. Even Tameka rolled her eyes and crossed her arms behind him. A response Korac could get behind. It was Sagan's response who worried him. Her eyes shifted from Atramentous black to mauve to normal. They never left Korac's body, Razor's eyes.

Inside the mindscape, a terrible grin spread across Razor's lips as he answered Xelan with Korac's mouth, "I'll answer any question you ask if the Seamswalker answers one of mine."

No fucking way was Korac about to sit by and let this happen. "You miserable son of a bitch—"

"One question," Sagan said in a voice of three pitches.

Razor sneered smugly at Korac inside the shared space before informing her, "I'll know if you lie."

"Ask."

Tameka tossed her hands in the air and sat on the bed with a sulking huff, sharing Korac's sentiments. Xelan narrowed those midnight eyes ever so slightly. He didn't like it either.

Oh, but the Pain Curator enjoyed it. The terrible grin transformed into a wicked smirk when he asked, "Have you dreamt of me?" Sagan opened her mouth to answer, and he cut her off. "Sagan, have you dreamt of me the way I said you would?"

Finally, Xelan showed some sense. He shook his head and raised a finger to give Razor a good lecture—

"You know I have."

Sagan.

Her voice trembled, and her eyes shifted. Her breath left her on a shaky sigh, and she squeezed her eyes shut. "Now keep your end of the bargain and answer their questions. You know you hate to go back on a deal."

"There, you see? I'll take her from you yet. Soon, she'll request me in the bedroom, and I can put this inferior body of yours to good use—"

"You still can't see it." Korac frowned, incredulous and perplexed. "Any chance you ever had with her, and I'm not saying there ever was one, you lost the day you revealed your true nature. She will never want you, Razor, because her love, affection—everything about her—is founded in trust. And you shattered however much you developed between the two of you. Look at her."

Razor gazed out at Sagan, and she looked away, swallowing hard, as if she found the taste of something bitter. Tameka rubbed comforting circles in her back. Pablo and Xelan offered her something to help with the anxiety.

Korac shook his head, aching to end this cycle and soothe her, but this interrogation mattered. Still, he continued, "You broke her heart, and I hate that you ever possessed enough of it to hurt her. She wanted a friendship with you, and you betrayed her. There is no coming back from that, and I think it strange you want to at all. I'm almost convinced, after spending this time with you in my bones, that you don't pursue her to hurt me. I think you pursue her because you realized what you lost, and you're desperate to get it back. Like with T.A.O. If that's the case, do the right thing. Help them. Help Sagan save Rayne and finally finish Celindria's game."

Razor stared at him the entire while without an outward response, but Korac felt him in his bones. The genuine reactions. There was desire there for Sagan. Possession. And the bittersweet twinge of happiness. Sagan brought him some joy during their brief rapport, but same as T.A.O., Razor's world punished sweet things for their innocence. Razor did little in life to correct that.

Without a word to Korac, Razor returned his body to the seat at Triss' bedside. He made a show of straightening out Korac's jeans and ripped t-shirt and spared one poignant assessment of his black-painted fingernails.

"Ask your questions, Prince Xelan."

{REIPON}

Xelan sat on the bed to face Razor in Korac's body. The curious Prince wanted to know so much about the process. Was Korac still conscious? Were they communicating somehow? And what must that be like? Instead, Xelan focused on the situation at hand and asked, "Where in Enki would Imminent take Rayne?"

Razor stopped gazing at Korac's nails with a tragic longing and met Xelan's eyes. "Either New Cinder or the Pantheon."

From behind Xelan, Tameka pressed, "New Cinder?" Her frown was in her voice.

The Pain Curator sighed, bored with the tedium of the interrogation already. "All of Enki's continents are test sites for planets within the Vast Collective. New Cinder bears the same ecology as Cinder before they forced Li's expansion."

Sagan and Tameka exchanged something that made Xelan glance back at them. Sagan spoke up. "When we went before the Tribunal, they took us to a weird place with vegetation like how you and Nox's Verse described Cinder. Before..."

Tameka completed Sagan's sentence, "Before they used the nacre inside Li to destroy it."

They all looked at Razor, who narrowed his eyes with a twitch. "Yes."

"Do all the stars have nacres?" Tameka stepped closer to him until she looked down to maintain eye contact. Her disdain overrode the curiosity in her tone. Xelan didn't dream of holding her back as she took over this interrogation. She asked, "Did the Aegis put them there?"

Razor stared up at her, unthreatened by her tone or proximity. More fascinated by it. "You're... not what I expected, Tameka. While I appreciate your intellect, I agreed to help Sagan save Rayne. The stars and their potential nacre affiliation have nothing to do with that."

Tameka looked ready to escalate this, and given her history with Korac, she was the one most likely to hurt him.

Sagan touched Xelan's shoulder, and he asked, "Is Imminent collecting gas from Monarch 3 hives?" That ought to change the subject and save Korac's face.

Razor kept his eyes locked on Tameka's, but his words were for Xelan. "Your genius was so perfect for us. I wished I was successful at recruiting you. Yes, they are. And they harvest it for the reason you've guessed."

Sagan gasped.

Xelan shook his head in regret. He'd wasted time not warning the Progeny about Imminent and Enki before his death. Surely an army of generated soldiers was their ambition all along.

Tameka asked Razor the hard question. "How many—"

"Millions. Possibly tens of millions by now, but none of them possess the same unique talents as you and the rest of Xelan's Progeny. It's one reason Celindria works day and night to unlock her brothers' and sister's abilities. At the time of my death, the army only consisted of trained fighters Celindria could pilot through volition control. That's if they still exist."

"What do you mean?" Sagan sounded suspicious.

Razor tightened Korac's lips in a thin line of disapproval. "When she's dissatisfied with a batch, Celindria often eradicates them and starts over. Like an artist with a fresh canvas. Remorse tries to keep her in line, to stop her from wasting soldiers, but she has her own ways, as I'm sure you know."

Xelan held out a tablet. "Can you draw me a map?"

Razor finally broke contact with Tameka. He sounded bemused as he asked, "You want another one?"

Tameka looked behind Xelan to Sagan. They shared a surprised look.

To them, Xelan promised, "One day, I'll explain everything in my Verse." To Razor, he held out a tablet and said, "Please."

Razor accepted it with laughter sparkling in his eyes. "Where to?"

Xelan ticked the items off, tapping his fingernail on the tablet. "Anywhere you know I need. The progenitor, New Cinder, Celindria's lab—"

"The control bridge?"

"It exists?" Xelan felt his brows go up. This was monumental. If it exists, and they found it, they might save Rayne. Unfortunately, there was no evidence of it. "I never found mention of it in the Pantheon."

Razor's amusement once upon a time was infectious to Xelan. After everything he understood the Pain Curator capable of in the last few months, Xelan found it unnerving. What made his eyes shine so? "Yes. It exists, but I have a request before I lead you right to it."

Tameka groaned.

Sagan took a step forward and visibly shored herself as a sacrifice to this interrogation.

Xelan was *not* happy.

Gazing up at her, Razor shook Korac's head. "No. I'm... done with that. This is for Triss. I want to be there when the baby is born. She'd want me to hold our girl at least once."

Xelan blew the air from his cheeks. "That's a big ask, and we have other questions." He looked up at Sagan. "What do you want from this? We'll go with whatever you choose."

Sagan glanced back at Razor, who acted on his best behavior. No leering glances and searing smirks. He left Korac's face and body neutral. To that, she said, "It's an acceptable request if Korac agrees."

After a pause, where Razor's eyes darted about as if searching for something, he returned to them, saying, "He wants everyone to know he doesn't like it, but agrees." Rolling his eyes, Razor sighed. "He also wants everyone to know—wants me to say this—that he thinks I'm an asshole for putting you, Sagan, in this position."

She actually broke into a smile meant for Korac. For Razor, it fell as she said, "Answer their questions and draw their map to the control bridge."

"Anything for you, Seamswalker."

As he stared at her, Razor's eyes filled with such intensity that Xelan intervened by jabbing the tablet. "Map. Now."

Tameka grimaced as if disgusted with the entire affair as she pressed the interrogation forward. "Who is Silence, and why does she want Rayne?"

Razor spoke while drawing. "I don't know all the details. She was Primary Quet's project that he established once the Tritans found us. The Aegis designated some space in Enki for a lab to make things right between them. Surra—"

"Surra?!" Xelan gaped.

"—Escaped. She fled to Cinder, met Elden, and well... I suppose she's—"

"My grandmother."

Tameka smoothed her hand over Xelan's shoulder and kissed the top of his head. He leaned into it, grateful to share this revelation with her. All of them with her.

"Uhm..."

They both turned and looked at Sagan, whose eyes were wide and her mouth was open. After gaping like a fish for a few seconds, she confessed, "I told your grandma I thought she was hot."

Pablo, who quietly checked in now and again, barked out a laugh from the doorway. "Same, Sagan. Same." At their glares, he returned to working quietly.

Even Razor chuckled in Korac's voice. "No one would blame you. If I recall correctly, she was quite beautiful. Nacres preserve regular beings for millions of years after maturity. It's a gift that has led to more than one comical, romantic encounter—"

Razor tilted his head to the side as if listening before sharing, "Korac tires of my musings and would like to continue the interrogation or cycle me so he can quote, 'Take Sagan back to our room and cleanse her of this unpleasantness.'"

Sagan blushed.

Tameka groaned. "I don't need to know this."

Xelan muttered, "How do you think I feel?" He'd expected to share any information regarding Silence directly with Kyle, but right now, he squirmed at the notion. Pushing all that aside, he asked on a long shot, "Do you know how to end the Weapon in Rayne without killing her?"

"Don't you know? You perfected it, after all."

Xelan closed his eyes. The room went very quiet and very still. A vacuum built pressure in his ears until they begged for sweet relief.

Someone else please say something first.

When no words came, Xelan opened his eyes to find Razor glancing between the three stunned friends and beyond to the one in the doorway. He didn't look entertained or smug, only curious. He didn't know the damage he'd just caused.

"I wanted to wait for my Verse to tell you, so that I could explain everything in context."

Tameka inched while turning away from Razor and looking down at Xelan where he sat on the edge of the bed. She looked hurt, and it killed him. She said, "I accept knowing you on your terms. I have enough faith in you to know that if you could save Rayne, you would have shared that information by now. Anything else is a distraction and not helpful to our mission."

Sagan reached out from his side and squeezed his shoulder. "After working with Korac on his Verse, I understand not everything can be told like a confession. There's a story, and yours must be very complicated. We'll wait for you to feel ready."

Xelan's heart expanded until he sighed with relief from the guilt he carried. It was his greatest sin, and he didn't want to share it this way. How ashamed he was at the hands of that manipulation. How wrong he'd been about everything.

"Thank you for understanding."

Tameka glared at Razor with contempt as she asked, "So, do *you* know how to end the Weapon or not?"

Razor gazed up at Tameka with respect transparent on his face. He contemplated for a long stretch of silence before answering, "It depends."

Tameka's eyes flashed. She ground out, "On what?"

"Was Imminent successful in infecting her with Dr. Suarez's virus?"

"Fuck me!" Pablo cried from the entryway.

Xelan nodded.

Razor's eyes went grave, and he sobered completely. He looked only at Sagan as he said, "I'm afraid there's no way now. You can't even remove it. The Weapon will detonate if you try, causing maximum devastation in the event of her death. That virus is so thorough you can't even affect the fuse. She *is* a Weapon."

"I don't believe you."

{REIPON}

Just when Pablo felt like complete dog shit for ever developing that virus, Tameka spoke up and saved him. She was trembling with all her might. For love of her sister. For hope. Xelan took her hand in his and squeezed.

The warrior known as Fury repeated, "I don't believe there's no hope for her, and I say that because Pablo is brilliant—as you've mentioned. With a mind like his and Xelan's and the technology we'll find on Enki, we can save her."

Sagan reached over and squeezed her other hand.

Razor stared at them from inside Korac's body. He still looked grim. "I wish you luck. Here is your map. Are there any other questions? Korac grows impatient at the Seamswalker's suffering."

Sagan asked next, "How do we care for Triss through Echo's delivery?"

Pablo muttered, "Thanks. I wanted to know."

"It's one reason I've asked to be there—to guide you. She'll need Aegis blood from the Seam. There's nothing to treat the pain. The coma seems to be working and was quite an impressive idea. Thank you, Dr. Suarez." Razor gazed down at Triss with so much emotion in Korac's face. "Not much longer now."

"I want Korac."

Pablo couldn't blame Sagan. This must put her through the wringer. Especially given Razor's reaction. When she spoke, Razor snapped to her with those extremely alien eyes. The torment in them softened as he said, "And he wants you. Sweet dreams, Kitten."

Sagan winced, Xelan consoled her, and Tameka grumbled about bad guys having the last word. Pablo startled when Korac opened his eyes to their usual white with gray flecks.

"Sagan."

Korac bolted from the chair and swept her in his arms. She clung to him, and everyone else in the room stepped out. Except Pablo. He checked Triss' bones. Half-glass, they were broken shards earlier. Now they solidified and strained her tendons. He clenched his jaw at the state of her. "Sagan, I hate to ask, but can you please get her some Aegis blood soon?"

They parted enough to spare him an appreciative look. She assured, "Of course. We'll leave now. Do you have—"

Pablo handed her several IV bags to fill. "Thanks. Sorry, Korac."

He nodded at the doctor. "Thank you."

Poof. They were gone.

Alone, or so Pablo thought.

A knock sounded from the doorway. He stopped checking Triss' vitals to find Lynn standing there in jeans and a tight t-shirt that almost melted him. "Hey."

"Hey. Can I help? Never mind. I see something I can do." She pushed away from the door and went through the drawers in the nightstand. Retrieving some fresh sheets, she went to change the bloodstained linens. "How is she? Did Razor help her?"

Pablo changed the subject and stopped Lynn from her chore. He took her hands and kissed both palms. The ambiguity of his actions frightened her, judging by her wide eyes and parted lips. He couldn't think of how to soothe her because he was scared himself. "Lynn, for once I'm not worried about you in danger on a mission, but I am worried about me." Brushing his fingers down her cheeks, he assured, "Don't worry. I won't break our vows again, but do you mind giving this letter to The Brethren? It's for mi madre. She hasn't heard from me since we fled Earth and Cinder."

Lynn took the letter, and a tear rolled down her cheek. Breathy, she said, "We'll be fine, Pablo. I'll give this to The Brethren, but you'll see her before too long."

He pulled her close and kissed her forehead. "I know, but this means so much to me. Thank you, Lynn."

They stayed that way a while, holding each other—

Scratching sounded from the Infirmary's door. Lynn offered, "I'll get it." She took off, and from the hall, Pablo heard her say, "There you are, Thubgy. I lost you in the kitchen to Bones, you traitor. Now you want back in?"

"Let him in," Pablo called.

The hefty Hellkitten waddled into the room with a belly so full he had to spread his little bat wings to fly onto the bed. There, he panted up at Pablo, waiting for praise.

Which he got, of course. "You're such a good boy." Pablo even scratched the scaly belly. After which, Thubgy melted into a puddle at Triss' feet and snored immediately.

Lynn laughed in a way that Pablo loved. "I'm so glad Andrew talked us into keeping one of Pisces' kittens."

"Yeah, but what happens when he gets as big as Pisces?"

Pablo was finished in the room until Sagan and Korac returned, so they worked on their research. "I have to cure this virus and reverse the Weapon mechanics in Rayne's nacre."

Lynn prepped med-kits for Phase II. "Did anyone ask Razor about it?"

Pablo swallowed and tried to say this without alarming her. "He said the virus was permanent and that any attempt to tamper with Rayne's nacre would detonate the Weapon."

Lynn hissed.
Pablo understood.
This sucked.

{REIPON}
Tameka left Xelan to prepare for Phase II and went to collect Pax from the lounge, but found him nestled in with all the boys and the Lyriks playing board games.

"Mommy," he whined cutely. "Pleeeeeease."

Andrew waved her on. "Don't worry, Tameka. Earth team is prepped, and Pax isn't bothering us."

Bones chimed in. "Go relax or something, Fury. Enjoy the alone time."

Alone time.

What a concept.

"All right."

What would Tameka do with herself? With no clue, she wandered up the stairs toward her suites and bumped into Tumu. "Hey, I thought you and Xelan were meeting for Mon3 prep."

All the way up his seven feet compression, Tumu said in a voice which still hurt her ears and she never fully acclimated to, "He was upset about something, Peaches. I don't suppose you know what."

Oh. "Razor brought up some stuff Xelan wasn't ready to talk about." That gave her a notion. She tilted her head at the Tritan. "You've known him a long time. Did you know he worked on the Weapon project?"

Tumu leaned against the balustrade as he considered her question. Eventually, he said, "I never knew of the initiative to make nacres into Weapons until they gave it to Rayne. I knew he worked on some experimental nacres for Enki in return for aid to fight Nox. It's possible, even Xelan knew nothing of the Weapon itself, but still contributed to it. Am I making sense?"

Tameka nodded. "I think so. You're saying that he was tricked into it."

The old Primary's almond-shaped voids widened slightly despite the lack of eyelids. "Yes, and no. He worked under Lance and Wiw's sentencing, so I doubt even they knew. Is it deceiving another when you've been manipulated as well?"

Sighing, Tameka dismissed his logic with a wave. "You Tritans have a way of washing your hands clean of your messes. Leaving the rest of us to clean it up. I still can't get a simple answer as to how many of you there are."

"The answer is 'We don't know,'" Lamassau said as he entered the foyer from the kitchen. "We believe there are fewer and more than we assume."

Tameka pinched the bridge of her nose and squeezed her eyes shut. "Huh?"

Tumu explained, quieting his voice for her distress. "No one has seen Primary Xhi and Lon since we came to Enki. We don't know if they're alive."

"But we *do* believe they stored some of our people in resurrection caskets on Enki." Lamassau, the only Tritan Tameka ever saw eat food, stuffed a whole tomato in his mouth and busted it in his sharp teeth while saying, "Unfortunately, we found no proof."

Tameka looked between the two of them, incredulous. "I'm sorry. I know Enki is tremendous, but how can you—you, Tumu, a Primary—not know so much about your race."

The Tritan couple shared an exchange. Lamassau shrugged. Tumu confessed, "You think you can trust your own. It's never the case. I know Enki—the Tritans—want to restore our race using women from across the galaxy in a reproduction program. They also desired security, so they employed the Icari, constructed the Lyriks, and eventually developed the Weapons. I know Imminent interlaced their operations, lending to the more sinister projects of which we are still unsure what they are and how far they reach. For that, I'm sorry."

Softening her combative tendencies, Tameka smiled sadly at Tumu. "I know you're doing everything you can to make it right." She looked at Lamassau. "You, too. Thank you both. Sorry if I still get… you know… Anyway, I'm heading off to clear my head. See you two in a few hours."

Lamassau waved while shoving another tomato into his mouth.

Tumu called after her, halfway up the stairs, "Peaches?"

She turned. "Yes?"

"We will make it right."

Lam punctuated the affirmation with two thumbs up and a messy face.

Laughing felt good, and it relieved the tension between them. Tired and stressed out, Tameka headed to the weight room on the second floor. Her suites could wait until after she relieved some tension—

A present waited for her inside.

Xelan, shirtless and glistening, executed a perfect one-handed push-up with Pil platinum plates on his back. And the gym was empty. No one to ask to leave or to force awkward interactions.

Just them.

Door locked without a cackle. It was a wonder Tameka managed.

She stripped out of her shirt, leaving only her sports bra beneath. She could work out in the cut-off shorts. Her only complaint was all the mirrors in the room kept her from sneaking up on him.

When he spied her approach, Xelan explained to her reflection between grunts. "Needed to… relieve some… tension."

Tameka grinned at him in the mirror. "I'm here to help." As she lifted the plates off his back with some significant strain, he stopped mid-push-up with a quirked brow. Before he could guess, she climbed on his back, much to his chuckling delight.

"What're you doing?"

Tameka positioned herself on top of his push-up position with her head at his calves. Gripping his ankles, she planted the toes of her shoes between his shoulder blades. "I'm working out, silly."

"Silly, eh?" Xelan's grin in the mirror meant the world to her.

"You do your push-ups. I got mine." Tameka nodded encouragingly, with a wicked challenge in her eyes.

Xelan pushed down, and so did Tameka, using his ankles on top of his back. When he pushed up, they both laughed at the wobbliness of it all, but after a few reps, they found their balance.

Two hundred of those.

Xelan got slippery along the way, and Tameka laughed at their ridiculous antics. Once they completed a set, she asked, "How was that?"

"Interesting. I'll admit." Xelan's grin crooked into a smirk. "My turn to help you."

That sparkle in his eyes almost made Tameka lick her lips. "Yeah, okay. Sure."

Xelan stood in the center of the room and reached out to her. "Wrap your legs around my hips."

Tameka was fine with this. She jumped into his arms and wrapped her arms and legs around him. Xelan smiled and this close, she fixated on that midnight ring outside the black of his eyes. "I missed this." Her voice came out breathy, but she meant the significance of the feeling behind the words.

"Get ready to see it two hundred more times."

That made Tameka blink. "Huh?"

With her wrapped around him, Xelan bent his knees into a perfect box squat. "It's your turn, *Tameka*." He said her name the way she liked.

Oh. Uhm. Okay. Tameka figured it out. She locked her legs securely and fell back for a sit-up. All the way up until she met his eyes again.

Xelan waited for her with his signature grin. "One."

He squatted again, she fell back, and so they went. The friction of Tameka's shorts against Xelan's sweats added an intimacy to the exercise with his eyes so close. They almost kissed several times, but prolonging it increased the want into a need. A craving to kiss him.

At one hundred and fifty sit-ups with no interruptions—people needing guidance, ex-lovers, or Pax—she growled, "Fuck it," and kissed him.

Xelan tasted Tameka's lips and went to his knees, pinning her to the floor. Shiny from their exercise, they gripped each other. Him clutching her legs; her squeezing his arms. Bergamot, honey, and leather mixed in the air. They both moaned along their tongues and lips. Afraid to let go.

Xelan parted only enough to pop the buttons on Tameka's fly and looked at her. They were both flushed, him blue, her red. Roughly, he pulled off her shorts, staring at her. "I had plans. Ideas. Fantasies—"

Tameka swallowed her pulse.

"—But I can't wait for the weeks I want to spend with you. Not anymore. I'll make it up to you."

Tameka opened her mouth to dismiss it and beg him to take her now, but he kissed her hard enough to press her head against the tile beneath. Easily, Xelan pushed down his pants and found her ready. Found home waiting for him there.

He closed his eyes and groaned when he entered her, stretched her, even with her eagerness and desire. It almost hurt, and she loved every second.

Tameka cried out and arched her neck. Xelan kissed over her nacre and across the swell of her breasts. Impatiently, he freed them from the confining bra and tended her in time to his thrusts. She opened her eyes to glimpse them in the mirror. The length of their bodies pressed together. Her legs spread wide for him, and him taking—

Xelan caught her looking and grinned—playful and sexy. "Don't close your eyes. Keep looking."

Tameka nodded for him because she couldn't speak.

He twisted with the next thrust, and her eyes almost fluttered shut. Their sensual, heavy gazes looked back at her. Xelan did it again, and she called out his name, looking like a hungry animal. Once more and Tameka lost.

Her eyes closed, and she cried out. Spine bowed. Lip bitten to bleeding—

That changed the moment entirely.

"Yes. Tameka. Now." Xelan purred in her ear.

She granted his wish and bit into his shoulder. The nanites in his blood fed the deprivation in hers. The sensation of the bite ruined his careful control. Xelan lost the twisting rhythm and forgot caring for roughness. He simply fucked her.

Tameka loved it.

The bite healed, and she drew her tongue across his skin. Made her way down his collar bone. The straining vessels in his neck. Kissing over his nacre sent Xelan over the edge.

He let go, and she went with him.

Still, Icari could go for days. No matter how many times Xelan could finish, he would keep going. So, Tameka clasped his face in her hands and made him look at her, while she said, "I want more. Now. But we've got a war to win and a kiddo to see."

The lust cleared in Xelan's eyes, and he grinned. "I care about at least one of those two things." He sat up. Tameka thought he meant to stand, but he took her legs and shifted them to one side. In easy, languid draws, he moved for her. "But both can wait a few more times."

In this new position, Tameka suddenly lost the need to care about anything outside of this room.

Pax was fine learning all the cuss words that came with playing games in the lounge.

The war couldn't happen without them.

Sex with Xelan was now. And necessary. And good.

So very, very good.

FOURTEEN

THERE'S A TIME AND A PLACE FOR OPTIMISM

{ENKI}

PHASE II HAD COMMENCED COMPLIMENTS OF PRIMARY REM. Lucy was ready. So ready that when her shift started that night, she wasn't surprised Yito approached her separately from the Second Half-Day team.

"Yes?" Lucy forced every ounce of unassuming innocence into the high lilt of her voice.

The Tritan guard fidgeted with his arm behind his head, scratching nervously. "Well, Remorse asked if you'd consider working on another project for them in Enki proper. He was so impressed with your enthusiasm here, he thought it was an honor to extend the privilege to you." Yito added an abashed grin. "It's really a good thing for you and Matt. I'm glad I put the word in for you."

Lucy knew better, but also understood that Yito did not. "Of course, I accept. Matt will be so excited. Can I tell him now?"

"Sure. Yeah. Before you get your things together."

Lucy paused. "What?"

He grinned with all those sharp Tritan teeth, still not understanding. "They want you to start immediately. Isn't that great?"

"Truly. Excellent." Lucy beamed at him while her heart fluttered in her chest. "I'll let Matt know." She moved through the equipment panel in the shrine with the other team members looking on. Their faces were full of smiles as she'd already charmed them all. She nodded and waved. "Sorry. I need a second to talk to my husband."

One day, the couple would make time for a wedding. Maybe.

"Ginger. This is Morning Star. Over."

There was a pause until Puk came on the line. "Hey, Morning Star. Don't worry. Your boy will be on the line soon. You caught him after he fell into a pile of—"

"I'm here, Morning Star. Over." There was a squelching sound in Matt's background that made Lucy snicker.

She glanced at Yito's earnest face before sharing the good news. "They reassigned me to Enki. I don't know for how long, but I'll reach out as soon as I can. Over." Matt never gave Lucy cause for concern. He understood how she hunted.

In a wry voice, he said, "Don't have too much fun without me. Over and Out."

Lucy's smile in response was real and filled with how much she loved him.

Yito practically vibrated with eager energy. "Great. Get your things, and we'll head further into Enki."

She grabbed a pack and followed him through the Shrine's conduit. It led to a platform surrounded by a flat ocean. The Shadow called these "landings," and there were supposedly hundreds of millions of them designed into a maze. Lucy followed Yito through three more conduits, making note of... not much. Everything looked the same. Either ocean or white stone and glass hallway.

"Here we are," Yito said as he entered the last conduit.

Lucy straightened her hair and adjusted her suit to best display her assets before following him inside.

Primary Rem waited on the other side in an amphitheater. White, like everything else, it could sit several hundred audience members. Instead, it was her, Yito, Remorse, and a woman who could only be Celindria.

Lucy waved in a friendly gesture. "Hello again."

The Gargantuan Tritan and his Imminent colleague exchanged a look. Her with one eyebrow raised, and him with a firm nod. Celindria approached first in a sweep of her breezy white dress. She circled Lucy as she said, "Morning Star. Lucy. Primary Rem passes along high praise of you."

Lucy lowered her eyes and shifted her weight awkwardly. "Thank you, ma'am and thank you, Primary."

"I am Eminent Celindria. Address me by my title." The beautiful woman's voice took on an icy edge that nipped Lucy's usual composure.

This was a contender. "Yes, Eminent Celindria."

Yito gave Lucy an encouraging thumbs up from across the theater.

Celindria stopped circling her and stepped back to get a better look. "Do you know why you're here?"

"To help with some work in Enki."

Primary Rem took over. "That's right. We're launching a special measure to decimate the half of Gait on its way to Enki's hull. Eminent Celindria will brief you on the schematics."

That wasn't entirely the truth. Lucy tried different approaches with Remorse, but the Tritan retreated rather than took the bait. Resisted. It intrigued her, and she wondered if he somehow learned of her tactics. If that were the case, Celindria was here to test as a female participant.

Lucy raised her chin. "I'm ready."

An hour passed after they transferred Lucy to an adjacent arena where she came face-to-face with a familiar sight. The colossal Tantamount occupied the entire space with its ominous capacity for planet-wide destruction. Eminent

Celindria explained the purpose of it, not realizing Lucy understood it perfectly. All the while, Lucy kept her eyes down in deference and smiled kindly when it suited. She wanted to come across as interested, but not suspicious or conspicuous, but she knew what this solo conversation was actually about. It was her mission.

"You're a perfect candidate for the program." Celindria wasn't smiling. Her blue eyes were dead. She faced Primary Rem and delivered in a flat, hard voice. "Good luck with this one, Remorse." She disappeared through a conduit.

Meanwhile, Yito itched and fidgeted beside Lucy. She tried to shine him a reassuring smile, but something about the briefing bothered him.

Remorse walked over to Lucy, where she sat in the stands. "Well, she approved of you. Once you've finished with this assignment, I'll call you in for another. Of course, if you can part from your husband for that long."

Lucy smiled warmly. "We've worked separately in the past, and everything turned out fine. I look forward to our next encounter, Primary."

He almost shrank back from her, as if unnerved.

It amused Lucy. This close, she smelled the coconut and pineapple aroma of Tritan blood in his black veins. She wanted to slice him open now, but that wasn't the mission. Besides, she knew without a doubt, Primary Rem would squash her like a bug.

So this hunt went on.

Yito escorted Lucy to the conduit where the Tantamount-installation team waited. He was quiet and a little squirmy. Gently, she pushed, "Is everything all right?"

Yito stopped and grabbed Lucy by the shoulders, pulling her into a hug she wasn't sure they were ready for. In her ear, he whispered, "Don't mind the hug. We are being monitored. They want you in the breeding program. That's why Eminent Celindria was there. I've lost so many women I've liked to them, friends and confidants. I respect you too much to let you die that way."

Finally.

Lucy squeezed him in the perfect imitation of a genuine embrace. "Don't leave me. Help me when it's time. Until then, let's keep working to avoid their attention." A thought entered her head, and she asked, "How do they die?"

"Used up and spat out."

This was Lucy's mission.

"Here's what I'll need from you, Yito. The rest I can do on my own."

{REIPON}

So much hustle and bustle in this place. Busy people gathering and preparing. Bethany stayed out of their way, sitting with her legs dangling from the banister of the foyer's second floor. Pax grinned at her with all his baby teeth and kept asking her to play with his toy train. No matter how many times she declined, it seemed to only make him more determined. The massive tree that spanned all three floors played sentinel to it all, reaching to hug Bethany in its branches.

That was fine with her. Bethany only left her room to appease Kyle and Ross. If she shut herself inside, they'd come looking for her. She hated that. It made her feel without a choice of how she wanted to spend her time. How she wanted to heal.

Korac understood. He always walked Bethany to her room and left her alone, without letting Ross know when they finished their walk. It bought her some time. Like the last Quarter night. She'd heard Ross open the door and check on her, but Bethany kept her back turned until the door latched on a mournful note.

One day at a time.

Sagan rushed by behind Bethany, calling below, "Xelan, let Tameka know I borrowed her boots. After we separate. She'll know which pair. Oh, and am I getting Legir or is he already on Earth?"

Xelan craned his neck to answer her from the lounge entryway. "Is that the pair with X's blood on it from that one time on Pil? At the Caprent restaurant? And Legir's waiting for them with The Brethren. Stop worrying. I—"

"—Got you," Kyle and Andrew mocked him from the third floor banister.

"Nice one, boys." Lynn rushed down the stairs with three more packs. She nodded to Bethany and Pax on her way by.

Lamassau followed behind her, saying to Xelan, "Have you considered rebranding?"

The Prince of Cinder grinned, and Bethany swore he winked at her. "Why change when I'm known for such a positive and reassuring catch phrase?"

"Maybe because it applies no small amount of pressure on you to live up to it." Tumu tossed him a rifle. "You and Tameka might want one."

In his gravelly voice, Caedes said, "Firepower. Everyone got it?"

Lamassau patted his ribs beneath his robes. Bethany made out the guns in his shoulder holster.

Andrew and Kyle both shouted from the stairs behind Bethany. "Got mine!" "Yup, C-man!"

"C-man…?" Sagan's nose scrunched. "I don't think that works. Caedes, what do you think?"

The gruff man scowled.

"Too generic," Bones announced from the third floor stairs. "What about Gravel-nator? Yeah? What do you think, 'the Chef?'"

Lamassau shook his head. "Lame, Icarus. So very lame. Clearly he's Master Graveller."

Bethany held her breath as Caedes glared at Bones.

Xelan smiled into his task of checking his gear without contributing.

Tumu rolled his eyes. "Children."

While they carried on, Kyle knelt beside Bethany. "Hey. We might be gone a while. Caedes, Bones, and Pehton are here if you need anything. Put them to work, okay?"

For the first time in… Elden, she didn't know how long. Bethany wanted to hug Kyle. She sat in on the mission discussions. She knew how dangerous and involved this was for him and the others. For the people she came to like, who made so much noise in this big house. Andrew's friendly smile beyond Kyle's patient openness was further proof of that.

But Bethany just couldn't. As she thought about reaching for him, her skin itched and burned. Instead, she returned the friendly smile to them both and nodded. That was her best.

"Hee. You're pretty," Pax said beside her.

Kyle held a stern finger out to the boy, but exaggerated his "mad" voice. "I already gotta keep my eye out on one delinquent after another sister in this house. I don't need a second one."

Pax gripped the finger and bent it back into Kyle's hand, making Bethany's brother raise a brow. "Strong, aren't ya? Okay, Bethany. You're in Master Graveller's—"

"Quit that."

"—hands now."

Bethany liked the way Kyle beamed extra big with Caedes' interjection. Andrew even snickered.

She loved them.

Ross stopped by next. "I shouldn't get into any trouble while I'm out. We're helping locals clean up after a disaster. One day, you can come along and help, if you'd like."

Bethany nodded. She might.

Beyond Ross, Korac left the suite he shared with Sagan. He gave Bethany a nod of mutual understanding.

Her sister saw Bethany's reaction and turned. "Oh, hello, Korac." Ross' cheeks glowed like a nuclear reactor.

Korac offered her a polite nod. Completely different from his gesture to Bethany. It wasn't dismissive, but it didn't invite further attention. The Icarus majestically swept by them, down the stairs, and into the waiting arms of his lover. Sagan got on the very tips of Tameka's boots to peck him a kiss and mutter something in his ear that made him smirk.

Ross sighed beside her sister. Bethany nodded.

Staying on task was hard in this house with all the pretty people to distract observers. Which was Bethany's primary occupation, as far as she was concerned. Maybe next time, she'd ask to go along. Put herself to good use. She could look out or something. Was she able to whistle? She should try.

Pablo blundered in from the Infirmary hall, arms filled to the brim with supplies. He even made Iuo and Devis help carry it. Jack, Miy, and Twenty-One followed.

Tameka appeared in tactical gear and kissed Pax. "Be a good boy for Peh Peh and Uncle Caeda."

"What about Uncle Bones?" Pax swung his legs emphatically with his question.

His mother smirked and ruffled his curls, saying, "Give him hell."

"Looks like it's time. Bye, Bethany. I love you." Ross made to hug her.

Bethany leaned away. Instead, Pax jumped in Ross' arms and squeezed her around her neck. It hurt to see the dismay in Ross' eyes. The rejection. But that reaction only sent Bethany further into retreat.

Korac was easy because he held no expectations for her. When would her siblings ever see that and take note? Carrying Pax, Ross gave one last wave to her little sister before heading down the stairs.

"What a parade." A voice muttered behind Bethany. She turned to see Pehton approaching the banister. Leaning against it, she said, "Look at all those brave people."

Lynn, Lamassau, and Andrew stood to one side with various bags, empty and full, between them. Xelan, Tameka, Sagan, Korac, Kyle, Pablo, Tumu, and Iuo stood across the open foyer from them, letting the tree keep them apart. Ross, Jack, Miy, Devis, and Twenty-One formed the last corner of the triangle. Bones and Caedes waited at the bottom of the stairs.

Everyone looked brave. Everyone looked ready.

Bethany wished them luck, knowing they would need it.

{EARTH}

Andrew and his team stepped out of the Seam, in its varying shades of majestic purple, and entered a pagoda made of dark wood and white stone, cushioned in the snows of northern British Columbia. Tempest, a female Icarus with a chic sense of style, and Legir, Leader of Yu, with stick arms and a triangular body attached to his perfectly round head, waited for the Shadow. They both smiled and welcomed them with hands outstretched in greeting.

Andrew couldn't—He just couldn't find it in him to trust them. He swept their intentions.

Discuss the nacre situation. Brainstorm how best to proceed. Elden, I hope their samples return clean, but when have we ever been so lucky?

Tempest's kindness and dedication made Andrew grind his teeth with guilt. What about Legir?

They need to eat more. And rest. Skin and bones and dark under eyes. Poor children. At least these nacre experiments will ease their minds.

Andrew wanted to cry. How could he doubt all these people? He knew the answer. The people he never doubted were the last ones to betray them.

Lucas...

In Andrew's silence, Lynn introduced Lamassau officially to Tempest. She also asked, "Where's Cypher and Colton?"

Legir smiled knowingly and spoke inside their heads. "In the kitchen, preparing for you."

Tempest waved for them to follow. "Dolor is down there, too." When Andrew shivered at another mind to sweep, she mistook it for a chill. "Some people find it quite cold here with no windows, but we find it refreshing. If you like, we can shutter it?"

Andrew dismissed her kind offer. "No, thank you. If you don't mind, I'd like to ask about the state of Cinder. How many refugees remain?"

They took the stairs as she answered, "None. With Sagan's help over these last few months, we evacuated the remaining Icari to Earth. Of course, we couldn't let the Tritans know. They think we finished before Imminent took Rayne."

"So we completed that mission at least. How are they integrating?"

Tempest nodded, as if approving his questions. "Well. They're doing well. Especially once the nacres disseminated on a global scale—Which I know is not everyone's favorite subject, but it's done wonders for relations."

Lynn overheard from the bottom of the stairs and asked, "How many were distributed already?"

Dolor sighed behind her and explained in his boring professor's voice, "Unfortunately, two billion. That's almost the entire population of Earth since Invasion Day."

Both he and Tempest, the two Icari in the room, darted their gazes away. Not everyone liked the reminder that the Icarean invasion wiped out half of the human populace. Andrew checked Dolor's intentions.

I wish so many things were different. For Earth, for the Shadow, and for the Brethren.

Aloud, the tall, slender Icarus asked, "How is Caedes fairing so far from home?"

Lynn answered, "He's Shadow now. He's doing fine—"

"Get in here! There's cheesecake!" Lamassau called from further out of the stairwell. Presumably from the kitchen.

Andrew smiled. How could he not? Especially as he entered the stainless steel paradise and paid witness to the absolute patisserie of a kitchen. Cakes and cookies lined every surface.

Lynn gaped. Legir chuckled in their heads. Tempest said, "We thought to prepare a surprise for you and the rest."

Lam pouted. "Rest? No. This is all for us three, right Lynn?" He nudged her from his compressed height of seven feet.

She laughed. "Don't lump me in with your piracy. This is Shadow fuel. They should all—"

"Hear about the awesome desserts we ate on our own," Andrew interrupted. "I agree." He and Lamassau bumped fists.

"Has anyone found Rayne?"

Cypher, the mood killer.

Now that Andrew thought hard about it, the soldier's fixation on their King was a little odd.

I can't stand the thought of anything happening to her. She can hear in the Martyr Complex. Is she afraid for her life? For ours? That's awful.

Well. It's not anything they weren't all thinking.

Lynn placed a friendly hand on Cypher's shoulder and smiled at Colton, who gazed on in an apron. Lynn said, "This was Rayne's mission. She knows what she's doing. There is no one safer in the galaxy than our War King."

Borrowing her fugitive name for emphasis. Nice.

Some time and at least two cheesecakes later, they gathered in The Brethren's lab. Another world of stainless steel and sterile white-washed walls. Nacres filled the space like the pastries in the kitchen. Tiny pearls of amber glass waiting for examination.

"There must be a hundred thousand," Lynn said, plucking one from a countertop and holding it in her palm. "Have they shown any unusual characteristics?"

Dolor sighed, probably to relieve some tension. "Not yet. Humans are experiencing the predictable benefits of nacre assimilation. Increased stamina, speed, and strength. Nothing outrageous. No overall enhancement to their senses, which was expected. They *can* hold their breath unusually long though."

"But we don't suspect that's part of Imminent's sinister plan." Tempest sounded amused, but looked wrung out. "We'll keep surveillance here and notify the Shadow at the first unusual observation."

Legir, who ran the family business of helping people afflicted by Tritan intervention through their nacres, looked at Lynn. "Are you ready to start?"

"Yeah. We have some space back at the house, too, but I'm afraid these might explode in the Seam or something.

Boys," She glanced between Andrew and Lamassau, "How will you keep busy?"

Andrew knew why he was here. Xelan wanted him to test The Brethren's intentions. Now that he had, and they proved sincere, he didn't have a clue what to do with himself or how to distract from the Probabilities in his mind. He'd have to wait until they return to report, because the radios couldn't span interplanetary communication.

The Chef was muscle. Backup. But fortunately, he knew what to do. "Do you Brethren types have any crawlers here?"

Dolor and Tempest shared a quizzical glance before Dolor said, "Four of the small ones. Why?"

Now Cypher and Colton glanced at one another, both grinning as if they'd figured it out.

"Oh, you know… No reason."

{MONARCH 3}

Kyle didn't like it here inside this ancient tree filled with flowers and grasses. The unbelievable diameter of it made his head spin. He also wasn't sure how he felt about a tree with multiple floors and residences. No cool rope bridges and ladders. No highly flammable thatch huts in the branches—where even were the branches? How big were they? How high were they from Mon3's "ground" if there was one—

"Breathe, Progeny," Iuo muttered beside him. The snake man looked equally itchy in this environment. "A day—maybe two—is all we'll need in here."

Tumu shuffled through the grass to add, "Tree caissons cause a sickness that often affects the claustrophobic this way. For as vast and mighty a tree this is, you're still inside it."

"The opposite sensation to agoraphobia," Xelan contributed his two cents. "You'll get used to it within the hour."

Pablo offered, "I have some anxiety and motion sickness remedies. If you'd like?"

The powerful aroma of flowers—akin to lilies and roses—hit Kyle like a truck, dizzying him. "Yeah. Please."

"I'll take some," luo got in line. The snake man's muscles rolled unsteadily with him as he walked in bipedal form across the spongy "ground." Kyle sympathized.

Tameka gawked at the ceiling—wherever it was. "It's beautiful."

Kyle chuffed. Sure, and the resulting vertigo nearly killed him.

Sagan and Korac went through the conduit last, discretely opened and closed far from civilization. Everyone wore a hood or wrap to hide their pricey features. Kyle borrowed a gray one from Devis which matched his favorite carbon fiber jumpsuit. Tameka wrapped her hair back in a yellow bandanna that looked autumnal with her red cropped jacket and black tactical pants. Xelan and Korac both braided their hair back to make it shorter. With opaque black goggles, Wingmaster got by. But not Korac. That conspicuous son of a bitch hid his white hair under the hood of his expensive custom-made combat coat. Pablo wasn't a named fugitive, but he didn't want to stand out, so he borrowed a fedora from Korac. It just needed a feather in it. Tumu wore—gasp—Tritan robes over his compression suit. Hard to hide an alien that couldn't compress less than seven feet. No one owned clothes big enough to disguise him. The Seamswalker built a hood into her tunic top that fell to the knees of her leggings.

Gazing out at the place with her eyes hidden behind blue-tinted glasses, Sagan asked, "Is this like the one from Nox's Verse? With the hive?"

Xelan glanced at her and spared a look for Korac who answered, "It's the very same." He pointed further into the tree. "The lights on the horizon are where the hive was."

"Now it's the Queen's Fare. A hideout Razor established not long after Umbra tried to kill the queen." Xelan waved for them to start walking, with Tameka at his side.

Kyle loved when the group ruminated aloud about the celebrity Verses. It totally didn't make him think about Silence and her place in all this. He clicked his tongue and kicked a rock.

"Hey, that queen survived, right? Is she still around?" Sagan asked perfectly reasonable questions.

Tameka asked better ones. "What were you doing around that time, Tumu?"

Korac crooked a brow at the Tritan. Iuo and Xelan went over some aspect of entering the "establishment," leaving Tumu to fend for himself.

Curious, Kyle almost peeked into Tumu's memory, but there wasn't a way without alerting him to the invasion. The last time Kyle tried to plunder that treasure trove, it led to a stern sit down and talking to with Kyle apologizing to Lamassau in the end.

Tritan memories were off limits.

"Well, first. She did survive, and she still rules somewhere on this planet. Second, I was already demoted to Eminent and assigned the case of Gait's missing children. May I answer anymore of your intrusive questions?" Tritans applied sarcasm extra thick to their deep voices, leaving little room for more teasing.

Pablo was undeterred, much to Kyle's amusement. "Now that you ask, can I get a physiology lesson when we return? I need to understand the location of your major organs and blood vessels. You know? For science."

Xelan, still walking ahead of them, barked out a laugh without turning back.

Tumu sighed, incredulous.

Iuo patted the big man on the back. "Be grateful they know you're one of the good ones, Tumu."

Korac changed the subject. "Speaking of vital points, how confident are we that they don't frisk for weapons here?"

The Lamia said, "They never checked me, but I'm prince charming."

Kyle made a disgusted sound. "You're the Porn Baron. The only weapons they think you'd carry are bedroom toys."

Sagan snickered. Tameka rolled her eyes and clicked her tongue.

They walked the rest of the way in silence. The crowd grew thicker as they drew closer to the wooden carving of what Kyle suspected was a hive. No bouncer at the front, and the place was packed. People from all across the Vast Collective—Caprents, Luks, Dwarves, Icari, Lamias, and drones. No queens, though.

Kyle frowned and asked, "Why don't we ever see Mon3 queens outside?"

Iuo volunteered, "They're busy sustaining the hive."

The crowd migrated between the bar, restaurant, and dance floor. Lounged in pairs or larger groups. The polished wood surfaces reflected surrounding faces like mirrors.

Classy.

Xelan ordered, "Split up. Blend in. Remember, we think the factory is beneath, but we aren't sure how to access it. Speak into the earpieces if you get a bite."

Everyone followed, dividing into smaller chunks. Pablo went with Tumu. The couples opted to stick together. Tameka and Xelan. Korac and Sagan. That left Kyle with Iuo. They fist bumped. The A-Team.

Opting for the burlesque show in the back of the establishment, they both got some drinks and sat in the thick of the crowd. The ladies on stage danced with their elbows and knees bent backward. Pasties and transparent skirts. It was… eye-opening.

After about five minutes of it, Kyle tugged his ear at Iuo, who discretely scanned the crowd.

Go time.

Kyle opened his ability and brushed the people nearest him with it. Memories carried a flavor that he tested. Tasted. Bounty hunters to their right. Closer to the stage were some mercenaries. Icari in the back, they—

He grit his teeth and clenched his fists.

"What's wrong?" Iuo whispered into his earpiece.

It was hard to share information on serial rapists in the middle of a show without someone picking up on it.

Kyle shook his head and promised himself to kill the shit out of them before leaving.

Another cluster of peeps hid on the balcony. When he scanned their memories, Kyle smiled. "Got us some contenders."

Iuo nodded upward. "The three drones?"

"Oh, yeah. They're who we're looking for. No doubt." As he stared into the hive plant hidden in their memories, Kyle spoke into the Shadow channel. "We got some bites, and some vermin that need exterminating."

Without irony, but probably with a grin, Xelan responded, "I got you."

{PIL}

Ross' head hadn't hurt this much since she and Kyle scanned all the memory drives Tumu brought back from Razor's Emporium. The vein pounding along her temple felt close to exploding. And why shouldn't it? She'd only scanned a million people since arriving at the promenade on Pil.

All their memories returned to the same image. A sixty-five foot Tritan stomping along their homes and businesses.

But their words said something different.

"Rayne."

"The War King and her accomplice, Primary Tumu."

"That damned Progeny woman escaped her box and destroyed our people."

All of them liars.

Ross frowned, on the brink of tears. Hot, frustrated tears. She caught Devis across the main thoroughfare. He shook his head in disbelief. Both of them knew better.

She muttered, "This is exhausting."

X shrugged beside her and whispered, "They're frightened."

Twenty-One stood behind them, taking the role of bodyguard literally. "They make a mockery of King Rayne's sacrifice."

"King Rayne makes a mockery of her own sacrifice, saving the likes of Cinder after what they did to Earth." Miy was a ray of sunshine.

Even X glared at her.

Ross was all too happy Jack accompanied Devis and didn't hear that blasphemy.

The Lyrik blew the air from her cheeks and crossed her arms in indignation. "They don't want our help here, big surprise, but they'll easily take Jack's head. We should leave while we can—"

"Help! Help! My husband is alive under here!" a Dwarf cried into the streets.

Ross and Twenty-One shared the same smug look for Miy as they all lugged over to the lady. Hopefully, they wouldn't need Jack's strength. Ross asked the big Icarus, "Can you do this?"

"I can try, my lady." Twenty-One climbed further down into the building, avoiding debris and structurally unsafe scaffolding. He called out, "I see him."

"Help me!"

Ross called down, "We're coming, sir. Twenty-One, can I help?"

Miy clicked her tongue. "Better not try. What're the odds it'll hold both you and him steadily?"

X whispered, "Twenty-One has him, Ross. Look!"

They all gazed down into the basement, where the mighty Icarus hauled the injured man on his back. "Go, Twenty-One! You're my hero!" Ross cheered and met Miy's rolling eyes by sticking out her tongue.

Twenty-One brought the man to the basement's entrance and laid him inside a safer zone in the building. The man's wife fell to her knees beside him. With tears in her eyes, she said, "Thank you! Thank you!"

"I'll grab a doctor." Ross turned and rushed to one of the rescue stands Jack helped organize. Two doctors were treating survivors and pointed her to a stretcher. She was halfway back to the others when a sight stopped her dead in the street.

Para.

In a carbon fiber jumpsuit, the smallest Valkyrie almost looked inconspicuous, but the way she stood in the middle of the street implied menace, a challenge. That was before her eyes went Atramentous, and her black wings opened.

"Jack! Miy! Do you see this?"

The others spilled into the street, which emptied fast.

It was Para's voice that spoke, but not her words. "You Progeny work fast, but do you really think you can sway the people from those heavy rewards?" Louder, she announced to the onlookers, "That is Jack, King Regent of Earth, the War King's brother. And that's Ross, Story Taker's sister. The Tribunal would reward such leads to the bounties on their siblings' heads."

Murmurs throughout the crowd made Ross uncomfortable in her own skin. Desperate, she reached into Para's skull and scraped for anything—

Walking around Enki naked. A lab with a woman that could only be Celindria. Pain. Shame. Anger.

"Keep your mouth shut, Para. Or I'll force you to watch Karter perform on Abresson again. Will that render your obedience?"

Ross fell to her knees in the debris. Her heart opened and collected the hearts of those around her. That couple barely hanging on. The shop owner down the way who lost his son. Everyone who lost their sons. Daughters. Wives. Mothers. The world. The entirety of Pil spilled into Ross until it rushed together in one beautiful, colorful funnel of memories.

Reverse. Flood. Fill.

Every single memory over the last seventy-two hours washed back into those bystanders Ross lived every moment with. All the loss. All the unity. But most importantly.

Remorse. Primary Rem's sixty-five foot figure crashed into the hundreds of thousands of people that surrounded Pil's once proud promenade. Now not a single one could deny it.

"You'll die if you go on much longer," Devis murmured. Apparently, he held her in his arms. "Let them back to themselves. We need you, Ross."

Finished. Complete. Ross let go.

In a haze, she watched Jack face off with Para. With that leadership voice of his, he announced, "Imminent committed this atrocity. Not my sister. Certainly not us. We're here to help." He picked up a beam that bisected the entryway to a shop. Easily, Jack rested it on his shoulder. "We want to rebuild. That Valkyrie is Primary Rem in control over an innocent woman's body. He only came here to weaken your efforts. If you want us gone, we'll leave. But if you want our help, we have to force him out. Capture her, unharmed."

The crowd pressed in, and that was the last Ross saw before her migraine took her.

FIFTEEN

KNOW I'M BY YOUR SIDE THROUGH IT ALL

{MONARCH 3}

XELAN PACED A CIRCLE AROUND KYLE AND THE THREE UNCONSCIOUS DRONES. They followed the goons into a private VIP corner and disabled their nacres. Tameka drained them unconscious, and Pablo laid them out with heavy sedatives. They all said a prayer or two to Elden.

Milling about a room full of soiled couches, Iuo observed, "That bought us ten minutes at the most before someone discovers us."

Tumu nodded in agreement with the assessment.

Kyle immediately went to work.

Now Xelan paced, sweeping his coat and biting his thumbnail. Tameka spared him a pitying glance that stopped his anxious habit.

"Everything looks fine out here," Sagan said over the earpiece.

Korac insisted on playing lookout from the dance floor with her, and to Xelan's recollection, he'd play the part well. But that was far removed from his mind.

Xelan stared at Tameka. Her frown. For the last five minutes of the memory walk, Tameka was frowning, deep in her thoughts. While Xelan liked the intelligence in her eyes behind it, it still bothered him. "What is it?" He almost included her name, but those weren't safe in public.

Tameka kept the frown as she stared down at Kyle sitting with the unconscious men. "I don't like this."

Tumu agreed. "Me neither."

Iuo shrugged in one muscular movement. "What's to like?"

Pablo glanced between all of them before nodding at Tameka. "I feel it, too."

Xelan knelt and looked into Tameka's sharp eyes. "Tell me."

She bit her lip before saying, "They have nacres. That's suspicious on its own. If they have memories of this mysterious plant... Why would Imminent let them keep those—"

Kyle startled on his return and fell back on his hands. "Joint. Joint. I need a joint."

Pablo shook his head. "No medicinal marijuana in public. You kinda marked the smell as a distinctive trait."

"Fine. Someone buy me a drink then." Kyle held out his hand for help up, and Xelan took it as the young Progeny said, "They work there all right. Huge facility with hundreds of these nasty pulsing things behind a wall of nacre glass. Hidden lifts throughout the place will take us right to it. If we can trust them."

Xelan nodded for Tameka to see.

With little change to her outward appearance, Tameka drained the three drones dead. After a few seconds, Xelan felt recharged and awake at the brush of her power. Tumu and Iuo perked. Pablo's brown eyes sparkled as he checked on Kyle.

Xelan said, "Practical but callous, we stash these bodies and return to recon. I'm with you. I don't like this. One group stays in public while another goes with Sagan to investigate. Understood?"

"I volunteer to stay upstairs with the booze. Iuo, are you with me?" Kyle nudged the Lamian Prince.

Iuo bowed with his head. "Of course."

"Good. You're the only one with any real sway around here. Get me something top shelf," Kyle said while the light evacuated from his forest-green eyes. Just vacuumed off. Story Taker swallowed before saying, "If you could see what was in their heads—the things they've done and the people they've hurt—"

A tear blinked from Kyle's lashes before he shook his head as if ridding himself of the images.

Pablo squeezed his shoulder. "Let's get you a drink, man."

Tameka squeezed his other one, snapping him out of it. Xelan appreciated they worked out their differences over the last few months. He was especially proud of her for learning to let go and forgive. It was good for morale to bolster the greatest strengths in the outfit. Truth be told, there wasn't a single person here who wasn't a strength. Good leaders should always acknowledge that. Despite her impressive ability to hold a grudge, Tameka was learning.

When Kyle reached up and patted her hand, Xelan felt the old wound mend. As the liquor-bound trio left the room, Xelan made sure his respect showed in his smile for Tameka when she turned around.

She returned the expression with warmth in her eyes before looking around and blowing the air from her cheeks. "Right. Bodies."

Xelan, Tumu, and Tameka spent the next ten minutes hiding the drones, each of them quiet in their own thoughts. Mostly, the Prince of Cinder wanted to arrange some group healing time once they finished Phase II. Any more of this constant grind, and they'd drive good soldiers away.

As they hid the bodies behind a maintenance alcove, Tameka remarked, "The construction of this place is seamless. No joints or frames. It's amazing."

Tumu humphed. "Yes. For all that Razor was a monster, he had an affinity for gorgeous architecture."

"It's seamless because it was solid once." As Xelan spoke, the other two turned to him at their work. He elaborated, "Razor programmed nanites to hollow it out—cut it from the wood to create his design. I know because that's how I dug out the stronghold on Earth, among other hideouts."

Tameka's eyes glittered with admiration. "Is there anything you can't do?"

Tumu snorted. "Return a phone call."

Xelan barked out a laugh and tucked Tameka into his side as he got on the earpiece. "We're ready, Seamswalker. Kyle said there was a lift behind the burlesque stage. Do you copy?"

"Aye, aye, Cap'n." Sagan Seamswalked into the VIP room with Korac at her side.

The fair Icarus nodded once to the group. "I can't tell you how honored I am to walk into this trap with you fine fugitives."

It chafed Xelan how much he still appreciated Korac's humor and how easily Xelan fell into it. "You certainly dressed for the occasion."

Tumu chuffed.

Tameka didn't get in the way of the compliment. Instead, she asked Korac, "Is there anything you don't look pretty in?"

"It's quite the curse."

Yes. It was. So Korac's Verse said so. Xelan nearly winced at the thought. Especially as he recalled how many times the Icarean General made the same joking confession over the years. Always embittered. Now Xelan understood why.

Sagan hopped with anticipation, looking exceptionally young in the over-sized tunic. "Ready?"

It made more sense to explore the lower floors, but Sagan understandably struggled with uncharted spaces. Xelan was grateful she recognized the Mon3 tree from her pre-Razor journey across the Vast Collective before the disaster with Gait restricted her travel. Sometime soon, Xelan would chat with her about how she was processing it all.

Entering a room with only the lift, Xelan grinned. "Nice work." He refrained from calling Sagan Planet Breaker. Instead, he ruffled her hood.

Sagan huffed in exasperation and fixed her hair.

Korac hid a smirk at her expense. It was enough to broaden Xelan's grin. When Tameka entered, she raised a brow at the scene until she got the joke with a warm shake of her head.

Tumu was all business. "The lift is unguarded. Not exactly what I imagined when Remorse promised to 'triple security.'"

"This is a trap." Korac ground the words in his teeth.

Tameka sighed with an unenthused, "Yup."

Xelan kept his reservations to himself. They were the Shadow. They had each other. And a nifty Seamswalker to help them escape if anything went wrong.

On high alert, they took the lift down to the uncertain below.

{Earth}

"Hey, I thought you might want a snack."

Lynn turned to find Lamassau in the lab's doorway. The space was empty save for her since Legir went to bed. She was surprised the boys had finished with Battle of the Crawlers so soon. He held a plate of nibbles and a glass of milk. She set down the nacre she examined and smiled for the Tritan.

"Thanks. I'm starving."

That wasn't true. Lynn could still feel the cheesecake in her gut, but maybe she wasn't digesting it well because she needed something with meat.

Lam handed over the provisions, looked around the lab, and blew the air from his cheeks. He asked the obvious question. "Learn anything yet?"

Feeling suddenly heavy, Lynn sat down. "Not one inconsistency so far. Legir's results are the same. I'm better at building weapons against nacres. I think Pablo and Xelan are more suited to find if anything's wrong. We'll need to take all these samples back with us." She took a second to look over the expansive room littered with the amber glass pearls. "It's a big job."

"Worthwhile." Rolling a nacre like a marble, Lamassau continued his explanation. "I told Conscience back when this conversation started, I didn't think it was a good idea to trust Enki-supplied anything."

"He sure did," Andrew called from the door. "Mind if we come in?"

Lynn smiled at her boys. "By all means." Then she noticed the frown on Andrew's face. "What is it?"

Cypher and Colton followed with similar expressions. Colton's heavy dreads swayed down to his waist, and he recently added some more muscle to his already considerable bulk, preparing. "Sorry to bother you, Chief." That was probably the most words she heard from him in a single conversation.

"But we need to show you something." The hazel-eyed soldier, Cypher, still passed as a blond frat boy. He plugged a drive into one of the lab's many terminals.

Lynn checked their grim faces before settling to watch the footage on the screen. It was of the Iona Arsenal's observation room outside the Faraday Cage. The day the detainees and Inanis copies attacked. There was Lynn, John, and Caedes carrying Devis out. Smith volunteered to stay behind and guard the...

"No."

Was all Lynn managed to say before T.A.O. appeared further down the corridor, followed by Celindria and an entire horde of black-clad operatives.

Smith let them right inside the secret weapon room.

Lynn was oblivious to her tears until they scalded her cheeks. Her voice sounded detached from her as she said, "That son of a bitch." His betrayal continued to masticate her already raw wound.

Andrew, the only other person she knew who understood, placed a gentle hand on her back. "What did they take from there?"

Cypher looked expectantly at her. Colton was generous enough to keep his lids low. Lamassau narrowed his eyes at the screen, watching as operative after operative transported the weapon from the most secure facility in the Shadow.

Lynn swallowed a dry lump of heartache before answering, "The colossal Tantamount."

Andrew cursed. Cypher's eyes doubled in size. Colton shook his head.

Lamassau shrugged. "Well, I guess it's a good thing they detonated it yesterday on L. Capra—"

"No." Elden, this hurt Lynn to say. "That wasn't the colossal. That was a regular Tantamount. This one is a hundred times more catastrophic—a hundred thousand if placed on a tectonic singularity. Nox meant to use it on the Yellowstone caldera, on the North American continental divide. Earth was facing volcanic winter if we'd lost on Volcano Day."

Pausing the footage, Andrew asked, "Do we have any idea where they might use it?"

Lynn dragged a hand down her face and shook her head, bewildered and horrified all at once. "For all I know, they may stick with Nox's original plan. To force us out. That's a smart strategy. But so many other planets are tectonically unstable. They could use it on any of them."

"Then we'll need to prepare," Tempest said, entering the lab from the hall.

Dolor followed behind her. "We'll spread the word to monitor any volatile sites. They won't get the chance to use it here."

Cypher asked a scary question. "Do you know if there's any way to diffuse it?"

Lynn certainly did, and she still relived nightmares of that day.

Wasting no time, Lynn ran to the Tantamount's lift.

Bones called out to her, "You don't need to do this."

"Yes, I do. I won't let him do this alone. He'll die." She reached to hail the elevator when it suddenly whirred from below. "What's happening? Is he down there?"

Bones' tone went from somber to impatient. "That's what I was trying to tell you—" Caedes put his hand on Bones' shoulder to stay the warrior.

Pablo stood inside the lift. "Hey."

She punched him in the shoulder, and he cried out. "Fuck! You're strong." He grinned at her sheepishly as he rubbed the site.

Her voice cracked on a sob. "I thought you were planning on dying like some hero without me."

Bones confirmed, "He was."

Lynn punched him again, half-heartedly.

"Ouch. Baby, I'm all right."

"Blood. It's always blood. A good deal of it, if I recall correctly. Where the sacrifice of nacre energy arms the weapon, blood signals the machine to abort." Lynn felt haunted by her mistake of trusting Smith. Haunted by her lineage of poor decision-makers. Were her parents blind cultists CoN members in every Probability? Or was there one out there where she wasn't condemned with trust issues?

Lamassau picked up the snacks he brought her and started to eat. "Well," he began while smacking, "Chief of Weapon's Engineer, what's our prognosis?"

Without another moment's hesitation, Lynn took out the envelope in her pocket and handed it over to Tempest. "Will you give this letter to Pablo's mother?"

The woman's eyes widened before she bowed with her head. "I'll ensure she receives it." She left the room, presumably to deliver it.

Dolor stayed, glancing over Lynn and Legir's failed research into the nacres. Cypher ejected the drive. Colton went to work on researching possible Tantamount locations. Lamassau finished eating the food he'd brought her.

It was Andrew that checked Lynn back into reality. "We'll solve it. We always do."

If Lynn was haunted, then that made Andrew another house full of ghosts. She took his hand and asked, "How do you manage?"

He squeezed back with a vacancy dulling his eyes. "Sarcasm and cheesecake. You know... like a *Golden Girl*."

Laughter escaped Lynn, unexpected and full. And why not? This family was held together by nacre, and that sufficed for now.

Fuck Smith.

Fuck the Tantamount.

And fuck Imminent.

"Yo, Colton? Is there any cheesecake left?"

{REIPON}

Pehton scoured the trim surrounding the foyer's third-floor window. No sign of Imminent. What a strange calling card, to carve their name into the windows of a building they'd infiltrated. Was it meant to represent something or simply announce their sinister presence? Why leave one at all?

It gave Pehton the chills.

The emptiness of the house didn't help. With only Pax, Bones, and Caedes playing on the first floor and the Lyriks outside, the rest of the estate was so quiet.

Damn.

She grew accustomed to the comforting noises of others living and being around her. Sagan and Korac's constant kissing. Ross and Jack's unbeatable optimism. Andrew, Kyle, Lamassau, and luo's play. The warmth of Pablo and Lynn's pure love. Gossiping Lyriks. Devis and Twenty-One's hilarious culture shock. Tameka and Xelan tip-toeing around the awkward tension in their relationship—well, at least that ended recently. Congrats to the couple. Life was too short not to enjoy a partner's company.

There was that subject again.

Pehton ran fingers through her feathers in frustration. Blowing the air from her cheeks, she moved on to the next window. She carried on this way—on autopilot—for the entire third floor. Negative of Imminent's presence.

The need for air hit her, and Pehton welcomed it on the wraparound veranda. Below, the Lyriks meditated in the garden. It was part of their required rehabilitation regimen that Xelan helped Pehton establish. And it was working. They looked centered and peaceful. Even Miy, who initially fought tooth and feather against it, looked less begrudging of the ritual when she wasn't busy with the Shadow.

Before Jack's team left for Pil, Pehton had noticed Miy was frowning. She figured Miy should be glowing after spending a quarter night with Caedes—

No.

Stop going there.

Caedes wasn't Pehton's. She made it perfectly clear she wasn't ready yet.

Quiet settled over her thoughts. Salty air breezed through her feathers as reedy as the truth—Pehton sought this drama as a distraction from her children. Their empty faces haunted her dreams, so she refused to sleep. The exhaustion compromised her. She needed...

Elden, what could distract her from what mattered most but wasn't so outside her reach?

"I've been looking for you."

Pehton whirled from the scenic oceanside garden to find Caedes standing in the door to the foyer. He dressed the closest to casual he ever went in a long-sleeved black shirt and tactical pants. Some combat boots, because what other shoes could he possibly own? The relaxed but "at the ready" look worked terrifically for him—

How long did Pehton stare at Caedes without responding? Or blinking? What had he said—Oh...

"Why?"

There, that was intelligible. Pehton even softened her initial frown at his arrival to avoid sounding rude. Although things were complicated between them, she'd prefer they stayed cordial. Because, dammit, Pehton needed more friends than Korac and Sagan.

Gravel rocked around in Caedes' voice as he asked, "First, am I intruding?" He nodded beyond at the view of the Lyriks in a stretching pose.

"No. I'm—You're fine." Yes. He was.

As if he heard her thoughts, Caedes reached both hands for the top of the door frame and leaned into the opening, making for an enticing picture. He should go into modeling, and Pehton rarely thought that about men who kept their heads shaved. Eventually, she stopped focusing on how he looked and listened to what he was saying.

"I wanted to get this out of the way instead of putting it off until things grow tense. Like at the Phase II meeting—"

Pehton concealed a wince.

"—Words aren't really my preferred way of communicating. I like fists and knives, as you might have noticed. With that in mind, I like the way we talk—You and I. Words or punches, I enjoy spending time with you. Miy said you were always rather solitary, which I commiserate—"

"Miy said? You... you talked about me?" Dizzy or nauseous or both, Pehton couldn't decide, but her head was spinning for sure. Gut punched. That's how she felt. She gripped the railing to compose herself.

Caedes talked through her episode. "We talked all night. I'd mentioned to you she needed the distraction from Oleen's death."

Mid-panic attack, Pehton let Caedes' words seep in and frowned. All night? "Uhm. You mean... Did you two not... ?" Hope made her dizzy for a different reason.

"We talked, Pehton."

She liked the way Caedes said her name with his rough voice. Stunned, she licked her lips before saying, "I... I assumed..."

Although the Icarus rarely smiled, when Caedes did it suited him right to the spark in his dark green eyes. "I know what you assumed. Miy and I aren't compatible that way. That's one thing we learned in our talk."

"Compatible?" Pehton tried the word in her mouth. It seemed like such a strange choice. How could two physically fit and mature beings be incompatible for casual sex? Especially after expressing interest in one another.

Caedes cleared his throat into his fist before elaborating with… was he blushing? "Well, we're both bottoms."

Oh.

Pehton's eyes widened.

Ohhhh. "No way!"

Almost shyly, Caedes nodded.

"But… you're so… I mean…"

Caedes laughed, and it was a rich and masculine sound. All too uncommon. "I appreciate the compliment. But no. That's why I like redheads. You're all so bossy. The shorter, the feistier. And Pehton, you're the shortest redhead I've ever met."

Pehton opened her mouth. Closed it. Truly, at a loss for words, which was funny given her company. As if he met his own limit, Caedes let go of the door and closed the distance between them. His proximity was comfortable to her after all their intimate training sessions. Suddenly, it made sense why he wanted to keep them in the room as he reached out and cupped the nape of her neck, leaned down—

And stopped.

A hairbreadth from kissing her, Caedes whispered against Pehton's lips, "Tell me what to do."

Pehton's heart pounded against her chest, and she had to admit—this was properly diverting. Letting go of the weight that chained her, she breathed, "Kiss me."

Normally, when she kissed men this tall, Pehton reached for them on her tiptoes. But not Caedes. She let him come to her. She was the boss, after all.

Practically preening, Pehton felt exhilarated by this new power until Caedes kept leaning forward and collapsed on his face without kissing her.

"What the fuck? Caedes, are you all right?!"

Pehton went to check on him when the ground switched places with the sky as she fell on top of Caedes' solid build before her vision went black.

{REIPON}

Bones regained consciousness with one hell of a hangover. Elden, he couldn't remember the last time he felt this much like a steaming pile of Hellkite droppings.

One minute, he was teaching Pax poker in their fort, the next...

How did Bones even get outside? And why were all the Lyriks unconscious, too?

He hopped on his feet despite the fatigue begging him to stay down. This was high alert time. Clearly, something went down.

Check the rest of the people in the house, including Bethany and Triss.

Search for Imminent carvings.

Foremost, find Pax.

"Pax? Kiddo, where are you?"

Bones neglected the unconscious Lyriks to run back into the lounge, where he found the most epic fort ever built standing empty. Again, he called, trying to keep the edge of panic from his voice, "Pax? Answer Uncle Bones, please!"

No response.

No.

No. No. No.

This felt all wrong.

"Pax?"

Bones searched all the rooms on the first floor, calling for the toddler. On the second floor, he found Bethany passed out at her desk. Triss was still breathing steady in a coma with perfect vitals. Or as perfect as Pablo said to expect with how much pain she was enduring.

Second floor clear.

This was bad.

Third floor found only Pehton and Caedes in a somewhat compromising position. The gruff Icarus was already stirring by the time Bones discovered them. "Hey, man. Wake up and help me find Pax. Now."

That got the bald Icarus on his feet. They all seemed equally exhausted. It was familiar.

Gently, Caedes lifted Pehton and laid her out on a patio chaise. It was cute, but neither here nor there. When the bald Icarus turned to Bones, he already knew.

Damn it, Bones knew what the other man would ask.

Please no.

"Have you checked the windows?"

Fuck.

Bones avoided them because this couldn't be it. This... this wasn't happening.

Swallowing, he clung to faith—faith in the Shadow, in the Icarean Prerogative, and faith in Elden—that the windows would be clear. With all that in his heart, Bones checked the nearest window.

IMMINENT.

"No." All the "no's" that were in Bones' insides came onto the outside. "No. No. They took him. They fucking took Pax."

Caedes checked all the windows in this room—this floor. With each one he checked, his face grew more grim.

Meanwhile, Pehton roused with a groan. "What... what happened?"

Bones knelt to check on her and tried to think of the best way to break it to her. "Somehow it's worst-case scenario without it being the worst-case scenario. No one's dead this time. But..."

Pehton gripped his wrist. "But. What?"

Caedes returned to the veranda. "Imminent was here, and Pax is missing."

Hearing it said that way, drained the blood right of Bones and almost laid him low again.

Pehton paled, too, and swallowed hard before asking, "How... how were we all unconscious? We were... We...

" She looked at Caedes and revealed the nature of their prior conversation with only the look in her eyes.

Good for them, but again, neither here nor there.

"The house is compromised. We have to evacuate. We have to—" Bones stopped panicking as the nightmare peaked. He breathed, "I'll have to tell Tameka and Xelan."

Caedes frowned.

Pehton gave Bones a pitying look.

Bones wiped a shaking hand down his mouth. "I'll have to tell them I lost their son to Imminent." He'd rather the sadistic fuckers had killed him than leave him to this fate worse than death.

{MONARCH 3}

"I can't believe... Look at all of them."

If Tameka's eyes grew any wider, tears would spill from them. Xelan's mouth was agape as he tentatively touched the nacre glass barrier, as if afraid it might shatter. Korac took in the horrific view with an icy glare. Angry but not surprised. Unlike Tumu, who lost some of the depth in his blue complexion.

Aghast, Sagan cupped a hand over her mouth. Her muffled voice trembled when she said, "Hundreds. Thousands. Do they even know what life is like outside that cage?"

"In fact, they don't."

They whirled on that deep feminine voice in fear, in trepidation, and in hope, of all things.

Karter, T.A.O., Chris, and Abresson spanned the corridor behind them. Each of them in combat gear. Because of Korac's Verse, Tameka glanced between Karter and Korac, checking the resemblance. His proud carriage was all they shared in common, loaning credence to Triss' insistence that Aegis genes were dominant.

Their expressions certainly weren't similar. Karter, or whoever controlled her, looked patient and calculating.

Korac went straight to his frosty Atramentous and clenched that angular jaw of his so tight it made hollows of his cheeks.

Tameka wasted no time and warned the others. "A-Team, we've got contact down here. Red alert. Over."

Celindria as T.A.O. gave a single nod. Karter and Abresson disappeared.

With so much calm that he impressed Tameka, Tumu observed, "Still failed to perfect Seamswalking without a Seamswalker, Celindria? Still limited in range?"

T.A.O.'s eyes moved to assess Tumu almost unnaturally. She tilted her head to the side. Listening.

Tameka and Sagan exchanged a look, ready to pounce, when the woman reanimated so suddenly that their entire company startled.

Xelan shook himself and took a step forward. "Celindria, please. Release T.A.O. to her own volition. She doesn't deserve this."

Again, with that avian and robotic nature, the small damaged woman said, "What about what I deserve, father?!"

Korac swept back his coat to reveal those signature dual axes of his and two nacre disabling rifles.

One of which, Tameka snatched and aimed happily at T.A.O. It frustrated her that Xelan insisted on reasoning with the crazy woman when the rifles would take her down. In theory, T.A.O. would wake with her volition restored. A little Tritan blood from Tumu would see her nacre operational again in minutes.

So why this melodrama? Elden, Tameka trusted Xelan too much to shove him out of the way and shoot T.A.O. against his orders. There was a reason. She believed it. In the meantime...

A tremor possessed Xelan's entire body. He was ahead of her, so Tameka couldn't see his face—couldn't fathom his emotions. But even as he trembled, he compelled Celindria, "I know you were wronged. Don't you think it's time to stop punishing the world for my mistake?"

What. Mistake. Was. That.

Celindria made T.A.O. sneer, but the stilted action of it added true menace to the smile. "There are so many worlds and you love each one. Even now, you suffer without realizing it. Finding this place amounts to nothing. Even a Seamswalker cannot breach it. All you've done—all you ever do—is invite misery onto yourself. Stand aside. Cease this pointless crusade, and we will consider returning what you lost this day. When we finish with it, of course."

Sagan held out a hand, and Korac passed her an ax with a warmth Tameka could only describe as pleasure. Everyone relished a chance to take Celindria out. Tumu looked more cautious and concentrated on Xelan.

Tameka took a risk and stepped up to his side, finding him frozen in shock. Unnerved, Tameka asked, "What, Xelan? Do you know what she took—"

"Hey, B-Team, we got a problem." Over the earpieces, Pablo sounded frightened. "Abresson just blew our cover in the middle of this bar." At least he was proportionately frightened.

Tameka tried to reach him again. "Xelan, what did she take?"

T.A.O. answered, "I *wanted* to take you."

Glaring over the rifle's barrel, Tameka shrugged. "Too bad." Wait. That was the answer, wasn't it? If Celindria couldn't have Tameka—

"Tameka . . ." Xelan turned to her as a horrifying reality dawned. He gripped her shoulders. "Be strong. Don't shoot. We don't know where she took him. If you free T.A.O. now we may never get him back."

"Him."

Even as Tameka spoke the word, it sounded removed from her. Lost in the vacuum that opened in the room. It *was* a trap, but not for them.

"Wingmaster—" Korac growled. "I detest that you make us call you that. What're your orders?"

Before he answered, Kyle came over the earpiece. "We are sincerely fucked here. Karter and Chris are about to kill us. Sagan, help!"

They continued to ask Xelan for orders, but Tameka focused on his eyes and tuned everything out. Those black eyes with a midnight blue ring. They sparkled when he smiled and glistened when he cried. So sweet in their son's little face—

So many nacres.

So much energy.

Tameka knew she'd slipped into Atramentous when she fell to her knees and her wings opened. How much Pax would delight in that.

This was all too much...

When the well opened and siphoned those sources of energy, T.A.O. wasted no time and vanished. Tameka stayed on her knees and filled.

Filled.

And filled.

The forty drones waiting for orders down the hall, and the thirty-two scientists beyond. Lamian princes and rich Luks on the dance floor. The seventeen people in the burlesque lounge—five Caprents, eight Dwarves, and four Tritans. The thirty people at the bar surrounding Kyle, Pablo, and Iuo. Male, female—it didn't matter. All of their nacre energy filled into Tameka.

Only the Shadow remained untouched. She stole the life of every creature in the Queen's Fare until she was close to bursting with it.

"Tameka?" Xelan's warmth. It was almost too much for her. "Tameka, what will you do with all that?"

The sun? No. Not the sun.

They took Pax.

Death was all they deserved. But how?

All the energy in Tameka swelled, gorged, and waited. Alive to the point of burning, she funneled the energy through the same channel she stole it from. Fed them, at first, with their own power. But, again, it was too much . . .

All of it.

Even the sun.

All nacres—aside from the Shadow—Tameka filled that amber glass to shattering. Including the walls beside them. All the walls around the gas farm blasted open. "Unbreakable" no more.

Around Tameka, people talked, but she could barely hear.

Xelan was closest to her. "She's in shock."

Sagan sounded breathless. "I got the others. You won't believe it. All those people upstairs . . . I think they're dead."

Concern filled Korac's voice. "Karter and Chris?"

Iuo sighed with relief. "T.A.O. fetched them first. As if Celindria knew."

Xelan fell to his knees in front of Tameka and took both her hands. Softly, he said, "Come back to me. Please."

All the energy swirled inside her. None of it touched the pain of returning to the house to find Pax gone. To moving everyone to another location because Imminent compromised the home they'd made. Pablo's infirmary. Sagan's nursery.

Pax.

Tears spilled down Tameka's face and evaporated. The power burned so brightly—

"Thank you for confirming my hypothesis."

They all faced the unwelcome voice.

Celindria returned T.A.O. to the corridor. The fearless woman inspected the broken glass wall. Contemplatively, not at all concerned, T.A.O. said, "Yes. This will do. Surely the son is as strong, if not stronger. That's exactly what Mother needs."

Xelan lunged at her, but T.A.O. Seamswalked back, shaking her finger mockingly.

Tameka found the strength for words. The strength to plead, "Take me, Celindria. Give him back and take me."

"You're far too volatile. No, he's pliable and my blood, after all. My little brother." That demon gave one stony glare at Xelan before praising Tameka, "This demonstration here proved exactly what I suspected of your ability."

Frustrated, Tameka shouted, "What's that?! What could be worth stealing a child?!"

"You're the key to Ishkur."

Those unconnected words that meant nothing to Tameka brought more tears. Tears of frustration. Tears of fear. In her pain, Tameka swore, "I *will* end everything you stand for."

"You will try."

Merciless in her victory, Celindria Seamswalked away.

AN EPILOGUE TO STARVE

{CINDER | NEAR 150,000,000 YEARS AGO}

ONLY QUET CAME.

"You misunderstand me, Surra." Quet patronized to his Project from his full height of seventy-five feet. He liked to get tall when he talked down to her. "Your purpose is noble and lauded."

A breeze of orange blossoms filled Surra's hair and feathers. Outside. The world deprived to her for an eon. An eon working to form beautiful beings such as the several million behind her. No longer angry, only cold, Surra said, "You abused me. Took them from me. I never held… Not a single one. Can you not see the wrong you committed against me? Leave me in peace."

Quet reached out, beseeching her, "Girl, we have yet to finish. You are the only beacon of hope for Tritan civilization. Primary Rem threatened my life if I returned without you."

Of course he did. She was their simple solution.

Surra felt the tension of those holding the line behind her with a beastly hunger and a mind half as complicated. This conversation already went on too long. "Father, this is between you and me. Leave the Tritans on their borrowed continent in Enki."

As if this were a positive, Quet announced, "We plan to claim Ishkur soon, if we ever find it. You can continue your work there. Now. Come home."

Ishkur?

When her nameless companion touched her arm, Surra regained focus. She said, "No."

"Why? At home, you represent the salvation of our species. Here… What are you to these animals?"

Animals. He called them… animals.

Probabilities, the instances, they flashed through her mind. Filtered her vision until Surra saw only through the potential worlds and instances they promised. And in this instance, they always promised the same outcome.

Wrath, hot and consuming, burned through Surra. She let Quet see it in her eyes, and in a voice of six pitches, she declared, "I am Imminent."

Her nameless companion—her General—signaled the troops, and they swarmed. At first, Quet looked amused, but as the numbers continued to roll over the hill's crest, his eyes widened and he turned for the conduit. Surra flew over to distract him and almost laughed.

Busy fidgeting with his suit, Quet failed to compress so he could fit inside the conduit. All conduit maximum height capacity was only sixty-five feet. Again. And Again. In his panic, he turned horrified voids to Surra and screamed.

Now she laughed.

Even as the horde swarmed his feet and sunk their teeth to devour his Gargantuan form, Surra cackled. Laughed for all the mega-years of her life spent in stirrups, pregnant. Laughed for all the times she begged to have a short decade to herself and explore the worlds she helped create. All the times he said "no."

Quet was long dead when the tears stopped pouring. Now was the time to act. Before the others claimed it, Surra led her nameless companion to Quet's nacre, deep inside his massive carcass.

Surra gestured at her mouth. "This. Eat it."

The language-less man swallowed her father's nacre. He no longer needed her aid to understand the universe.

Elden, so named, spoke his first words. "Surra is Imminent."

{Enki | Now}

"Sissy!"

Pax had played in Silence's arms until Celindria entered Remorse's sanctum. Now he wriggled for release, and she let him go to her. The boy jumped into the "smiling" woman's outstretched arms. "Smiling" because none of Celindria's expressions were natural to her face.

"You did excellent, little brother."

The complicated web of relations in the room was enough to boggle Silence's mind. Lucas referred to it as a "catastrophic genetic tangle." That worked. He watched, standing at attention, beside Smith at the conduit. They were here for the big ceremony.

Silence wanted to scream.

Remorse approached his grandson with an outstretched hand, and the boy shrunk away to hide against Celindria's dress. Silence noted his good instincts, and observed the rigid movement of Celindria's face as she soothed, "Shh. It's fine. No hand will lie upon you that is against your consent."

A lost look crossed Remorse's face—genuine—but vanished in an instant. "Are we prepared to witness?"

Pax tugged on the First Progeny's sleeve. "Where's Uncle Nock?"

To Silence's surprise, Celindria's face fell. That was the first authentic emotion from her since Silence arrived. Celindria answered, "He's not coming, my dear. I'm sorry. I know how much you'll miss him." At the last, she glared at Remorse.

In a single day, Imminent suffered two blows. Razor's defeat and Xelan's resurrection. The latter perplexed the group. In all Probabilities before this one, Nox was inside the casket under the prison. And in all those Probabilities,

Silence would witness the rise of Imminent's greatest soldier. Her grandson, now dead at the hands of a twenty-year-old Earth girl. Until now.

Lucas spared Silence a glance, and Smith winked at her.

The Earth girl that represented hope for them all.

In the wake of Razor's demise, Silence noted Remorse's extreme apathy to the mixup. After reading how terribly he'd treated Nox, Silence wasn't surprised when the Tritan shrugged off Celindria's scorn. "I wasn't aware Nox kept Xelan's birth nacre. I'm not to blame for this."

Pax looked away from him and beseeched Celindria with those beautiful eyes. "Who will be here with you, sissy? Daddy?"

Celindria brushed a tendril of his hair behind his ear. "That's entirely up to you. If you choose me, I'll shape you into Imminent's finest leader. If you choose your father, I'll never awaken you to the Probability Matrix. Say the word, and Auntie T.A.O. will return you to your parents."

Silence wanted little in this world. Ishkur, Kyle, and for Pax to say "no."

In a guise of agency, Celindria set him down to make his choice. The toddler glanced at every face in the room before staring up at Silence for a long moment. Could he sense her reticence for him? She hoped so—

Pax turned and crossed the columned temple to the cascade of black flames. Remorse smiled like a proud grandpa that stole the privilege from Silence's unconscious daughter. Celindria's eyes widened with what Silence imagined was delight, but nothing was in them. Lucas and Smith both watched on with a professional detachment that looked forced.

Once more, Silence wanted to scream.

But doing so endangered Ishkur. Endangered the Vast Collective.

Duty-bound, Silence watched on in horror as Pax reached out and touched Cascading Light.

Celindria muttered, "As always."

Remorse's voice was thick with pride. "He is Imminent."

For Pax, for Xelan, and for Savis—Gripping Pax's chain, Silence vowed to make this right.

Even if it killed her.

THE VAST COLLECTIVE CHRONOLOGY

7M BCE	Enki Terminates Li, Elden's Sacrifice, Umbra Seizes Control of Cinder, Nox is born
3M BCE	Xelan is born, Nox becomes a weapon
2M BCE	Gait's children disappear, Korac joins Cinder's royal family
1.7M BCE	Umbra invades Lacceirus Capra
1M BCE	Umbra invades Monarch 3
500K BCE	Valkyries & Lyriks Revolt
250K BCE	Savis & Umbra pass into eternity, Nox becomes King of Cinder
6K BCE	First Icarean invasion of Earth, Nox invades Thailea, Xelan creates the Progeny
5.5K BCE	Celindria's uprising, Disbursement of Progeny lines, Formation of The Brethren, The Vacating
100 CE	Celindria 'dies' in Thailea incident
400 CE	Razor introduces Nox to Cascading Light, Xelan is banished to Earth, Nox & Korac plan their next invasion of Earth
1987 JAN	Tameka Phillips is born, Xelan builds Iona-oo
1993 May	Xelan saves Rayne Callahan from a fateful car accident
2002 SEP:	Xelan trains the Progeny, Icari commence 'soft' invasion of Earth
2006 APR	Full-Scale Invasion Day
2006 AUG	Volcano Day Battle
2008 JUL	Gait's destruction

AUTHOR'S NOTE

"It starts with him *and ends with* her.*"*

We're getting closer to the end.

Keep reading for a sneak peek at *Levee*, Book X of the Vast Collective Series.

And sign up for news of future books.

Nicole Hayes

LEVEE

{Earth}

"ANDREW, WHAT'S WRONG?!"

Andrew knew it was Lynn without seeing her, but the rest of his brain couldn't make sense of what was happening in front of his eyes. Neon halos surrounded the woman kneeling over him in varying shades of her vibrant lives. Her skin shifted every saturation of brown. Her eyes were almond-shaped, perfectly round, hooded, deep-set, and almost feline all at once—every human color imaginable. Full lips on the verge of kissing, thin and bordering on angry, down-turned and surrounded by tears—every expression made on her shade-altering countenance at once.

Beyond Lynn, the scenery kaleidoscoped from a pagoda to a stone temple and into a Tudor palace. All of it grand, but none of it felt true. More faces surrounded him and churned in a cascade of vacillating features.

Andrew closed his eyes. Elden, what the fuck happened to the Probability Matrix?! What if Andrew reached out to Lynn and...

Get him some water.

Kiss him and tell him it'll be all right.

Check his temperature.

Did Imminent do something to him here on Earth?

When a hand touched his arm, Andrew jumped three feet into the air and scrambled back. All her voices—all the very different emotions behind them—felt too strong with physical contact. Lynn was all of those thoughts, but only one belonged to the friend Andrew knew.

With his heart pounding in his chest, Andrew opened his eyes. All the Lynns and all the Lamassau's held their hands up, trying for harmless. Colors lined their faces like Andrew forgot his 3D glasses at the movies. He squeezed his eyes shut again and shuddered against the solid surface behind him.

This was too much.

And to think, only yesterday Andrew died to see more Probabilities. Now...

"I take it back."

A silence filled the room, which could only mean Lynn and Lam exchanged a "what should we do" glance. Andrew was fresh out of ideas to offer them. Because this was it. What Zero described to Sagan. Razor to Xelan. What Imminent was all about.

Chaos.

At once, Andrew was terrified and alive—more alive than ever in his existence. He felt the birth of a new star in the fiery waters of Cascading Light, and the essence of their promise seeped into him. It married with his soul and exacted only the price of a hunger he ignored until now. A desire—a need—to create more. To feed on it as the light fed on him when he joined the ranks of Imminent.

And this line would never end.

Andrew licked his lips, took a deep breath, and let it out on more of a shiver this time. An electric tremor. He pressed his head back against his only solid anchor—whatever it was—grateful for its sentry as his mind drifted along the waves of black flame.

Who was this new initiate? Could he see them? See their place in this fragmented world—

Blue eyes found Andrew adrift in the future-seeking sea. Bright blue and filled with tears. Not tears of joy or sadness. These were tears of pure fear and loneliness.

Rayne.

Those eyes glared with a white light—true, magnesium white. Brighter still. And brightest, until that light consumed her. One last breath and the light released what remained of his best friend—his sister, really—in tiny fireflies of pure phosphorous sparks. All of Enki taken in her shine.

"No!"

A billion times, Andrew watched her die. The same way each time. It was the last sight on the edge of a lightning-struck horizon. Rayne dies alone and afraid, and she destroys Enki in the process.

It never changed.

"Andrew, how can we help you?" Lynn inched closer.

Andrew knew without opening his eyes that she stretched out a hand. By all that was Shadow, he took it this time. He opened his eyes to find hers wide and unsure. He pulled her in for a much-needed hug.

Lynn gripped tightly and muttered against him, "It's okay. We won't let anything happen to you. Can you tell me what's wrong?"

Lamassau waved his arms across the room. "Yeah, is it safe for me to move yet?"

"Please," Andrew started against Lynn's locs. "Please, don't let go yet." The two friends weren't really *this* close. But at the moment, her earthy moisturizer smelled like home. Like Shadow.

Someone entered the room behind Andrew. "Uh, does Doc Pablo know about this?" It was Cypher.

Lamassau dismissed the soldier with a wave. "I think her husband will make an exception just this once."

Lynn sounded like she rolled her eyes as she said, "There won't be any exception to make if Conscience, here, can tell me what the fuck is wrong."

Right. Andrew sniffled and let her go with an apologetic smile. "Sorry. I . . . I don't know how to describe it. Someone new touched Cascading Light, and I don't think this is the only Probability in which this particular person joins Imminent. It felt so familiar. Anyway, I guess I'm affected when someone dives into the Probability Matrix."

Cypher walked over into Andrew's line of sight and looked him over. "Are you okay?"

Andrew couldn't imagine how he looked. Was he pale from the shock or radiant from the feeding? Overall, the only way to describe how he felt was alien. "I'm… alive, but I don't feel quite right."

Lamassau leaned back against the far counter of the Brethren's lab facility and crossed his arms. "Well, can you tell us who it was? Or what you saw?"

Ashamed of his shortcoming, Andrew shook his head and grit his teeth. "No. Nothing, but the end."

They all shared a glance. Everyone knew "the end" meant Rayne dying. Everyone looked equally sick about it, too.

Andrew met Cypher's eyes and said, "We need to get back to the villa on Reipon. I think something's gone horribly wrong with our plan." He checked with Lynn and Lamassau. "Any protests to returning?"

They exchanged a glance before Lynn answered, "You won't see me complaining about checking on Pablo right now."

Lam shrugged with a look of pure understanding. "Nor me on Tumi."

They knew not to fuck with the Probabilities ever since Razor attacked the Shadow with copies of themselves from alternative universes where they defected to Imminent. Repeatedly stabbing someone wearing their own face scarred them, with a particular trauma impossible to replicate outside of their special brand of bullshit.

Cypher headed for the door, where he paused and turned to say, "I'll let Tempest, Dolor, and Colton know. We'll pack you some goodies for the trip home. I hope everything's all right." With that, he left.

Lynn stood and shuffled around the lab. "I'll pack these samples. Lam, grab the rifles."

Lamassau did so without sass. Things really were taking a turn for the worst.

Each of them moved with a nervous energy and vibrated with apprehension. They felt it, too.

Something... momentous waited for them at home.

Something that would change their lives.

Andrew only wished he could see it before it took them by storm.

www.ingramcontent.com/pod-product-compliance
Lightning Source LLC
Chambersburg PA
CBHW020459310726
48979CB00016B/2715/J

9781737837954